To Kate and Kara. I love you both so much, and couldn't do it without you!

Well here we are again. "Took you long enough, lazy!" Yeah, yeah, yeah... Well regardless, here's the standard disclaimer: This is a work of fiction. If it's not painfully obvious that any of the characters within are just that— fictionalized characters— and not meant to be actual representations of any persons, living or dead... well... I'm not sure what to tell you. Get a sense of humor (or "humour," as Dr. Templeton might say).

Cover Art by J Caleb Design, 2019. www.jcalebdesign.com

Orion's Comet logo designed by Grant Gelner, 2012.

ISBN: 1-939417-07-7

ISBN-13: 978-1-939417-07-7

Corcoran Was a Time Traveler

A Thought-Provoking Time Travel Adventure Tale In the

"Was a Time Traveler Series"

D.J. Gelner

Orion's Comet | St. Louis

CHAPTER ONE

Should I break the empty bottle of Macallan 18 and slit his throat? Or would it be more satisfying to rip out his jugular with my teeth?

I decided on the former and, in one motion, dashed the empty scotch bottle on the curb, and brought the jagged edge to the exceedingly cool-looking man's throat.

"Aw come on, Doc, we ain't got time for this!"

He made a casual attempt to swat away my erstwhile hand, which had formed a claw around the bottle's neck.

Yet my resolve was steeled. I was more beast now than man. Fueled by hatred, I pushed through his half-arsed defense, though his parry forced the bottle *just* far enough away so as to graze his cheek.

Damn! How close I had been!

"Shit!" he checked for blood. "So we're gonna do this the hard way then?"

I let out a primal scream (or what I imagine as such—I was in a state of somewhat less-than-complete sobriety) and lunged for the Commander again.

I felt sick as he lodged his fist squarely in my gut. I heaved in gulps of air between near-wretches as I crouched to draw in breath after breath.

"God *damn* it Doc can ya let me—"

The mere sound of his voice re-lit my fuse. I spun out of the crouch in a backhand led by the jagged bottleneck. He sidestepped the attempt as I thrust the bottle toward him repeatedly, backing him toward the corner of the alleyway I had been "fortunate" enough to call home for the past several weeks.

His eyes darted around the surrounding area. I had been in battle with this man enough times to know he was looking for an advantage—*any* advantage—he could press as I forced him toward a somewhat indefensible position.

He set his back foot and used it as leverage to bound forward, his open palms straight out, on their way to the sides of my head, presumably to box my ears.

I reached both hands up to block his assault, then leveled a kick at his leg.

It connected flush, and as he reeled, I steadied myself into my boxing stance. I jabbed at him twice, connecting on both and brought my rear hand back, ready to unload a devastating cross (along with what remained of the bottle) on the side of his face.

I could sense the now hot, moist glass nearing its target. The jagged edge of the bottle practically smiled as I thought of spoiling that well-crafted chin.

Suddenly, I heard a loud "RIIIIP!"

The man had managed to raise a leather-clad arm to repel my final blow… though I must admit I was somewhat pleased it had utterly ruined his fine-looking jacket.

"That!" He punctuated his exclamation with a right cross.

"Was!" He followed it with a jab.

"My!" His right hook connected and sent me reeling.

"Favorite!" He grabbed the remnants of my sleeve and pulled me toward him as his off-hand somewhat curiously held my wrist. What the devil did he have in mind…?

"JACKET!"

<CRACK>

I felt the blood drain from my face as the sickening noise coincided with an otherworldly pain in my arm.

I instinctively released the bottle, which shattered on the cobblestones of the alleyway, and watched as my arm dangled lifelessly at a funny angle, broken at the elbow.

My eyes went wide. I must've screeched like a schoolgirl as I ran around in circles, lamenting the grotesque break in my joint.

"It's gone! My arm—it's gone!"

Corcoran straightened his jacket and leaned against the wall with a sigh.

"Oh come on Doc. It ain't gone… just broke a bit."

"I can't feel it! I can't use it! It's *gone!*"

He rolled his eyes and reached into his pocket.

"Here you go, ya big fuckin' baby…"

He reached up toward my mouth and squeezed whatever was in his hand. Within seconds, I tasted the familiar, vaguely pineapple taste of medigel.

"Shhhh… there, there, sweetheart…" he chewed the words like nails. The bastard had the gall to mock me!

He reached into another pocket and produced a bottle of (rather cheap, mind you) whisky.

"This oughtta even ya out a bit…"

I seized upon the bottle like Smigol upon the magic ring and started chugging it down.

"Christ Doc, I woulda settled for 'Good to see ya, Rick!' or 'Wow, how long has it been bud?'"

"How about 'Thanks for ruining my life! Stealing my fucking legacy?!" I spat the words at him.

He harumphed. "Figured there might be some hard feelings leftover. Didn't you get my—"

"Yes I got your fucking note. Thank you." I nodded at him.

"Well… it was all in there, ain't it?"

"About how Helene employed you to steal my time machine? To abscond with it and the outrageous fame and unfathomable riches that was rightfully *mine* for having discovered time travel?"

"Yeah… yeah I guess it *was* kinda about that…" he rubbed his chin.

"And now that you've come back in time to gloat, to show me just how awful I am, what a wretch I've become. To lord it over me, and add injury to insult in this case."

He shook his head, "Why you gotta be such a fuckin' drama queen all the time Doc? Look I came here for two reasons, and rubbin' your face in it or 'lording it over ya' ain't neither of 'em, okay?"

I must have literally taken a step back, and the surprise must have been evident on my face.

"First of all, I figured you might still be sore about what all happened back in 2042." He took a couple steps toward me. "So I wanted to offer you the chance to take one free shot at me, right on the—"

He had begun to point at his chin, but my fist anticipated his words. I launched a perfect left hook with my good arm that connected flush with his face, and sent him reeling toward the piss-stained wall that doubled as my urinal.

"Owww! God…*fuck!*" He covered his face for several seconds. I don't know why, but as satisfied as I was at getting my God's honest revenge on him, I couldn't fight the urge:

"Are… are you okay, Ricky?"

"That fucking *hurt* Doc!"

"Yeah… I know. Months of repressed rage and so-on and so-forth?"

He nodded. "Got it… Christ, and here I was thinking Bloomy was just a pussy when you whalloped him one…"

Though I normally wouldn't pass up an opportunity to make a joke at Steve Bloomington's expense, with him not in present company, over half the fun was drained from said opportunity.

Corcoran finally staggered to his feet and brought his hands away from his face.

"How do I look?"

A large purple welt had developed around his cheekbone, raising the usually taut skin into an unsightly mass of pulsing flesh.

I shrugged, "Hardly can tell…"

"Allright… we square now Doc?"

I thought for a moment. It *did* feel surprisingly good to both enact some small measure of revenge on Corcoran and show him that I was a more than capable adversary when pushed.

"I suppose that depends. What was your second reason for coming here?"

He wiped his shredded jacket sleeve over the deepening purple skin on his cheekbone.

"Well for one…" he paused, "I couldn't in right conscience let you rot away back here in history, just so you could wave 'Hi' to daddy a couple'a times a week."

He delivered the final part in a rather grating, mocking baby voice.

My expression must have been suitably off-put.

"Come on Doc, look at yourself! You reek of shit and piss!"

I straightened up. "I thought the whole idea was quite moving, almost poetic even. Become the very vagrant my father warned me about on all those long walks by the Thames. A cautionary tale to young Phineas, week in and week out, forced to face my deepest fear and shame like—"

"Spare me the goddamned 'woe is me, daddy hates what I've become' psychobabble lecture, awright? It's fuckin' selfish is what it is."

"I *beg* your pardon?!" I had half a mind to slug him once more.

"Look, I fucked up. I can't say I'm sorry enough. I'm sorry. I'm sorry. I'm sorry. Does that help?"

"Wise ass. Only about 999,997 to go…" I said, emotionlessly.

His uneven stare lowered on me for a moment… and I saw just how serious he was.

"Truth is, what's up there—" he pointed at my ragged hair, "Is probably one of the most valuable commodities in history."

"You… want to make a wig?"

"Your brain, dummy! You're one of the greatest human minds of all time, damn it! And to wallow in self-pity like a damned pig in slop is downright fuckin' tragic… when you could be helpin' so many people all throughout history."

I tried to take in the Commander's compliment in the best manner possible. And unless he had added "Oscar-Winning Actor" to his repertoire (I was legitimately afraid to ask him if he had), then I believed his apology to be sincere.

"Very well then—for what do you require my assistance now?"

He scrunched his nose momentarily before he shook the awkward sentence construction out of his head.

"I have a job offer for ya."

I rolled my eyes. "Oh really? Need some sap you can pin the Kennedy Assassination on? Perhaps I could be nailed to the cross in

Trent Fucking Albertson's stead?"

"No, nothin' like that."

He didn't even chuckle.

Corcoran continued, "Anyway… does the name Klaus Thurbur ring a bell?"

I was (quite literally) taken aback—I shuffled backward a half step.

Klaus was a dear old friend of mine, and perhaps more importantly, was one of the few people on the planet whose intellect could even begin to rival my own. We had spent many gin-soaked nights together in Leipzig opaquely talking around key concepts of my time machine in coded vagaries like a couple of mobsters planning a hit.

He was especially keen on optics, and I had enlisted his help more than a few times tweaking the time machine's cloaking device to get it to perform up to spec.

"What in the devil does Klaus have to do with anything?"

Corcoran shook his head. "He's in trouble back in the future. I guess he got involved with Chronosaber somehow, and then the Nazis got word of it, and they ended up coming to his lab in 2032, and—"

"You *cannot* be serious." I forced my most deadly serious stare. "Who in their right mind would ever do business with Chronosaber?"

This time I at least got what I can best describe as a "huffed guffaw" out of the Commander.

"Damn it, Doc, this is serious stuff. Last I saw, Klaus was pinned down in his lab, under heavy fire from Dolph, Gerry, and the reunion tour of the survivors from our little jaunt into Paris circa WW2."

"Klaus… is *seriously* being attacked by Nazis? He's in trouble?"

This time it was Corcoran who rolled his eyes.

"Yes! Fuck it, Doc! And as soon as those Hugo Boss-wearing assholes goose-stepped their way into his office, he sent me to get you."

"Why?" I shot back.

Corcoran shrugged. "Beats the tarred shit outta me. Somethin' about he wanted you to have somethin'a his? Or somethin'?"

I narrowed my eyes in the hope that the Commander would realize how unhelpful his description was.

"Anything more than that? Like an invention? Or piece of equipment?"

Corcoran shook his head. "That's all I got. He said you'd know what to do with it when you got to Leipzig—"

"And fought my way through an army of Nazi thugs?"

"Fought *our* way through an army of Nazi thugs!" Corcoran couldn't conceal the glint in his eye from the glee he felt at an opportunity for unchecked mayhem against the fascist horde.

I stroked my chin. If Klaus was truly in trouble, then it would logically follow that he had *something* that only I could understand. Should someone of lesser intellect, like the Commander, for example, try to use or decipher whatever Klaus had prepared, it would be much akin to a chimpanzee in a lab coat trying to operate a fission reactor.

My only worry was the mention of Chronosaber. Obviously that old crone Helene was cooking something up, and had employed Klaus to help her do so… but what? And was this some ruse concocted by her to further humiliate me? And make me the clown's arse of history?

Or would it allow me to cross paths with her once more and set history "right?" Sure, "what happened, happened," and whatnot… but nothing I had seen had shown me definitively that I couldn't off the old bat in both of our futures.

For all I knew, she would have travelled directly from our meeting in 2042 back to 2032, and now I would have the opportunity to exact revenge from her, much as I had already from the Commander.

With eyes greening by the minute, I nodded my head.

"Well then, if Klaus is in need of help, then help him we shall."

A broad grin crossed the Commander's face.

"Awesome! Put 'er there pal!"

He extended an outstretched hand to me.

I shot away from it as if it was a loaded gun.

It took him a second to realize it was the same hand that had damned me to become a vagrant all those months ago when he had inadvertently used a "memory glove" to capture my handprint.

"Ah come on Doc—no glove, see?"

He raised his bare hand in what I imagine was supposed to convey a sense of comfort.

I steadied myself, sighed, forced an overbroad smile, and clasped the man's hand in my own.

"Very good then. To one more adventure, just like old times!"

Perhaps it was the medigel taking hold, but I must admit it was invigorating to contemplate a proper adventure like the ones we had previously undertaken!

The sad truth was, sitting in this alleyway, pickled as a mummy in formaldehyde week after week, wasn't nearly as therapeutic as I thought it might be. I *longed* to recapture that sense of adventure, that *joie de vivre* from our previous travels. Even more so than I wished to come to terms with my father's shame…

My father!

"Um… one more thing Ricky?"

"You name it." Corcoran nodded.

"I…err…well…you see, it's my father and I."

"Look, Doc, if you really want to come back to this time period when you're done to be a damned bum and see your Pop, we'll see what we can—"

"No, no—seeing him these few times was thoroughly therapeutic," I said. "But the simple fact of the matter is that we saw the bum every week when I was a child, and if I leave now—"

"Won't someone take your place?" Corcoran asked.

It took me a moment to catch on, but eventually I realised what he was saying.

"Ah yes… 'whatever happened, happened.'"

"Right. No matter what you do, the past is fixed. You leave, and someone else should be right there to take your place, just as the universe intended..."

As if on cue, the sound of a stream of water impacting brick resonated out from behind the dumpster in front of us.

"OOOOOOHHHH YEAH MATE!" a voice yelled after it. "GET AFTER IT, POP, WHYDONTCHA?" the booming voice asked no one in particular.

We circled around quietly to find one of my alleymates urinating loudly on the facade of the building next door.

"He been there the whole time?" Corcoran asked.

"That's Horace. Real piece of work, that one," I shook my head.

As the man continued to pound the wall with a torrent of urine and groaned, Corcoran walked over to the far side of him and stared at him in profile.

Hopped up on God-knows how much gin and barbiturates, I doubt Horace even noticed.

"Sure," Corcoran said.

"What?" I asked.

"He'll do just fine."

As Horace shook out the final drops of what I imagine he considered his greatest masterpiece, Corcoran grabbed him under the arm and guided him the several steps back to where I had previously made my home.

"Absolutely not!" I protested. "Horace takes all of the aluminum cans for himself out of the bins. Furthermore, he's an *incessant* bore. I will *not* have that man represent me on my—"

"Your what? Your wall? Who the hell knows it's you, anyway? Not your Pop, that's for sure. Not little Phineas Templeton. Look at him—he's a dead ringer."

I hadn't had the good fortune to admire myself in a mirror lately, and though grudgingly I must admit that Horace was somewhat of a "handsome homeless," if I was in as poor of shape as he was, it was probably a good thing I was getting back to work. The Commander waited for Horace to finish his semi-orgasmic urination.

I offered Corcoran a tight smile and a nod, "Very well then, Commander. I am officially, if reluctantly, in your employ."

The familiar broad grin worked its way over the Commander's face.

"Outstanding. Thank you, Doc. I mean it—won't let you down again."

I nodded, perhaps too-grimly to betray my suspicion. "Indeed. Now about these Nazis…"

CHAPTER TWO

We arrived at the intersection perhaps some fifty metres later. The buildings that formed the corners were somewhat recessed from the alleyways, which provided ample room and privacy for what I imagined was Corcoran's means of conveyance.

Corcoran motioned for me to wait at the exit of what had previously been "my" alleyway as he continued forward several steps. I remembered that my spectacles, sullied as they were, were, ostensibly, still smart spectacles. My motor skills were dulled a bit due to the quantity of whisky that I had imbibed over the past several days, but after several seconds of fumbling I hit the button on the temple.

Sure enough, the lenses appeared to tint green, and the familiar outline of the time machine, *my* time machine came into view. I never thought I'd see the damned thing again, but doing so brought a flood of emotions to the forefront. I was certainly proud and relieved that the old girl had survived so long and was still in one piece. I was also furious at the traitorous computer inside, which Yanks would describe as a proper Benedict Arnold. The damned thing had been in cahoots with Helene the entire time, but continued to allow me to believe that *I* was the one ultimately in charge.

Oh how mistaken I had been!

Curiously, Corcoran continued walking toward the hand panel that allowed entry to the vessel without any kind of sight aid. He placed his hand on the plate and the door opened and turned into the familiar gangway to allow entry to the ship.

"How did you—?" I asked.

"Smart contacts. I think Google makes 'em. Or Apple. Not entirely sure on that one. They're an improvement on those…those 'things' you insist on keepin' around." He nodded at my spectacles.

My head involuntarily seized upward, "I'll have you know that these were a gift from my *father*, thank you, and engraved as such! Plus with the beating these frames have taken, they should be the model of ruggedness and utility. A prototype for proper vision the world—"

"Yeah, yeah—save it for the commercials, Doc," Corcoran didn't so much as turn toward me as he ascended the ramp into the ship.

"I see you've properly reprogrammed her to respond to *your* handprint now?" I asked, my indignation growing by the minute.

Corcoran nodded, "Yup. Still responds to you, too. Which brings somethin' else up—" Corcoran reached underneath his t-shirt (which I believe was the same comfortable maroon number Victor Burnham had provided him during our visit to 1985-86 St. Louis, Missouri) and produced two old-fashioned keys on long, metallic chains. He pulled one of the keys over his head and tossed it to me.

"I figured your anti-theft system was a little lackin'. So now, just like a missile sub, both of us have keys, to go along with a biometric retinal scanner for both of our eyes. No more foolin' around, no more mistrust."

"What if one of us…you know…?" I asked as I slipped the key over my head.

"Croaks?" Corcoran asked in reply.

"Perhaps not quite so eloquently, but yes."

Corcoran sighed, "It gets kinda grizzly, Doc."

"I'm a bum who's been living for months using the out of doors as his collective toilet and fighting others for favored urination spots along buildings. I think I can take—"

"There's a contingency plan, but let's just say it's even more unpleasant than that, okay? Look, it's a gesture of goodwill, Doc. I'm showin' you that neither of us can just take the time machine," he pointed inside the device with both arms, "and fly away with it, and leave the other guy stranded in the past. First of all, since I'm even *here*, I would think that'd be enough to dissuade you from doin' likewise. But just in case it's not, we're a team now, you and me."

I nodded, steeling my head so as not to belie my apprehension. To be perfectly honest, it was rather refreshing that he would so "graciously" put these measures into place, even when he had so callously made off with my pride-and-joy, the time machine, those several months ago…or years in the future…however one wished to consider it.

"They made a coupla' improvements that I think you'll like, though honestly, Doc, some of the stuff you came up with is still state-of-the-art, even by future standards," Corcoran said.

I followed Corcoran up the gangway and into the ship's interior, which *was* remarkably familiar, albeit with a few structural changes. The seating area opposite the bunk had been removed and relocated next to the kitchen; in its place was a wall that matched the material and colour of the rest of the ship perfectly. Immediately curious, I turned right inside the door and ducked my head in, to find three sets of bunk beds instead of the lone, military-style bunk I had placed in there practically on a lark before that jump to visit Jesus, or "Trent Albertson," or whatever you wish to call the man whom ostensibly was the focus of Christianity.

"We increased crew capacity from three to six, 'case we pick up any hitchhikers along the way."

"Do we?" I asked Corcoran, knowing that he was more than likely well aware of the answer.

He pursed his lips and angled his head toward me in reply. "We also added a second head there," he pointed toward what used to be the seating area past the wall, which now housed a door similar to the one that partitioned off the head I had installed.

I exited the quarters and sauntered toward the cockpit, which now consisted of three command seats, my own, in the middle, flanked by two others situated perhaps a foot behind the lead chair.

"Thought it might help if we had three experienced time travellers workin' the controls this time, especially given the other 'modifications' we've made."

"I'm quite capable of driving the ship myself, Commander. I don't need your assistance, nor do I require the assistance of any other flunky you may bring along on this—"

Corcoran chortled before he raised his hands in mock defence, "Sure, sure, Doc—you get to drive the boat. I get it. That crazy control…hologram'a yours—"

"The omniyoke." I said through gritted teeth.

"The *omniyoke*," I hate to admit as much, but Corcoran's mocking British accent had improved even more since the last time I had heard it, "that's still how they pilot these things. Most of the changes are in the guts, things you can't see from the flight deck. The computer's been upgraded as best we can, though it still has the same 'winnin'' personality," Corcoran grimaced as he said the words, and the panels flanking the center seat came to life with an affected 8-bit-like display of a crude, blocky face sticking out its tongue.

"*Great* to see *you* again, *too*, Commander!" The display read in block lettering before the jagged face turned into a smiley. "Doctor Templeton!"

"Don't you 'Doctor Templeton' me, you traitorous glorified eight track!" I moved to hit one of the displays, but the Commander easily subdued me with one arm. To add to the insults, the square-like face with its tongue sticking out flashed back up on the displays.

"Hey, come on now, play nice, you two!" Corcoran yelled.

"This isn't over!" I spat the words at the computer. The smiley face returned. I turned to Corcoran, "Dare I say I enjoyed it better when Helene monkeyed with that damn thing."

"As for other changes," the Commander ignored me and lowered his arm, "we can jump pretty much whenever we want, no questions asked—"

"How the devil is that—?" As soon as I asked the question, I realised that the answer likely involved my Benefactor's previous artificially limiting of the computer to conform with her whims.

"—With a couple of exceptions," Corcoran must have understood as such, "biggest one is that once we jump somewhere, jumpin' close to that time again gets a little dicey. You can't guarantee you'll show up exactly when you want to show up."

"The ripple effect," I whispered without thinking. The "ripple effect," as Trent Albertson (of all people!) had described it, was the idea that because of the quantum computations involved in time travel, there was always some uncertainty involved in the calculations made by the computer, no matter how advanced. As a result, upon arriving in the past, the residual tearing of spacetime acted like the ripples formed on the surface of a pond after casting a stone inside, making travel to and from that point somewhat more challenging.

Corcoran nodded, "Yeah, somethin' like that. I don't know the specifics. Where we're goin', uh…*someone'll* be able to answer that a little better."

Corcoran looked like a schoolchild asked to answer an advanced algebra equation before he brightened, "Other things—the reactor's improved; only takes six hours to recharge give or take, and the cloak works a lot better. We even added some bad ass weapons, real *Star Wars*-type shit. The places we're goin', we may need a little more than some tunnelin' lasers, which are well and good if you're carvin' up spacetime, but if you're in a firefight for your life…well…they ain't exactly useful, 'less you wanna turn the Earth into a black hole…" Corcoran looked at me for a response for several seconds.

I shook my head.

"Didn't think so."

Suddenly, an awful thought hit me squarely in the head. I practically ran off to the kitchen.

"What? All the talk about laser guns and smart-ass computers borin' you?" Corcoran asked.

"It *has* to be here!" I made my way into the pantry and no doubt tossed aside a number of amazingly advanced delicacies that Corcoran had procured for this voyage in search of a solitary box, packed away long ago.

"What? There's plenty of—" Corcoran must've realised what I was looking for and raced over to help me. "All right, all right, it's in here somewhere…yeah…yeah, there it is," Corcoran pulled out a case marked "Ramen Noodles" (whatever the hell those were) and opened it.

Inside, I witnessed the most glorious sight a man who had spent several months on the street could possibly imagine:

Macallan Eighteen.

An entire case of it.

"Thank *God!*" I heaved, and wrapped both arms around the cage in an enormous bear hug.

Truth be told, as with everything I encountered on this ship, I had somewhat mixed feelings upon seeing the stuff. Part of me recoiled at the bitterness I had felt first at being betrayed by Helene when she poisoned my drink, then by Corcoran as he left me a bottle as the only lasting souvenir of our previous excursions.

Then again, bygones being bygones and whatnot, how could I hold a grudge against the most perfect drink that the universe had ever created? There was nothing quite like a glass or three of Macallan Eighteen at the end of a thoroughly stressful day to relax the mind and debrief the senses on a job well done.

Judging by the Commander's unwillingness to discuss our impending mission, there may be a few occasions when we may find the whisky's services so valuable that we may think of it as an indispensable member of the crew…

…or maybe that was the gin-soaked bum in me talking.

"Right. God forbid you don't have your sippin' whisky, Doc. It's the right brand, ain't it?"

The beaming smile on my face and my eager nod must have tipped Corcoran off that he was indeed correct.

"Great. So…anything else now, Doc? Or are we good?"

I thought for a moment before answering, "I think you covered most of the obvious areas of improvement. I suppose we can always address other changes—"

"*Fan*-tastic," Corcoran interrupted. He sauntered over to what was the gunnery seat and inserted his key into the box that had been placed next to the command console. It turned with a satisfying, firm "click," and he looked at me.

"If you'll do the honors…" Corcoran said.

I approached the odd-looking little box and tilted my head; it was certainly anachronistic, a dark, ugly, grey rectangle in the otherwise sleek, modern interior. I suppose to rig up such a device for something as simple and "old-fashioned" as non-electronic keys required a little bit of ingenuity, albeit by people who obviously lacked the ship's creator's design sensibilities.

I inserted the key and twisted to the right until it clicked. The blocky face that the computer had put up on the main console was replaced by the *Star Trek: The Next Generation*-inspired time travel interface, as the other panels awoke from dormancy.

The command console to the left of the chair already had coordinates punched in:

"20-7-2032: Leipzig, Germany"

"No cryptic note from Helene this time?" I muttered under my breath.

"Don't worry, Doc; there'll be *all* kinds of goofy *shit* for you to deal with here in a sec. For now, though, I'd recommend we head to those coordinates I was kind enough to punch in ahead'a time."

"Two weeks after I left? Certainly didn't waste any time in getting back to work," I said.

"Christ, I can't keep track of it all anymore. It's probably been close to six months for me, give or take a few days, since I left Montauk. Don't know how I'll be able to have a real birthday ever again…"

I briefly considered changing the date on the console to a mere fourteen days earlier, to try and warn myself of the impending frustration and doom I faced before embarking on the most foolish of temporal scavenger hunts. A warning to naive younger me moments before I took off on this oddest of oddessies.

Then I realised how ridiculous such a notion was, and that should I attempt to do so, some horrible fate would likely befall the Commander and I before we reached our intended destination, so as to preserve the natural order of the universe.

I sighed and saw that most horrible number displayed in the upper right-hand corner of the display:

"99.9%"

"You wouldn't bugger me again on this one, would you, Computer?" I asked.

The blocky face appeared on the non-command side of the console. It shook its head and frowned.

I rolled my eyes before I looked over my shoulder at the Commander once more.

"All set then?" I asked.

"Yes—*Jesus Christ,* just hit the damned button already!"

I grinned at the Commander's frustration.

"Now, now, no need to bring Trent Albertson into this." My quivering finger hovered over the green "Engage" button for several moments. Oh, had I the opportunity to go back and do it again knowing now what was in store for us! Needless to say, I likely would've torn out the key and run back to the darkest, most anonymous corner of 2002 London I could find, content to live the rest of my days in a blinding alcoholic haze.

Sadly, though, my curiosity once again got the better of me. I dropped my finger onto the console and the engines whirred magically to life.

May God have mercy on my soul…

"Oh yeah, one more thing," the Commander interrupted my momentary reverie. What words of wisdom could he possibly have now? Perhaps another apology? Or maybe another betrayal?

"Take a shower, will ya? You stink like shit!"

CHAPTER THREE

After a self-assessment proved the Commander correct, I showered and shaved, as well as engaged in a third bodily function beginning with an "s" that completed the "three 'S' tonic" about which Grandfather Templeton (my father's father) always raved as the "cure for what ails a man."

I put on the comfortable casual clothing offered by the ship's closet (though, I'm afraid minus the stylish leather jacket that the Commander wore) and made my way back to the flight deck.

While previously the "wondrous" colours of the time vortex had become downright boring, I now savored their presence as a comfortable, warm reassurance that I was putting my little jaunt into the past behind me.

After all, what *had* I accomplished by haunting that alleyway with my gaunt, unkempt visage for all those weeks?

Who was I proving a point to? Myself? Younger me? The ghost of a long-dead father, as great of a man as he may have been?

And what *had* that point been exactly? I suppose my father's words had quite the profound effect on me at that early age:

That's a bum Finny... you want to work hard so that you don't end up like him...

Truth be told, perhaps I was seeking to turn my father's words into their own self-fulfilling prophecy. Especially since if the entire universe was pre-ordained, it *had* to happen that way.

And yet... somehow the whole excursion seemed empty. Hollow. I couldn't rightly explain it... but deep down, in my gut, it seemed *wrong* for me to be there, out of place, out of time.

Regardless of my own navel-gazing, we emerged from the time vortex to the comfortable sight of that enormous blue globe of earth in the distance, in its familiar, 2032 form.

"Who would've ever thought I'd be coming home to fight Nazis?" I said, to no one in particular.

"Yeah," Corcoran punctuated his statement by chambering a round in the holster of his sidearm and grabbing what appeared to be a ghastly laser rifle, based on that awful contraption I had used to fell the T-rex 65 million years in the past. He flipped his shades down dramatically onto his nose.

"But ain't somebody gotta do it?"

I nodded, and wasted no time availing myself of the armory. I found several copies of my trusty old Beretta nine millimetre, as well as two (admittedly more advanced) copies of my prototype laser pistol that Steve Bloomington had appropriated for himself toward the end of our previous voyage.

I decided that given the potential torrent of Nazis that we'd be facing, there was no such thing as "too much firepower," and loaded one of each into a holster on each shoulder.

I followed that up with a chest plate of (I must say rather light) body armor that hung in the armory closet.

Bavaria of my own time period was coming into view, and I had forgotten just how hard-hit the Continent had been during the war.

The ship's computer overlaid red "no go" zones over the landscape, presumably where low-yield nukes and dirty bombs had been dropped.

Fortunately, Leipzig had generally remained untouched. By 2032, it was perhaps the largest remaining city in Germany, and widely considered one of the continent's leading centers of culture and scholarship.

In fact, despite three world wars, it was amazing how little had actually changed since Steven, the Commander, and I had visited the city during Bach's time. Old buildings still dominated the landscape; even newer construction had been done in a way to try to recapture the architectural style of "the Old World." In a way, I suppose it was also an attempt to recapture a simpler time, an easier time, without the wanton destruction of the present era.

Little did they realize just how brutal life had been even during a supposedly "cultured" period such as the Renaissance!

In fact, my travels had opened my eyes to just how brutish and "base" human nature could actually be. What frightened me wasn't how much buildings and weaponry changed through the years. Rather it was how *little* humanity's appetite for destruction had wavered from century to century.

I pondered all of this as we descended toward the university. I recognized the building that housed Klaus's office almost immediately. It was "modern" not so much as meaning "of the times," but rather in that way that most academic buildings were rectangular and looked to have been built around 1976.

The computer plotted a tight approach, and as we came in for a landing, we shot out of the way as another brushed metal saucer almost threw us off course.

"Sunday driver…" I raised my fist at the passing craft for maximum effect.

The craft landed imperceptibly; only the main viewscreen gave any hint that we had, in fact, hit the ground.

"Alright Doc, ain't no time like the present, am I right?"

I don't know if it was meant to be a joke or not—I simply nodded and turned my attention toward the door, where I steeled myself for whatever awaited outside.

Corcoran nodded in kind. "Okay, let's do this. Computer, open the main door."

The gangway extended into what I immediately saw was a sort of civilized wilderness. At first, the only "Nazis" I saw were a bunch of skinheads, the likes of which had been known to join gangs targeting those unfortunate Muslim migrants who remained in Europe in my own time. This was a rather horrid fact that I had put out of my mind in my drunken stupor, and for several moments, I once again felt downright *had* by the Commander.

But as I looked past those ugly foot soldiers currently undertaking this half-assed "siege" against the science department at the University of Leipzig, I noticed several of the honest-to-Satan World War II-era Nazis that we had previously been face-to-face against, directing the assault.

Even more oddly, another group of black-uniformed Nazi thugs was emerging from a large bell-shaped craft, that appeared to be covered in some kind of script that looked eerily like hieroglyphs of some sort.

The Commander and I disembarked our own ship, and took cover behind a nearby pile of benches that had been assembled as a makeshift barricade. This must have drawn the fascists' attention, as our position was almost immediately torched by a tongue of fire unleashed by one of the World War II-era Nazis wielding a proper flamethrower.

Ricky cocked an eyebrow in annoyance. He shouldered the laser rifle and levied several bolts of plasma at the *flammenwerfer*, leaving three rather large holes in the man as he fell limply toward the scorched earth.

I could've sworn the Commander raised the laser rifle to his face and smiled before laying down more covering fire to help us get our bearings.

I fired several rounds at two approaching skinheads. They cried in pain as I hit one squarely in the knee, and the other in a shoulder, halting their advance, temporarily at least.

"Come on!" Corcoran motioned toward an entrance, guarded by two hulking figures in black jumpsuits. They wore what appeared to be incredibly advanced gas mask contraptions on their faces, with glowing yellow eyes that made them appear somewhat "less-than-friendly."

I instinctively reached out for Corcoran's shoulder. "Are you—?"

He shrugged my hand away and bolted for the door. Amid the chaos outside of the building, I had little choice but to follow Corcoran toward the menacing pair.

As we approached though, the two soldiers merely nodded and waved us through.

"Appreciate it fellas," Corcoran huffed as we made it inside the comparatively quiet hallway. In fact, I was quite amazed by how little damage the building had taken during the firefight. I assumed that meant the fracas hadn't been going more than a few minutes before we arrived.

Corcoran stopped and surveyed the hallway. It took several seconds before I realized he was looking at me.

"Well?"

"Well *what?*"

"Where is this Klaus fella's office?"

"I thought you said that *Klaus* sent you back?"

Corcoran looked at me, widened his eyes, and shrugged. It hadn't occurred to me that the Commander had given me less-than-perfect information, though in hindsight I suppose it should have. I shook my head, gathered my wits, and tried to remember where we had crunched those equations all those long nights ago.

Truth be told, it likely would've been easier had I had a stiff drink, situational "muscle memory" and whatnot. And while I craved a glass of Macallan 18-Year, if I was honest with myself, it was likely equally for my nerves as it was in any attempt to remember where Klaus's office had been.

It finally clicked in my head, and I motioned for Corcoran to follow me. We navigated the maze-like corridors of the science building quite easily in hindsight. Though I suppose the soldiers with the yellow, glowing eyes were ensuring that no stray Nazis entered the building as of yet.

We finally came to the door with "K. Thurbur, Professor" next to it on a rather plain, unassuming nameplate.

"Here it is!" I tried to wrench the door open, but it held fast. "We may need some sort of—"

"Move, Doc!" Corcoran motioned me away from the knob. I took several steps behind him as he squeezed the trigger on his laser rifle, and dispatched the door handle with little trouble.

He put his shoulder into the door, and we found ourselves in Klaus's predictably unkempt office. Old-fashioned notepads littered the landscape, each one filled with priceless knowledge ranging from the equations explaining quantum entanglement or negative index of refraction optical physics to a series of (I must say rather clever) dirty limericks Klaus came up with after our various visits to one of the nearby pubs.

One thing that seemed a bit out-of-place was the foot-tall leprechaun that appeared on his cluttered desk seemingly when it heard my voice.

"Hoi-toi-toi-toi! Oy, Finny! Just the man I was looking for!" The fantastical little creature let out in a delightful Irish brogue.

While I momentarily thought my foray into the past had driven me permanently mad, I then remembered how Klaus had amassed his small fortune. Unlike me, who had a fabulously wealthy (and in hindsight utter fraud) of a billionaire benefactor, Klaus had trouble securing funding for his wildly speculative and theoretical studies.

So instead, he brought to market a rather clever concept called "holopaper," that served as a programmable gift wrap of sorts, whereby a holographic figure was projected above a wrapped present and invited the recipient to open it with whatever message the gift-giver desired.

In this case, Klaus had (quite correctly) assumed that I'd be enchanted by the hilarious little leprechaun. While I would've thought under more normal circumstances he'd delight in the thought of me chasing the little guy around the corridors of the college, it stayed put as I approached. He had quite clearly deployed it just to get my attention.

I unwrapped the green-and-gold paper from around the rectangular package. It was, unsurprisingly, another notebook. And while this one was filled with more than a few dirty limericks, it also contained hundreds of seemingly partially-finished equations, most of which were tantalizingly close to those that had unlocked time travel for me, though oddly only about 90% of the way there.

"What is it?" Corcoran asked.

"I'm not entirely sure…" I replied.

"Well, whatever it is, just pocket the damned thing and let's get the fu—"

His curse word was interrupted by a loud "CRASH!", and we were both thrown back against the wall. The blast left a cloud of dust and debris at the other end of the room, and as it cleared, a large opening became apparent.

"Hang on to your ass and grab some cover, Doc!" Corcoran toppled over several thick tables to provide us with some protection from the shots that were beginning to fill the room.

I threw myself against one of the felled tabletops and peeked over its precipice. Several stormtroopers adorned in black "SS" uniforms streamed through the new access way into the outside, spraying the room indiscriminately with automatic weapon fire.

Their machine guns were deafening. Albertson, I can still hear the sharp, "RAT-TAT-TAT-TAT" ringing in my ears to this day, each second bringing the horrible cacophony closer and closer to our position, even as Corcoran and I returned fire with our own, somewhat more advanced energy weapons.

The awful noise was followed by cries of "*Snell! Snell!*" There must've been a dozen of the highly-trained shock troops now. Though we may have clipped one or two of them as they advanced on us, it was becoming quite apparent that we were in for whatever horrible punishment these ghastly Nazi animals had in store for us.

A sharp whistle caused me to raise my gaze upward.

I was met by a horrible old Nazi, his face made up of a seemingly hideous combination of sharp angles, his uniform adorned with shiny metals for committing who-knows what kinds of heinous atrocities.

The old Nazi raised his Luger at my face. I held my breath; my pulse quickened. It felt like the room was an oven that had just been turned on as sweat ran down my brow, and started to soak my t-shirt collar.

As the old Nazi opened his mouth to spew whatever horrible things were to come forth, a curious thing happened:

There was another whistle, though this one was from the doorway to our left. It was rather weak and ineffectual, but it drew our attention, as well as the attention of the decorated Nazi and his horrible compatriots.

In the doorway stood two figures dressed in the black jumpsuits and futuristic gas masks with the glowing yellow eyes we had seen outside. One was tall and lean, and moved swiftly like a ninja as it bounded across the room to our position, snapped the Nazi Commander's neck with an almost stunning grace, and unholstered two desert eagle magnums and opened fire into the crowd of fascists, all in seemingly one fluid motion.

The shorter figure in the doorway opened fire on the Nazis almost immediately. It wasn't necessarily "stout" as it were, but surprisingly agile for its frame; it scurried about the room plugging Nazis with its laser gun like a little wombat of death, leaving hole-strewn Nazis like Swiss cheese in its wake.

The two were a magnificent sight for the sorest eyes, and allowed the Commander and I to regain our bearings and open fire on the remaining stormtroopers.

We stemmed the tide and began our own advance toward the gaping hole in the wall. The powerful energy weapons whined with each pull of the trigger, and while their bolts of focused energy didn't always hit their intended targets, I was surprisingly accurate despite having (quite literally) shared a piss-soaked hell hole with several other bums but less than a day before.

Finally, only one stormtrooper remained. The taller figure in the black jumpsuit backflipped across the room, seemingly through a hail of gunfire that the stormtrooper unleashed at it.

The shorter figure scurried from side-to-side, dancing through the bullets as it made its way toward the Nazi, whose wide eyes belied the panic it felt.

As the taller figure got behind the fascist soldier, it grabbed under his arms and caught him in a firm body-lock.

The wombat of death arrived in front of the soldier and put its laser pistol up to the Nazi's chin. It said a few muffled words through its glowing yellow facemask, its tone dark, low, and ominous as the words started becoming clearer and clearer.

"Take *that*, you douchenosed, Nazi fuckface!" the smaller jumpsuited person exclaimed in its deep, altered voice.

The Nazi closed his eyes and winced… and waited… one second… two seconds…

Nothing happened, and eventually he opened his eyes to see what sort of sick trick this shorter figure had in mind.

The taller figure kept its hold, and cocked its head to the side.

Something clicked in the shorter figure's head. He tapped the laser pistol's safety into the "off" position.

"Oh yeah," it said, almost matter-of-factly. It pulled the trigger, and a puff of ash followed the laser bolt out through the top of the gaping hole that used to be the stormtrooper's brain.

The shorter figure shook its head. "I *always* forget that part."

"I just thought you were being dramatic," the taller figure said in the same, altered, monotone voice.

"Yeah… yeah, that's it…" the shorter figure said.

"Yeah right…" the taller figure responded.

"Hey, Rowan and Martin," Corcoran emerged from our spot behind the tables. "This is great and all, but we gotta mission to accomplish here."

"We?" The shorter figure took a short step back. "So you mean he—?"

I took several cautious steps out of my hiding place, hands raised (though still on my guns) to show that I meant the deadly duo no harm.

"Oh my God!" The shorter figure reached for something on the side of its head, and pressed it to no avail.

The taller figure did the same, though the first time it did so, the face mask began stripping away from its face. "We got here just in time," a female voice greeted us from where the contraption had been previously. I racked my (still groggy, from the medigel, I supposed) brain for where I had heard the velvety tones before.

And then it hit me. It seemed like so long ago since I had seen her… though I suppose it actually had been, in both senses of the phrase, all that time ago back at Chronobase Alpha during dinosaur times.

"Commander Sanchez?" I asked.

"It's Captain now, actually," she responded, in the same, down-to-business, matter-of-fact tone I had known her for previously. "And I think you'll remember my colleague as well…"

She pressed the button on the side of the shorter figure's mask. Before the face mask could disappear back into the sides of the figure's face, its arms were outstretched, and it was running toward me, with more alacrity than I ever imagined possible given the jumpsuit's inhabitant.

"Doctor Templeton!"

Steve Bloomington wrapped both arms around me in a big, genuine bear hug.

And for the first time in recorded history, I was glad he did.

CHAPTER FOUR

"Steven?! Is… is that you?"

While it may seem rhetorical to you, dear reader, I legitimately had to ask. You see, this short, remarkably thin man with unkempt dark hair and stubble slowly teetered toward me. For a moment, I didn't even recognize him despite his pale skin and agape mouth, which normally would have served as dead giveaways. Though his visage, now suitably sunken and almost like a half-inflated version of his former self, was unmistakable.

He had lost a *tonne* of weight. And even though I mean that in the rhetorical (and not literal) sense, it certainly *seemed* the obese scientist had lost *at least* fifty to sixty pounds.

Bloomington held me there and patted me on the back for well over ten seconds, the only soundtrack Corcoran's occasional snickers.

"I'm *so* sorry, Doctor Templeton," Bloomington whispered, his nasally whine unmistakable, "I tried to tell this douchetard not to leave you," he nodded over at Corcoran, "but he just wouldn't listen to reason."

"I, uh, it's quite alright, Steven," I exerted all of my strength to extract myself from his vice-like grip as I affected a smile, "Great to see you, too. Appreciate the help with the Krauts and whatnot…"

Bloomington laughed, "Yeah, if there's anything Sophia and I know how to do, it's mow down *Nazi assholes!*"

He unloaded about a dozen more laser bolts into the jack-booted corpses surrounding us before Sanchez restrained him.

"Easy Steve…" she shook her head at him, as if he were a child misbehaving in a toy shoppe.

"What? Is ChronoSaber charging by the laser bolt now?"

The mere mention of the company's name sent a shiver down my spine.

As if on cue, five or six of the similarly black-clad individuals with glowing yellow eyes swarmed around the edges of the room. They surveyed what remained of Klaus's lab, raising their ghastly laser rifles at Nazi corpses and piles of rubble…

… And Ricky and me.

Even though we were rather clearly *not* a threat to either Steven or Sanchez, one of the seemingly sinister figures stopped and jabbed me in the face with his rifle.

"I *beg* your pardon?!?" I asked him.

"Identify yourself!" The figure commanded with that same radio-hollow, deep voice.

I sighed, "Not that it matters, but I'm Doctor Phineas Templeton," I shot a sideways glance at Corcoran, "inventor of time travel."

Corcoran shook his head and raised his arms, "It's okay! He's all right! Lower your weapons!"

"Sir, all due respect sir, but you are *not* my commanding officer, sir!"

Corcoran narrowed his eyes, "It was my understandin' that during this mission, Private, the government was to have the full cooperation of ChronoSaber, and not the other way 'round."

"He's right," Sanchez shook her head.

"You heard her—stand down, soldier," Corcoran said.

"I wasn't talking about you, Commander," Sanchez continued to ignore me, "I meant *he*, Private Marquez, is correct in that you aren't his commanding officer. *I* am. Stand down, private."

The black-clad figure lowered his weapon.

"I'm doing just fine, thanks for asking," I offered with a wry grin, hoping to ease the tension.

"That's odd. I thought for sure he'd wanna take orders from a *real* soldier, you know, one who actually rose through the chain'a command instead'a someone with a shiny uniform who got her rent-a-merc trainin' on a damned *weekend*."

"I guess ten years of sterling service in the Marine Corps doesn't count for anything anymore?" she asked.

Corcoran steeled his jaw, "A thousand pardons, princess. Where the hell are my manners?"

Sanchez affected a mocking grin, "Ever the charming Past-ie, as always, Ricky. Perhaps after this, you can jump back to a time when NASCAR was popular."

Corcoran affected a shiver, "Is it cold in here? Or is it just me?"

Sanchez ignored him and turned her attention toward me.

"Where are my manners? Doctor Templeton, so nice to see you again. It's been far too," she exhaled, "long."

She extended a lovely hand, which I took in my own. Despite its dainty profile, and contrary to Ricky's assertion, her entire presence seemed to fill my thin, spindly fingers with warmth and welcoming.

"My goodness, Captain Sanchez, I...you're...you look fantastic for being some sixty-five million years old."

She allowed a thin smile to wash over her normally down-to-business face, "I apologize for our last encounter, Doctor. I was under strict orders from HQ to—"

"Nothing of it, Sophia," I felt a wellspring of confidence within, "you do look lovely, though."

"See there, Ricky," she smiled fully, "some men *do* know how to treat a lady properly." She motioned for the soldiers to lower their rifles.

Flummoxed, Corcoran tilted his head for several moments, searching for something to say before he pointed directly at me.

"He was eatin' outta a *dumpster* when I found him yesterday!"

Sanchez raised an eyebrow at me.

My eyes went wide as I shrugged.

Corcoran shook off his previous statement, "Look, I did my job, now can we *please* get some details on why we're gettin' the band back together for the reunion tour?"

Sanchez raised a hand to her ear and waived Corcoran off. She talked to what I presume was some sort of intercom.

As we awkwardly waited for her to finish her conversation, I decided to turn to Bloomington and change the subject.

"My Steven, you're... uh... looking well."

I suppose it was only a half-lie. He had certainly lost *a lot* of weight, though it appeared to be in the unhealthiest way possible.

Bloomington beamed, "You like it?" he asked.

I didn't really know what to make of the question, and decided he was speaking of the extra sixty to seventy pounds of visceral fat that had somehow melted off his body.

"It suits you."

This most assuredly *was* a lie; Steve Bloomington was a creature meant to carry some heft. Absent the extra tonnage, his features became overgrown for his slighter frame, and dare I say downright grotesque.

I nearly retched as he reached to unzip the black jumpsuit that covered his stomach and pulled it apart, to reveal…not the grotesque pastiche of pasty skin and dark hair that I expected to find.

Instead, all skin on his stomach had been replaced by a device made out of some sort of alloy sunken into the remaining thin, rippling layer of flab overlaying his abdomen. Even more curiously, two three-pronged standard A/C outlets protruded from the curious instrument, as well as four other connectors that I couldn't recognize, but that seemed to be some future iteration of USB cable inputs.

"This is the Personal Electric Biomaterial Burning Lipophilic Equipment, or the 'P.E.B.B.L.E.' for short."

Corcoran raised his eyes skyward, "Aw, *shit*, Bloomy, why don't you just call it what everyone else does?"

"Commander, please don—"

"Fatteries."

"I *beg* your pardon?" I was shocked.

"Fuckbreath!" Bloomington thundered.

"What? No one calls it a 'pebble,' or whatever you do. They call 'em 'fatteries.' They burn fat and make energy from 'em. Somethin' about the country gettin' so fat that we had tons of excess energy just sittin' around, doin' nothin'. Food industry *loved* it. Big-time winner for them, since folks can still stuff their faces and be decently thin. As you can tell," Corcoran smirked, "business is boomin'."

I struggled through my nausea and tried to project a diplomatic air, "Well, I, for one, find it admirable that you are…controlling your weight problem, Steven."

Bloomington nodded at Corcoran with smug, "I told-you-so" satisfaction.

I hope they have to good sense to hook him up to the grid, I thought. *Electric bills would fall like a stone, post-haste.*

The oddly-proportioned scientist lowered his shirt and leaned his head in toward me, "I assume Ricky has already showed you the improvements we've made for the trip?"

Corcoran nodded.

"I was a bit shocked by the addition of weaponry and the decreased recharge time, Steven. Is that," I mustered all of my courage, since I dreaded the answer, "*your* handiwork?"

Bloomington shook his head, "Nope. I'd like to take credit for it, Doctor T, but it's from a bunch of lameshit eggheads in the future. At least these ChronoSaber pricknoses let me fix the old girl up—two weeks of non-stop repairs and retrofits to get her ready for the mission."

I cocked my head, "And *what,* pray tell, *is* the mission, my good Steven?"

He nodded over at Sanchez, "Hey Sophie, you about done?"

I couldn't believe his tone—it was as if he was addressing her like some kind of annoying kid sister. Meanwhile I could barely keep my composure around the lovely, deadly Chronosaber Captain.

She briefly raised a finger, clicked off the device near her ear, and took several quick steps over to us.

"Gentlemen… if you will follow me back to your ship, all will be explained once we're safely back in Baltimore."

Almost out of habit, I looked at Ricky for confirmation.

He nodded, "You heard the 'lady.' Move out!"

We emerged through the hole in the building to a rather grizzly mop-up scene. Chronosaber troops in black jumpsuits were lining Nazi soldiers up in single file, then firing a single high-powered laser bolt through a group of five or so German soldiers at a time. The all-too-familiar scent of singed flesh permeated the scene like a bad air freshener as line by line, group after group of grey and brown-shirted fascists hit the ground, lifeless, like bags of meat.

I felt momentarily bad for the thugs until I realized that they had done *far* worse to the Jews, Slavs, homosexuals, and pretty much *anyone* whom didn't conform to their "ideal" vision of humanity.

Other soldiers escorted white-coated scientists toward the odd bell-shaped craft that Corcoran and I had seen upon our arrival in Leipzig. I squinted—I could've sworn that Neil DeGrasse Tyson was among them. The white-coated men poured over the craft, scanning them and taking measurements as if they were fitting the bells for suits.

We arrived at our ship and received a full escort aboard (with a salute to boot!) from the men who had held me at gunpoint only minutes earlier.

We set a course for Baltimore, and within minutes we were whizzing effortlessly through the sky. Exercising my right as "co-captain" as it were, I insisted in playing Eric Clapton's "Layla" for the duration of the brief flight there.

It took five, maybe ten minutes to reach our destination, and as we did, I realized that my invention may have opened up an entirely new travel industry; clean, comfortable, and fast as the dickens.

One more trillion-dollar industry that was stolen from me, I mused.

We had already broken through the atmosphere, and Baltimore—*my* Baltimore, the 2032 version—stretched before us. It was right around sunset, but even the shades of orange, purple, and red couldn't seem like anything but the cheapest of lipstick on the most grotesque of hogs. Blocks of abandoned buildings stretched in every direction away from Hopkins, the product of years of decay spurred on by the government funneling every last shred of available funding into the foolish enterprise known as World War III, the deadliest conflict in human history.

My laboratory was on the outskirts of campus, situated in a quiet, if formerly desolate part of town. I say "formerly" desolate because much to my shock and surprise, the several blocks immediately around my building were a hive of activity. Athletic-looking men and women scattered about in plain beige coveralls, unloading trucks bearing a rather plain-looking "Corrigan Solutions" logo, with both the "C" and "S" large and unmistakable.

"I see Helene is so ever-subtle," I mused.

Corcoran shrugged, "Yeah, never really did get a good answer on why they were buildin' stuff here, 'specially since they're gonna' tear it all down and move it downtown once the tower's ready."

"Let's just say it's a temporary staging location for something… important…" Sanchez said.

Corcoran and I raised an eyebrow at each other.

Bloomington rolled his eyes, "Oh *that* fucking thing?"

Corcoran and I stared at him.

"What? You'll see soon enough."

I turned my attention back to the massive changes that were scarring my formerly quaint lab. In fact, I had secretly been hoping that somehow, someway, it would eventually be turned into a museum of some sort: the birthplace of time travel…

"They didn't just run a quick hand up her skirt, did they?" I nodded at the lab with gritted teeth.

Corcoran rolled his eyes, "Boy, you're the damned *dumbest* genius I've ever seen! *You* didn't *own* the lab, remember!? It was given as part of the salary of the—"

"—Jacob Harvey Chair of Adjunct Faculty Advisement, yes, *now* I recall," I said.

Fortunately for my bruised ego, Corcoran thought the better of pressing the issue.

The autopilot glided us over the busy disguised ChronoSaber employees and toward the roof of my building. Corcoran's brow furrowed and dampened with the faintest hint of sweat. He raced to the cabinet and rifled through it, searching for something much as I had desperately fumbled for whisky minutes before.

"Come on…come on…where is it…A-*HA!*"

He emerged with the rather crude, old-fashioned garage door opener that functioned as the "controller" to open the roof of my laboratory.

"Well *that* was a close one," I deadpanned.

"Let's just say I've had a bad experience or two," Corcoran let his gaze linger on me with an arched eyebrow for an extra beat.

The ceiling of the edifice below began to retract as the time machine hovered, waiting patiently as the ancient chains and gears removed the ballistic steel ceiling over the lab.

Without the floor of the ship to stop it, my jaw may have well dropped all of the way to the floor below. My lab, my beloved sanctuary that only Avi had managed to infiltrate for going on close to a decade, now teemed with Chronosaber soldiers, each holding an LR-15 laser rifle, trained on the craft (*our* craft!).

"Helene certainly doesn't waste any time, does she?" I asked.

"No she does *not*," Sanchez replied, eyes forward.

We descended to the floor below, which was being converted into a proper landing pad for time machines much larger than ours. Brilliant arcs of electricity welded metal and what appeared to be gravity-controlling plates together, so as not to nick the bottom of the ship, which I gather was fashioned in a somewhat less workmanlike manner to my own careful "old world" craftsmanship, even if said work required the use of quantum computers and 3D-printers.

As we set down, the walls automatically seemed to disappear as the ship brought itself into 360 degree view mode. We opened the ship's door and let Sanchez take the lead, lest we get the same kind of "hero's welcome" we had experienced from the ChronoSaber troops in Leipzig.

Instead of the yellow-eyed, blck-jumpsuited thugs we had seen while fighting the Nazis, these ChronoSaber soldiers were dressed in generic camouflage uniforms with a somewhat gaudy "CS" patch on both the left front breast pocket and the sleeve. The half-dozen men and women saluted Sanchez as she made her way into the ongoing renovations.

Corcoran followed, and then notably their salutes lowered as Bloomington and I followed them.

Ungrateful prigs... I thought.

One of the ChronoSaber soldiers, a rather clean-cut Latino fellow, saluted Sanchez crisply.

"Welcome back ma'am, and congratulations on completing your mission."

Sanchez returned the salute, "At ease, Private. And thank you. Though honestly, the 'fun part' of the mission is just about to begin."

I rolled my eyes. "The 'fun part?' Honestly? As if engaging in gunfights with time-travelling Nazis' wasn't 'fun' enough? What's next? A coterie of knife-throwing horses? Or perhaps a Volkswagen filled with zombie clowns?"

"How in the *fuck* would they get horses to throw knives?" Bloomington wondered aloud.

"It's a simple matter of cattle prods and voltage, Steven," I replied.

"They have hooves?" he shrugged, and waited silently for my reply for several seconds.

I shrugged back at him, not overly concerned with my rare miss.

"So Sophia, this is quite lovely, being escorted from ChronoSaber base to appropriated ChronoSaber base… goons prodding me with laser rifles every opportunity… but what *is* our mission?"

I steeled myself for some kind of cutting remark, delivered in a silky voice with a Stephen Wright-like deadpan.

Instead, all I heard was a slow clap coming halfway across the room, from atop a catwalk that had been hastily placed about halfway up my rather tall former laboratory. Eventually, the clap subsided, and it was followed by an all-too-familiar cackle.

In the low light of the laboratory, or facility, or whatever the devil it was by then, a distinctive, shapely, female form sashayed down the stairs, followed by two somewhat larger gentlemen.

"Typical. So bloody *typical*, my dear Finn," the sultry, middle-aged British lilt intoned.

I balled my fists with a mix of rage and frustration.

"Always in such a hurry. Always demanding to know what's going on *right now!* Only enough time for a witty one-liner or retort before prematurely moving on, failing to *grasp* the full gravity and import of the situation."

At that moment, my erstwhile Benefactor, I should say my *true* erstwhile Benefactor, Helene Tottenham-Clarke emerged from the shadows into the lab's bright, shining lights.

"Miss me, dear?"

CHAPTER FIVE

I had half a mind to pop her one right there, in direct contravention of a previous oath I had taken to never lay hands on a female in an aggressive manner (though I will forgive you, dear reader, given my rather non-existent sexual exploits if you thought I may have initially omitted the "in an aggressive manner" prior to my encounter with one Cynthia Albertson during the previous mission, but I digress…).

Unfortunately, the presence of the heavily-armed team of ChronoSaber commandos ensured that nothing of the sort could occur.

Instead, my only ammunition was my keen wit and prickly tongue.

"You *tart!*" I spat the words at her.

This only elicited a haughty laugh and a smile from Helene.

"Oh, posh! Come now, Finn, though we've had our disagreements in the past, I *knew* you'd find your way out of that mess back…or I should say 'forward' ten years from now."

My face reddened as I took two steps toward her, fists clenched all the while. I plumbed the depths of my unrivaled brainpower for a pithy comeback, a witty retort.

"You *scurrilous* tart!" It was all I could muster through clenched teeth.

The two men behind her emerged from the darkness. One was a heavily-decorated, bald, black man in an American military uniform.

The other appeared to be a flustered, unkempt bumpkin of sorts with an unstylish tweed blazer to match a similarly grotesque haircut. An untrimmed mustache completed the atrocity against style and common decency.

I was shocked that Ricky brought his hand to his brow in a crisp salute toward the soldier, though I suppose Bloomington's limp-wristed, backhanded attempt at the same was equally jarring, if for other reasons.

"General Carter, *sir!*" Corcoran barked the phrase out like a drill sergeant.

"General Carter, *sir!*" Bloomington did his best to copy his superior officer, though his nasally whine was somewhat less-than-impressive, and almost sarcastic-sounding.

The man strutted over to Corcoran and looked him over, as if inspecting his strong chin for defects. To his credit, Corcoran stared straight ahead throughout the entire odd, wordless exchange.

After several moments, the decorated soldier brought a hand to his brow and returned the salute, "At ease."

Corcoran broke into a grin, "Well I'll be damned—General Carter!"

The General flashed an equally broad smile as he extended a firm hand, "Bet you thought you weren't gonna see me again, eh Ricky?"

Ricky's eyes narrowed with mischief, "Eh, when you're in the line of work we are, ya begin to expect the unexpected."

The two exchanged a vigorous handshake for several moments before the General disengaged and turned to Bloomington, "Specialist."

"Hey General," Bloomington's cracking voice betrayed the affected nonchalance of his tone.

I raised an eyebrow at the display, "If your little reunion is over, I'd like to know what in the devil's oven this…this *succubus* is doing here!" I nodded at Helene.

She shook her head and sashayed her way in front of me. She reached to grab my chin, and though I moved to prevent her from doing so, she rapped me hard on the wrist before her fingers came to rest on my freshly-shorn jaw.

"My, *my*. *That's* how you repay me for all I've done for you? The *billions* that I, and my business partners," she nodded at the shabbily-dressed man behind her, "invested in you? This," her free arm motioned around the room in a wide arc, "*wonderful* lab space, leaving you to work, undisturbed, in," she snorted, "perfect anonymity? And not to mention the rather *hefty* amount of money we're willing to pay you now to make you *whole*."

She practically spat the last word at me, though I raised an eyebrow, intrigued.

"Don't forget Avi," I said, half-sighing.

"Ah yes, the private Aramaic lessons that were of," she chuckled, "*so* much use to you in your quixotic little quest to visit Jesus, Trent, whatever you wish to call him. And what do I receive in return?

Name-calling and temper tantrums?" She squeezed my cheeks in like an overzealous aunt condescendingly explaining something to a child.

This time, I raised an arm to force her hand off of me, but Helene caught it mid-flight.

"I'd gladly give you more if you'd let me?" I quipped.

She grabbed the hem of her skirt and raised it an inch with an arched eyebrow, "Oh? That can be arranged…"

I shuddered with a mix of revulsion and arousal.

"Are you two *through* yet?" Corcoran yelled. He made his way over to Helene, "Now I got Bloomy, and I got Doc, and I got 'em both here."

Sanchez cleared her throat behind the Commander, though it did little to interrupt his train of thought.

"That's the last item on your little list. Now I'd like to know what in the," he turned to the General, "no offense, General, sam *fuck* our mission is here."

"Perhaps we should go into the conference room to discuss it," Helene said. She clapped twice and Carter, as well as the man in the ill-fitting jacket, followed closely behind her. Sanchez was behind them, and half of the contingent of soldiers surrounded them.

The other half flanked us and forced us forward, up the freshly-built stairs, and into a room at the top that was a part of an entirely new level of my laboratory.

I caught Corcoran's eye during the forced march, "Remind me to thank you for the *wonderful* trip into this *fabulous* ChronoSaber police state," I hissed.

"Ain't like I had a choice, Doc. The way she sold it to me, this is end of the world, end of *time* shit we're talkin' about here." He nodded at the room ahead, "Not to mention they seem to think your old pal Klaus is pretty important to this whole deal."

"What did they—" I reconsidered my volume and raised a free hand to my mouth, "—what did they tell you about Klaus?"

"Eh, not much. Basically just that mentioning him would get ya to come along on the mission. Plus, ya know, all the Nazis raidin' his lab stuff obviously."

"So then why are *you* going on the mission?"

Corcoran's smirk dropped, "What? 'End of the world' not good enough for ya?"

I shook my head slowly as we entered the conference room.

What I saw next caused me to nearly dislocate my jaw so suddenly did it swing open.

There, in that very conference room, stood Ben Franklin, pounding a gavel on the table in front of an assembled coterie of additional poor facsimiles of historical figures. One of the actors was even dressed in a bright green dinosaur suit, presumably to be replaced by something computer-generated in post production.

My mind immediately raced to the hospital bed I had occupied at Chronobase Alpha back in the age of the dinosaurs. None other than the fetching Captain (nee Commander) Sanchez herself had shown me this very ChronoSaber orientation holovid, complete with ridiculous, British-accented anthropomorphic dinosaur in a short-sleeved, button-down engineer shirt, to prepare me for my "dinosaur hunt," which in reality had been an elaborate way to (quite literally) scare the shit out of me.

"Should Frank's wife apologize for calling him a fat slob? Socrates!" Franklin barked at a toga-ed actor at the end of the table.

I glared at Commander Sanchez.

She met my stare and shrugged.

Helene clapped twice, and the director (a scruffy-looking fellow with a large beard and even larger midsection) snapped to attention.

"Uh…cut! Everyone, take five. Take ten. Take *whatever*!" He eyed Helene nervously even as the old shrew refused to acknowledge him. The actors and crew shuffled out of the room as the director hastily pushed them out the door.

Within thirty seconds, the conference room was completely empty once more. Helene took "Franklin's" former spot at the head of the table, flanked on either side by General Carter and the dowdy mustachioed fellow. Two guards stood near the entrance, though Corcoran, Bloomington, Sanchez and myself were allowed to select our own seats.

Needless to say, I took the one furthest away from Helene.

She pointed her mobile at the holoprojector on the wall behind her. Immediately, a picture of my dear friend and colleague, Klaus Thurbur, filled the front of the room, his icy blue eyes accented by the silvery streak in his thinning, grey hair. Underneath the picture was a perfunctory bio of his numerous known accomplishments.

Helene didn't waste but a moment before beginning, "Klaus Thurbur. Theoretical physicist, University of Leipzig Department of Physics. Known to associate with," she focused her gaze on me, "obnoxious, deviant, utterly mad—"

I cleared my throat and leaned in an arched eyebrow.

Helene waved the gesture off, "—contemporaries, with outlandish, crackpot-like theories."

She tapped another button on her mobile, which brought up a picture of a standard-looking time machine (who would have *ever* thought I'd write those words down when I was studying with Avi those months ago!?).

"This is the *C.T.S. Saint Germain*. Exactly one year from today, Professor Thurbur will," she paused and took in a deep breath, "abscond with it."

The room fell deathly silent for several seconds.

Bloomington raised his hand.

"Klaus *stole* it? A *time* machine? From *ChronoSaber*?" I asked in an effort to save Bloomington the embarrassment of asking the question I knew he would.

"What's abscond mean?" Bloomington blurted out.

Apparently I had inadvertently worsened it.

Helene rolled her eyes (likely in unison with Corcoran and myself) before she narrowed and steeled her gaze, "He *took* it. Made off with it. Just, 'poof!' It's gone." She looked at Sanchez, who hung her head and frowned.

I brightened, "But I thought ChronoSaber security was unmatched? Absolutely un*paralleled*! Practically MI6 and the Secret Service rolled into—"

"Are you *quite* finished? Or shall I have you shipped back to the gutter in London where you can argue with your fellow bums about canned *beans* and *gin* for the rest of your *miserable* existence?!"

My mouth went slack. I reflexively pulled on the collar of my t-shirt and swallowed.

"Well!?"

"I'm still pondering it…" I managed.

"Take all the time you need," she affected a thin smile.

I squinted; clearly she wanted to hear me give a verbal answer, to allow everyone in this hodgepodge of a group to know who was in charge.

"I'm finished," I was willing to comply.

For the moment, I thought.

Her smile became more taut, and downright serpentine, "Good. As you might recall, the only other security breach we had was when a vagrant *was allowed,*" she chewed the words, "to stowaway on a machine bound for 2002."

Bloomington raised his hand again. This time, I politely patted him on the shoulder and shook my head.

"This *other* pilferage by Dr. Thurbur was decidedly *not* by design, and represents an enormous threat to our security. Regardless of what that fool Hank Fleener may have told you—"

I raised an eyebrow. *How could she possibly know who Hank Fleener is*? I thought.

"—this is the sole blemish on all of ChronoSaber's otherwise sterling security record."

Corcoran squinted at Helene, "So why don't ya just, you know, go back and stop him 'fore he steals it?"

Helene looked as if she was about to leap over the table and castrate the Commander, "Commander, you of *all* people should understand the impossibility of such an idea!"

"Right—whatever happened, happened, I know. But I mean, we were just *in* Leipzig, right? Why the *fuck* didn't you tell us to get Doc and Bloomy there like a day sooner, before he boosts it?"

"I assume you also forget the idea that the universe wouldn't allow such an event to happen? That some horrible tragedy would befall your motley little…" she eyed Bloomington with equal parts shock and revulsion, "…*crew*… well before you got access to the man himself?"

"So if we can't find him before the fact, how in the devil will we be able to uncover when and whence he absconded with your 'misplaced' machine?" I asked, perhaps with a twinge too much condescension.

The unkempt-looking hayseed at the front of the room finally opened his fuzzy-lipped maw, "We were hoping that *you* could help us with that, Dr. Templeton."

His voice was deep, with a perfect Americanized elocution that threw me; I was certain that I would be speaking with Uncle Goober from Mayberry. The voice that greeted me was far closer to that of Alec Baldwin.

The man slid a file folder down the table toward me. I appreciated the nod to tradition, even if, admittedly, my tablet was one comfort of my era with which I could scarcely be without.

Sanchez's eyes went wide. She let out a low whistle.

"Wow…" she exhaled.

I looked around the table with incredulity before I nodded at the lovely Commander Sanchez, "Has she reviewed this already?"

Helene rolled her eyes, "Commander Sanchez is *marvelling* at the *vast* quantity of paper she sees before her."

Sanchez nodded, "It's pretty rare…I mean most of the time we just use tablets. Or even just holograms."

The formerly-disheveled man next to Helene now looked anything but; his hickish cow-lick had been shrugged into place, and his eyes, formerly dull and uninspiring, came to life, focused intently on my own.

"These are all of Dr. Thurbur's files found in his laboratory, shortly after his departure."

I thought the better of patting the journal in my pocket the little holographic leprechaun had given me.

Instead, I thumbed through the file folder. It was utterly remarkable! Many of the equations were familiar to *me*, but I had never told another soul about them before my rather abrupt departure, and though Klaus and I had touched on some of the concepts tangentially in our conversations, he demonstrated a mastery of several topics that far outstripped my own genius. Most notable of these topics was optics, which was hardly a surprise to me given our discussions.

More troubling was the fact that within the labyrinthine arrangement of equations upon equations, just when he was about to make a breakthrough that would have allowed *him* to crack the code of time travel, he stopped. Instead, several large "P.T."s in Klaus's handwriting were highlighted on the pages.

"See anything interesting?" The barely-mustached man asked.

"How the devil did you *get* these?" I looked up, indignant for my colleague. "This is tantamount to stealing!"

"It's not stealing when you pay for it," the unkempt man said. He eyed me, then Helene.

I could have reached out and popped the man in the face.

"Allow me to introduce myself. I'm Gabe Marlow."

He paused, as if the name should have struck me like a laser bolt.

Instead, I merely tilted my head with confusion, along with Corcoran and Bloomington.

"Gabe Marlow? Marlow Aerospace?" Marlow continued.

"That some kinda airplane part-maker?" Corcoran asked, his own rural affectation in full force.

Marlow rolled his eyes, "You might know me from my various space-based endeavors. I was one of the first private companies to explore sending a rocket to space. Wanted to build a big, modular space station / hotel / casino in space, charge millionaires *exorbitant* prices for in-orbit entertainment?"

I certainly hope that wasn't the tagline, I thought.

"Oh…*that* Gabe Marlow." I hoped my delivery was wry enough for the tidal wave of sarcasm to flood through.

Marlow shook his head, "Of course, officially, the government awarded some key contracts to other, higher-profile private spaceflight companies." He paused and turned to General Carter, "I told you we should've gone with something bigger—higher profile! Something with explosions!"

"Since you wanted 'Marlow' to be associated with 'explosions in space?'" The General snorted.

Marlow waved him off, "No matter. *Un*officially, we went into business with General Carter here, Army black ops. The stuff we were doing was very cutting-edge, very 'hush-hush.' Not only space stuff either—advanced propulsion, nanotech—" he met eyes with General Carter and put his hand up to the side of his mouth, which I found curious given that his booming baritone voice was still quite audible, "—alien contact. I don't even think Commander Corcoran over here knew what we were doing behind the scenes during Project Omega."

All gazes in the room turned toward the erstwhile "hero."

"Hey, don't look at me," Corcoran shrugged. "I ain't got a *clue* who the hell this joker is."

"That was... by design, Commander. Though not by *my* design, mind you! I wanted to be more hands-on, more into it! It was quite some time ago—I was younger. Dumber. More foolish, perhaps, but DAMN—" Marlow banged loudly on the table, "—if I'd take *shit* from anyone."

We all jumped out of our seats. I heard a shriek and looked at first Sanchez, then Helene, but both women remained unfazed.

It was only when I turned to Bloomington and saw his hand cupped over his mouth that I realized the source of the banshee-like utterance.

Marlow smiled smugly for several moments until the room calmed down once more, "Alas, General Carter here kept a nice buffer between me and my projects. Between me and my pets. And you know what? It was probably for the best. It allowed me to focus more on my business, and as I continued to gain money and power behind the scenes from my forays into black ops, I decided to take on a promising academic as a protégé, a German physicist who was doing incredible things, experiments that, at least I thought—" he glared at me, "—were on the vanguard of manipulating space and time itself."

"Klaus?" I whispered.

Marlow nodded, "Indeed."

"But...*why* would you need to 'manipulate space and time?' What exactly were you working on?"

Marlow raised an eyebrow, first at Carter, then at Helene.

They shook their heads.

"Let's just say you'll find out soon enough, Doctor Templeton."

I collected myself, "All due apologies, Mr. Marlow, but I think you owe me a little more explanation that that. We have the finest, most experienced crew in history ready to work for you...shouldn't we have a bit more briefing here up front?"

I very much hoped that Bloomington wasn't picking his nose at that moment.

Marlow shook his head, "My cash, my rules. Besides, given the nature of this little expedition, I think you'll thank me later for keeping you in the dark. Plus it makes it easier to get you your payout, no questions asked."

"What do you mean?" my eyes narrowed.

"I've put up 1,000 Bitcoin to be delivered to you directly upon successful completion of this mission."

He leveled a steady gaze at me.

"Yes but—" It took a second for the full force of the words to hit me. "1,000 *Bitcoin*?"

Corcoran and Bloomington looked at each other, dumbfounded.

Marlow noticed their confusion, "It's the equivalent of about $3 billion in 2012 dollars."

Bloomington's hand shot up.

"And 100 Bitcoin each for each of the rest of you."

Steve, Ricky, and Sophia looked at one another.

Bloomington's hand shot up again.

"That's $300 million in 2012 dollars for each of you."

Bloomington's hand came to his chin, deep in thought. Or I should say, "as deep in thought as possible for him."

1,000 Bitcoin? For me? Surely it wasn't *quite* as nice as the notoriety that I so desperately craved… though I suppose it was a "passable" consolation prize.

"Of course, I asked ChronoSaber to match it, but unfortunately Helene refused."

She glared at the unkempt, gravely-voiced billionaire. He returned her look with a sharp smile.

"Cheap bitch," I muttered under a cough at Helene.

"Fancy prig," she shot back.

"And why would I ever work with this…this *hussy* on *anything*?" my rage boiled to the surface, ready to erupt in a tide of invective.

"I suppose 'billions of dollars of compensation' isn't good enough now?" Marlow asked.

"The reason I declined your offer, Gabriel," she sighed, "Is that I know what Doctor Templeton *really* wants. And not only that, but I can *give* it to him…" Helene took a draught from a nearby glass as she leaned over the table. As I steadied myself to make another quip about her unwanted sexual advances, she produced a smile.

Then, her eyes went steely, her expression almost grave as she gritted her teeth, "I *promise* that when this is all over, we will host a 'Doctor Phineas Templeton Day,' at ChronoSaber's expense, in order to get you the—" she sighed, "—*fame* and recognition that you so crave."

My mouth, which had been ready to unleash the full fury of my sharp tongue on its erstwhile target, went slack. I truly didn't know what to say; I looked first at Sanchez, then at Corcoran. Both officers nodded their assent, even if Sophia's was somewhat reluctant.

"R—*really*?" I asked. I didn't know what to do—all residual vengeance directed toward Corcoran (if not Helene) melted away, as I considered all of the wondrous possibilities: entire museums and universities named for *me!* Lecture series, bestselling books (*bestselling* books! Not drivel written by some hack on my behalf), the whole nine yards! My eyes went starry with thoughts of the opportunities that—

"Look, we don't even know what the damn *mission* is yet!" Corcoran blurted out.

Marlow snorted, "Flip to the back of that file, Doctor."

I shook my head to collect myself (and did so), and found a package that looked like it had been torn into by a couple of hungry pit bulls trying to get into a butcher counter. Despite its condition, I could clearly make out the salutation, which I read aloud.

"To: Doctor Phineas Templeton. From: Your Friend Klaus." My laboratory address followed.

"We went ahead and *inspected* it. Hope that's not a problem," Carter said without a hint of emotion.

"No, no—far be it from me to worry about your federal government committing federal crimes," I said. I hoped my tone didn't betray the *other* journal Klaus had left for me in his lab.

Inside was one of the tiny notebooks that Klaus was fond of using to jot down errant thoughts.

Instead of the dirty limericks and edge-to-edge equations that I had come to expect from Klaus's books, there were five specific dates and locations (in very neat handwriting, might I add):

25-4-2580 B.C., Giza, Egypt: The show must go on!

13-5-9203 B.C., Jerusalem, Israel: A miner annoyance…

5-1-13872 B.C., Latitude: N. 38 degrees, 43 ′, 18 ″, Longitude W. 27 degrees, 13′, 14″: Bust a "Cap"

23-12-1749, Paris, France: Count Your Blessings R.I.P.

But perhaps most jarring of all was the final line, a date that caused Sophia's eyes to widen and her mouth to utter a curse even before it came into my field of view.

When it did, my jaw went slack. I reached for a handkerchief to wipe my dampening brow, but found none in the clothing that the Commander had provided. My skin went pale and clammy even as I read off the final line, chilling in both its brevity and meaning:

20-4-2102, Cairo, Egypt: Bye Bye…

I could only form two words, awful ones that foretold the fresh hell I was about to enter:

"Oh goody."

CHAPTER SIX

The snark and amusement quickly drained from my face as I levelled narrowed eyes at Helene.

"*You* put Klaus up to this, didn't you?!"

She raised a cold, calculating eyebrow, "Of course—*that* makes sense. I somehow engineered the theft of one of my proprietary time machines by one of the few people to ever exist on this planet who *might* be able to reverse engineer it, and ruin the outrageous monopoly I have so fiendishly worked to engineer!"

I shook my head, "But you *know* he doesn't!"

Helene wrinkled her nose, "Do I? That last entry—the end of the world?!"

I looked at Sanchez, "Is she right, Commander Sanchez? That wasn't more ChronoSaber propaganda designed to mislead me?"

During my previous jaunt through time, Commander Sanchez had been the one to inform me that April 20th, 2102 was the date beyond which no time traveller had returned.

More troubling, people from her time onward had no idea as to why.

Sanchez nodded, "I'm afraid she's correct. That information was absolutely true."

Helene subsumed her scowl beneath an affected grin, "As much as you must think I'm simply a cruel, heartless bitch hellbent on making your lives a living hell—"

Corcoran and I exchanged a knowing glance.

"—I'll have you know that you—*especially* you, Finny—are of far less import to me than this Thurbur fellow potentially *ending the world!*"

She spat the final sentence across the long conference table with such vigor that I reached for my non-existent kerchief once more to wipe my face.

"Oh, *spare* me, Helene—" I started.

Carter pounded the table, "That's *enough*, God *damn* it!"

He let the rich bass tones of his voice reverberate around the room for several seconds before nodding at Corcoran, "Now you and I both know that Army Black Ops finds working with private industry somewhat distasteful," he eyed the two billionaires at the head of the table with suspicion, "but we've made exceptions in the past, Ricky. Namely for you to end the Third World War later this year."

I scowled first at Corcoran, then at Carter, and opened my mouth to speak.

Carter's glared right back and stopped me in my tracks; the veins in his neck strained against his dark skin as his jaw jutted out taut, giving me the distinct impression that he was chewing on nails.

"By all reports, if this Thurbur has anything to do with whatever occurs in 2102, for good or ill, then we need to find out what that might be."

"So what are we to do then? Go on *another* scavenger hunt through time, with little more than Klaus's *ridiculous* clues to guide us?"

Marlow nodded, "That's *exactly* what you *will* do."

"Yes!" Bloomington pumped his fist like an adolescent on his first trip to a whorehouse.

I shot a sidelong glance at the artificially-thin scientist.

Helene interjected, "This time, though, the gloves are off: no restrictions on jumping, and no restraints on the QC. You may tackle the list in any order you like, though I would suggest that you four start with the first entry on the list, since it's a ChronoSaber operation."

My eyes bolted upward momentarily before they settled on Helene, "Four?"

"Awesome!" Bloomington practically squealed with glee, "I'll tell Marie to get her shit packed—"

"Commander Sanchez will be accompanying you as the ChronoSaber attaché on the mission."

For once, Corcoran, Bloomington, Sanchez and I all yelled in unison:

"What!?"

Sanchez shook her head, "Ms. Tottingham-Clarke, with all due respect, my responsibilities at ChronoBase Alpha will likely preclude me from—"

"Suzy-Q here doesn't even know how to operate one'a these things!" Corcoran interrupted Sophia.

"I have to say, I agree with the Commander on this one—" I tried to get a word in edgewise.

"Do you know how many Nazis Marie's mowed down? Seventeen. I counted every last *fucking* one of 'em!" Bloomington screamed.

"And how many have *I* mowed down, Steve?" Sanchez narrowed her eyes at the skinny-fat man child.

He thought for a second and sighed, "Forty-three… I guess…"

"Shut up. *Shut up!*" Helene barked. She blinked and covered her ears, "Christ on *Christmas,* it's like dealing with *children* in here! Am I the only one who sees the grave import of this?" she looked at Sanchez, "Sophia, the Army already has a representative on-board, and as much as I…" she looked at Marlow, "…*tolerate* Mr. Marlow's involvement with this mission, I need someone from ChronoSaber to serve as my own eyes and ears onboard, and keep the, *ahem, others* on board on the straight-and-narrow."

Corcoran rose from his chair, "I'll be *damned* if I have some stuck-up soldier *wanna-be* lookin' over Doc and my shoulders on this trip!"

He nodded at me, and I dipped my head in return.

"And, uh, Bloomy over here, too, a'course…" He must have noticed Bloomington's peculiar, face-drained-of-pudge scowl.

Carter shook his head, "No 'ifs,' 'ands,' or 'buts' about it, Rick—Sanchez is going. It's a concession we had to make to get use of the time machine for this mission."

Corcoran turned to Sanchez. Sophia narrowed her eyes at him in reply, "Thanks for the vote of confidence, Commander."

Ricky didn't skip a beat, "Don't mention it."

Helene rose from her chair and shook her head, "If we're *quite* through here, I have times to go, people to see."

She paused before completing her thought, eying the four of us at the end of the table much like a lion would a wounded gazelle.

"So that's it? 'Oh, let's get right into the scavenger hunt,' then, isn't it? Send dumb old Dr. Templeton out to be embarrassed once more, one more time—?"

"Oh, for the love of *God*," Helene rolled her eyes, "*Must* we listen to you throw *another* tantrum, Finny? Isn't Marlow here paying you enough to just go along with it for once without being an obstinate, hard-headed *bore*?"

I thought about her assertion for a moment. I knew Helene was up to *something*, but as of yet, I wasn't sure what. I doubted that Klaus was in cahoots with the wily old shrew; after all, Marlow, though no Helene Tottenham-Clarke as far as net worth goes, still seemed to be fabulously wealthy, to the point that he could entice me to join this voyage by flashing a stack of Bitcoin at me.

Nonetheless, I wasn't likely to tease out what she had up her sleeve in the presence of either Carter or Marlow. More importantly, perhaps Sanchez knew more than she was letting on, and could be pumped for information on the voyage.

Not to mention that I utterly *abhorred* seeing my beautiful laboratory reduced to such a monstrosity of ChronoSaber goons and gaudy technology from who-knows-how-far in the future?

"Actually, I'm told people find me rather charming," I said, with the faintest hint of a smirk.

Helene sighed,"Now, if there's no more *bullshit*—" she turned toward me as she said the word, "—or nothing else terribly pressing…"

She allowed the silence to fill the room for a good two seconds.

"Good enough for me," Helene walked out of the room, flanked by the ChronoSaber guards that waited outside. The two soldiers stationed at the door preempted any impromptu Q and A between the erstwhile time travellers and General Carter.

We made our way down the staircase toward my time machine. No matter how much ChronoSaber had violated the old girl with all manner of "improvements" (though, truth be told, I *was* grateful for many of them), she still looked utterly remarkable, with nary a scratch on her shining, brushed alloy finish. I allowed myself a moment to admire the ship with a hearty sigh before I made my way toward the gangway.

Marlow followed directly behind me, and though I didn't know what to make of the man, I was heartened by the somewhat frosty tone with which Helene had referred to him. Though now, more than ever, my guard was ever-raised—on the lookout for further traps and feints—I thought that anyone who bankrolled Klaus (and who offered such a princely sum to myself) couldn't be *wholly* irredeemable.

That's likely what others think of you and Helene, you dolt! I chastised myself.

It was only later that I realised that my likability (or I should say lack thereof) likely painted a far different picture of our relationship than previously considered.

As we approached the ramp, Corcoran stopped and saluted General Carter with his right hand, while his left pulled Bloomington back toward him even as the now-svelte and grotesque scientist let out his familiar (if out of place) squeal.

"Guess this is goodbye again, General."

Carter returned Corcoran's salute, "Maybe. Maybe not, Rick. You be careful out there. You're far more than a desk jockey, shit, more than even a soldier. You're an icon now. America needs you. Get back in one piece, whatever the cost."

Corcoran nodded. I craned my neck to get a better look at the Commander. His eyes were dull; they stared straight through the General to a place far, far away. It was the same expression he had after he witnessed the carnage we had unwittingly wrought back in the Mayan village on our first trip.

Of considerably greater import, it was the same vacant, yet understanding, stare that he had given me so many times over the course of our first journey, almost *willing* me to understand, to figure out the con he was running against me.

I never did.

This time will be different, I assured myself as I followed Marlow onto the now-narrow entryway to the ship. I found it odd that the billionaire was making his way onto the ship alongside the crew, but I rightly suspected he had his reasons for so doing.

One of the features of my design on which I had most prided myself was the open layout of the craft. Though I wasn't a proper architect or interior designer, I knew enough about the subject from my father's short lectures on ancient Greek and Roman buildings to know that the single room with small alcoves off to the side gave individuals the sense that the craft was larger.

Now, though, with expanded living quarters, another head, even more chairs on the *bridge*, the ship felt downright claustrophobic.

Hopefully that feeling will be offset by Bloomington's decreased tonnage, I thought with a chuckle.

"What's so funny?" Marlow asked.

"Pardon?" I asked. Perhaps I hadn't realised entirely how audibly proud I was at my mental jest at Steven's expense.

"Forget it," Marlow shook his head. He arched an eyebrow and looked me over slowly, deliberately, almost as if he were a jeweler inspecting a diamond for flaws.

"Take a holopic, it would last longer," I quipped.

"I'm sorry it's just… I read your book you know."

"So *you're* the one," I rolled my eyes.

"Phineas Templeton himself," Marlow ignored my jest. Instead he extended a warm hand, "It is an honor, sir."

"Forgive me if I don't take your hand; given my *history* with *scoundrels*," I threw my voice toward Ricky, who remained steadfast in his procession toward the cockpit, "in the past."

Marlow's jaw dropped open, "Oh of *course!* Stupid old me! I forgot what that snake in the grass she-devil had done to you. My God; the father of time travel, relegated to history's dustbin, all so Helene could make a few extra bucks."

I gritted my teeth and forced myself to pat the frumpy billionaire on the back, over that *hideous* brown tweed blend he attempted to pass as a jacket.

"Indeed, indeed…" I took a breath.

Marlow pulled me close and grabbed my forearm. "We will meet again, Dr. Templeton. I know time travel scrambles the old noggin a bit—gets you feeling nutty sometimes. Just remember, if you're ever in a pickle, I've always got your back."

The unkempt billionare patted me a bit too forcefully, almost as if he was manhandling me before awkwardly shoving his hands in his pockets.

I rubbed my chin with my free hand before I opened my mouth to speak.

"Wish I could be more specific, but you'll know what I mean when you need it. Until then, I'll just say, 'until next time."

With that, he patted me twice on the back, the second so forceful that it halfway propelled me into the command deck as he made his way back down the gangway.

Or I suppose you could frame it that he gave me a running start to the bar! Even though I had seen the woman mere moments before, the mere sight of Helene's face (along with the veiled poison the words clearly held for Marlow) led me to take the few short steps over and fix myself a Macallan Eighteen, neat.

I took down several swallows in a single draught and craved more. Though one might think that my time in the past as a bum had caused my habit drinking to cross the line into "problem" territory, I still blamed my unquenchable thirst for scotch on the medigel and my harpy of a Benefactor more than anything else.

I sopped up the stray whisky from my freshly-shorn chin with a cocktail napkin, sighed, and turned to wave a hearty goodbye to Marlow with an affected smile.

Instead, I found wild whisps of dark hair standing half on-end before I looked downward and saw Bloomington's gaunt-yet-gooey smiling face next to an empty glass.

"Hey, save some for me, crapface!" Bloomington nudged me with a limp elbow, in what I suppose was designed to be an attempt at camaraderie.

I smiled thinly and poured him a healthy swig.

"Whoa, whoa, whoa—I'm not all medigelled-out anymore!" Bloomington held up his hands in mock protest.

I shrugged and dumped two-thirds of his glass into my own before I took another hearty pull off of it.

A sharp snort echoed around the cabin, "Jesus Christ (I resisted the urge to correct Sophia by saying 'Trent Albertson;' it had become a bit of a habit of mine to interchange the two names), is this all you people *do* on these trips of yours?" Sanchez couldn't hide the incredulity of her uncharacteristically judgmental tone.

Before I could reply, the glass in my hand clinked as Steven shot his hand out and connected it with his own.

"Just like old times, eh Doctor Templeton?"

As I rolled my eyes, Corcoran turned around from the flight deck and grinned.

"Hey Doc, if yer hungry, trash can's over there." He pointed at a corner of the kitchenette.

I harumphed, somewhat less than amused.

He grinned, "If you're done bein' a wino for the time being, I could use ya up front to, you know, pilot the *damned ship!*"

I bristled, then refilled my glass for a final time, and made my way over to the flight deck.

Corcoran motioned toward the two-key contraption on the dashboard. Ricky's was already in place; I removed mine from my neck, inserted it into the fitting, and turned.

The console came to life with the familiar "home" screens I had installed, even if several more options for weapons and the engines had been added.

"Think ya can remember how to fly this thing?" Corcoran asked.

I calmly reached out and hit the "auto-pilot" button on the console.

"Yep," I said.

The computer flashed all manner of icons and text on both screens. The familiar time travel display popped up, complete with the map of the world and "dial" icon that controlled the target time period.

I must confess, dear reader, that my initial instinct was to program the ship to go anywhere *but* one of the time periods provided by Helene, just out of principle. After all, it was her ridiculous little scavenger hunt that had not only driven me utterly mad, but also had been *designed to do so!* Oh, what I could do with an untethered time machine, the places I could go, all of the fantastical historical figures with whom I could interact, set timeline be damned! My eyes gained a mischievous gleam as I continued to turn the dial toward parts unknown.

My head tilted involuntarily as I considered what all that would truly mean; being a mere observer to God-knows what kind of a historical travesty, another important person torn from the pages of history and revealed to be yet another ChronoSaber puppet, playing out a role until a preordained death, when thousands more mourners from the twenty-first century would show up to simultaneously celebrate the poor wretch's life and pay ChronoSaber handsomely for the privilege to do so.

I shuddered at the thought of contributing to such a vile enterprise, albeit tangentially.

Besides, all thoughts of revenge aside, Klaus almost assuredly needed our help, whenever he was. Though Helene, and, by extension, Sanchez might have some idea of how Professor Thurbur operated, neither had the faintest idea how the man thought, of what a brain so overpowered with intellect was capable. Only someone with a similarly outrageously bright mind could even hope to do so, and, at least according to some of history's greatest businesspeople, there was only one man who fit the description.

Even if they had to dispatch another paper hero to an alley in London to find him.

Speaking of Ricky, his gruff, Southern twang rang in my ear.

"Hey 'puter, can we get some tunes on in here? Maybe…oh, I dunno…'Magic Carpet Ride,' by Steppenwolf?"

My eyes nearly shot through the roof of the craft; how utterly predictable, given that it had been the "runner up" as the first song I chose to play whilst taking off to times unknown on my first voyage back in time.

The (admittedly catchy) tune played throughout the ship. Corcoran grinned like an idiot who had discovered a piece of "half-chewed" gum stuck under a park bench (or I suppose I could just say "Steve Bloomington" to save us all some time and trouble).

"I could get used to this…" Corcoran leaned back in his chair, hands folded behind his head.

"I had no idea you were such a *First Contact* fan," I muttered.

"What now?"

Instead of answering, I merely shook my head knowingly.

"Wow…talk about ancient…" Sophia startled me from over my right shoulder. "Even the *Star Trek* movies with Chris Pine are *old*, old."

My face went flush.

She broke into a rare smile and put her hand on my shoulder as she leaned over. "It's okay—I'm kinda a Trekkie too." she whispered at me.

I do believe the temperature in that cockpit rose a good five degrees centigrade at precisely that moment, as I was compelled to pat my brow with a handkerchief.

Sophia's elegant hands deftly maneuvered over the controls. She pulled up the first set of coordinates:

25-4-2580 B.C., Giza, Egypt: The show must go on!

This time, the computer barely hesitated in its calculations:

"99.9%"

The red "engage" button flashed up on the screen. As I pushed it, an involuntary reflex pushed a cough through my lips, almost as if in vain protest of where we were headed and what we were doing.

As we ascended through the lab and into the clouds, even I couldn't begin to fathom the awesome, terrible events that were to come.

CHAPTER SEVEN

We emerged from the wormhole to find the earth cloaked in calm, quiet, blissfully *empty* space once more. Gone were the dozens of saucers cribbed from my own design and ferrying multiple different versions of the same rich, slack-jawed millionaire from time A to time B.

In their place flashed thousands of wondrous specks of starlight, each one a sparkling testament to just how tidy, how utterly *boring* our view of the rest of the galaxy was.

The ship continued its descent, and first Africa, then, more accurately, Egypt came into view. I don't know if it was the medigel toying with my emotions or something else entirely, but I blinked several times as silent tears wandered their ways out of my eyes.

My mind flashed back to one of the last conversations I had with my father before his death in the mid-teens.

"Well, father—"

"What ever happened to just plain old 'Dad,' Finn? I mean, my God, just because you grew up in England doesn't mean you have to talk like some kind of a Limey ba—"

I cut him off rather curtly, "—I was thinking, now that you've retired, and I'm on the precipice of graduating, perhaps we could take that holiday to see Giza: the pyramids, the sphinx, et cetera and so forth. We both *so* love the Egyptology exhibit at the British Museum—I'd like to think I learned more on those walks we took when I was younger than about that pitiable wretch who sat on the side of the road like a lump of—"

Father interrupted me with a deep, weary sigh, "It isn't safe, Finn. Not yet. All'a the chaos over there, we'd be liable to get kidnapped or killed. Besides," I could almost hear him fidget more deeply into his chair, "We'll have plenty of time for that later. For now, I wanna sit back, relax, and enjoy not screaming at some piss-pants MBA types for a year or two."

He died within the month.

I shouldn't have been shocked; if anything, I was surprised that his body didn't give out sooner under the mountain of stress and cigarette ash he heaped upon himself.

We continued to descend toward a surprisingly verdant Egyptian landscape, the unending desert just another subverted expectation of time travel, a concept with which I was becoming far too familiar through my travels.

The craft lowered itself beneath the clouds and my mouth must have dropped, practically unhinged.

There stood the three Giza pyramids, as barely visible specs carted heavy blocks of stone up a nearly-complete faceplate to the largest of the three edifices. In stark contrast to the enormous, crumbling blocks of granite I was used to seeing in countless pictures and travelogues, a bright alabaster material coated the surface of the great monolith.

As "awe-inspiring" as those pre-War photos were that set the monuments against the various fast food establishments that littered the modern suburb of Giza, dare I say that the *actual* sight of the pyramids was jarring. Thousands of blocks of stone, weighing in at millions of tons, representing one of the early pinnacles of human achievement.

And we'd get to witness some of the final blocks being put into place.

The collector of antiquities inside me could hardly contain himself!

Of course, leave it to ChronoSaber to ruin a majestic, mind-expanding cultural experience. As we continued our descent toward the valley floor, I noticed several brushed-metal discs similar to our own baking in the midday sun.

I blinked twice when my eyes fell upon a man with a golden head in the shape of a hawk with sapphire eyes; he waved us in with a couple of stick-like devices that projected beams of light toward our craft. Almost like something out of *Stargate* or some other similarly awful B-movie.

As I strained my eyes, I felt Ricky's hand on my shoulder as he looked toward Sanchez and Bloomington in the back of the room.

"Hey, JLo, Bloomy—"

"JLo?" Sanchez narrowed her eyes.

"What did the old English broad mean by this is a ChronoSaber base'a some sort?"

All eyes on the craft turned toward Sanchez.

"I'm under strict orders to let you see this one for yourselves."

Sophia reached for her sidearm, her reflexes much quicker than mine, which I suppose may have been dulled by my multi-month-long bender, medigel be damned.

"Shit!" Bloomington cried out.

It was only when I turned to face Corcoran that I realised that she was only preemptively drawing on Ricky, so as to prevent him from forcing her to tell at gunpoint.

"Still need to work on our quick-draw skills, do we?" I asked. The corner of my quivering lip betrayed my bravado.

The Commander squinted at me, perhaps remembering his confession to me at the First Ecumenical Council on our previous voyage regarding his decided lack of quick-draw ability—perhaps the only aspect of combat in which he was not utterly a killing machine.

Ricky dropped his hand to his side and sighed, "Guess we oughtta get to seein' what's out there, then," he affected a thin, wise-arsed grin.

He turned to me and nodded at the key box on the dashboard. My eyes widened as I scampered over to the contraption, pulled out the key, and replaced it securely around my neck.

I discreetly made my way to the armory cabinet and crouched behind Corcoran's now-vacant gunnery chair. "Computer, open armory," I whispered.

"ARMORY UNSECURED! ARMORY UNSECURED!" The wail of the alarm was second in annoyance only to the intruder alarm I had installed for the flight deck.

Corcoran winced as he strode over to me, "Turn off that damned noise!" he yelled at the computer.

It immediately obeyed his command.

He reached inside and grabbed one of the brand-new Beretta nine millimetres from its holster. He loaded a filled magazine into place and handed it to me.

"Commander, what if Commander Sanchez sees that—"

"Sees what?" Sophia's stern tone caused me to flinch.

I looked at Corcoran before I extended the pistol, handle-first, toward the lovely Commander Sanchez.

"I suppose you'll be confiscating this?"

She shook her head and chuckled, "No offense, Doctor Templeton, but I think I can handle whatever you might be able to do with that thing," her chuckle turned into a full-on laugh as she walked toward the exit.

"Doc's a killer, you know!" Corcoran shouted after her.

I narrowed my eyes at Ricky.

"Kinda…sorta…" he muttered.

I sighed and reached for one of the shoulder holsters in the armory. I fitted it snugly around my midsection and fastened it. It was only then that I realised that the Commander hadn't bothered to check the clothing file for new outfits for this stretch of the trip. I quickly shook the thought out of my head; it didn't matter. No matter what we wore, history would always record that we had dressed this way.

I snarled briefly at the memory of all of the ridiculous costumes Helene had made me wear during our first excursion as I followed the rest of the crew toward the doorway.

"Open the damned door, already!" Corcoran growled. I quietly fumed; despite Corcoran's earlier assertions to the contrary, it sure seemed as if my time machine had a new master.

We emerged in the bright, hot sun of the Egyptian afternoon. Though I had expected to see nothing but miles of sand, I was shocked by what seemed to be miles and miles of dark, rich soil filled with sprouting plants that dominated the landscape, marred only by the monolithic architecture of the pyramids and surrounding structures, the landing pad we currently occupied, and the boxy, stone-work building now in front of us.

The man in the ridiculous hawk helmet stuck out a hand, "Welcome to ChronoBase Igloo," he said, voice reverberating through the bell-like construct surrounding his head.

"What the fuck?" Bloomington snorted as he wiped his brow with his already-drenched shirtsleeve. "It's hotter than my asshole after eating P.F. Chang's!"

"Kind of a play on words, you know?" the man in the hawk headdress responded. He eyed the rest of us and issued a crisp salute when he reached Sanchez.

"Captain Sanchez, ma'am!"

"At ease, soldier," she responded with a glance over her shoulder at Ricky. "Where's Commander Rayburn?"

"He was on his way, ma'am. Must've gotten caught up with some—"

A chorus of horns interrupted the hawk-headed fellow, and directed our attention toward the side of the stone building.

What we witnessed astounds me to this day; there, seated on a damned *throne* carried by eight pasty-skinned, time-travelling morons, each grinning like an idiot, was a man dressed as an honest-to-God Egyptian Pharaoh.

I say "dressed as" since the man's large frame immediately gave him away as someone not of that time, though surprisingly the same could be said of the eager servants that carted him around like King Tut.

His dark skin glistened in the beating sunlight to the point that I thought he must have oiled himself up just for this eye-roll-inducing approach.

Corcoran, Bloomington, and I stood there, mouths agape, wondering what in God's name was going on.

As the garishly-adorned "pharaoh" approached, Sanchez placed her hands on her hips and shook her head.

"This assignment is going to your head, Cy."

The servants placed the throne on the ground and bowed toward the man in the ridiculous outfit.

He chuckled, "What? You thought shepherding millionaire assholes around on ridiculous dinosaur hunts was a better gig than lettin' them not only *worship* you, but *pay* for the privilege to do so?"

Sanchez's scowl softened, "Hey, I could've come here and played Cleopatra if I had wanted to."

Now, at this point, dear reader, I must admit that I must've swallowed several errant grains of sand. How else can one explain the rather loud and forceful manner in which I cleared my throat?

All eyes fixated on me.

"Sophia, I *do* believe you've mixed up your history. Cleopatra ruled in the late first century B.C. Perhaps you were looking for 'Nefertiti,' in which case you may have been more on point, but she, too, would be a bit of an anachronism in this era, as she reigned in the fourteenth century B.C."

Corcoran rolled his eyes, "Well that's fuckin' *great*, Doc. 'Preciate the history lecture."

Rayburn shook his head and scanned the group to address me, "Look fella, I—"

His eyes went wide as he did a double-take.

"Commander *Corcoran*?"

Ricky looked at me, eyebrow raised, eyes narrowed, lips curled into the rakish grin that had haunted my dreams for all those months—that very same grin with which he had greeted me in the London alleyway not but a day before.

Corcoran shrugged and stuck out his hand, "Yeah, s'pose so. You must be Khufu."

It must've looked as if I had been smacked squarely in the face with a frying pan as I stared at Corcoran with bemused wonder.

"What? You ain't the only one who knows his Egyptian history."

I ignored Ricky and turned toward Rayburn, "Careful!" I said, even as the man stuck out a thick forearm to grasp Corcoran's, ever vigilant of the swindle that Ricky had pulled on me when we first met in ancient Mexico.

"Lieutenant Commander Cyrus Rayburn, Chronosaber. Call me Cy. Damned honor to meet ya, Commander."

"Pleasure's all mine," Corcoran continued to grin like an idiot.

We stood in silence for several seconds before I cleared my throat once more.

Corcoran shot me a bothered glare, "These are my associates, *Doctah* Phineas Templeton, Steve Bloomington, and you know Sergeant Suzy-Q over here…"

I expected a bothered frown or withering glare from Sanchez, but I must say I was pleasantly surprised as she wordlessly took a step toward Corcoran, grabbed his arm, pulled it behind his back, and hit him precisely on the rear of the leg, forcing him to his knee.

"Ow—God *damn* it!" Corcoran yelled.

"Jesus *Christ*, Sophia, be careful—the man's an American treasure!" Rayburn shouted.

Sanchez took several mock off-balanced steps forward, "Oh dear—*clumsy* me!" She batted the lashes that covered those beautiful brown eyes, "I wouldn't want to harm such a *fragile* national heirloom…" she snorted.

Corcoran instinctively reached for his pistol. I had known the man long enough to realize that Sanchez had gotten dangerously close to squeezing Ricky's hair trigger a millimetre too far. I held my breath for one second…two…afraid to exhale save it would mean the end of poor Sophia.

Then it hit me: I couldn't just *stand* there. I sat in my haunches, ready to spring. Sweat beaded on my brow and flowed near my eyes, though I wouldn't dare to indulge in so much as a reflexive wipe of the face, fearful it might set Ricky off.

"Reauuggh!" I flung myself between the Commander and Sophia, arms outstretched, ready to take the bullet for the fetching leader of Chronobase Alpha.

Instead, Ricky put his hands by his sides and stood up, wry smile affixed to his face, "Nothin' of it," he said, as I flew past. He winked at her, "Long trip we got ahead of us. Good to know I have a *rasslin'* partner if I need one."

Oddly enough, Bloomington of all people rushed in to help me to my feet, concern plastered all over the slack skin of his face.

Corcoran raised his eyebrows, "He, uh—"

"Medigel sickness," Sanchez didn't miss a beat.

"Medigel sickness," Corcoran repeated, almost like Isaac Newton struggling to complete one of Hank Fleener's equations all those years ago.

Rayburn shook his head and motioned to the archway leading to the plateau, "Follow me."

CHAPTER EIGHT

The relief on the servants' faces was palpable when Rayburn clapped his hands twice in succession to dismiss them. They rushed out of the room into another building adorned by Egyptian hieroglyphics, but unmistakably also marked in large, bold English words:

"Fuck Den."

The awful, orgasmic sounds coming from that room seemed to confirm that it had been properly labelled.

I cleared my throat once more.

Rayburn held out a large, dark hand toward me.

"Cough drop?"

I waved him off.

"They're lavender-honey flavored."

I looked around quickly to see if any of my comrades were looking, then snuck one of the lozenges into my mouth.

"My, my… usually they don't show me the 'Fuck Den' on these trips until the *second* fifteen minutes."

"Five hundred grand you ain't *never* seen a Fuck Den in your life, Doc," Corcoran shot back dead serious for a minute before breaking into a wide grin.

"So is this some sort of whor-whorehouse," I half-choked on the word, "lost to time?"

Sophia and Rayburn laughed.

"Something like that," Rayburn shook his head. "We have a very particular clientele. Sure, the," he paused, "pleasures of the flesh are part of that. But… we also cater to a… how do I put this? A 'BDSM' crowd."

"*Realllllly?*" Bloomington said, perhaps somewhat too creepily.

The rest of us stared at him.

"What? Marie and I've been trying some new shit in bed. Now that I'm," he stretched his arms above his head, "more svelte and limber."

I'm surprised Sophia and I were able to hold our lunches in.

Rayburn changed the subject, "Helene told me to be expecting a group'a VIPs, but I had no *idea* Commander Corcoran would be involved in this little expedition."

"What exactly did she tell you about why we're here?" I dusted myself off and mustered as much confidence as I could; I was in no mood to mince words.

"Well, I know you're here to get the tour, ask me some questions, but not quite sure what the *hell* this whole…" he waved his hands in the air theatrically, "…to-do was about, 'specially if Ricky Corcoran and *you-know-who* are here."

I was more than happy to pry through the opening, "Oh? You mean a scientist, a German fellow, goes by the name of Klaus—"

Rayburn nodded, "Professor Thurbur!?"

I stopped and had to clasp my hand over my mouth out of bred politeness.

"You know—He was *here* already?" I asked, hand still firmly in place to muffle my words.

"Oh sure—great guy. *Great* guy. He was here with that cool-lookin' dog'a his—"

"Archimedes…" I whispered.

"Yeah—that's its name! He was pokin' around here, asking some crazy questions. I told him even though *I'm* from *his* future, he probably knows more about all this Egyptian shit than I do—I'm just the soldier they hired to run this operation. I have strict orders to show you exactly what he wanted to see, answer all the questions I can, you name it. Even have one of my Egyptologists meeting us up there to help explain."

At that moment, a couple of foul-smelling, absolutely filthy time-tourists walked by and bowed at Rayburn.

He clapped twice again and momentarily affected an overly-serious frown, "Quickly, make haste to the Fuck Den!" Rayburn ordered, and broke into a smile.

"Thank you, Pharaoh!" The man said.

"Your most benevolent command is my desire!" The woman followed. They broke off in a sprint toward the awful room. I realised I had pinched my nose and unclasped it involuntarily.

"So they just follow you around all day, doin' whatever you tell 'em to?" Corcoran asked a somewhat different question than I would have.

Rayburn nodded, "Yeah, pretty much. Hell, they signed up for it."

"Signed *up* for it?" Bloomington's distaste for any kind of physical labor bled into his tone.

Sanchez shook her head.

Rayburn chuckled, "Yeah, believe it or not, this is one of our most popular packages. 'Live like an ancient Egyptian building the pyramids.'"

I stroked my chin in mock thought, "I wasn't aware that the ancient Egyptians had giant orgy rooms where they heaved in a sweaty pile—"

"First of all, it's called the Fuck Den, okay?" Rayburn corrected me. "We're kinda *proud* of the term. Second, maybe they do, maybe they don't—the natives are over on the other side of the plateau. We try to stay out of their way, they steer clear'a us. They try to get too close, and one'a their 'gods' comes out to make thunder and lightnin' and all kinds of other *ruckus* to keep 'em away."

He patted what appeared to be a perfect replica of my laser pistol concealed beneath a garishly gigantic belt on his hip.

"That's proprietary!" I whispered.

"That's a badass gun, is what it is!" Bloomington carelessly flung his (though I should say more accurately *"my"*) identical sidearm from its holster and waved it around in the air.

Corcoran furrowed his brow at me and shook his head.

"Stop wavin' that shit around like fuckin' Yosemite Sam!" he motioned for him to put the laser gun away.

"You guys weren't such fuddy-duddies when I was using it to save your fucking prolapsed assholes back in Leipzig," he frowned.

With each step, the magnificent structures in front of us came into sharper focus. They really were enormous monuments, white and glistening in the Egyptian spring.

"A tomb truly fit for a King," I sighed.

Rayburn raised an eyebrow, "Tomb?"

I rolled my eyes, "Don't tell me that the Commander of a ChronoSaber outpost during the time the pyramids are being constructed doesn't even know that the Pharaoh Khufu, or 'Cheops,' as the Greeks called him, built the great pyramid as a funerary monument to honor his—"

Corcoran nudged me on the shoulder and pointed toward the incomplete portion of the pyramid's façade.

I don't know if I took in a breath for the next two to three minutes.

There were the time tourists, right as rain. Though a group of them was gathered in a circle near the entrance, most of them were carting enormous blocks into place, using sheer musculature and manpower to hoist the large blocks with ropes.

Though unsurprising, what was so baffling was the kerfuffle that followed them.

Close behind them, waving (as best as I could tell) fluorescent-colored whips in the air, were curious little creatures. Their large, black, oval eyes dominated their bulbous grey heads and slight frames as they snapped the whips directly over the tourists heads. Most of the idiot time-travellers laughed with glee.

"Aliens?"

I could barely croak out the word.

Now, as you likely are aware, dear reader, my childhood was dominated by reruns of all of the various *Star Trek* series. Not only did they serve as an inspiration for the look and feel of much of the interior of my initial build of the time machine, but those series were the foundation upon which my entire career in physics was built. Wonderful fables designed to expand the mind to embrace possibilities far beyond the current state of human understanding.

I often wondered what it would be like to be Captain Kirk or (more often) Picard (should one be able to get past that *awful* fiction that he was meant to be a Frenchman, and not an Englishman like Sir Patrick himself, but I suppose that's neither here nor there), zipping around the galaxy, solving problems and brokering peace treaties between different species.

And yet, as I gazed upon the scene, my analytical mind absolutely picked it apart.

Aliens? Aliens *can't exist!* Some part of my brain fully of this earth wouldn't consider the possibility.

For their parts, Commanders Corcoran and Sanchez reached for their sidearms.

"Too *cool!*" Bloomington exclaimed.

Rayburn laughed, "Yeah, pretty awesome costumes, right? Some'a these folks wanna be bossed around by aliens while 'building the pyramids.' Maybe they've been watching too much'a those crazy shows on H3 or whatever. Or *maybe* it's a—"

"An S&M thing?" I asked.

"An *alien* S&M thing!" Bloomington said simultaneously.

Rayburn nodded.

My heart began thumping inside of my chest cavity once more. "So they're *not* aliens."

Rayburn shook his head with a chuckle, "Fuck no! Shit, you think aliens are *real?* Don't be ridiculous."

My stomach sank.

Bloomington stomped the ground and threw his hands into the air. "Fuckers! Butt…shit…morons!"

"That's a new one," I muttered.

Rayburn ignored us. "No, we just give these 'overseers' 'close enough' costumes. We tried using holograms for a while, but those freaked the *shit* outta people, gave 'em nightmares, couldn't sleep, the whole nine. Not good…"

One of the "extraterrestrials" cracked a whip as his (I must admit, hilariously) high-pitched voice rang out into the clear sky, "Come on you *turds!* Pull harder! Mush! Mush faster!"

"Yes *sir!*" One of the tourists luxuriated in the words, tinged with sexuality.

"Must be some little fuckin' people…" Corcoran mused.

Rayburn nodded, "We use jockeys."

Everyone's, save Sanchez, eyes went wide, "Jockeys?!" we asked in near-unison.

"You mean like…like *horse riders?*" Bloomington asked.

"Sure—why not? They're short, athletic, follow directions, and are used to beatin' the shit outta things."

If it was supposed to be a joke, Rayburn offered no indication.

I looked around at the group, wide eyed, mouth agape, "Am I the *only* one who sees the sheer *absurdity* of all this? ChronoSaber built this…this *orgy camp—*"

"Fuck Den," Rayburn corrected me once more.

Despite the man's towering physique, I nearly reached back to acquaint him with my right cross before thinking the better of it, "—populated it with tourists that want to not only sell themselves into slavery to finish building the pyramids, but who also *pay for* and *enjoy* the supposed *privilege* of doing so, all while being chased by fraudulent extraterrestrials that were whipping dog food ingredients around a horse track mere weeks before?!"

Rayburn's face twisted into a bothered grimace, "Nothing could be further from the truth! They aren't building the pyramids!"

"*Oh,* so *now* it's—I *beg* your *pardon?!*" Perhaps I had been the one that had been caught by a right cross, albeit a verbal one.

Rayburn shook his head. He pointed at what appeared to be a settlement, barely visible on the far side of the pyramids. "You think those Past-ies over there built these things?"

Corcoran and I nodded yes.

"Who else built them, then?" I asked. "Wait, let me guess: the Stay Pufft Marshmallow Man? Or perhaps it was the Greek gods—I suppose you'll next tell me that *Zeus* and *Aphrodite* were just ChronoSaber operatives, as well?"

Sanchez nodded, lips barely upturned, "Chronobase Sigma," her words were drier than the desert I had expected to find upon our arrival.

Rayburn shrugged, "Beats the hell outta me. They've been here for a while, certainly before we got here, all sealed up and shit. We had to open 'the big one' up with goddamned lasers to get inside, and even then, well…we found some, to use a technical term, cool shit."

We shuffled through the sandy dirt of the plateau. The surprisingly abundant greenery not only set a far different scene than either the pristine desert of the photographs I had seen, or the bombed-out, nuclear wasteland that dominated my time, but it also provided a dewy, almost fragrant aroma that pleased my nostrils when not overshadowed by the horrendous B.O. that wafted over us in waves.

As we drew nearer to the monument, the din of the throng of

individuals gathered close to the entrance intensified. I craned my neck to see inside the huddle.

Rayburn lifted a large finger toward the group, "The other VIPs are here today. I wouldn't worry about 'em too much, if you wanna follow me, you can see…"

Cyrus's voice faded into the void of my racing mind well before he could finish his thought. For it was then that I saw through the great mass of people, and caught a glimpse of two figures at the front of the group. One was dressed in a flowing robe, his square jaw covered by an ample beard, a Charlton Heston look-alike, albeit a poor one.

Next to him was a spindly fellow with long, brown hair and ice blue eyes that peeked out from behind expensive Ray Ban sunglasses. His broad smile framed an affable, yet harmlessly slow face as he formed his right hand into a "Live Long and Prosper" sign and nodded toward the flash of a holocam. Even before I heard the dull, surfer cadence, I knew that Helene had decided to play an especially cruel and heartless joke on me.

"Jesus Christ," Bloomington said, breathlessly.

I shook my head and corrected him through gritted teeth, "Trent Albertson."

CHAPTER NINE

I suppose technically Bloomington *was* right, after all; the man whom he knew as "Jesus Christ" had been the first time-travelling tourist I had ever encountered.

That I had eventually shared a bed with one of his ancestors, the lovely Cynthia Albertson, on a later time jump, only further complicated the situation.

As we approached, Albertson's brow furrowed. He lifted the sunglasses off of his nose and lowered red eyes at me. Our gazes met, and Trent bid adieu to the elderly couple who stood next to him.

"Alright Chuck, I'm gonna take five here, bro," Trent said. The fellow next to him nodded and trudged off to the side.

My throat tightened as Trent made small talk with the crowd even as he made his way toward us. As if he already knew what to expect, Rayburn tried to steer us clear of the hapless twit, but Albertson was not to be deterred.

"Hey…hey man—" he extended a bony finger toward me, "—you're that guy—the science guy! The guy with 'his own time machine!'"

I wanted to belt the miscreant right there, right in front of everyone else, though I suppose titling this travelogue *Jesus Had a Glass Jaw* likely wouldn't endear myself to certain segments of your quaint Pastie society, but no matter.

Instead, I bit my tongue and extended a hand toward the man as I affected awed surprize.

"Trent Albertson? So nice to see you again!"

"Doctor…'F' something…Frank? Fausty? Furball?…"

"Furball?" Even Sanchez couldn't help but chuckle.

"Phineas Templeton," I hope the sound of my molars grinding against one another didn't drown out my speech.

Trent snapped his fingers and pointed at me once more. "Right! Was gonna be my next guess. How are you, bro? You ever find—" he surveyed the group and broke into a broad smile when he came across Ricky, "—Commander *Corcoran?* Nice!"

I rolled my eyes, "Commander Ricky Corcoran, meet Trent Albertson, also known as 'Jesus Christ.'"

"Hey there, Trent, nice to meetchya," Ricky stuck out his iron grip and took Trent's very fragile-looking hand in his. "I, uh, I ain't much the church-goin' type, but—"

Albertson laughed, "No worries, bro—to each his own. Just live by the golden rule and shit, that's all I ask, man."

"As you can see, Mr. Albertson here has a rather 'unique' perspective on theology," I said. I turned toward the rest of the group, eager to expose this charlatan once and for all.

Instead, what I found were awe-struck, gaping maws on everyone save Sophia, who dare I say was downright *swooning* over this miscreant; she batted her eyelashes at him like a trollop on the pier who had caught wind that the fleet had finally come in.

I introduced my colleagues in turn (hoping that the dry air had caused Bloomington's 'gold-digging' efforts in his nostrils to strike it rich before taking the man's hand in his) before Albertson stood back, arms folded nonchalantly across his chest.

"So what the hell are you doin' here, man?" he swung a hand out and hit me playfully on the shoulder.

I forced my right fist down to my side and attempted to affect a pleasant tone, "I could ask you the same thing."

"Chuck…err…'Moses' and I—"

"So Moses was a time traveler too then?" Bloomington blurted out. He shot me a knowing wink.

Trent beamed, "Right on! Yeah, Chuck… you know…Chuck? He was in some movie or something?"

I had to squint but I'll be damned if it wasn't *actually* Charlton Heston accompanying Trent!

Trent nodded in his direction, "Chuck took over for the original Moses at the top of that mountain or whatever—"

"Sinai?" I asked.

Trent sniffed several times, "Naw, my allergies are fine out here—desert air, ya know? Anyway, Chuck wanted to, like, pull a Jesus and me but, like, with *Moses*, man, so he had ChronoSaber bring him to the top of the mountain, and, like, waited for the real dude, and then like *totally* threw him in the time machine and sent him back to the future!

It was *hilarious*!"

"So you were there, too, then?" I asked.

Trent nodded, "Yeah, it's like…" he stared off into space for several seconds before he shook his head and snapped to, his gaze focused on me once more, "…like right after you showed up, not even like fifteen minutes later, a bunch'a ChronoSaber soldiers, kinda like her," he nodded at Sanchez, whose caramel skin turned more of a burnt sienna with the acknowledgement, "came by, and they told me if I made a buncha appearances for 'em throughout time and stuff, then they'd take me home after the crucifixion and resurrection and stuff.

"So I say fine, and they had me sign something, and I packed up the Brainenator and—"

Corcoran opened his mouth, but I placed my hand on his shoulder and shook my head at him to discourage any further elaboration with regard to Trent's enormous cannabis pipe.

"—off we went. So here we are, takin' holopics with—" he looked around and brought a hand to his face as he thumbed the other one behind him, "—these assholes, shootin' the shit, you know, the works, bro."

"Like a mascot?" Corcoran asked. He looked at Sanchez, who nodded, mouth drawn taut.

"Whoa, whoa, whoa, Commander C—*exactly* like a mascot!"

"So where's the real Jesus then?" Corcoran asked.

"What?" Trent was taken aback.

"The real Jesus Christ, you know, the Past-ie version of him. What'd you do with him? Him and Moses just chillin' in the future somewhere?"

Trent looked at me, eyes hollowed with disappointment. "You didn't, you know, tell him, *man*? About the no Jesus thing?"

"The *what*?"

Corcoran and Bloomington stared at me, Corcoran with intrigue, Bloomington with some sort of sad form of betrayal.

I sighed. "What? Didn't I mention that back in Mexico? Where you crashed?"

Corcoran and Bloomington shook their heads.

"'Fraid not, Doc. I think I woulda remembered something that big."

"There's no *JESUS?!"* Bloomington asked, late to the party as ever.

Sanchez wrapped a hand loosely over her face and shook her head.

"I *definitely* told you both. And you!" I turned to Sanchez, "*You* of all people should know *exactly* who ChronoSaber sends *when*—"

"*Easy,* bro," Trent stuck out his hands, "*I'm* Jesus, 'kay? Don't get all wrapped up in, like, *labels,* and stuff. I can still do all of the miracles and shit…just with, like, *technology,* and stuff."

I was eager to change the subject, "So why exactly did ChronoSaber bring you *here, today?* Did they say anything about me, or—"

"Nope," Trent shook his head.

"—Or Commander Corcoran being here?"

I waited several beats as I could practically smell the cannabis smoke clearing from betwixt Trent's ears.

The erstwhile Messiah snapped his fingers, "Oh yeah—they *did* mention something about Commander Corcoran being here."

I rolled my eyes.

"Something about…like…how he and some chick from ChronoSaber might be by, and I should just play it real cool-like, send 'em along to the Egyptologist and whatnot."

"I think that'll be enough, son," Rayburn said.

"'Course, she's the reason I'm here—to see Gram-Gram," he nonchalantly cast a slender finger toward the entrance to the monolith.

As my attention turned toward the doorway, I took in a deep breath, ready to exhale in a deep sigh.

Instead, I found myself standing utterly rapt, like Odysseus returning to the shores of Ithaca.

There, shaking her hair out in the dry air, was Cynthia Hess.

Or I should say, the former Cynthia Albertson.

My jaw hung utterly slack and useless for seconds until I regained some control over my faculties and composed myself enough to whisper.

"How?" I hissed, both pleasantly surprised at this serendipitous turn, and absolutely gobsmacked by the temporal implications of a woman from 1985 somehow finding her way to this most depraved of ChronoSaber freak shows that I had seen thus far, well in the past.

She walked toward our coterie of misfits clad in a white linen shirt that showed off her still-beguiling figure. Though she was perhaps several years older than when we had our New Year's dalliance, she was still every bit as "ravishable" as I recalled.

I struggled for words lodged at the back of my throat, hoping against hope that something witty, some semi-intelligent phrase could make its way to my lips.

"Finny? Is that you?" Her smile lit up the sun-baked plateau.

I gave her a curt nod, "Cynthia—you look well."

Curse my eternal Britishness! It was the same half-compliment I had given Bloomington for crying out loud! Had I any control over the timeline, I would have surely hopped back in the time machine alone, killed myself on the spot not but five minutes before, taken his place, and done the whole thing over.

Alas, due to our accursed universe and its wishes, no such suicide-homicide was to be.

"Finny? My God, it *is* you! How long has it been? How many years?" She ran to me and flung her arms around my back.

It was all I could do to catch her, and cradle her head on my shoulder.

"There, there," I actually clasped my hand over my ignoramus of a mouth.

She pulled away from the embrace, "I believed you, you know! All of that…that crazy talk about inventing a time machine, and how my grandson would become Jesus Christ."

My collar seemed as if it contracted two sizes; I yanked on it twice to allow some steam to escape even as I felt the heat of Corcoran's glare.

She chuckled that lovely, semi-sobbing chuckle of hers. "At first, I thought you were some lunatic who just wanted to get in my pants—"

Corcoran brought a hand to his face and bit down hard on his knuckle to keep from laughing.

"—but then you gave me this—" she held out a folded piece of paper, deeply creased and ever-so-slightly yellowed, "—some of your equations were just—just mind-boggling!"

The noose of the collar around my neck tightened ever so-slightly as I surveyed my own drunken handiwork. Sure enough, not only were the maths impeccably plotted, but gripped in the throes of my blackout, I had written down perhaps the two or three most important equations to achieve time travel! The very ones that even Klaus Thurbur himself somehow fell short of, even when knocking on that most sacred of doors in all of physics.

My self-satisfied smile quickly dropped as I came to a startling realisation, "You…you didn't show these to anyone at ChronoSaber, did you?"

"Why…why no, I didn't. Why do you ask?" She batted her eyelashes at me.

I shook my head. "No reason…I—it's just so *good* to see you again!" I wrapped her up in another embrace.

Over my shoulder, I heard the distinct sounds of someone clearing their throat.

I turned to find Sophia shooting daggers at me.

Corcoran extended a hand toward the great sloping side of the pyramid. "Look, if you two lovebirds are through, I'd like to get to checkin' out the inside'a this thing."

My eyes met Cynthia's as I nodded softly, "We can catch up more later, my sweet. Can you be a dear and point us in the direction of the Egyptologist?"

Without skipping a beat, Cynthia pointed to herself.

Corcoran nodded at Cynthia, "I think your ladyfriend's sayin' that *she's* the Egyptologist, Doc."

"I know *that,* Ricky, but I…how?" I attempted my most reassuring smile toward her.

She smiled back, "Why Finny, it was because of *you.*"

What kind of fresh hell? I thought, even as I affected a grin.

"Whatever do you mean, darling?" I asked, saccharinely sweet.

I may as well have conked her over the head with a brick, "Why, it was all of that pillow talk—"

"Okay—that's enough!" Corcoran held up his arms.

"—you, sobbing like a baby—"

"Go on," Corcoran made a rolling gesture with his forearm. Sanchez smiled curtly, and I thought Bloomington might excuse himself to "use the facilities."

"Sobbing like a *what*?" I felt the blood rushing toward my face.

"You know, talking about your father, and how you two never got to see the pyramids and whatnot. After *I* got done crying, I think it was only a few seconds before…well…you know…" she stuck her tongue in her cheek and twirled around a lock of hair.

Bloomington's saggy mess of a body sidled up to mine, flaccid, clammy hand stapled to his face, "Way to go, Doctor Tee!" he jabbed me in the ribs with several flabby elbows. Sanchez struggled to maintain her composure.

Cynthia waved their reactions away, "Never mind them. It just got me thinking how much *I* wanted to be an Egyptologist back when I was a young girl, hunting for tombs and treasures all through the desert, like Indiana Jones. I figured when I caught my husband with that hussy and divorced him, it was time to start a new life for myself, but I had no idea how to go about doing so.

"Oddly enough, as I left the Adam's Mark that New Year's Day, this ridiculously put-together English woman told me she was some kind of a relative of yours, maybe your sister or cousin or something—"

I reflexively convulsed at the thought of being somehow related to Helene, even if only by her own false association.

"—and she said that you'd be happy to pay my way to become an Egyptologist, as if she could read my mind or something. When she took me to a warehouse with an honest-to-*God* flying saucer in it…well, let's just say that's when it all sort of crystalized for me. After I graduated, your cousin or whatever put me in touch with ChronoSaber, gave me the opportunity to work hands-on with these pyramids without all of the ridiculous 'myths' surrounding them, she said. I said, 'What myths?' She said, 'Why don't you come to Baltimore and we'll show you.' So here I am, five years later, all thanks to you and your cousin's generosity, studying under one of the finest Egyptologists to ever live!"

She flung her arms around me once more. Despite the softness of her skin and the intoxicating aroma of her (somewhat more modern, mind you) perfume, I couldn't help but stroke my chin. I knew that

Helene was up to something—unsurprisingly, she had already been proven to have lied innumerable times during our "briefing" the day before, but for the life of me, I couldn't figure out *why* for the moment.

Corcoran and Sanchez looked at one another, then raised their eyebrows toward me.

I widened my eyes and shrugged at them over her shoulder.

"I...think nothing of it, love," I said. I winked at her, perhaps in an overly awkward and theatrical manner, and placed my hands on her shoulders.

Rayburn's deep voice melted the silence, "Much as have a soft spot for all this mushy shit, I *do* have Fuck Den duty tonight, so if we could, ya know, *get on with it*, Miss Hess..."

She tightened her grip around me, but already the gears were beginning to turn inside of my head. I pulled away to meet those beautiful blue eyes once more.

"One question, darling—you mentioned studying under one of the finest Egyptologists to ever live?"

Her eyes widened. "You mean, you haven't heard of—" she paused, if only momentarily before she placed a limp hand over her chest, "—I apologize, Finny—I always forget what a mess this time-travel stuff gets to be. She's from your future, her mind is—"

"Brilliant and unburdened by the ridiculous preconceived ideas advanced by morons digging through trash pits with rock hammers and toothbrushes?"

A gruff female voice advanced the question from up the ramp leading to the pyramid's doorway. Though her accent was plainly American, forgive me if her brash, plain-spoken manner reminded me more than a little of Kathy Bates back in the day.

A fairly squat, if powerfully-built, woman stared back at us, her previously-scarlet hair turned orange and silver by the passage of time. She held her chin high, with more than a touch of arrogance belying the implied pride in her work, in all meanings of the word "descending" to our level.

She marched toward us and stopped, perhaps five metres away, and looked each one of us up-and-down. When it was my turn, her eyes, magnified by her thick-rimmed glasses, slowly washed over me, from the ground up, then back down once more. She narrowed them for a moment or two in contemplation, though I haven't the faintest clue what of to this day.

"Dr. Templeton, I presume?"

CHAPTER TEN

"Never heard *that* one before…" I muttered under my breath.

"Well ain't you just the prom king today?" Corcoran mocked.

"Actually, at Eton, we didn't have a—" I stopped myself, hopefully limiting my own ridiculousness before I turned to the odd little woman in front of me and extended a hand.

"*Doctor* Phineas Templeton. And you are?"

"*Professor* Potter Amaranth," she mimicked my own (admittedly haughty) tone, "Head Egyptologist, Chronosaber." Potter's southern accent was bold and brassy. She extended a veiny, muscular hand and squeezed my own with such force that it was all I could do to steel my jaw and fight through it.

"Pleased to meet you," I gritted through my teeth.

She introduced herself to each group member in kind; Corcoran acted as if the handshake were from an annoying fan. Unfortunately, Bloomington was next.

"YEOOOW!" He yelped as she crushed his hand.

I could've sworn a sly smile crept over Amaranth's face before she raised her hands to her face.

"Goodness, where *are* my manners?" She said, wholly apologetically. Sanchez must've received a somewhat less intense grip, as she went through the customary pleasantries with this colourful figure. Or at least as "customary" as Sophia could be in her own aloof, distant way.

When all were finished, Cynthia nodded, "Professor Amaranth is something of a celebrity in her own time. Her analysis of—"

"Yes, I suppose *someone* has to do some real science around here, while most of the tourists are content to play around in that awful 'den' that I refuse to name."

"The Fuck Den?" Bloomington blurted out.

Corcoran shook his head as I rolled my eyes.

Amaranth affected a sweet smile. "No, dear—the cub scout den. Of *course* the 'f' den!"

The force with which she yelled the non-swear surprised the lot of us, even if she had plastered the smile on her face once more before she turned her attention back toward me.

"Now, now, my good doctor, I received Helene's brief on your…shall we say 'peculiar' time travels over the past few months, even if for the past several weeks you had been arguing with another bum over which dumpster to urinate behind."

"We had agreed-upon *spots*, thank you very much, and they were—" I clasped a hand over my mouth, indignant that my thoughts had escaped my head. Corcoran managed a chuckle while Sanchez covered her mouth.

"Professor, I think it would be helpful if you could tell them everything you know about that German guy that came through here and what all he wanted to find out."

She squinted, "You mean Dr. Thurbur?"

Rayburn nodded.

Amaranth rubbed her chin, "Actually, I can't say I had much contact with the man—thought he was a crackpot, totally nuts. I passed him off to Miss Hess."

We waited for a minute as Cynthia nodded along, well after Amaranth had finished, and she realised she was being addressed indirectly. "Oh, okay! He was a charmer—he had the cutest little dog and the most endearing half-accent you had ever—"

Rayburn cleared his throat and nodded at the pyramid entrance, "Let's just stick to the facts, shall we?"

Cynthia nodded, her lip barely trembling. In my schoolboy-with-a-crush state, I half wanted to pop Rayburn a good one to let him know that such roguery with regard to Cynthia simply would *not* be tolerated.

Instead, I nodded at her and she sighed.

Corcoran stuck out both hands, "And he wanted…?" he bobbed his head with frustration.

She looked at Amaranth, who gave a terse, thin-lipped smile and nodded.

"I suppose that it would be best if I could show you. If you want to follow me, we can begin the tour."

She turned and made her way up the rough concrete staircase

toward the precisely-carved entrance; it was obviously a modern addition for the benefit of whatever visitors dared to wander over from their "Fuck Den" to actually observe these wondrous structures up-close and hands-on.

Despite Cynthia's invitation, Amaranth took the lead, nose stuck ever-skyward, "The great pyramid of Giza was allegedly constructed around 2580 B.C."

"Even if Jesus is right out there?" Corcoran asked.

Bloomington stared at him blankly.

"B.C.? *Before*...Christ, Bloomy, I swear sometimes..."

Amaranth ignored him, "Obviously, pre-time travel archaeologists got this date wrong, namely because Khufu's royal seal and name appear a number of times in some of the passageways of the pyramid. We now believe these to be add-ons at a later date; as you can see, none of them are present right now, and the structure is very much constructed—"

"And what of the various trading records? The accounts of pyramid construction found in the worker's camp nearby?" I asked.

Cynthia shook her head.

Amaranth snorted, "You mean the projects?"

"Projects?" Corcoran interrupted.

"Yes," Amaranth dug around in the satchel over her shoulder, "You don't think that all these tourists do is get beaten like rented mules and jump each others' bones, do you?"

Bloomington nodded, "Doesn't sound too bad to me."

She produced a crumpled sheet of papyrus littered with hieroglyphs.

I instinctively reached for it.

"You're ruining a—"

"An art project, and a second-rate one at that." She waved at a group of slave-driven tourists on the face of the pyramid, "We tell them what 'pretty symbols' we want inscribed on the papyrus, and they make two copies—one for us, and one that they can take back with them to whenever they're coming from."

She yielded the coarse, fabric-like sheet and I held it in front of my face, squinting at the (admittedly shoddy-looking) hieroglyphs that littered the page.

"I believe that one is supposed to be a purchase order for beer for a group of workmen, but no matter."

"And the worker's camp?" I asked, though I shuddered to think at what the answer might be.

She pointed at the ChronoSaber compound, "You think we're gonna leave that as is, sugar?"

My eyes widened as my chin rose reflexively, "Forgive me—I forgot about all of the mentions of the workers' *Fuck Den* in my *numerous* trips to the British Museum!"

"That's enough, Doc," Ricky put his hand in front of my chest and offered a cautionary glare.

I nodded.

He grinned at Amaranth, "Makes perfect sense to me, Professor. Now, if you don't mind…" he motioned toward the door of the pyramid.

I marvelled at the sheer *size* of the structure. Each block was the size of several large lorries. And that was just the exterior blocks!

Yet there was one more thing that seemed out of place… or I should say "the lack thereof" seemed very out of place.

"I say, Dr. Amaranth. At the top of the pyramid—" I adjusted my smart spectacles and pointed at the pyramid's apex. "There's no—"

She nodded, "Capstone?"

"Quite," I nodded in return.

"Yes—it's very odd, isn't it? Why build this pyramid without putting a capstone here on top? And even weirder, there's nothing really that indicates that there ever *was* a capstone there. It's one of the biggest mysteries of this *very* mysterious structure."

I shook my head. This is *exactly* the kind of thing my father was great at figuring out. Had we been able to take our trip to this massive structure back when I was a teenager, I could almost hear the questions he might ask me, to get my brain properly rolling:

"Was there a capstone at all?"

"If so, what did it do?"

"And what was so special about it that it's no longer up there?"

I pondered these questions as we ascended the final few steps of the ramp and made our way through the entrance. It was an opening in the rock, perfectly rectangular, with incredibly sharp, well-hewn edges.

"The stone-work is *remarkable*." I mumbled.

Amaranth chuckled, "Where we just entered was, somewhat paradoxically, carved out by an army of ChronoSaber soldiers with precision laser rifles specially designed for the task. We cut right through several feet of thick, polished limestone, which was to be expected."

Cynthia nodded, "What we didn't expect, though, were the series of gold gates beneath the façade."

Amaranth shot her protégé daggers.

"Gold? Like 'gold,' gold?" Bloomington perked up.

Amaranth narrowed her eyes and nodded, "Of course. We took pictures of them before sending them to the Corcoran Museum back in 2042."

I shot Ricky a look dirty enough that he should have had to take a shower afterward.

Of course, that bloody rake smirked with his eyes and nodded, "Ever been there? 'Should really see the movie if ya go."

"I'm sure I'd see it with a snack—some rotten fruit, perhaps?" I gritted the words out.

Fortunately, Amaranth continued on up the rather lengthy makeshift stairway, "You might not know some of the amazing architectural facts about the pyramid. For instance, each of the faces is almost perfectly aligned with one of the cardinal directions, and the base is completely flat, within—"

"Within an inch," I muttered to Sanchez, for no reason in particular.

Everyone else in the group's eyes shot skyward.

"That's right, Finny," Cynthia nodded. She ducked inside the entrance, and we all followed suit in turn.

Amaranth waved toward the passageway, "We're about to head down a shaft, all the way to the bottom, and—"

"A secret entrance to an underground city?" Bloomington's hand shot up, presumably trained as one of Pavlov's dogs from years within the American public school system.

"Priceless antiquities and treasures?" I thought Ricky, on the other hand, might know better.

"—a dead end," Amaranth completed her thought.

"Too cool!" Bloomington yelled out far too loud for the claustrophobia-inducing hallway. Though it was presumably dark as night in there, in a rare show of consideration, ChronoSaber had lined the inside of the passage with LED lights to help us find our way.

We came to the "dead end" chamber. It was dusty and cramped, with only a line along the floor and a large granite block of any note.

Cynthia motioned toward the empty room, "So I brought Dr. Thurbur down here, and he spent some time making measurements of some of these different things."

"He ask you anything in particular 'bout it? Have anything to say 'bout what he found?" Corcoran asked.

Cynthia frowned, "All he said was, 'interestink.'"

"Interest*ink?*" Sanchez asked.

I immediately recognized Cynthia's little joke (or I should say "joke attempt"); it would be how Klaus might say "interesting," given his slight, endearing German accent.

I chuckled as I shook my head, "Nothing else? Nothing about what he expected to find, or what he *actually* found?"

Cynthia shook her head, "Nope, not a word. He did spend some time fiddling around with that line in the middle of the ground—scanned it about fifteen different ways before he just stood there and said—"

Sanchez interrupted, "Lemme guess: 'interestink.'"

Cynthia nodded, "That's right. If you'll follow us into the King's Chamber…"

We began the short trek back up the passageway to the tiny landing area where the hallways branched off from one another, then began the trip up a similarly tiny passageway toward the next level. Somehow, Bloomington had ended up behind me, and despite his comparatively lighter frame from the "fatteries" attached to his grotesque stomach, he made all kinds of awful wheezing and choking noises, tongue lurching about as if a camel was being hanged.

We approached another vertical division in the path, though curiously there was a hole off to the side on the landing. It was huge; far wider than the passages had been to that point, and seemingly straight down for many metres.

"What the devil is in there?" I asked our guides, even as I leaned over to inspect the gaping hole carved into the masonry.

No sooner had the words left my lips than I heard an exasperated sigh, followed by a flabby elbow in the small of the back.

My stomach dropped as my eyes went wide. It was all I could do to dart out a quick jab at the wall to steady myself.

Unfortunately, I am unable to say that the interruption was without its casualties. As my torso was thrust forward and nearly over the edge into the enormous shaft, my smart spectacles flew off of my face into the abyss, the only evidence that they had ever existed a muted "thwack!" of titanium-on-stone as they must have caught on a ledge well below the bottom.

I heaved out several deep, choking breaths as the colour rushed back to my ghostly face, turning it beet red with fury. I levelled my gaze on the source of the elbow, who himself continued to wheeze, albeit more out of a general lack of physical fitness than of the same type of rage that built within me.

Bloomington's face went blank for a moment before his lip trembled, his eyes went wide with fear before he narrowed them and shrugged his shoulders at me.

"Sorry, Doctor Tee—couldn't stop in time."

"Doctor *Tee? Doctor TEE!?*" I raised my fists in self-defense, ready to pop the nincompoop squarely in the jaw. "Those were my *only* spectacles, you dolt! You…you…you…pernicious *squid* of a human!"

"I said I was sorry!" Bloomington implored.

"Oh wonderful—*that* will bring my smart spectacles rushing back to my face! Those were a gift from my *father* you muddlebrained alleywhore! Engraved specifically for my last birthday before he died!"

I took a swing at Steven. It connected, but surprisingly he didn't crumple in fear and pain as he had back during our little excursion to Mexico.

"Don't make me push you in the *fucking hole!"* Bloomington raised his forearms in front of him and started to lurch out toward me, as if in slow-motion.

I hate to admit it, but I likely had a glint in my eye and a smirk on my face. Like a bullfighter ready to give way to the most pathetic *toro* he had ever laid eyes upon, I took a step to the side, ready to let Bloomington's momentum carry him over into the yawning opening next to me.

Fortunately (or unfortunately, depending on one's perspective), he was bluffing, and took a step backward.

"Nobody's going in the fucking hole!" The command with which the phrase was said perhaps jolted me even more than the firm, but feminine voice that released it. Sanchez reached into a well-concealed pants pocket and threw a small business card-sized package at me.

Though I may have juggled the package several times, I eventually came up with it and held it up proudly, my scarlet complexion owed more to embarrassment than my slowly ebbing rage. It was covered in fluorescent letters and numbers that for all the life of me made it look like some sort of futuristic rubbish.

"What the devil is this?"

"Holo-lenses. Smart ones. Try 'em on."

I could see how Sophia had risen to the rank of Captain at such a young age.

"I'll have you know that I positively *loathe* contact lenses, Captain San—"

You'll forgive my irritation, given the maelstrom of emotions I was experiencing at the time.

Unfortunately, the Captain did not, though she dismissed my insubordination (if you can call it that) with an elegant, yet no-nonsense, wave of the hand.

"They aren't contacts, *Doctor*," her condescension was likely well-earned. "They're holo-lenses. Tiny chips with holo-emitters designed to simultaneously project a field of energy to scatter light rays that conforms precisely to your eyes, and a heads-up display, providing all of that information from your archaic smart specs, and then some." She punctuated the statement with a wry smile.

I frowned, "But how does it know my—"

She rolled her eyes, "They're designed to automatically detect your prescription and adjust accordingly."

I thought for a moment, "Well I simply *can't* put them in without—"

Before I knew it, another small projectile was hurtling through the air toward me.

In a flash, the ball emitted a pane of perfectly reflective glass. As Corcoran stood over Sanchez's shoulder, I envied his view.

"Find Doctor Templeton," Sanchez ordered. The mirror quickly hovered its way in front of me.

"Remarkable," I whispered.

"It'd be even *more* remarkable if you would shut the fuck up for once and put in the goddamn lenses," Corcoran muttered.

I pouted, indignant, and tore open the package. Somewhat trepidatiously, I placed the lenses on my eyes and blinked several times. Much to my chagrin, not only did I not feel a thing, but I also was happy to find a far more advanced heads-up display beamed directly into my field of vision, as well as sharper focus on the entirety of my surroundings, than my smart spectacles had ever provided.

"So whattaya think?" Sanchez asked.

"Still a bit *bothersome…*" I lied and rubbed my eyes several times for effect, "…but I *suppose* they'll do for now."

"Ahem," Amaranth cleared her throat, "If you folks are done, now—"

Cynthia shot me a mock-disappointed glare.

I bobbed my head back and widened my eyes.

"—we will continue up into the King's Chamber." Amaranth peeled off into the extraordinarily tall passageway upward at a forty-five degree angle. This time, Sanchez ran her hands along the wall, as if somehow by touching the side of the passageway, it made it more "real" to her.

"This is called the Grand Gallery. It's obviously taller than the rest of the passageways, and ascends into what is commonly thought to be the resting place of the Pharaoh Khufu, though," she flipped her hair and looked over her shoulder, "As you'll soon see, that's impossible."

"Why the *fuck* do you say that?" Bloomington asked.

I couldn't help but smash my palm into my face.

"Because, Steven," I was amazed Amaranth remembered his name from their brief introduction, "Khufu is comfortably ruling the Past-ies of this time on the other side of the pyramid, as we speak."

You may as well have told Bloomington that Khufu's mummy had come to life and was roaming the halls, thirsty for blood. His face went from "ghostly-white" to "near-translucent."

I debated whether or not to talk him through the logic of the situation, though I decided that his ridiculous terror and confusion were ample punishment for his earlier stunt near the hole that now served as the crypt for my engraved smart spectacles.

We reached the end of the passage and emerged in a chamber that, though comparatively larger than the rest of the rooms we had been in, with "lavishly" high ceilings of about five metres or so, was somewhat underwhelming if meant for a ruler.

Don't get me wrong; the masonry work was absolutely impeccable, with blocks fitted together into tight seams that seemed impossible for all but the most advanced civilizations on the planet. But there were no hieroglyphs, no regalia, no hint that it was a room intended to convey the soul of a king to the afterlife. Appropriately enough, a large stone sarcophagus sat empty and uncovered in the middle of the room.

"*This* is the King's Chamber," Amaranth turned to face us.

"*Laaaame, prrrrrrt,*" Bloomington blew his lips together in a loud "raspberry," that echoed amazingly for an enclosed chamber in the middle of a massive stone monument.

Cynthia frowned.

I leaned toward her and placed the back of my hand over the side of my mouth, "Still time to throw him in the chasm," I whispered.

She raised her eyes skyward in mock thought for several seconds before she offered a nearly-imperceptible shake of the head.

"I can't believe I'm gonna say this, but I agree. Where's all the gold and jewels—the King Tut shit?" Corcoran asked.

Amaranth shook her head, "We don't know."

Cynthia's voice broke, "We think it was devised as a tomb, but for a much earlier civilization than Ancient Egypt."

"Shouldn't you know?" Corcoran squinted at the four

ChronoSaber employees with frustration.

Rayburn shrugged. "Actually, we don't know exactly when these things were built. Up through about 28,000 B.C., it's just primitive tribes around here, nothing spectacular. Then, there's a 'dark spot,' lasting—"

"*Dark* spot?" I inquired.

Rayburn rolled his eyes, "No time travel expeditions that involved this area during that time came back, thus we have no information—*that* kind of dark spot."

"Now, don't you talk down to me like a common…a common...*Past-ie!"*

The vitriol with which I spat the final word surprised even me. Rayburn's enduring glare indicated it was best for me to keep my mouth shut for the foreseeable future of our conversation.

Cyrus continued, "Anyway, there's a dark spot lasting from 28,000 B.C. to, oh, about 6,000 B.C. or so. Forgive me for not looking into it personally—maybe you can take a look at that yourself, *Doctor.*"

"Pretty fuckin' big dark spot," Corcoran said while surveying the masonry work.

"Yeah, it is. Maybe you should ask Commander Sanchez about it—she's a bit more plugged in here. All I do is run the Fuck Den, remember?" He finished the statement with a pointed stare at me.

"What did *I* say?" I asked, mustering as much false outrage as I could.

A sharp whistle interrupted the budding melee. Sophia lowered her fingers from her lips and took a step forward, "You really think this was still used as a tomb? After all, as Commander Corcoran so astutely noticed—" Ricky cocked his head and grinned, "—there are no funerary artifacts in here. Not even carvings—just one or two inscriptions that could've been added after the fact. Just this big granite box that may or may not be a sarcophagus."

"What else would it be for?" Amaranth placed her hands on her hips.

Sanchez stroked her chin, deep in thought.

I cleared my throat, "So what did Klaus want to see in here?"

Cynthia frowned, "He just kind of bolted for the sarcophagus and took some measurements with some doohickey he had. As you can see, in this corner of the room—" she made her way toward the corner behind the sarcophagus, "—the blocks aren't fitted as tightly together. He knocked on it a few times and took some measurements, and that was kind of that."

"Well hol-ee-*shit*, 'fasinatin'… knockin' on walls…takin' measurements…" Corcoran turned to Sanchez, "Glad your boss is puttin' the A-Team on this one."

Sanchez looked at him blankly.

"Oh, *come on!* The A-Team? Like the show? Made a movie outta it and everything?"

More blank stares.

Cynthia smiled and walked back toward the tall passageway, "What Dr. Thurbur really wanted to see was down in the Queen's Chamber…"

"Gee, guess we could've started *there* then," Sanchez muttered.

Cynthia's glare was met with a too-tight smile.

We trudged back down the tall hallway into the narrow passageway down. A whirlwind of emotions swirled in my head—I was overjoyed to see Cynthia once more, and eager to rekindle our budding (if one-night) relationship.

More than that, though, I was at once thrilled to finally see the Great Pyramid with my own eyes (even if covered by holographic projections emanating from computer chips hovering millimetres from my pupils), dismayed at not being able to experience it with my father, and oddly shocked at how wondrous and underwhelming the whole experience was.

Before you go slamming your book or tablet down and having a proper fit, dear reader, know that the wonder of the structure was simply unmatched. It is patently impossible to convey the sheer size of some of the blocks, the fit of the masonry, and even the size of some of the rooms hewn from stone deep within the structure.

However, even as a man of science, I somehow expected the "wow" factor to be even greater. Call it being oversold, but I think there was something *more* there, perhaps a spiritual connection that I expected to find that simply wasn't. I had never been a man of God previously, and I still had my questions as to a supreme being's existence, but my first journey through time with Corcoran and Bloomington had at least instilled a proper respect in me for the wishes of the universe, especially given the fact that nothing we could do could change the past. I found that fate and inevitability, as much as anything else, were comfortable, if not comforting, proxies for God.

We descended the passageway to the landing with the giant hole.

"Last chance," I asked Cynthia. I rolled my eyes toward Bloomington, who still gulped air behind me like a fish flopping around on land.

She smiled and shook her head, politely and gracefully as ever.

We entered another short passage, though, thankfully, this one was orientated horizontally, and proceeded down it toward a well-lit room at the end of the hallway. There was a step close to the end, and even though most of us cleared it without issue, Bloomington stubbed his toe and acted as if he had been knifed.

"Shit muffins!" he yelled.

"That's a new one," Corcoran cocked his head.

"This is the Queen's Chamber," Amaranth waved around the room proudly, almost as if she had constructed it herself. It was an odd room, not as cavernous as the King's Chamber, yet again, rather spacious for being in the midst of thousands of tons of stone arranged so tightly one would be ill-served to fit a finger between the masonry-work.

Oddly enough, as we entered, a large portion of the wall to our left was carved out in the shape of a stepped lighthouse. The only other interruption in the well-fit-together masonry was a one foot square hole in the wall opposite us, which appeared to be far deeper than the odd indentation to my left. The roof sloped upward to a point that ran along the room, cutting it in half.

Without further thought, transparent green and orange shapes floated through my field of view.

"The *devil*?" I swatted at the invisible shapes as if they were angry mosquitos.

Sanchez raised her forearm to her face, ostensibly to cover her laughter.

The rest of the group was not nearly so polite.

As my face reddened yet again, I tugged on my collar, then on the front of my shirt as the colourful shapes fixed on several points of interest around the room, complete with short snippets of information.

One of the reticules flashed rather wildly near the rectangular shaft on the far side of the wall. Eager to be free of ridicule, I marched rather brusquely over to the rectangular hole and peered inside.

Seconds later, a bright light illuminated the tunnel.

I rubbed my eyes, "Commander Sanchez, these damned things are more trouble than they're—"

A tender hand came to rest on my shoulder, followed by an object fluttering next to my ear. I removed my head from the cavity long enough to find Cynthia's lovely blue eyes matching my own, her kind smile tugging at the slight dimples of her high cheekbones.

Oh, how easy it was for her to make me happy once more! For a moment, I forgot all about Klaus, about our mission, which, I reminded myself, was in furtherance of some cockamamie scheme of Helene's. I even allowed any animus I bore towards Corcoran and Bloomington to fade to the wayside, a remnant of a past I so desperately wanted to forget.

I longed to grab her there and kiss her deeply, passionately, in a manner befitting such a wondrous creature, something jarring that would set her very *soul* alight with uncontrollable desire.

Instead, I likely just grinned like an idiot and rubbed my thoroughly confused eyes as whatever had buzzed my ear hovered in front of them. It was a curious enough little contraption, a distant cousin of the floating… mirror…thing that Sophia had shown me moments before. Though it was more insect-like, more mechanical, designed almost purely to fly.

"When Dr. Thurbur came here, he took a lot of pictures of the room, but was most interested in this shaft."

Corcoran put a hand up to his mouth and barely made an effort to whisper, "Bein' a friend'a Doc's, I can see how he'd be interested in a *whole* lotta shaf—"

"If you're *quite* through!" I turned and snapped at Ricky, sneer dripping from my face at his relentless homophobia.

He smirked and patted his Beretta underneath his jacket.

Cynthia frowned and raised her voice, though it remained steady and sweet, "He pulled this thing out—" I stared at Corcoran and raised a mock fist, though this time it was Bloomington who snickered, "—and sent it flying into the hole."

"This *ventilation* hole," Amaranth interjected; she raised her eyebrows at Corcoran like a stern headmaster at a misbehaving child, "is far from unique. There are four of these shafts in the pyramid, two each in the King's Chamber and Queen's Chamber."

She pointed to a similar hole on the opposite wall, though this one hadn't been pointed out by my smart lenses.

I snorted.

"What is it, Doctor?" Amaranth's exasperation was beginning to rival my own.

"You say 'ventilation shaft' like it's an accepted fact. But the crazy part is that—"

"The crazy part is that," she snapped twice, and the small mechanical contraption raced into the hole without hesitation. Immediately, a small window popped up in the upper left corner of my field of view, ostensibly showing what Klaus's mechanical gizmo was seeing.

The tiny robot rushed through the opening at what I thought to be ridiculous speeds, illuminating the tunnel all the while and providing such sharp video that as it approached the end of the tunnel, and a wall popped up, I winced to brace for the seemingly inevitable impact.

Fortunately, it stopped and hovered in front of the sandstone wall. The ceiling was scratched and chipped in several spots, which made the space look much older than the rest of the complex. Two metal plugs were fused (and flush) with the slab, though narrow cracks around the edges betrayed it as a true wall and indicated that it was, in fact—

"A *door?*" I thought aloud.

Amaranth nodded, "Bravo, Herr Doctor! The most fascinating part is that each hole is capped off by a door, complete with a pair of iron fittings. Now, the Past-ies of *this* era don't even know how to manipulate iron, let alone those miserable fools from thousands of years ago."

Cynthia nodded, "Crazier still is that each shaft points toward a different star in the night sky of that era: Beta Ursa Minor, Alpha Draconis, Mintanka, in Orion's Belt, and, for this shaft, Sirius, the brightest star in the sky."

We all stood, marvelling at the information we had been given. Everyone, that was, save for Corcoran. He furrowed his brow and took several slow, cautious steps toward us, hands at his sides, nose wrinkled. It was almost as if he was *begging* for a reason to reach for his sidearm.

I clenched my hand into a fist, eager for whatever smart-ass remark might provide him with one (I blame the medigel).

Instead, his voice was even and largely free of his Southern affectation, "How the hell do you know?"

"What's that?" Cynthia frowned.

"You say 'Of that era,' like you know when this thing was built. But I thought you just said you don't *know* when this thing was built. Which is it?"

Amaranth grinned and clapped her hands, "Well *done*, Commander!"

I rolled my eyes.

Amaranth reached into her bag and removed a tablet very similar to my own, circa 2032. It lit up and projected the view from the robot that I saw in my own private "theatre," if you will, into the middle of the room, in exquisite holographic detail.

She swiped several commands across its face. The robot's view shifted upward, now pointed at the ceiling of the tunnel next to the door.

"Great—a bunch'a scratches," Corcoran deadpanned.

"Tablet, run program Amaranth Iota," Amaranth said.

Immediately, a map of the night sky overlaid the dimples on the ceiling. The dimples themselves were illuminated by bright neon green points of light to contrast with the stars in view.

"Of *course!*" I whispered, "YouTube!"

"Fucking *YouTube?*" Bloomington whined.

"A video on there—forget it…"

I shook my head and pointed to Amaranth. Several red lines began to connect the green dots on the ceiling.

"As you can see, these aren't merely random scrapes and dents," Cynthia said, proudly. "After Dr. Thurbur sent this gadget up the tunnel and it flew back, he smiled at me, put it in my hand, and said, 'Keep it—you *need* it now.' Real kinda creepy-like, but not, like, *creepy* creepy, more European creepy, but in that—"

Amaranth cleared her throat.

Cynthia sighed. "I figured out the controls and ran it up there again and analyzed the data. The Quantum Computer had a rough time figuring it out, but it eventually did—"

As the lines fully materialised, I couldn't help myself. "The Big Dipper!" I blurted out.

Cynthia nodded and pointed at another formation, "And that, there, is Draco the Dragon. These aren't imperfections—it's a—"

"A star map," Sanchez took two steps toward the projection. She reached a hand out toward "Draco the Dragon" and dragged it through the particles, almost as if reaching out to the various stars themselves.

"So we're back to aliens?" Corcoran's tone remained unimpressed.

"Not exactly," Amaranth said. Yellow lines connected the corresponding stars on the actual star map overlaying the stone carvings, though, curiously, they were nowhere close to matching up with one another.

"The actual star map—the one that looks like the night sky—is how it appears now…err…in 2051 A.D. As you know, Earth is moving through the Milky Way, which changes how the night sky looks over the course of hundreds, or even thousands of years."

I stole a glance at Bloomington, who remained slack-jawed and silent, but for the loud, huffing breaths he took as a course of habit.

A yellow line bisected the holo-projection of the star map as "2051 A.D." flashed up on the side of the screen.

Cynthia smiled and met my gaze once more. "Wanna see something *really* cool?"

I smiled. *Seeing your lovely eyes are quite enough, darling,* I thought.

I feared, though, that had I actually *said* those words to her, I would have been mocked mercilessly by the rest of the crew, Sanchez included.

Instead, I merely nodded.

She cleared her throat. "Tablet, match the orientation line of the projection with the one on the ceiling of the pyramid, accounting for stellar drift over time."

The tablet took a brief moment to calculate, then began manipulating the map in a manner which I can only refer to as a drifting spiral of sorts. As the stars shifted, the years began ticking off in the display, well past 1 A.D., then past 2580 B.C. as the map continued to move.

I found the whole scene poetic, really. I had been through a lot over the course of the past several months, from the brink of fame and fortune to the depths of despair. All the while, I had *been* to a goodly number of those time periods; given the expense of time travel to future-dwellers, likely more of them than perhaps even Commander Corcoran himself.

And yet there were so many that I hadn't been to, countless lives that had begun, been lived, and ended, without even half a blink of a thought given to their existence. Perhaps *that* was what had driven me to construct the time machine in the first place—not reverence for a father taken from me far too soon, or abject arrogance, which, though in ready supply in my case, was not enough to justify my expense and life's work.

Perhaps it was the desire to rise above the rest of the forgotten masses, to be *remembered* for something, something grand, something that would never even have the potential to slip from the minds of future generations.

Even still, as I stole a glance away from the dwindling numbers, and found the same reflected in Cynthia's wide eyes, so proud at having figured out a centuries-old mystery on her own, I couldn't help but wonder if I had it all wrong.

In contrast to Cynthia, Amaranth nodded, her eyes narrowed. I could've sworn that she licked her lips, fully embracing the other realisation I had made during my first voyage: whenever an apparent solution to a mystery popped up, it was almost always followed by a new puzzle to solve.

The numbers finally slowed as a red line appeared across the face of the stone carvings. As the yellow line came to rest on the red one to form a flashing orange line, with a perfectly-aligned star map, I knew it could be only one of two dates.

"9203 B.C." the display flashed.

I looked at Corcoran and steeled my gaze, "It appears we have a winner, Ricky."

CHAPTER ELEVEN

We made our way past the time tourists getting horse-whipped by jockeys in grey alien costumes, past Trent Albertson, past the (ahem) "Fuck Den," and back toward the ship.

Rayburn, Cynthia, and Amaranth were kind enough to see us off. I pulled Cynthia aside.

"Are you quite sure you can't join us, darling?" I clasped her hands together.

"I'd love to… more than anything else in the world…"

Her lip trembled for a moment.

"But…"

"But there's just so much to do here! I have to check the other pyramids for any corroborating evidence of this star map, *then* I have to come up with some sort of a working hypothesis on who—or *what*—built these things, and oh yeah, that's aside from taking whatever tourists can tear themselves away from the damned Fuck Den for a couple hours on a tour of the plateau."

"Is that all?" I arched an eyebrow.

She laughed that delightful laugh of hers.

"Oh Finn…I know. But hey, it's not like you're leaving forever, right?"

I arched an eyebrow at her. "I honestly don't know."

A thin smile crept across her face. "Well, provided you succeed in finding Dr. Thurbur, why don't you just come back and visit me here when you're done, hmm?"

The distant crack of a whip broke the silence.

"OW! I THINK YOU HIT MY *SACK!"* an unfortunately male voice shouted out.

I steeled myself and allowed my head to bob slowly. I placed a hand on Cynthia's shoulder, and she threw her arm around me in a desperate hug.

"I'll see you again," she said. "I can feel it."

"Of course, my dear," I lied. "Of course…"

"Oh my *God…*" Sophia rolled her eyes. "Get a freakin' room, you two…"

We ignored Captain Sanchez as I held Cynthia tight to me. We pulled away briefly and studied each others' eyes, both pairs glistening from the low sun. I moved my hand to the small of her back and drew her in swiftly, yet confidently, for a short, but passionate kiss.

"*Au revoir,*" Cynthia nodded.

Bloomington sighed, more with nostalgia than annoyance.

I hoped I hadn't cringed at the mere mention of a French phrase.

"Until next time."

I brought my hand to her shoulder and let it linger for a beat too long before I turned and hustled up the ramp to be with the rest of the crew.

"Take care," Rayburn nodded at me and extended his hand.

I ascended the ramp onto the ship and took my spot at the controls. I would've just as soon buried myself in some make-work or another on my tablet given my druthers, to avoid myself from dwelling on my departure from Cynthia *too* much, but I had a ship to fly—

—or at least on which to engage the autopilot!

"Jesus *Christ*, Doc, I think you just went and gave me diabetes." Corcoran threw himself into the gunnery chair next to me.

I squinted at him, "Steven? Is that you? *My* how you've changed…" I feigned.

"*Nuh-uh!*" Bloomington yelled out. "I'm right here, mongoloid-wart!" He followed that rather colourful slur with a coughing fit, presumably from guzzling down the Macallan Eighteen-Year that he held in his hand.

Sanchez looked on disapprovingly.

I quickly poured myself a glassful of the whisky, neat, and took a healthy gulp before raising it toward the Captain.

"Don't worry Sophia—I'm driving."

I looked over at Ricky, and as we both broke into broad grins, for the first time on the entire trip, everything seemed back to normal.

I set the navigational computer:

13-5-9203 B.C., Jerusalem, Israel

"You thinkin' what I'm thinkin', Doc?" Ricky asked across the center console.

I nodded. Because I knew *exactly* what Ricky was thinking:

I hope this goes better than our last trip to Jerusalem. Granted, there may have been a "rootin' tootin'" or other colloquially vulgar offense to the English language scattered elsewhere inside that head of his, but I got the gist of what he meant.

If you'll recall, that trip ended with us digging a shallow grave for a rather resilient fellow who called himself "Kayoss." He was a reprehensible creature with a penchant for "trolling" his way through history, causing as much trouble as he could within the universe's somewhat persnickety parameters.

I decided to lighten the mood.

"Computer, play Redbone's "Justify Your Love."

The familiar tune I enjoyed so much from *Guardians of the Galaxy* filled the cabin.

Corcoran and Bloomington looked blank for some reason. At least Sophia shot me the thinnest of smiles (I think).

I shook my head as I removed the ship's key from around my neck, and inserted it into the fitting. I looked at Corcoran, who sat, staring through the ship's "window" of transparency directly in front of us.

I cleared my throat and pointed at the second keyhole.

Corcoran shook his head. "Gets me every time…"

"That's funny—you only got me once."

He inserted his key, we turned them, and I pressed the big, green "Engage" button on the screen. Before we knew it, we were gliding through the sky above the fertile plain below, watching those tiny "aliens" that had been tenderizing animals destined for low-rent fast food mere months before whip those time tourists into submission below.

We coasted through the atmosphere until we were in the blissfully empty expanse of space once more. The tunneling lasers kicked in, and before we knew it, we were on another routine trip to the past through a rip in spacetime (ho hum).

Sanchez and Bloomington passed the time by regaling us with (admittedly incredible) tales of their exploits against the Nazis. Best I could gather, they had spent some two years on commando-like raids in the past that had quite the effect on the war—World War *Two*, I should say.

"So then Steve says, 'Hope you can breathe out yer asshole, Fritz!' and pulls the trigger!" Sanchez and Bloomington erupted in howling laughter, while Corcoran and I just smiled.

"But yeah, seriously… he couldn't." Bloomington shook his head.

"Really?" I said, overly serious.

I freshened up my drink and made my way back to the command deck. As we were pulling out of the time tunnel, I heaved myself into the command chair, adopted a healthy slouch, and heaved a "too bored" sigh into the cabin.

"Warning! Warning! Collision Alert! Collision Alert!"

"What the hell?" Sanchez raced up to the front of the ship.

I instinctively yanked the omniyoke down. For an instant, I cursed the moon once more for having nearly bludgeoned my time machine to smithereens.

As I was about to curse Neil Armstrong himself though, I looked outside the craft to find that Earth occupied far too much space in our field of view to be anywhere close to the moon.

Instead, what I saw caused my jaw to quite literally drop.

A large, bronze, pyramid-shaped craft hovered over what appeared to be the entire continent of Africa. Its surface was pocked with shallow gashes from what appeared to be some kind of energy weapon.

"Well I'll be *god*-damned… ol' Giorgio Tsoukalos wasn't bullshittin' anyone…" Corcoran let out.

Sanchez and I looked at each other, then back at the craft in front of us. It rotated very slowly, almost like a top, and held our gazes, almost hypnotically as it made a quarter turn in the foreground.

Suddenly, what sounded like an incredibly loud, out-of-tune

trumpet blast racked the ship. It was so discordant that it scrambled the inertial dampeners momentarily, and caused the ship to vibrate fiercely.

"Ever see one of those before Sophie?" Bloomington asked.

She stared at him. "Only once. I was hitching my way across the galaxy with the Loch Ness Monster and the Easter Bunny."

"Whoa… they exist?" Bloomington asked, too earnestly.

Before I could implore them to cease their somewhat childish banter, a large triangular space opened in the pyramid-like craft, and three smaller pyramids emerged from it. They bore down on us at incredible speed; within seconds, they were mere kilometers away.

My brow went damp as a bright, orange light powered up on each point of the smaller pyramids, glowing almost white-hot after mere moments.

"Somethin' tells me they ain't powerin' up their radios…" Corcoran strapped himself in and furiously pawed away at the weapons console.

The smaller craft tumbled through space, and I must admit, I was absolutely transfixed. Even as I heard the first discernible note of a whine coming from one of the craft… it was like an eerie elegy… almost like I had heard it somewhere before.

"Move, god *damn* it!" Sanchez dove at the omniyoke and swung it in a wide, quick arc. The smaller craft zoomed past as three lasers carved a path through the space that we had occupied only a split-second before.

She wrenched the ball of the omni-yoke down, then up, then zig-zagged it randomly. White-hot bolts of energy danced around the craft, each one seemingly closer than the last.

"For fuck's sake Ricky, where are those weapons?!" She commanded him.

"Hold your horses, Sunshine…" his fingers danced across the targeting console and hit three different red buttons.

We unleashed our own volley of laser fire at one of the pyramids. It hit its mark, and carved a soft trench into the side of the ship.

"Yes!" Bloomington clenched his fist.

Corcoran waved him off. The smaller pyramid spun for a second or two, then regained its bearings. While one of its lasers appeared to be offline, it spun up the remaining two and came about as Sophia continued to dodge the laser bolts from the other ships.

KABOOM!

The inertial dampeners failed for a brief moment, and the ship rocked from side-to-side. A strong wave of nausea washed over me while the ship's center-of-gravity was rocked by the blast.

"Status!" Sanchez commanded again.

"They hit us pretty good!" Corcoran responded. "We can't take too many more like that!"

"Computer, evasive maneuvers!" I yelled.

Sanchez slapped me.

"What was *that* for?"

"There's three of them, with three lasers each. Assuming their computers are at least as advanced as ours—"

"Then they can probably anticipate anything 'random' our computer tries to do," I completed her thought. "So then what the hell do we do while Ricky's little 'pop gun' is recharging?"

VALOOM!

At that moment, a large, gooey, green blob emerged from our ship. At what had to be close to light-speed, it tracked one of the smaller pyramid craft through space. It zigged, zagged, and dodged as best it could, but the pyramid was no match for the green blob, and the weapon connected with its target and utterly vaporized it.

"Pop gun, eh?" Ricky shook his head.

"We need more'a *those!*" Bloomington screeched.

"Where the devil were you hiding that?" I asked.

Ricky glanced over, "This old gal is just full'a surprises, ain't she Bloomy?"

"Please tell me you aren't just some one-shot wonder…" Sanchez arched an eyebrow at Corcoran.

"Don't worry sweetheart—there's *plenty* more where that came from. Just…takes a sec to recharge is all."

Silence for one second… two…

"So are you two going to *fuck?* Or are we going to win this god damned space dogfight?!" I finally broke the silence.

Both Corcoran and Sanchez composed themselves at their stations.

"Plasma cannon recharging. Antimatter torpedoes… still charging."

"Uh… yeah, let's try those!" Bloomington sounded like a fat kid in a candy store… though in hindsight I have no idea why that should surprise me.

Still, antimatter torpedoes *did* sound pretty fantastic, so I turned to Sanchez.

"Let's give him enough time to use his new toys, shalln't we?"

She nodded. "I have an idea."

She grabbed the holographic ball-shaped controller of the omniyoke that hovered in space.

"Computer, engage manual navigation controls, gravity on omni-yoke set at 100%!"

Manual navigation controls engaged. Omni-yoke gravity at 100%.

The computer flashed the words dutifully in its blocky lettering on the main console.

"Dr. Templeton, get up!" Sanchez commanded.

I unbuckled myself and stood up, across the omni-yoke control panel from her.

"Catch!"

She tossed the ball toward me, a perfect strike at my chest.

Unfortunately, I had little use for "ball games" of any type, and after hitting me in the chest, the ball dropped straight down to the ground.

The ship did the same. It plunged down toward the planet below. The two small pyramids that tailed us were caught unawares, and circled around each other momentarily before diving down to catch us.

"Now toss it back!"

I pointed at the ball, and she nodded impatiently. I seized it up (it was quite a bit "heavier" than anticipated with the gravity turned on within the holo-mechanism) and slung the ball toward Sanchez.

She fielded it with ease. The ship shot back up again.

"Antimatter torpedoes charged."

I believe Bloomington and I both squealed a bit with anticipation!

Corcoran slammed his hand on a bright blue button that appeared on the console. Almost immediately, a tiny blue speck floated out into space in front of us. It flitted about, almost like a tiny blue firefly set against the backdrop of infinite stars, as it tracked its "prey."

One of the smaller pyramids paid it little heed as it pursued us back away from the planet. It continued at full speed, directly on course with the blue speck. We waited… one second… another…

Until the ship flew right through it.

And… nothing.

I cocked my head, waiting for something to happen.

"Well, *that's* fucking great. We get a piss-soaked fucking *dud*—" Bloomington snorted.

The smaller pyramid-shaped craft began to twist. Not the focused circular drift that I was talking about earlier—this was an actual twisting of the metal of the ship, so that it appeared to be an inverted 3-D ninja-star of sorts, as the points all twisted toward one-another.

The ship's surface cracked under the stress, and while it should have been impossible, I could've sworn I heard the shit-brown craft groan before it buckled under itself, was turned inside-out, and imploded into a fantastical core breach.

We were all silent for a moment. Then Bloomington opened his mouth.

"That… was… *awesome!*"

I nodded proudly at Sophia, and she returned the nod. Corcoran grinned like he had woken up between a pair of tits.

KABOOM!

Another shudder, followed by that sickening wave of nausea.

"Let's not start suckin' each other's dicks yet," Corcoran turned toward the front again.

I checked the control panel. What appeared on it soon blared throughout the ship.

"Low Power! Low Power!"

We began diving toward the surface, at an awkward pitch. Klaxons blared as the cabin filled with an even, on-and-off red glow.

"Computer—resume autopilot!" I shouted above the various alarms.

"Unable to resume autopilot at this time."

"For fuck's—computer, engage manual navigation controls."

"Manual navigation engaged."

"Finny!" Corcoran shouted above the increasing din as the planet raced toward us. He pointed toward the back of the ship. "Turn us around so that I can shoot up!"

I nodded and sprung out of my seat. It was then that I realized that the artificial gravity was beginning to wear off; I landed on the ground with a pronounced thud in the nose of the ship.

I could barely lift my arms through the pronounced g-forces. I managed to wrench my leg up against a large support rod underneath the control panel. I steadied myself to pounce up toward the omni-yoke…

Underneath me, the ship listed sharply to the right. Sanchez had placed a delicate hand on the omni-yoke and started turning it. However, she too had lost her footing, and was now stapled next to me under the command console.

"Dr. Templeton!" She pointed at her foot. Not only had she lost her footing, but her boot was wedged between a loose panel and another support rod under the console.

I nodded. With Corcoran manning the weapons, and Bloomington God-knows-where, I was our only hope. I forced myself up to the support rod once more. This time, I was extraordinarily careful to "catch" the rod in the arch of my shoe's sole, which gave me enough leverage to pull myself up onto the omni-yoke.

I started turning the holographic ball against gravity one turn… two turns. Slowly but surely, the ship began coming about.

"Need more, Doc!" Corcoran shouted above the din.

"Almost… there!" I wrenched the ball three more times, and the ship faced the opposite direction.

Of course, with artificial gravity failing, this caused all of us (except Corcoran, who was strapped in) to fly to the back of the ship.

"Fire!" Corcoran shouted as he hammered the green button, which I presumed indicated he was firing the plasma cannons.

The green bolt of plasma shot out in its majestic arc into the blue sky of the Earth's atmosphere. We must've been falling for quite some time by that point, as the sky was almost as lush blue as it often appeared from the ground.

The bolt of plasma raced toward the copper-coloured ship that pursued us. As it gained speed, it had no real shot against the charged energetic goop. The mini-pyramid tried to spin at the last second, but the plasma cannon met its mark, and the enemy ship exploded into a fireball of awful-sounding twisted metal.

My heart skipped a beat. Just how close were we to the ground? I turtled on my back, and clamored for the dining table of the kitchenette, which was bolted to the ground.

"Computer… engage breaking thrusters!" Corcoran shouted.

I squinted my eyes tight, prepared for the absolute worst.

CHAPTER TWELVE

It's amazing what runs through one's head when one think he is about to be strewn across the landscape in a fantastically high-speed crash.

For the briefest of moments, there I was, back in the alleyway in England. My father chuckled, carrying six-year-old me on his shoulders. He bumped my younger self up-and-down a bit for what he called a "horsey ride," and they passed my pitiful, wretched, booze-soaked form.

"Now there Finny, that's a bum. You want to work hard in school so that you don't grow up to be like *him* some day…"

Little Finny on my father's shoulders turned to me. His smile turned into a deathly serious stare, the icy blue eyes I had seen for thirty-six years haunting me in what I thought was to be one of my final moments.

"Not yet…" younger me said.

I immediately snapped to. My jaw was clenched so tightly that wrenching a single tooth off its bottom neighbor seemed like an entire ordeal.

As I slowly opened one eye… then the other… I quickly realized that I was back laying on the floor of the ship, which meant that somehow the ship had righted itself.

"Computer, engage three-hundred sixty degree view!" The words came out in a somewhat high-pitched, Bloomington-like staccato.

The top of the craft seemed to cut away to three plumes of white smoke coming from the bottom of the craft.

Well I'll be damned… the breaking thrusters did *fire!* I thought.

The breaking thrusters were three good-old-fashioned rocket engines with a limited amount of fuel to be deployed in an emergency quite like this. Along with several maneuvering thrusters on each side (little more than "forced air" micro-jets), they were designed to right the ship, and then counter-act gravity should the ship become disoriented during flight.

As the rockets ran out of fuel, the smoke eventually cleared to reveal a fairly stark landscape. The ship had found a hill upon which to descend. To the west was a large mountain, which almost appeared to shine even as twilight descended on the rest of the plateau.

In the other direction, between two rivers, sat a rather impressive town. While the architecture was somewhat blocky, it was clear the landscape had been set out in an advanced grid pattern. Wide channels appeared to guide water from the rivers into the town, and fed into a series of lush, terraced gardens that gave the city a sense of serene life.

"Computer, report current location."

A map flashed on screen (I never received a good answer on why the pleasant voice of Majel Barrett had been discontinued), and showed that we were somewhere in the middle of what appeared to be modern Pakistan.

Forgive me for my momentary panic! If you'll recall, dear reader, when I had left 2032, World War III was still ravaging that part of the world, and Pakistan had been turned into a radioactive wasteland, along with most of Iran and the Arabian Peninsula.

"Son of a *bitch*," Corcoran rubbed his head as he came to.

"My thoughts exactly, Ricky."

He nodded at me, "You okay?"

"Nothing a trip to the bar can't fix." I made my way back toward the kitchenette.

"Jesus, you guys drink a *lot*," Sanchez had staggered to her feet as well.

I ignored the rather judging comment and instead shook an empty glass at her.

She nodded, "I like it!"

I doled out a couple of generous pours of Macallan 18 Year, and shot one over to the fetching Captain.

"Thank you, Dr. Templeton."

"Please my dear—call me Finny."

She smiled. Perhaps it wasn't the first time I had caught her in the act, but it was certainly the first time I had detected any sweetness, any joy, underneath one of her sly grins.

Amid this rather uncharacteristic show of emotion, Bloomington rose almost immediately to a ninety-degree angle. He surveyed the scene almost like a robot before he popped up, much like the wombat-like phantom he had first appeared to be back in Klaus's lab.

"Whoa! Close one, eh Doctor Tee?"

"Err… yes I suppose so, Steven."

"Who remembered to fire the breaking thrusters?"

Corcoran raised a hand, half-arsed. "Yours truly."

"Well then, Commander," Sanchez pulled on her uniform top, which had the unintended effect of accentuating her rather lovely figure underneath. "I guess… how should I put this…?"

"She's trying to say thanks for saving our mouth-breathing asses!" Bloomington interrupted.

She frowned, "Not in so many words, but yeah. Thanks."

"What's the matter? They don't teach ya, you know, what all these things can do in rent-a-cop school?"

The semi-scowl returned to her face, "You'd be surprised at what ChronoSaber keeps from its top officers."

I felt like a child of divorce torn between two outlandishly selfish parents.

Or in other words, "At home."

"How much damage did those… those *things* do?"

"What? You mean the UFOs?" Corcoran shot back.

I chuckled, "Now, now Commander, let's not jump to any conclusions…"

"First of all, I don't know what in the sam *fuck* those were, so by definition they were UFOs," Corcoran explained. "And second of all, they sure as shit didn't look like anything I've ever seen before from this planet. How 'bout you?"

The three of us stood silently.

"Yeah, that's what I thought…"

I sighed, "Computer, damage report?"

A long list of errors and downed systems filled the command console.

"Oh goody…" I mused. "How long are we going to be waylaid in Pakistan then?"

The computer flashed several numbers and letters on the screen.

As part of this, it became readily apparent that the antimatter containment unit had sustained some damage.

Not only that, but the computer output an 8-bit-like picture. It showed the flashing lining of the gravity drive with big block lettering underneath:

NEED RHENIUM

"Damn!" I pounded the console with my fist. When I had built the time machine in the first place, I had vowed not to make the same mistake that Doc Brown had made in *Back to the Future.*

If you haven't seen the film (and if you haven't, I *don't* know why you're reading this book now), Doctor Emmett Brown designed a perfectly-working time machine with one flaw: it ran on plutonium.

And while plutonium was semi-available (at the expense of some gullible Libyan terrorists) in the 80s in the original film, when going back in time, plutonium was anything *but* readily available.

Hence there was a fatal flaw in the machine that was extremely difficult to overcome without much hand gnashing and a bolt of lightning hitting a well-placed rod at *precisely* the right moment to get Marty McFly back to the future.

In this case, I thought I had accounted for pretty much any scenario that might face the time machine in the past. Even the antimatter that powered the ship had a failsafe backup that was programmed to release in case of failure.

However, there are only so many contingencies I could "bake in" to the ship and its computer. So I had to leave some physical backups to contain the antimatter reaction should the primary containment (a mix of plasma and directed magnetic fields) fail.

The result was a reactor chamber lined with an alloy containing rhenium—a particularly robust metal that not only stabilized volatile molecules, but when arranged properly with other molecules, presented quite the heat shield, enough even for an antimatter reaction.

Unfortunately, the computer was now saying that since the primary system (the antimatter containment unit) and the backup unit (containing rhenium) were both offline, it would be impossible to start the ship without either.

Even worse, rhenium is extremely rare in nature. It's a byproduct of copper minning, and we were in a pre-copper era, if one was to believe the history books.

I sighed and took another deep pull on my Macallan 18. Of all the stupid, completely foreseen ways I could have gotten us marooned in the past… this one took the cake.

"Fucking Rhenium!" I excalimed.

"Fucking *what?"* Corcoran responded.

I explained the situation to Corcoran, Bloomington, and Sanchez.

"So unless we find some of this 'Rhenium,' we're pretty much S.O.L.?" Sanchez asked.

I nodded, "I'm afraid that's correct, Sophia. And if this time is anything like my own, in this part of the world, I'm afraid that Rhenium is quite difficult to come by."

I let my statement hover over the room for several moments, like the wet fart it was meant to be.

And yet… all of a sudden, Bloomington raced to the front of the ship. Upon hearing about my royal fuck-up, I was shocked to find him grinning from ear-to-ear as he scampered off to the pantry.

"Yes! We can use it!"

"Use *what?*" Corcoran asked.

I followed the formerly-portly scientist as he dug through the mass of food that had been displaced by our "rough landing," toward one of the crates at the back of the pantry.

"Steven, I assure you, while we may have had a few glasses so far, there is *plenty* of Macallan for at *least* another couple of days in the crate. I already—"

"Here it is!"

On the bottom shelf, he grabbed at an ordinary-looking crate and dragged it toward the pantry entrance. It must have weighed a decent amount; it probably took him a couple of minutes to lug it into the kitchenette. When he did, it became clear that the word "POLARIS" was stenciled on the outside of the crate in big, green block letters.

"Help me open it, would ya?" He motioned at Sophia. She

grabbed a crowbar out of the armory and started separating the lid from the rest of the box.

After some finagling, it finally gave way, along with the sides of the box, which fell to the ground in a tide of styrofoam peanuts.

I couldn't believe what was left.

Folded up into a seemingly excruciatingly uncomfortable position was a terrifying-looking robot.

Its skeleton was some sort of bright alloy, and colored wires made up its "veins" running up and down each appendage.

What made it so grotesque, though, was the fact that it was covered almost entirely in a clear plastic epoxy of some sort, from head-to-toe. That included the robot's face, which showed two full-sized, spherical eyes, a nose cavity plastered over with some sort of cheap rubber-cement-looking compound, and a maniacal grin of exposed teeth.

I shuddered involuntarily.

"Perfect. A gen-u-ine terminator. That'll help us fight off the aliens—thanks Bloomy!" Corcoran was less-than-amused.

"Ha—I wish! Though… I never really thought to give him a gun before… it'd be pretty cool to see what he could—"

"Damn it, Steve!" Corcoran put his hands on his hips. "Get to the point, will ya?"

"Okay… okay… for now…" the last part was barely audible. "Ladies and fartnozzles, let me introduce you to POLARIS. He's a working prototype service droid."

The ghastly machine sat in its position with the same sick grimace on its face.

"This is about… 2050s era tech. Or so I'm told—I dunno. I just think it's pretty fucking cool is all."

"It looks like… it's going to murder us in our sleep," Sanchez flicked it a couple of times with her finger.

"Hey, so do you, Suzy Q, but we keep you on board, ain't it?" Corcoran grinned.

Bloomington ran his hands over the robot. "If I can just find the On/Off switch…"

He flipped the switch and jumped away from the grotesque collection of metal, wires, and epoxy, almost as if he expected to achieve the same results as Dr. Frankenstein himself.

Instead, his wide eyes waited several seconds before fading into bewilderment.

"What the *dick?"*

Sophia rushed over to inspect the machine. Corcoran followed soon after. Both scoured its anatomy for some sign of anomoly.

And yet… I knew what was wrong.

I saw an indicator light where the robot's lat should be, right on top of its shoulder. While it was blank, a small lightning bolt adorned the space to the lower right of the light.

I steadied myself for what was to come with my next uttterance. Nonetheless, I took a deep breath and started:

"I *do* believe it's out of power."

I looked at Bloomington. His expression went from excitement, to dour disappontment, to one of hope once more.

And then, for the first time ever, a sly smile crept across Steve Bloomington's face.

Without a word, he semi-waddled off into the pantry, and emerged seconds later with an extension cord.

Before I could utter a word of protest, in a single maneuvre, he removed his t-shirt, revealing his shrunken (yet flabby) midsection, and the three outlets that now protruded from it.

He plugged one end of the extension cord into the three prongs in his stomach. And then, he knelt down between POLARIS's legs. I couldn't tell where exactly he was meddling on the robot, though it seemed to be closer to the arse than to where you might think the robot would otherwise have three prongs.

With a flourish, the freakishly pallid scientist jammed the prongs into the robot's arsehole.

Immediately, the robot's eyes came to life. It unfurled itself and staggered, head jerking side-to-side, trying to gain its footing while letting forth a string of staccato words and phrases like Max Headdrom on methamphetamine.

Corcoran and Sanchez reached for their sidearms, ready to add lead to the metals used in our newly-discoverd companion.

Then, all of a sudden, the robot ceased its convulsions. Its eyes glowed red, and that same twisted, maniacal grin remained plastered on its face.

It leaned in toward me, those teeth—those *teeth!*—looking all-too-ready to take a big bite out of my face, or perhaps skin my face and take it for itself.

"*Masssster?*" It said to me without moving its mouth.

"Uh… well… I *suppose* I am…"

Truth be told, I was doing everything I could not to piss myself.

Bloomington snapped his fingers twice at the awakening contraption.

"Hey fartnozzle, you answer to me, okay? I jumped you, I gave you life, you are *mine.*"

The formerly pudgy scientist made the proclamation with a startling amount of authority. I could only imagine it was because it was a machine and not an actual person—otherwise I can't imagine Bloomington having such bravado when dealing with anything *remotely* sentient.

"*Yessss Masssster…*" The machine's cadence was frighteningly serpentine.

"Now, Doc Templeton over here needs something called Rhenium, okay? Do you understand?"

He punctuated each of his statements with pauses, almost as if talking to a child. I had distinct flashbacks to Hank Fleener "educating" Sir Isaac Newton in my earlier travels.

"*Yesss Massssster….*"

I was beginning to think that was all the machine could say.

"Now get out there and find us a pile of Rhenium, alright?"

"*Yessss Masssster…*"

And with that, the grinning menace extended the gangway and went off the ship to survey the scene.

My relief forced out an enormous sigh.

Sanchez nodded after it, "Hopefully that… that *thing* doesn't come across any Past-ies while it's out th—"

"Analyssssissss complete. Rhenium deposit found..."

The robot boomed its proclamation from outside the ship, to the point where even Bloomington startled a bit and jumped an inch or two off the floor.

"Re—really?" I half-expected a *"Jussssst kidding"* to follow, though none was forthcoming.

We rushed down the gangway toward POLARIS. The machine had its arm pointed straight out toward a village in the distance.

"Well I'll be sam *fucked*..." Corcoran whispered.

"Are you *quite* sure?" My surprize overcame my fear as I addressed the robot.

It turned its head around, 180 degrees to face me. Then it nodded, a little too quickly for comfort.

Sanchez dug into one of the pockets on her fatigues. She produced a pair of what appeared to be compact binoculars and surveyed the general direction POLARIS pointed.

"Hmm... yeah... yeah the robot's right. There's a *bunch* of it in that village over there."

She handed the binoculars over to me. I brought them to my face and felt a distinct sucking feeling as the eyepieces comfortably latched onto my eye sockets.

Instantly a wireframe mesh overlayed the exterior surroundings in true 3D-VR. An icon came up over the village in the distance, flashing "Rhenium supply found!"

The view zoomed in to the largest hut in the village. It was built from stone (unlike the rest which were made of mud brick), and it had a tiled roof, which seemed more than a little anachronistic for this time period.

I suppose my "surprize" was tempered a bit by my previous dealings with mischevious, misanthropic, or otherwise unpleasant time travellers.

I removed the binoculars from my eyes and nodded.

"Indeed—that should be *plenty!"*

Bloomington patted POLARIS on the shoulder. "Good boy! Good

boy POLARIS! Who's a good boy? *Who's a good boy?"*

"I am a good boyyyyy," the robot hissed.

"We ain't gonna take that thing to town with us, are we?" Corcoran nodded at the robot.

Sanchez and I arched an eyebrow at one another.

"I don't know Ricky," I said. "He *has* been quite helpful so far. Plus he might, to use a technical term, 'scare the ever-living shit' out of the locals."

Sanchez nodded, "And it might be good to have an extra gun around."

Corcoran arched an eyebrow, "You're gonna give that *thing* a fuckin' *gun?"*

Sanchez's eyes narrowed, "Why not? Some of the finest soldiers I've commanded have been robots. Granted, they aren't quite as—" her eyes widened as she examined the robot's insane visage "—unique… as this one… but tell them to do something and sure as shit, they'll do it."

Corcoran gritted his teeth. "Okay then. Yo, robot!"

POLARIS's head twisted slowly about 270 degrees around the other way to face Corcoran, at a thoroughly odd angle compared to its body.

"Here's an order for ya: don't shoot any of the four'a us, no matter what. Got it?"

The robot's head squeaked as it rotated to face Bloomington.

Steven nodded. "Do what he says, POLARIS."

"Yessssss Masssssterrr…" The robot hissed.

"Excellent!" I said.

"Well ain't that somethin'?" Corcoran grabbed one of the Baretta nine millimetres from his shoulder holsters and flipped it to the robot.

Almost too quickly, POLARIS's arm shot out, grabbed the gun, loaded a round into the chamber, and removed the safety, all in one fluid motion.

The subsequent low shriek that was let out may or may not have been my own…

"Yeah, this is gonna be *real* great…" Corcoran sighed. He closed the gangway and we headed toward the village.

CHAPTER THIRTEEN

We arrived in the village, and received the requisite cock-eyed looks from the locals.

Upon seeing POLARIS, gun outstretched, maniacal grin on its face ever-present, one short, portly woman who was carrying a pot of water back to her hut simply dropped it. She didn't seem to care when the pot cracked into a dozen different pieces and her days' work slaked the thirsty ground.

Several nearby children started crying, and for once in our travels, I was quite certain that Bloomington *wasn't* the source of their consternation. Groups of villagers recoiled in horror, brought to their knees by this totally foreign spectre.

"Yes, that's right—bow to your god!"

Being in the company I was in, I wasn't shocked necessarily that *someone* had made the obvious crack at the expense of the Past-ies.

However, I was more than a little surprised that Sophia was the one saying it.

I furrowed my brow at her, and she only responded with a devilish smile and a shrug.

I couldn't decide if I was incredibly turned on, or dismayed that she seemed to be adopting more and more of Corcoran's mannerisms by the hour.

We arrived at the staircase leading to the central, stone hut. In terms of materials used and overall level of craftsmanship, it was little different than the Newton household in 16th century England.

Well-fitted stones were held together by what appeared to be strong mortar. Keystones outfitted with relief carvings of animals dotted the tops of glass-fitted windows. A bank of tiles served as the roof.

I could only imagine how this relatively modern building had come to exist in such a distinctly far-away time period.

Then I considered the giant "pyramid of death" we had encountered perhaps an hour before, and thought the better of asking too many questions just yet.

We ascended the stairs. While two guards stood on either side of the doorway at the top, POLARIS bounded ahead and flashed his gun at both, causing them to kneel in a mix of fright and reverence.

"You see Ricky? You don't *always* need to shoot someone to get what you want…" I lectured him.

"What can I say?" He chambered a round (likely for effect), "I'm just a friendly guy with this robot around!" He smiled his broad grin and walked up ahead to the front of the party, and into the structure.

Inside the structure, more guards surrounded a well-appointed throne. These men weren't so easily cowed as their comrades at the front door; many raised their spears which, though primitive, appeared to be tipped with an almost liquid-looking metal.

Upon the throne sat an odd-looking, portly fellow, who appeared to be in his fifties (or perhaps slightly older even). His face was covered in tribal tattoos that, while once probably quite striking, had faded with age and wrinkles. His jet black hair was thinning, though his garb was a one-piece tunic with a gold-threaded pattern adorning its fringe.

"Ball-o-way! De-de-ano parchescu rom mac deelano!" He said. He waved at the guards to lower their weapons.

"Oh great…" Corcoran rolled his eyes. "Anyone got one of those nicotine-patch thingys?"

Before he could finish asking, Sanchez had reached into her pocket and produced several holotrans.

"Standard issue. All rent-a-soldiers get them," she deadpanned at Corcoran. She unwrapped one and threw it to the tattooed fellow, and patted her neck to show him how to apply it.

The tattooed fellow tilted his head and eyed the patch suspiciously. Sanchez batted her eyelashes at him a couple of times (she could be *quite* charming when she wanted to be) and repeated the gesture with a sly smile.

Finally, he brought the disc to his neck, and pushed down on it.

Sanchez handed them out to the rest of us, and we did the same.

"Now speak. Say something. Anything." Sanchez practically commanded the tatooed fellow.

"Whoa! Hey! I can understand you!" The tattooed man was downright giddy. "Amazing!"

"We got you too, stretch!" Corcoran said. He stuck out his hand, "Ricky Corcoran, nice to meet you!"

I thought about warning the tattooed fellow against accepting, and then reconsidered.

"I am Chief Octoc, ruler of the prosperous village of Mohenji-Daro."

The name of the village sounded familiar, but for the life of me I couldn't figure out where I had heard it before.

"Nice to meet you—name's Richard Corcoran, United States Navy. You can call me Ricky."

"Very firm handshake, Ricky!" the Chief turned toward one of the head guards, "Always trust a man with a strong handshake who can look you in the eye."

I wondered if both men could perceive the steam I felt shooting out from my ears.

"And I'm *Captain* Sophia Sanchez," Sophia extended a hand.

The Chief gave a low whistle. "My goodness…what a lovely name, Sophia… Sophia…" He kissed her hand.

"Really? It's pretty common when…er… where I'm from…" I could've sworn Sophia blushed.

I rolled my eyes.

The Chief's attention turned to me, "And who is this academic-looking fellow?"

I suppose I should have been flattered, although I took it as somewhat of a slight, as most of the academics that I knew were slovenly fellows with a rather dreadful fashion sense.

"I'm Doctor Phineas Templeton, very nice to meet you, Your Highness."

"Your Highness? Haven't heard that one before… but I like it!" He turned to the guard once more, "Can we make that a thing? Calling me 'Your Highness' from now on?"

The guard nodded slowly, his expression stoic as a secret service agent.

The Chief shook my hand vigorously. He certainly exuded charisma, combined with a warm, exciting energy for a man of his age.

I found his general personality and comportment reminded me of the legendary comedian Mel Brooks.

Bloomington was the last human to be introduced to the Chief.

"Steve Bloomington. I'm a scientist. I kill Nazis."

The Chief took his hand, "Well, judging by your handshake young man, I certainly would *not* want to be these Nazis you speak of, that's for sure..."

He turned away from Bloomington and rolled his eyes in an exaggerated manner.

Finally, his attention turned to POLARIS.

"And of course, you must be the Sky God."

"Sky God?" We all said in near-unison.

"I am POLARISSSSSSSSSSSS..." The machine hissed.

"Yeah, yeah, "POLARIS," "Sky God," whatever the last traveler who passed through these parts said. Noble Sky God, you have no use for your weapon here. Can you please put it down so my guards can relax a bit?"

POLARIS looked forward, I have to say quite dumbly.

I nodded at it, as did Bloomington, and the robot lowered the weapon.

"Yesssss masssster..."

"Excellent!" The Chief clapped his hands. "And now—"

"This previous traveller—was it perhaps a German man?" I interrupted. "Yay high, grey hair, somewhat of a 'lively' personality?"

The Chief stroked a tattoo of a particularly hostile-looking totem on his face.

"Yes, the traveler you speak of was through here several days past..." he scratched his head, "He wanted to know more about the language of the ancients...come to think of it, he had one of these too," he scratched at the holotran on his neck. "I thought he might be a little bit—" he whistled several times, seemingly to indicate that he thought Klaus was somewhat off, "—when he kept pointing at things and being like," he pointed at one of the guards, "Soldier," he turned the other way, as if he was Klaus. "Soldier. Spear. Spear. *Everything* he wanted to know the word the ancients used. And then eventually, we were able to speak ancient to one another. Say… you don't think it has anything to do with *this*, do you?"

He patted the holotran on his neck.

"I'd say there was a *very* high probability of that," I said.

The Chief shrugged, "I dunno. With all of these travelers coming through here recently, it's tough to remember who's who…"

"Really…?" I arched an eyebrow. My curiosity got the better of me. "Of which other travellers do you speak?"

"Well let's see now… there was that beautiful raven-haired woman who was by here recently—" presumably he spoke of Helene on one of her many time travel errands.

"—and your friend… and there was one other, but I dismissed him as an agent of the Anunnaki."

My eyes went wide.

"Anu-what now?" Corcoran asked.

I turned toward the Commander, "The Anunnaki? Zechariah Sitchin?"

Blank looks plastered Corcoran and Bloomington's faces.

I rolled my eyes again, "According to a somewhat 'questionable' interpretation of Mesopotamian myth, the Anunnaki are supposed to be a race of ancient aliens who came to Earth thousands of years ago on a planet called Niburu or somewhat more creatively 'Planet X.' Allegedly, Niburu has a long, irregular elliptical orbit of the Earth, and only comes around every 12,000 years or so.

"Some folks, including the late Zecharia Sitchin, think that the Anunnaki were here in search of gold to somehow fix their ozone layer."

Now it was Corcoran and Bloomginton's turn to roll their eyes. Though curiously, Sanchez nodded, as if to say that in her time, fixing the ozone layer with gold was about as controversial as replacing a solar cell that doesn't work.

"The Mesopotamian legends say that the Anunnaki found a race of primitive human-like beings living here that they made mine the gold. Of course, after a while, the Anunnaki mated with the local women… and gentically modified the offspring, creating human beings as we know them today."

Bloomington widened his eyes at this revelation.

"Most think Sitchin was a bit of a crackpot, but there's compelling evidence even to this day that there may have been some kind of genetic manipulation done with early humans by, shall we say, 'outside forces.'"

The Chief sat in his throne, lazily eating something that looked like grapes from a basket at his side.

"Yeff, yeff, 'ats no wegend," he talked with his mouth quite full before he swallowed. "This other traveler came by and asked for men for the mines and women for… uh… the *other* mines, so to speak."

Sanchez shivered.

"But I told him to fuck off!" the Chief added with a flourish. "Honestly, I think they would've just wiped my whole tribe and the rest off the map if not for one thing:"

He paused, first for effect, then to consider whether or not to let us in on his little trump card. He motioned for us to come closer, as if he was sharing a secret so powerful it couldn't even be shared with the guards.

"The capstone on the triangle building."

Sanchez arched an eyebrow, "Triangle building? You mean the Great Pyramid?"

"Pyramid? Pyramid… yes the large building with triangle sides, many miles away. Several times in my youth I accompanied a caravan to the Nile valley for trade, and feasted my eyes upon the great triangle building—and oh how the rumors hardly did it justice! Gleaming white limestone, polished to a sparkle lining the perfectly-made sides, a true marvel to behold!

"Yet there was one thing that was so oddly out of place I couldn't help but notice its absence:"

"The capstone," we all said in unison, harkening back to my observation back in Egyptian times.

"*Capsssssstone…*" POLARIS was a bit late to the party.

"Yes, yes indeed—the capstone was missing! Rumors swirled among the merchants gathered that the Annunaki had taken a particular interest in the triangle building—that they had discovered something inside that could give them wondrous power beyond even *their* wildest dreams… but it required the capstone that had either gone missing or purposely been hidden.

"I asked around trying to figure out what had happened to it, but most people thought I was an Annunaki spy. Me! Can you believe it?

"I finally encountered a toothless old Egyptian who spoke a dialect of the language of the ancients that I could understand—"

"And who were these 'ancients' again?" I couldn't help but interrupt.

"Before the time of troubles," the Chief continued. "The nations of the Earth were unified into two competing empires according to legend. This is thousands and thousands of years ago—few records of the civilizations, let alone their languages, even survive to this day. Though a dialect of it has been passed down to my father, from his father, from his father, from his father—"

"We get it," Corcoran held up a hand and disarmed the Chief with a toothy smile.

"And on, and on. I'm one of the few people who can even *understand* the language of the ancients, let alone speak it. So I see this toothless old man and ask him, 'Hey pop, what's with the capstone?'

"And he proceeds to tell me that the capstone went missing long ago, right before the time of troubles. In fact, according to his people, the capstone *caused* the time of troubles."

"Caused the time of troubles…" I mused aloud. I stroked my chin. Perhaps Klaus was trying to avert this 'time of troubles?' Though surely he knew that to do so was but a fool's errand given the "whatever happened, happened" nature of the universe.

The Chief shook his head, "Anyway, that's all a long-winded way of saying that I've hinted to emissaries of the Annunaki that I have some," he whistled and made the "okay" sign with his hand, "primo information about the capstone and its whereabouts. Though truth be told, if they had a laser gun to my nuts—"

Corcoran, Bloomington, the guards and I all involuntarily winced.

"—I'd tell them the exact same thing I just told you all, which is bupkus. So when the emissary last came for more women, and I told him to get bent, I *also* mentioned the capstone thing again. So I've been awaiting their next messenger… and I thought it was maybe that woman, or your friend… or you, but judging by your reactions, you haven't dealt with the Anunnaki yet?"

I looked at Sophia. It was clear we were thinking the same thing.

Since no one in the future had come back from this time in history, even future time travellers likely thought the Anunnaki to be "just a myth."

But what if "Planet X" wasn't a planet at all? What if it was that giant pyramid-shaped UFO that we had just narrowly escaped from? The Chief seemed to indicate that the Anunnaki were a very real threat to him.

"Perhaps we have… up near Niburu?"

The Chief's eyes went wide. "You've been up by Niburu and lived to tell the tale?! Tell… me… *everything!*"

I proceeded to recount our dogfight with the three fighters in space.

"Deities! I have heard of more boats like yours in the sky, but Niburu has destroyed all of them as far as I know. If you've defeated their fighters, they'll surely be back soon. Of course, any enemy of the Anunnaki is a friend of mine. How can I help?"

"Funny you might ask," Sanchez straightened her posture. "We have reason to believe you have a large quantity of shiny metal somewhere nearby—maybe something one of the travelers gave you?"

The Chief lit up, "The Moonstone? Yes, of course—that was the raven-haired woman! She said that sky god here would need some."

"*Obtainnnn Rhennnnium...*" POLARIS started moving toward the far end of the hut. The guards moved in its way. Undeterred, the robot reached for something on its back.

The Chief nodded at his guard, who hurled his metal-tipped spear through POLARIS's knee joint. The robot buckled to a kneel immediately. Somewhat pitifully, it kept trying to move its good leg to drag itself along toward its target, to no avail.

"Jesus CHRIST!" Corcoran pulled his gun and levelled it at the guard.

The guards surrounding us raised their spears in kind.

I put my hands out, palms down, "Okay, okay… everybody settle down now… no need for heroes…"

The Chief remained remarkably cool and collected given the circumstances.

"She said this would happen too. Moonstone makes *great* spear tips. Even ones that can cripple the mighty sky god."

"*Owwwwww...*" POLARIS said dryly as it continued spasming on its knee.

"Put the gun down, Ricky," Sanchez put her hands on her hips.

"Ain'tchya know this *same exact thing* happened back in Mexico last time we were there? And they ended up chasin' us through the jungle, tryin' to kill us."

The Chief shook his head, "Commander, I assure you, I mean no harm. My guards will not spear you like pigs unless attacked. So if you'll lower your weapon..."

Corcoran's eyes dotted back and forth across the room. Telling him to holster his sidearm in a potentially dangerous situation was like letting a lion into an enclosed pen of gazelles and telling the beast to watch over them while the zookeeper took a leak.

The angel on his shoulder must have finally won out, as Ricky engaged the safety on his weapon and put it back in its holster.

The Chief breathed a sigh of relief and wiped his brow. "Whew! That was a close one! Now of course I'm happy to help you out. I'll give you all the moonstone you'd like. But I'd like to arrange a parlay of sorts—a trade if you will."

"Whatchya have in mind?" Corcoran snorted. "Our busted-ass robot for it?"

"Hey!" Bloomington appeared to be personally insulted. He rushed to the robot's side. "It's okay POLARIS. It's okay buddy. You can stop for a bit."

The robot ceased its pathetic protestations, "*Yesssss massssster...*"

The Chief beckoned his head guard to his side and whispered in the man's ear. The guard nodded again and again—for what seemed like minutes, even though it was likely only 30 seconds or so. When the Chief had finished, the head guard ordered most of the rest of the guards in the room to follow him into the village; only 4 remained with the Chief.

The Chief clasped his hands together and turned his attention to us.

"Very good them. By now, I assume many more Anunnaki are on their way. They definitely haven't met any worthy foes in this era, yourselves and potentially my moonstone-tipped-spear equipped guards nonwithstanding.

"I have just made arrangements for the villagers to hide in… how should I put this… a nearby 'ark'? Is that the word?"

"You mean… like a big boat?" Sanchez asked.

"Lemme guess—one'a your guys' is named Noah?" Corcoran asked.

The Chief shook his head, "His name is No-ayeh, but that's beside the point—" We looked at each other and rolled our eyes. "By 'ark,' I mean a 'safe place.' There's a complex of man-made caves nearby from the time of troubles—before the Anunnaki came."

"Wait a minute—the time of troubles was *before* those alien assnozzles came?" Bloomington asked.

"Yes. Legends say it was a time of great sorrow. Never-ending storms with constant thunderbolts that turned the desert to sheer glass."

I rubbed both hands over my face, sufficiently exasperated.

The Chief caught himself and smiled, "I'm sorry. I'm rambling. The point is, the villagers will be safe. And I will happily give you everything I own—all of the moonstone, all of my gold, silver, and jewels, if you allow me to indulge in one thing:"

The Chief's eyes went wide. We waited two seconds… three… four.

At one point I thought he may have had a stroke or died on the spot.

"The thing you came here in—this great craft. I assume if you fought the Anunnaki beyond the sky, then it can fly in the air, soaring like a bird?"

"Sometimes…" Sanchez said wryly.

"Hey!" Bloomington and I for once said in unison.

"Jinx! Personal jinx! You owe me coke!" the fat-drained, annoying scientist said.

"Didn't you forget the 'a'?" I asked.

The extra skin hanging on his face contorted into a confused grimace, "What?"

"I owe you *a* coke."

He shrugged before turning away, "Cheap ass…"

I shook off the junkie's apparent slight.

"You were saying, Your Highness?"

"I would like nothing more than to have one ride," he punctuated it by wagging a finger somewhat gratifyingly in Bloomington's face, "in the flying machine that brought you here."

Corcoran nodded, "Sure, no problemo."

"*Excuse* me?" I couldn't help myself.

Corcoran leaned over and whispered, "What does it matter if we give the old codger a ride? We're up, we give him a thrill, we're down, badda bing, badda boom."

I stroked my chin. *Was* it so bad to give the chief a ride? Especially since we needed the rhenium to get moving again? Otherwise I feared we may become the next victims of an anachronistic nuclear explosion.

At the same time, I found it a bit odd that the man was willing to trade all of his earthly wealth for a single ride in a flying machine.

Then I recalled my own wonder upon making my first voyage through time. Adrenalin coursing through my veins, senses heightened, not knowing exactly what to expect as I hit the "Engage" button, and the swirling wormhole tore free of the fabric of spacetime, and produced some of the most wondrous shapes and colours I had ever seen.

Perhaps more than anything else, I remembered the thrill of doing something *different*. Something new. Something literally incredible to most people, of which I could only *dream* of for *years* and years.

And it all made immediate sense to me.

I nodded, "Your Highness, we respectfully agree to your terms."

The Chief clapped his hands together, "Splendid! Splendid! Now all we need is—"

His thought was interuppted by a loud semi-mechanical groan outside. Actually, that doesn't quite do it justice—it was a booming metallic wail, not unlike when hot metal is twisted under water, only with less whine and more ominous base.

The room darkened, and we all ran outside to confirm our deepest, darkest suspicions.

There, against the bright silhouette of the sun, was a pyramid-shaped eclipse.

And it was growing larger.

CHAPTER FOURTEEN

I don't know if I've ever seen Steve Bloomington run so fast in his life.

It was a feat made all the more impressive by the fact that he was helping to carry POLARIS along with Corcoran, Sanchez, and myself. The Chief followed closely behind with a football-sized lump of rhenium in the crook of his elbow.

"Come on you pigshits!" Bloomington goaded us on. As foul and juvenile as his exhortations may be, I found that in the moment, they were as motivational as if spoken by Tony Robbins himself.

We hurried back along the path from whence we came. All the while, the dark silhouette of the presumed pyramid-shaped ship "Nibiru" continued to grow larger, and obscured and then overtook the sun. It gave the landscape an eerie twilight look. Nocturnal insects began to buzz and fritter this way and that.

Worst of all, several colonies of snakes seemed to think their feeding time had arrived. They slithered out of passed-over cracks and crevices in the landscape that had previously gone unnoticed, so caught up were we in our revulsion of POLARIS on the way over. Some of the reptiles even made it into our path—I may have kicked one or two of them inadvertently, and though some seized up and hissed, we were moving too quickly for them to strike.

After what seemed like an hour, we finally arrived at the time machine and ran up inside. Bloomington opened the maintenance hatch and practically threw POLARIS down it.

"*Owwwwwwww...*" the robot said without emotion as it clanged to the floor.

"I'm coming! I'm coming!" Bloomington's "svelte" new physique benefitted him in this instance, as he grabbed the rhenium from the Chief and slid down the ladder into the guts of the ship right behind the robot.

"Form primary and secondary antimatter containment units from rhenium and install, fast!"

Bloomington's voice was more baratone, more authoritarian than I was used to.

I crouched over the hole on all fours, eager to offer my assistance.

By the time I had done so though, the robot's hands had transformed into a very advanced-looking 3D-printer of sorts. It would alternately heat the rhenium, and form it into the shapes needed for both the primary and secondary reactor containment units, almost like a combination of blowing glass and stretching taffy.

Once it had the shapes it wanted, POLARIS shot a coolant mist out of its wrists onto each part.

"*Ssssstand clearrrrrrrr…*" the robot croaked out.

Bloomington scampered up the ladder. Seconds later, the hatch closed, and we waited.

And waited.

Finally, I heard a sharp creaking and whining from down below. It was the familiar sound of POLARIS dragging itself across the floor, on its one good leg.

We all collectively cringed in the cabin as the nails-on-chalkboard noise continued for 15 seconds… then 30. Nibiru had to be getting close now, and there was no telling how little time we had left.

"Hey, POLARIS, do you have any excess rhenium left over?" Sanchez yelled through the closed hatch.

"*Yesssss Masssssster…*" the muffled reply came from down below.

"And can you use it to fix up your leg in the next, oh, say 30 seconds or so?"

"*Challenge acccccccceppppped…*" the monotone mechanical voice replied.

It was a positively brilliant idea—I wish I could say that I thought of the same thing, but to do so would be to discredit Sophia.

We waited as the taffy-making sounds of the robot stretching and cooling the rhenium continued from the maintenance room.

Still, despite the cabin not being in 360 degree mode, Niburu's presence loomed large above us. The Chief was noticeably sweating, and Sanchez nervously tapped her finger on the counter of the kitchen. Even Corcoran let out a small sigh and a "For sam *fuck's* sake…" at one point as the robot continued to repair itself.

"*Repairsssss complete…*" POLARIS croaked. "*Ssssstarting ssssssysssstem diagnossssstic…*"

Corcoran threw his arms in the air, "There's no *fucking* time for this shit! Just make the repairs and restart the goddamned reactor!"

"Yesssss masssster… diagnosssstics postponed. Reactor ressssssstarting in 10… 9… 8…"

While part of me was pants-shittingly terrified, I have to admit a more childish part of me was somewhat excited to participate in a real-life life-or-death countdown. I felt like I was in a proper spy movie!

A firm, yet feminine hand on my shoulder shook me from my momentary reverie.

I turned to find Sophia, face stern and down-to-business. She nodded at the command chair.

"Shouldn't you get over there so we can take off once the killer robot is done?"

"4… 3…"

I nodded, snapped out of my daze, and ran over to the command chair. I fumbled with the shoulder straps, desperately trying to secure myself for the shitstorm to come.

"2… 1…"

Suddenly, the ship came to life. Screens everywhere around us went live and lights flickered back on.

The familiar blocky face of the QC came back on the main screen.

Welcome Captains please insert keys to reboot system, flashed up on the screen.

I instantly regretted the fit I had thrown that had caused Chronosaber and Corcoran to institute the new security measures.

"Fuck—the key!" Ricky preempted my own comment.

He rushed over and grasped for the small key around his neck. I fumbled for the same, and after several seconds, we both inserted them and twisted simultaneously.

One Moment Please…

I wanted to punch whomever programmed the QC blockhead character doing casual summersaults as its "waiting" icon in the face.

The computer booted for several more interminable seconds, each one seemingly longer than the last.

Finally, the smiling QC's blocky face came back on the screen.

Within an instant, it was replaced with warning klaxons and sirens.

Warning: Nuclear Warheads Inbound!

I found the frowny-faced QC avatar underneath to be entirely unnecessary.

"Computer, start gravity drive and get us the fuck out of here!" I screamed.

Without hesitation, the QC's screen flashed:

ENGINES ENGAGED!

I was rocked back in my seat by the force of gravity for a quick moment before the drive's gravimetric compensators kicked in. The desert flew past us below as we held our collective breaths for one second… two…

A bright flash filled the window, almost like we were on the surface of the sun for an instant. My retinas burned and flashed bright green and pink for a second before I instinctively brought my arm up to shield my eyes.

The time machine shook—even the gravity drive and inertial stabilizers weren't enough to compensate fully for the force of the blast.

Corcoran staggered around the command deck like a drunkard. Cries filled the rest of the ship.

I even thought I heard an "*Ohhhh sssssssshiiiiit…*" from POLARIS in the maintenance bay.

At any moment, I expected the ship to disintigrate into a million pieces, for this little journey through time to evaporate out of existence in a blaze of glory!

Instead, after several seconds, the shaking stopped. The inertial dampeners came back online, and perhaps most shockingly of all, the QC flashed a notice of:

ALL SYSTEMS NORMAL!

"We're… clear?" I asked the cabin.

A bunch of unbelieving faces greeted my assertion.

Corcoran leaned over to look for himself.

"Fuck yeah! We made it!"

Bloomington, Sanchez, and the Chief erupted in a chorus of cheers. All three hugged while the Chief let out a loud "lalalalalalalalala!", which I assume was some kind of war cry from the sound of it, though I couldn't be sure—he could've been placing a curse on us for all I knew.

Our jubilation was cut short by another message on the QC's monitor followed by warning klaxons:

Warning: Nuclear Warheads Inbound!

"Fucking sweat fold lickers!" Bloomington yelled out.

"Computer, countdown to impact?" I asked.

3:18… 3:17… 3:16…

I cracked my knuckles and leaned forward in my command chair. The sky continued to darken in front of us—we were close to the cold emptiness of space, which was good. If the warheads managed to hit the ship, the last thing I wanted on my conscience was them vaporizing the ozone layer and turning the planet's surface bright green with fallout.

I snapped toward the back of the aircraft and held an invisible glass in my hand.

"Excuse me?" Sanchez asked.

I frowned, "Sorry darling, that wasn't meant for you. Steven, a drink please?"

"I'll give you a 'darling'…" Sanchez muttered under her breath.

Thankfully Bloomington was already ahead of me. Seconds later he rushed to the front of the craft, two overflowing glasses of Macallan Eighteen in hand.

"Can I get one'a those?" the Chief asked.

Bloomington opened his mouth to protest, but thought the better of it. He slugged down half of his own glass, and handed the remainder to the Chief, who did in kind before coughing up a fit.

"*Katunga!* Tastes like liquid smoke mixed with camel shit!" The Chief choked through it.

"How would you know that?" Sanchez asked, without a hint of emotion.

"It's an acquired taste, I suppose," I gritted my teeth and fumbled with the journal that I had been directed to in Klaus's laboratory by the dancing leprachaun.

Suddenly, another journal flew over my shoulder and onto the dash.

"Looking for this?" Sanchez asked. It was the journal that Helene had provided at our little briefing back in Baltimore.

I shook my head. "No, that's just going to tell us where Klaus *wants* us to go. I want to try to find where he *is*. That way I may be able to cut him off before the next jump and end this madness."

Corcoran snarled, "Great! Yeah, that's a fan-fucking-*tastic* idea! Only problem is, since you're such a fuckin' alkie, you got less than a minute to do so."

I glanced at the center console, which quickly turned into a double take.

0:48…0:47…0:46…

I heaved a sigh. There simply wasn't enough time to analyze Klaus's private journal he had left me in his lab. Though I made a note to do it the next time I had a few free moments.

Instead I quickly flipped to the page in the *other* journal that Chronosaber had obtained with the coordinates for the next jump (for once, my dreadful habit of dog-earring important pages in books made it easy to find).

5-1-13872 B.C., Latitude: N. 38 degrees, 43 ′, 18 ″, Longitude W. 27 degrees, 13 ′, 14 ″: It has risen!

I had never seen jump coordinates set out in pure GPS before.

0:29… 0:28… 0:27…

I started talking without thinking. "Computer, please set a time jump for the following time and coordinates and engage!"

I repeated the rather lengthy to say string of letters and numbers.

0:15… 0:14… 0:13…

In front of us, the tunneling lasers carved up space and time into the swirling dervish of a wormhole. My fingernails dug into the armrest of the command chair as I leaned forward, practically *willing* the ship to go faster, damn it!

0:08… 0:07… 0:06…

"Everyone hang on!" Corcoran yelled to the cabin. He looked up at me, his eyes steeled, dead-set. If he had any fear of death, his expression did well to conceal it; quite the opposite there was something zen-like about his countenance at a time like this, when the shit was about to hit the fan, or at the very least, the seat of my undergarments.

0:05…

We cleared the wormhole's event horizon. I all but *begged* for the swirling mass of spacetime to pull us forward and through to safety and took a deep draught on my scotch.

0:04…

For a brief moment I wondered whether the event horizon would stay open long enough for the nukes to follow us through. If that was the case, who knew what kinds of apocalyptic effects that could have had for the fabric of space-time…

0:03…

I cursed myself for every witty remark and snide aside I'd made that had cost us a precious second or two. Even if not nominally the captain of the ship, the people inside it absolutely felt like my responsibility.

Maybe it was being in the command chair. Or maybe it was my unrestrained arrogance and ego lashing out one final time before being snuffed out of existence.

0:02…

Then I thought of mum and father. What could mother have *possibly* seen in that Manyx fellow?

Suddenly I was on my father's shoulders next to the Thames, eating candy floss and looking at either myself or Horace hunched over in the mouth of the alleyway.

Then my perspective changed. I *was* the bum in the alleyway. I sneered at the well-to-do passerby, and the bright-eyed, naive youngster atop his shoulders.

0:01…

CHAPTER FIFTEEN

One eye was wrenched shut to the point where I had to consciously blink it open over the course of a few seconds.

Several more moments of disorientation followed. Was the swirling mass of colours outside of the ship the afterlife? No, no I had seen this before. We were still travelling through the wormhole, no explosion, no million pieces of time machine (and by extension, my companions and myself).

We had made it.

I heaved something more than a sigh out, as Corcoran simultaneously did the same. He arched an eyebrow.

"Ha ha!" he exclaimed with what I felt was an appropriate amount of relish.

"Yeah!" Sophia was next.

"Frothy mugs of piss!" Bloomington raised a fist at the back of the craft in bold defiance… even though I was quite sure he had screamed like a frightened schoolgirl not but moments before when the countdown had reached "one."

The Chief let out his prolonged victory cry once more, as the three in the rear of the cabin embraced.

I still couldn't bring myself to say anything. I stared at the console and heaved a few deep breaths in and out. Eventually I felt a meaty hand on my shoulder, and Corcoran's smiling face hovered over me, attached to it.

"Atta boy Doc!" He patted me on the shoulder several times before he clamped his meaty paw down and dragged me up to my feet.

Unfortunately, I was still strapped in to the command chair. I struggled, both for breath and to release myself from their unfriendly clutches.

Finally, I rose up and found myself in a hearty embrace. As Corcoran patted me on the back several times, some of the expensive scotch sloshed out of my glass and onto his (shoddily-repaired, I might note) "favorite jacket," though at the moment he hadn't a care in the world.

After a round of celebrations with the rest of my companions (and more than a couple rounds of scotch for all), I asked the QC to pull up footage of our dashing escape from the nukes launched from Niburu.

It pulled up a display with the "Time to Impact" conviently overlayed on it.

On it, the wormhole's event horizon was open at 4 seconds. Several objects with barely noticeable fringes of propellant plume followed behind us, and seemed as if they were gaining ground.

The ship moved forward into the wormhole more at 3 seconds, and more still at 2… but at exactly 1.4 seconds left, the event horizon abruptly closed, what must have been a fraction of an instant before the nukes could clear the mouth of the wormhole.

Several emotions tumbled inside me. Relief, obviously first and foremost. But also an uneasy sense that it sure seemed the nukes had been going fast enough to catch us before we entered the wormhole based on the video.

Perhaps it was a trick of the eye, or perhaps the wormhole accelerated us forward. But somewhat more unsettling was the idea that *something* out there—call it God, the universe, etc.—may have intervened to prevent such a catastrophe from occuring.

Then again, to believe so went against every analytical bone in my body. And while it was true that many of my rigid ideologies and beliefs had been challenged since my journey through time had begun, this particular one brought an entirely new notion into play: that of the quasi-supernatural.

I shook the stray thoughts out of my head. Regardless of how we had survived, we *had* survived. And that was worth having another celebratory drink.

I made my way over to the kitchenette. Bloomington was already doling out libations, and didn't even have to be asked to fill my glass comfortably.

Perhaps there was hope for Steven after all!

I butted into the conversation—the Chief was holding court, and the taste of fine scotch was apparently growing on him; he continued to take hearty draughts.

"You're the *only* humans I've seen who have spit in their faces and lived to tell the tale! The *only* ones! Normally they're quite vicious with those who oppose them."

"Vicious how?" Sophia asked. There was a newfound sparkle to her eyes that accentuated her natural beauty, and made her seem more human and approachable.

The Chief tensed up. "While mining gold, one man accidentally brushed up against his Annunkai overseer. They tied him up, cut him, and flayed the skin off his body while he was still alive until he had bled out."

"Ugh," I felt ill.

"Yikes," Ricky frowned.

"Ooooooo," Bloomington exclaimed, almost as if Zach Morris was kissing Kelly Kapowski on *Saved by the Bell!*

The Chief shrugged, "Eh, wasn't so bad… at least the overseer got a fresh human-skin shawl out of it. The Annunaki are—" he took a deep breath in, "—quite tall."

I swallowed something that had come up through my throat involuntarily, and decided to change the subject to something else I had been pondering.

"I say Chief, you were talking earlier about the capstone on the Great Pyramid… er… triangle building…"

His eyes widened. "Yes indeed I was. Imagine what the ruthless Annunaki could've done with that kind of power—"

I cut him off. "And you're not completely sure what the triangle building did with the capstone attached?"

He shook his head. "Nope. Was hoping such seasoned travelers as yourselves might have more info."

I shook my head right back at him, "I'm afraid not, Your Highness. All we know is that some 7,000 years in the future give-or-take, when we visited the pyramid in our past, there's neither remnant nor knowledge of the capstone at all, and the Annunaki are barely a crackpot's footnote in history."

He sighed. "A shame, that is. Damned shame."

"Why do you say that?" Sanchez asked.

"Because my dear, I am a great scholar of the time of troubles. Very interested—after all, my line has found it important enough to pass down the language of the ancient ones, yes? There must be some reason for that."

I stroked my chin. My mind raced in fifteen different directions.

"And rumor is the capstone unleashed the time of troubles on the Earth thousands of years ago."

"Indeed… tell us more about these 'ancient ones,'" I goaded him on.

The Chief slowly lowered himself onto a chair—either this was going to take a while, or his legs were shot from the harried escape we had made back in his time.

"Legend has it that the ancient ones formed two great empires. One was near my kingdom, and the other was *far* away—much too far for trade by my time without an Annunaki ship.

"Of course, that was no problem for the two empires—they both had technology to rival anything the Annunaki have, and in some cases if the rumors are true, they were well beyond what the Annunaki possess.

"Unfortunately, both sides went back and forth between being somewhat friendly, and fighting all-out wars with one another. One of these wars escalated to 'the war to end all others,' and somehow one of the countries used the capstone for something, and them BOOM!"

He raised his voice and clapped his hands together so loudly, Bloomington staggered backward several steps.

"Time of troubles."

The various thoughts in my head finally started to crystalize.

"And you say that this was several thousand years ago? From your time?"

The Chief nodded. "Yes. Long, long ago."

"Just spitballing here… but does 4,600 years ago sound right?"

The Chief thought for a moment. "I suppose it could be. However we don't have these fancy instruments you have—mostly we rely on generations and lineages to make out time, and I just know it was long, long ago."

I smiled. "What if I told you, Your Highness, that I think we're about to learn a lot more about both of these empires?"

I explained Klaus's journal entries leading us back to 13,000 or so B.C.

His face blanched, eyes wide.

"Are you serious?"

His tone lacked the customary wonderment I was used to from various other Past-ies whom we had regaled with tales of our journey.

"Deadly," Bloomington got in his face with *far* too much menace.

I easily pushed his heftless frame aside.

"You *aren't* looking forward to traveling back in time to the era you wish to visit?"

The Chief sighed. "Normally, what I wouldn't *give* for a trip back in time to that era! You saw how much I valued being able to simply travel in this ship… and it is *marvellous!*

"But if we're messing around with the time of troubles, or if you think we're going to the exact *time* of troubles itself, let's just say that's not something I'm terribly interested in experiencing first hand, if you know what I mean."

He nudged Bloomington with his elbow, which sent the just-recovered scientist reeling once more.

His expression brightened. "Unless of course you think that we could *prevent* the time of troubles from occurring in the first place?"

By this point Corcoran was joining our little gathering, and we all looked at each other, daring one another to tell him.

I figured best if he heard it from me.

"Actually Your Highness, there's something *else* we haven't told you quite yet…"

I explained the concept of "what happened, happened," and that try as we might, there was little we could do to impact the past. The Chief soaked it all up and nodded throughout my little dissertation.

"So we can go back to events that already happened… but we're just spectators?" he asked. It seemed that though he was far from stupid, he had little context for the idea of time travel.

The more I thought about it, the more I realised how much my own preconceived ideas about time travel had been coloured by numerous pieces of pop culture: *Star Trek* in its various incarnations, H.G. Wells, Dr. Ronald Mallett. Without these people and institutions, would *I* have ever pursued creating a time machine in the first place?

I sighed heartily, and felt Sanchez's gaze lower squarely on me. My face reddened; after all, what red-blooded straight man *wouldn't* blush when a strong, attractive woman such as Captain Sanchez would pay him such attention.

Several seconds went by, but I still felt Sanchez's lingering gaze fixated on me. I narrowed my eyes and turned toward her to find her not enraptured and taken with me, but rather more bemused.

She raised her eyebrows. "I've been waiting for the right time to mention it, but… well… now seems as good as any time."

She took in a sharp, deep breath.

I allowed my heart to flutter for just a moment, as a small part of me anticipated the beautiful soldier confessing her undying love for me.

"It's just… I read your book."

"Another one of the lucky dozen?" I deadpanned.

She laughed. "Actually listened to it on audiobook. The narrator was really quite good!"

"Better than that drunken *fool* I spirited the manuscript off to. I'll say, in a voyage *filled* with regrets, giving that… that *hick* my manuscript to mangle must have been the very—"

Sophia shook her head, "I thought it was remarkable—how someone could come up with something so ridiculous, so ludicrous in parts. I mean, if I hadn't lived it…"

I composed myself with a tight smile, "Yes, well the ghostwriter had a very active imagination…"

"I was just wondering—it got me thinking. Especially the end with Helene… something has been really bugging me… and seems *off*…"

"You're telling me," I gulped down another swig of Scotch.

"No—I mean." She paused and thought for a moment on how best to approach the subject. "When did you know—really *know*, for sure—that 'what happened, happened?'"

I arched an eyebrow. "Well Captain Sanchez, I suppose it was when I met you back in dinosaur times. The fact that Chronosaber had built an entire base to hunt dinosaurs was a rather convincing piece of evidence."

"Right, but—" she thought again, "Scientifically, how did you know it was true?"

I furrowed my brow. I thought I knew what she was getting at, and it made me uneasy. "Think of it this way: many people think that for what Ricky and Steven and I did to actually *have* happened, we would have to circumvent numerous so-called 'paradoxes' in the space-time continuum, correct?"

"Yes, that's absolutely right."

"You see, when Trent was explaining the whole system to me in his own, special way, my mind drifted off as to how, if he was right, the space-time continuum must actually be arranged. And when you think that there's this cannabis addict, this 'Trent Albertson' back there, possessing all of this advanced technology, then the true paradox would be to assume that whatever 'happened,' as he put it, could be changed."

"Now—see! Why? *That's* the key question, Doctor!" I hadn't seen Sophia this animated ever since she had joined the crew.

I smiled. "I'm so glad you asked, Sophia. Think of it this way: I built the first time machine ever, right?"

Sophia opened her mouth to speak, then frowned.

"I know, I know—technically Steven and Ricky were 'the first time travellers' in the rather absurd history books we have now, but hear me out: without my breakthroughs, allowing Ricky to steal this very time machine and bring it to your employer to duplicate, none of this—" I motioned around the interior of the vessel "—would be possible."

Sophia nodded.

"Given that that was the case, and we now know, fairly conclusively, that time travellers from ChronoSaber are *quite* prevalent throughout history, we know that the Commander's theft of my beloved time machine simply *must* occur, correct? No matter what happens, the universe *must* have that outcome for history to make any sense, right?"

Sophia squinted and nodded, somewhat skeptically.

"Consequently, everything leading up to that moment, everything throughout history, including young Helene and Victor Burnham meddling in our journey to get us to that point, had to happen, as well, correct?"

"Yeah," Corcoran nodded, perhaps only now catching up.

"As far as history's concerned, Ricky brings the time machine back, he's a hero, and that opens up this whole industry of deregulated time travel."

"You're right," Sophia said.

I took a deep breath, afraid to unleash the final part of the equation on dear Sophia—up until this point in my travels through time and space, I hadn't even revealed my concerns to you, dear reader.

"If that's the case, then not only was I destined to be made a fool of, not only was I destined to rot in an alley for the rest of time—"

Corcoran cleared his throat across the cabin.

"*Before* the Commander so kindly stopped by to get me and clean me up, but no matter—not only were all of those things true, but it was *also* true that countless moments throughout history had been preordained, as well. From Hank Fleener going back in time to wind up Sir Isaac Newton—"

Blank faces greeted me as I looked around the table, now all thoroughly engaged in what I had to say, and even more thoroughly perplexed.

"To you, Commander Sanchez, having to oversee a trophy-hunter's version of Jurassic Park gone horribly wrong. Now keep in mind, that was 65 million years ago, and it *had* to happen too!"

"So Finny, what exactly are you saying?" Sanchez interrupted.

Another deep breath. "I'm saying that if this is the case, and the *past* can't be changed, then not just all of *history*, but all of *time* is fixed. After all, your 'past' includes my 'future,' right?"

She nodded.

"So, had I blissfully stayed on my chosen career path, and indulged blundering idiots arrogant enough to call themselves 'academics' in their mindless drivel—"

Everyone in the group nodded along, even the Chief.

I shook my head, "My point is, if the past cannot be changed, and my future is your past, then there's truly no such thing as 'free will.' We're all destined to play our little part as cogs in the machine to get the universe chugging along to where it ultimately *needs* to go. In short, we are powerless."

A couple of my crewmates gasped. Bloomington may have shrieked again. Then absolute silence settled over the room.

I waited several moments for the thoughts to sink in. It had been quite an intellectual maelstrom inside my head, as well, thinking that no matter what I did, what agency I thought I possessed over my towering intellect, my unchained genius, that I was a pawn in a much larger game—not only to power-mad lunatics like Helene, but to a much larger, more formidable foe:

The universe itself.

After Corcoran had absconded with my ship, I had ample time to ponder my diminished role in the universe, that perhaps I had played my role and deserved to be mocked by my father and my younger self for all of eternity. I came to grips with how ultimately powerless I was, and accepted that my fate, whatever it was, was not truly my own.

Having done so, I simply smiled and clapped my hands together lustily.

"So…who's ready to go visit the ancient ones?!"

CHAPTER SIXTEEN

The rest of the voyage through the time vortex was relatively uneventful. I had a moment to myself, so I finally pulled out Klaus's "secret" journal he had the holographic leprechaun guard for me in his lab. (I suppose it looks a bit more ridiculous once typed out, dear reader, but I assure you, experiencing it in person was far stranger than any picture you might have in your head now.)

Much to my surprize, there was very little in terms of "science" in the journal. Sure there were equations here and there, but many of them dealt with optics, index of refraction, and bending light beyond it to create the "cloaking" effect that made the ship disappear.

For a brief scientific digression, every object has an index of refraction, which determines how much light bends when passing through it. If you can reduce this amount to somewhat below zero, it allows light to bend "around" an object entirely, and reform on the other side.

Klaus was an absolute genius about these types of things, and I must admit, it was only through his help, research, and quite a bit of scotch and hearty German beer that I was able to complete the cloaking device for my time machine.

But what thoroughly confused (if not "shocked") me were the reams and reams of limericks that filled the journal's pages.

Many of Klaus's limericks would be considered witty or even "bawdy," and had clever plays on words.

There were three limericks in the journal in particular, though, that stood out. These limericks were far more tame, far less "enjoyable" to read, and more cryptic.

Almost as if by that very fact alone, Klaus was trying to convey *something* to me in a way that, should the journal fall into Chronosaber hands, it would just seem like the pedantic musings of a frustrated (yet brilliant) scientist.

Take this one for example:

I cover the top of your head

But you never wear me to bed

I have many styles

Don't measure in miles

Use your triton and clock instead.

How did that "L" get in the last line? I thought. Not like Klaus to pass up such an extraordinary opportunity to use a little profanity.

It was clearly a reference to a "hat" or "cap," though the reference to "measuring" seemed a bit of a non-sequitur.

Or this one:

One on top of the other

Almost like brother and brother

They project all the power

From high in the tower

Red crystal the key and the mother?

What the devil did *that* even mean? One on top of the other? I felt like all the pieces were here to *mean* something… but what?

And "the tower"? "Red crystal"? We hadn't come across *any* of this in our travels as of yet…

Unless…

Was "the tower" supposed to be a veiled reference to the Great Pyramid? I'd keep an eye out and an ear open during this time jump.

Finally, there was one more limerick that caught my eye:

If you seek fortune and fame

The bottom one must be your game

Along for the ride

Get the stone to your guide;

Gabriel will be his name.

That last line stood out if only because I had met Gabe Marlow in my former lab a mere… day before? Two? Three? It was getting more and more difficult to track exactly how long we had been on this clever errand.

Yet if this limerick were accurate, then we were to deliver some kind of "stone" to Gabe Marlow? Perhaps a stela or "Rosetta Stone"-type relief that he could shine up for a few bits on the open market?

I didn't know that this was meant to be some sort of excursion to procure antiquities for a bumbling, eccentric billionaire, I thought.

I poured over Klaus's journal for the rest of the flight, though I was getting more than a bit tired, and I may have dozed off once or twice.

I was pulled out of one such waking reverie by the beeping on the main console.

Time jump complete, the QC said.

I looked outside, not knowing fully what to expect. Though I suppose the shock of what we saw next should have been expected, albeit a bit jarring.

As the globe came into view once more, the landmass upon it appeared to be completely foreign.

My mouth involuntarily swung agape as I surveyed the usual continents turned on their heads, and somewhat shrunken, swallowed up by what at first appeared to be a much higher sea level than the one with which you would be acquainted, dear reader.

North America was much smaller and tilted "down" a bit, so that Florida was pointed firmly southwest. Europe was further south, and the rest of the continents were oriented thusly as well.

The exceptions were in the middle of the Atlantic Ocean, where a large landmass roughly the shape of Germany (but much larger) dominated our field of view.

As we took an orbit around the planet, Asia was also much shrunken, and while part of inland China was coastal, the South China Sea had grown, and served as a gulf between the smaller Asiatic land mass, and collection of 3 large islands where modern-day Indonesia is.

Collectively, the islands' land mass rivaled that of Australia, though curiosuly Australia was still its basic size and shape directly "below" this new island grouping.

Sanchez and I shared a sidelong glance. Neither of us were strangers to seeing foreign landmasses on the planet we had called home for so long; both of us were quite familiar with Pangea, her from running Chronobase Alpha—the dinosaur hunting capital of time-travel, and me from visiting said dinosaur hunting capital.

However, something *this* foreign, within only a few thousand years of our previous time jump where everything appeared "normal," was certainly one of the more curious brainteasers presented to us by the universe to date.

And could it be?

The lost continent of Atlantis?!

I'll admit that I had more than a passing fascination with the lost continent ever since my father brought home a delightful book filled with Edgar Cayce's readings about it.

As a child, I marvelled for days and days about all of the advanced technology the mild-mannered (and self-proclaimed) psychic claimed this culture possessed, as well as the rather abrupt end to it under a deluge of flood waters.

For the longest time, I suppose I *wished* Cayce's book was true, even if one were to put the bright lights on me and rough me up a bit at an interrogation, I'd readily admit that deep down they were but the musings of a very creative, very "off" Midwesterner.

But now...was I actually *looking* at it?

"Holy shit—is that—?" Ricky was uncharacteristically incredulous.

Sanchez nodded & smiled, "Atlantis! My God… the rumors are true…"

I arched an eyebrow. "Oh *do* tell…"

She shrugged. "Not much to tell. Helene was mostly right when she said that no Chronosaber craft had made it back from this time period intact."

I rolled my eyes. "Of course. Why should *she* be expected to tell the *whole* truth?"

Sanchez didn't even so much as slow down. "There was one ship though—the *Poseidon*—that made an emergency landing at

Chronobase Alpha. It was a complete *wreck* by the time it got there--the purser was the only one left alive, and just barely."

I interrupted. "Sure. Why *wouldn't* Chronosaber have a purser to collect money for all manner of purchases on-board during one of their trips? If you have a wealthy audience, why not make an extra buck selling nice cocktails or souveneirs or knick knacks—"

"Is Doc annoying the shit outta anyone else right now?" Corcoran asked.

His own hand and 3 others shot up.

He shrugged and let the responses speak for themselves. I piped down.

"Anyway—" Sanchez shot daggers in my direction, "We rushed the purser to the medical facility, but he was already long gone. Refused to say anything about when he'd been. Even the computer was locked out—highest clearance. Helene only. There was one file though on the computer that mentioned 'Project Triton,' and spoke vaguely about making 'first contact' with inhabitants of this time. The coordinates were somewhere in the Atlantic, kind of close to here. So putting 2 and 2 together…"

We all nodded—even Bloomington made the requisite leap without hand-holding this time around.

"Fucking Atlantis, man!" he shouted out. He embraced the Chief heartily, clasping the man on the back so roughly that I thought he might collapse one of his lungs.

I rolled my eyes and shrugged. What was *I* supposed to do about perhaps the most ill-mannered time traveller in history?

As we approached the center of the continent, I was amazed at how clean and utopian it all looked. Lush, green manicured lawns dotted the landscape in-between densely-packed swaths of staple crops. Every so often in this idyllic countryside, a massive stone structure rose out of the ground seemingly out of nowhere, as if a mountaintop was peeking its head out to get a view of its surroundings.

Even more bizzare were the various craft buzzing around near the ground. At first glance one might think these were "run of the mill" high-speed monorails on elevated tracks.

Upon closer inspection however, as one whizzed by, it appeared to be made out of solid stone!

Even *my* vast, unquantifiable genius couldn't comprehend how such craft remained at such high speeds. Imagine the enormous amounts of energy it would take, not to mention how relatively fragile such a craft would be compared to one hewn fully from metal. And it still must have metallic components inside…

…right?

Several smaller structures also dotted the semi-pastoral landscape. As we inched closer to the ground, I made out several figures near each one adorned in bright, scaly metallic costumes. They held spear-like weapons in one hand, and motioned toward us with the other.

Next to them was a rather large rifled device that for the life of me appeared to be a meson blaster or rail gun!

Forgive me—you may not know what either of these contraptions are. Let's just say that it looked like a type of gun that accelerates an inert piece of mass (like a metal slug, for example) to very high speeds using some kind of magnetic or gravimetric propultion.

I looked at Ricky. "Do you see—"

He cut me off with a nod. He looked around to our companions and raised a single finger to his lips, as if to say he didn't want to panic everyone else on-board.

"Holy shit—is that a fucking *gun* pointed at us?!" Bloomington cried out.

I couldn't help but facepalm… and neither could Sophia.

"Yep—maybe a rail gun," she said dispassionately.

"And it's *tracking* us?" This time, Bloomington was the last across the finish line by a good mile or two, as per usual.

"Uh huh." Ricky said.

Then a wonderfully brief pause.

"So why isn't it shooting us down?" Steven wondered aloud.

"You know, I was *just* asking the Prime Minister of Atlantis that question myself the other day…" I said.

"Looks like they're wavin' us in," Corcoran nodded at the two figures who cast their spear-like devices about as if to guide us over the next hill.

We continued on over it, and what we saw thoroughly surprized us, even given the circumstances:

Vast tracks of stone buildings in strange shapes and sizes littered the landscape. Some had what appeared to be large fields of crops nearby. Others were tall and lean "skyscrapers," for lack of a better word, that were made out of shimmering quartz, and seemingly defied gravity by not collapsing over on themselves.

Past this inital shock of buildings were three concentric circles of water. Most remarkable, though, were the wide strips of land that separated each circle.

Though "land" perhaps doesn't do it justice. On each strip, thousands and thousands of the tall skyscraper-sized buildings were packed together like passengers on an economy airline. Each one was made of stone, though not the dull, dusty brown that you might imagine; many of the buildings were polished to a shimmering iridescence that dazzled the eye.

And many of them were in seemingly "impossible" shapes; true there were some of the traditional rectangular variety, but cylindrical, multi-faceted, and even fractal patterns were interspersed. Almost like a combination between the glistening glass of 2042-era Baltimore and the Fortress of Solitude from the old Richard Donner *Superman* movies of the 80s.

Perhaps more surprising, when the light caught the sides of these megalithic skyscrapers *just* right, it reminded me more than a little of the swirling vortex of colours in a time travel wormhole.

Almost as soon as the thought had crossed my mind, a piercing shriek filled the cabin. And for once, it wasn't Bloomington announcing that the cupboard was out of a given staple food.

We all covered our ears and recoiled in true pain. A cacophony of the shrill siren and weird, glutteral, clicking noises made the space practically uninhabitable. I was able to wrench my eyes to the front of the screen, where a flashing starburst symbol alternated red and yellow. Upon it were characters that looked just about as close to Klingon as anything else I had ever seen.

The only one not horribly affected by the noise seemed to be the Chief. He seemed mildly annoyed, and waddled in his very deliberate way up to the command chair.

I arched a quick eyebrow at him and nodded, still covering my ears.

He tapped me on the shoulder with a very firm finger, extremely unneccessarily.

"Uh, yes Your Higness?" I shouted above the din.

"Is there any way I can speak to the outside?"

I rolled my eyes momentarily before I realised that the Chief was perhaps the only person on the ship that had half of an inkling of what was going on, what with all of his talk about the "ancients" and whatnot.

"Computer, open a channel," I screamed again.

The familiar chime from *Star Trek: The Next Generation* was barely audible above the din. I'll admit, even given the dire circumstances we were in, a wan smile washed across my face.

I nodded at the Chief again.

He mirrored my nod for several seconds.

I gritted my teeth. "Go ahead, Your Highness."

He cleared his throat, opened his mouth…

…and started producing the same odd combination of clicks and glutteral noises as was overlaying the loud siren from the outside.

Within several seconds, the cacophony stopped all together.

"Brilliant!" I exclaimed.

Corcoran nodded at the Chief. "What the sam *fuck* did you say to 'em, hoss?"

The Chief smiled, "I told them to turn off that damned noise—I'm hard of hearing and it was even giving *me* a horrible headache."

Another series of glutteral clicks followed, and the Chief responded again. Interestingly, the more they talked, some words started to be interspersed in English, presumably as the holotran became acclimated to the new, utterly unkown-to-it dialect.

After the Chief went back and forth with the voice outside the craft for several exchanges, there was a long pause.

"*Hec tec isomay* land on *valious temptu* platform."

The flashing red and yellow starburst in the window faded away. Instead, a glide scope extended out from the ground with remarkable animation even given the futuristic holographic technologies I had seen in my travels. It led to a landing pad on top of one of the more regal-looking rectangular buildings on the central island.

"No time to waste I suppose—" I grabbed for the omni-yoke.

"Hold on." Sanchez paced to the front of the ship and turned to the Chief. "What exactly did you say to them that time? And what did they say to you?"

The Chief shrugged. "All I told them was that we had just escaped from the Annunaki, found ourselves in their time period, and were looking for a mad scientist. And that we had a rather attractive and badass young lady with us as well."

Sanchez may have been blushing, but if so she hid it well.

"So… the truth?" she smiled.

He laughed. "Exactly."

Sanchez composed herself. "I just… I get kind of a bad feeling about this place. I've seen some crazy shit, but this is next-level. An entire civilization that didn't leave a *trace* on the planet? Not to mention that extremely warm and open-arms welcome they gave us--"

I rolled my eyes. "Yes, since Chronosaber rolls out the red carpet for *anyone* who crosses their path in the past."

Her eyes narrowed ever so slightly. "We did for you at Chronobase Alpha, didn't we?"

Her verbal jiu jitsu may as well have been physical as I flinched back in my chair.

Perhaps sensing this, her face muscles tensed up momentarily before she sighed to relieve the tension.

"All I'm saying is, we need to be careful. And all of the cowboy shit—" she looked at Ricky and Steven before levelling her gaze on me, "—needs to be put away for this go-round."

Bloomington frowned. "Even POLARIS?"

"*Especially* POLARIS."

"Rats…" Bloomington kicked at the floor, only to recoil after stubbing his toe.

I decided to cheer him up. "You know, Steven, I believe Captain Sanchez is right. If nothing else, we need to be prepared for a quick getaway if need be. Perhaps you can prepare POLARIS to perform maintenance and ready the ship, just in case?"

Bloomington thought for himself for a moment. "I can ask him, but he's not gonna like it."

I found that particularly odd, given the extremely patronizing and degrading way Bloomington had spoken to the robot thus far in our journey.

He made his way back to the maintenance hatch, opened it, and shouted through it.

"Hey POLARIS, you *aren't coming* this time, okay? Lousy rustfart fuck—stay here, work on the ship, and be ready to come get us if shit goes sideways, okay?"

"*Yessssss Masssssterrr,*" the robot answered. Although shortly afterward I could've sworn I heard what was awkward, robotic sobbing coming from the bowels of the ship.

No matter! We continued toward the official-looking building. The graphics projected on the screen changed to what seemed to be some sort of "how to" of conducting oneself in what was presumably the Atlantean Empire. While it appeared to be in gibberish to us, the Chief was kind enough to translate what he could.

"Yeah, I'm definitely getting the sense that they don't care for visitors much," he said.

The ship shuddered as it approached the landing pad.

"What gives you that idea?" I asked.

The Chief was nonplussed. "All of this is saying you'll be under strict surveillance the whole time you're here, you agree to abide by the laws of the Atlantean Empire—see this one here?"

He pointed at the front of the ship, where several people dressed in blue and green garb were holding hands with others in purple and yellow. Though somewhat ominously next to them, other figures in blue and green were beating the ever-living daylights out of figures with purple and yellow clothing, though they had what appeared to be glasses and mustaches.

"This one says something like, 'Lemurians welcome, but Lemurian spies will be punished *severely*.'"

"Lovely," Corcoran sneered.

"You didn't tell them we were Lemurians, right Chief?" Sanchez asked.

He shook his head. "Nope. I specifically said 'travelers,' which means 'travelers.'"

We looked at one another. Apparently we had found a glitch with the holotran insomuch as he couldn't tell us the Atlantean word he intended while wearing it—it was automatically subbed out for its English equivalent.

Atlantean images continued to flash on the screen as the ship glided gracefully in. Somewhat tastelessly, I noticed several adverts sprinkled in among the "official" broadcasts and propoganda.

We finally came to a rest on the landing pad on the official-looking stone structure.

"Computer, 360 degree view," I ordered. Immediately the walls of the craft appeared to dissolve into nothing, and the full spectacle of the building we were on came into view.

I have to admit, up close it was even more magnificent than from the air! Ornate carvings of sea creatures covered almost all of the building's exposed surfaces. Intricate marble decorations that were the rival of anything the Roman world or Renaissance Masters had produced littered the area like they were tchotchkes.

Ominously, a platoon of tall-looking soldiers in blue-and-green uniforms pointed long, trident-looking weapons at the ship. The ends of each trident appeared to be covered in gold, though they sizzled with what appeared to me to be fairly "run of the mill" high-energy plasma.

A string of broken Atlantese sounded throughout the cabin.

"*Ak took sonerre* leave *hib* weapons."

The Chief motioned at our sidearms.

"They say no weapons allowed."

"Ah, bull*shit*," Corcoran cocked his sidearm for effect.

Sanchez put a hand on his shoulder. "What's the matter? Big old bad Commander Corcoran is afraid to get rough-and-tumble with a few Atlanteans?" she baby-voiced him and smiled at the end. She winked at Bloomington, then at me.

Corcoran shook his head. "You wanna see how SEALs do it? Guess I can dust off the old hand-to-hand moves, eh Doc?"

I scowled. "As I recall, I acquitted myself *quite* well in our little fracas, Commander." I turned to Sanchez. "I was actually runner-up in the boxing tournament at Eton back in—"

"Yeah, tell that to that arm'a yours there that was hangin' useless as a nun's cooter until the—" Ricky snorted, "—medigel fixed you up."

Sanchez banged on the console. "God *damn* it, I'm not interested in a dick-measuring contest right now!"

"You wanna measure?" Corcoran made a move for his belt buckle. "Let's do it."

Sanchez rolled her eyes.

"$10 on Ricky!" Bloomington called out.

I shot him daggers. Of all of the horrible things he had said, *that* had probably offended me most.

"My money'd be on the Chief…" Sanchez muttered under her breath.

We looked at him with raised eyebrows.

He simply smiled and shrugged.

I shook my head. "No weapons—we agreed?"

"Yeah, yeah…" Corcoran unshouldered his holsters, and I did the same. Admittedly, after spending so much time with the sidearms practically stapled to my side, I felt a bit naked after unbuckling it. That gave me an idea.

"I say, POLARIS," I called down to the maintenance shaft.

"Yessssss Masssssssterrr," He replied, the vaguest hint of hope in his voice.

"Just because we're unarmed doesn't mean that you need to be unarmed as well. So strap up."

"Yessssss Masssssssterrr," he scrambled out of the hatch into the armory. With alarming alacrity, he holstered two laser pistols, and grabbed one of the LR-15 laser rifles from there, and unsafetied all three with satisfying "clicks."

Bloomington sniffed. "Shouldn't we have a code word or something? In case these fishfucking shitbags pull something on us?"

Corcoran nodded. "Yeah, that ain't a half-bad idea, Steve."

Sanchez took a step forward. "We should keep an open channel to the ship too—POLARIS, if we say the codeword…" she paused in contemplation for a moment, "Care Bear, then you lock in on our position and come get us. Shoot first and ask questions later. Understood?"

"Yessssss Massssssterrr," the robot's grin, though probably unchanged, *seemed* more maniacal.

With everything set, I ordered the computer out of 360-degree view and to open the gangway.

One of the taller guards with a shiny, almost iridescent greenish blue uniform stepped forward, trident trained on us.

"Welcome *bit* Atlantis," he said with a big smile. "Prepare ti *die!"*

CHAPTER SEVENTEEN

"Goddamn it!" Corcoran cried out. He instinctively rushed back up the ship to get his sidearms.

Sanchez was close behind him, and Bloomington scampered back up the gangway to either grab his own weapons, hide, or berate POLARIS.

Only the Chief and I remained, and the Chief was smiling.

"Hey, whoa, where's everyone going?" the Chief asked.

"Prepare to *die?"* Corcoran asked.

The Chief chuckled and held his hand up to the guard.

"Forgive my friends, good sir. They have traveled a long distance—"

"*Not* from Lemuria!" Sanchez yelled from the cabin.

"—and they are not entirely familiar with your language." The Holotran was beginning to translate from Atlantean much more regularly as it was exposed to more of the odd dialect. "Would you care to rephrase? As if they are children who need things spelled out very simply and clearly?"

The arrogant smirk on the guard's face said it all. He was a hulking man—he must have been over seven feet tall, with dark olive skin, long, curly blonde hair and a goatee. He looked like he had stepped out of central casting for some weird mashup of *Thor* and *Aquaman*, though even now I hear Steven's voice in my head noting that such a combination is alltogether *mental* since one is in the Marvel universe, and the other is DC Comics.

He let out a hearty chuckle. "Welcome to this place," he tapped the ground with his trident. "At-lant-is," he drew out each syllable.

The Chief and I exchanged skeptical looks.

"Prepare to… how should I say… be awed by the greatest empire the world has ever seen. Though it's much easier just to say it all in one word: 'die'…"

"So you're saying," I said half to him and half over my shoulder into the ship's cabin for the erstwhile murderers to hear, "That 'die' in Atlantean means 'be awed by the greatest empire the world has ever seen?"

The various clicking of safeties and loading ammunition clips behind us suddenly came to a halt, followed immediately by silence.

"That is correct," the guard nodded. His smile broadened.

"My what amazing hospitality," I feigned excitement through gritted teeth. "I am Doctor Phineas—"

The guard nodded again, "Templeton, yes, we know! The Teuton who left mere hours ago told us you would be on your way. I am Vermoor, Chief Guard of the Imperial Palace of Atlantis." He stuck out his hand.

I went to grasp it, only to be pulled in to where he easily grabbed my elbow. In reciprocity, I latched onto his mid-forearm in a "Roman handshake."

"Bloody good to meet you Vermoor!" It was all I could do to not be lifted off the ground by the man's vigorous grip. Though to be fair, despite his initial arrogance, I was beginning to quite like the monstrous captain of the guard, if for no other reason than his "no bullshit" near-earnestness.

I turned to call into the ship. "It's alright! Everyone come back on out *without* your...uh...'emergency supplies.'"

I hoped to God that Steven would get the hint, and would leave his firearms on-board. Given that little display he had put on back in Leipzig, I fully expected him to emerge from the craft carrying a minigun or rocket launcher or some such sort.

Thankfully, even Steven wasn't quite so dense as to not pickup on my meaning, and he, along with Sanchez and Corcoran, walked down the gangway. Perhaps reflexively, their hands were halfway up.

Corcoran was (predictably) the first one to offer up a hand for Vermoor to shake.

"Hey there, Commander Ricky Corcoran, damned good to meetchya."

"Commander," Vermoor stuck out his meaty paw to grasp Ricky's forearm, and Ricky reciprocated. The captain of the guard winced slightly as Corcoran gripped the life out of his forearm, presumably as few others had in the past.

Sanchez and Bloomington each shook the man's hand in kind. Steven even did him the delightful courtesy of wiping his hand on his trousers before doing so, so as to remove any excess snot or earwax as may have found its way onto his pointer finger.

Once the introductions were complete, Vermoor beamed like a child at recess.

"So…" Sanchez offered to get us started. "You mentioned a Teuton you spoke with?"

Vermoor shook his head, while maintaining his grin. "I'm so sorry—usually, it's just that… we're under strict orders to shoot down any of those craft that come through that don't answer our hails—"

"Really?" Sanchez put a piece of the puzzle in place.

Vermoor wrinkled his nose. "Oh yeah, sure. We let trainees use them as target practice. Homing missiles, plasma rays—" he tapped his trident on the ground twice so as to indicate of what he spoke, "—they're good gunnery practice since the Lemurians don't care, and they just keep on coming…"

"Charming," I rolled my eyes.

"I always wondered what was in these things. And how whimsical it is to know that it's tiny little people!"

Corcoran scowled. "Who you callin'—"

I patted Corcoran on the shoulder and preempted him. "Oh indeed, little as we may be, hopefully you find our hospitality as guests to be appropriate-sized."

Vermoor nodded. "Yes, the Teuton was quite the gracious guest. He brought us an incredible gift, one that will make Atlantis into a global power that will strike fear into the hearts of her enemies!"

He snapped his fingers and four guards carried a platform on long slats out to the landing pad. A blue cloth draped over something that seemed to be the size of a large chest.

I could only imagine what kind of horrific weapon Klaus had brought and given to these odd giants. A laser rifle perhaps? A hydrogen bomb? Perhaps some wondrous new invention that I could scarecely dream of, having yet to be invented?

The guards removed the covering from the item on the platform to reveal something even more troubling.

It was a tablet that had Klaus's picture (and that of his trusted dog, Archimedes) on it. I remembered Archimedes from our long conversations back in Leipzig—for all the world, he looked like an extremely large (30-40 pound) shih tzu. Klaus had always claimed that he was the smartest dog to ever live.

I suppose the point of describing the wallpaper in detail is that it was surely Klaus's tablet, and even more surely, likely contained more than a few of his notes.

"Our scientists can't understand *half* the stuff in there… but they claim there is enough information to unlock the stars! And to fumigate the Lemurians once and for all."

We looked at each other nervously, even the Chief.

Vermoor's eyes widened. "Ah, another mistranslation perhaps? Fumigate—to prevent their ruthless expansion and spreading, and bring peace and order to all the lands of the world."

The five of us exchanged suspicious glances.

"Right…" I finally broke the silence.

Vermoor's broad smile returned to his face. He gave Bloomington two hearty pats on the back.

"Come now, come now—you have been summoned to meet Emperess Huron herself."

"A lady emperor?!" Bloomington coughed out after having been doubled over from the guard's hearty backslaps.

I allowed my palm to fly squarely to my face.

"Don't worry Steven—I'm sure she has an asshole just like anyone else," Sanchez didn't so much as crack a smile.

We took several steps down the path toward what was ostensibly the throne room.

"Gross." Bloomington muttered under his breath.

* * *

We entered what was ostensibly the palace to find a hive of activity. Giant Atlanteans scurried about, many of whom wore tunics of different shades of shiny materials. Every shade in the rainbow shone as the material flickered in the bright artificial lighting, which was somewhat warmer than the LEDs to which I was accustomed. The fabric of these tunics was of all sorts of different colours, though noticeably lacking was the presence of any yellow or purple on their garments.

Atlanteans were universally large, all well over seven feet tall, though otherwise they were very similar to modern humans. Dark skin tones were the norm, though given that, blonde hair and blue eyes were rather more prevalent than one might think. In fact, their hair was stylishly appointed and again, dyed many different colours, much in the way it was in my own time.

I will say that they also shared a musculature which I had only seen when visiting Sydney for a conference many years before. There I was shocked by the 6′4″ and 6′5″ men and women of "Down Undah" who all jogged through the botanical gardens, ostensibly training for their side gigs as Olympic athletes.

Aside from the size of the building's inhabitants, the other remarkable thing was the decor. The walls and floors were almost entirely hewn from solid stone. Marbles, limestones, and sandstones all adorned the walls and staircases. The stark, clean lines were interrupted only by wondrously-carved reliefs and cutouts for stunning stone pots.

Knowing what little I did about antiquities and architecture, I spotted influences on most of the other cultures of the world. A set of Greek columns here, some Indian-looking reliefs there, the clean lines of a Japanese interior from time-to-time as well.

I also knew that all of this stonework was impossibly heavy. Literally, there was no way for the building to support its own weight if these structures were traditionally-constructed. I knew enough about manipulating gravity to know that, yes, these Atlanteans were very much doing it already.

But if that was the case, why hadn't they already "unlocked the stars" as Vermoor said? And what the devil had Klaus bargained for with this Empress whom we were about to meet?

These questions knawed at my mind as we approached a very large archway. Two (what else?) marble doors that were likely 50 feet high guarded the entrance to what was presumably the throne room. Each one looked like it may only be moved by a giant—someone equally as tall as one of the doors with the strength of a titan.

Vermoor halted our approach, and nodded to one of his men. Seconds later, a melodious tune played on what sounded like an enormous conch shell of some sort heralded our arrival.

As if to make a point, Vermoor extended a single pointer finger and flung one of the massive doors wide open.

"Holy shit!" I thought it was Bloomington for a second, but Sanchez couldn't help herself.

"Remarkable…" I studied the door, pushing it with one of my fingers. It gently moved back and forth, as if perfectly balanced on its hinge, though to be fair, no hinges were readily apparent.

A dark, meaty hand reached out, grabbed my wrist, and gave it an ever-so-slight (and painful) twist.

"Please don't do that," one of Vermoor's guards warned.

I sheepishly thrust my hands back into my pockets.

The throne room was quite the sight—imagine a sixty-foot-tall room made almost entirely of solid, sculpted marble—though it was very much in line with the rest of the palace. A green carpet that seemed to be woven of fine hemp ran the length of the room, leading up to a large, marble-and-gold throne.

Seated upon the throne was a tall, Amazon-like woman with delicate features that belied her size. She appeared to be maybe in her mid-thirties, and quite obviously dyed her hair stark white. Her eyes were a stunning blueish green, and seemed to pull us toward her like a tractor beam from halfway across the room.

We walked down the carpet and were guided to kneel before the short set of steps leading up to the throne.

Vermoor banged the marble floor with his trident twice.

"Your Highness, Her Majesty Empress Huron, Ruler of Atlantis and its Free Colonies, Defender of the Crown and Trident, Protector of the United Peoples of Greater Atlantia—"

Corcoran, Sanchez, and I stole a gaze and rolled our eyes quickly.

"—Arch-Priestess of the Ancient Gods, Shrewd Businesswoman and Gold Doubler, Righteous in Both Heart and Deed, Mother of Aenon, Future His Majesty Emperor, Ruler of Atlantis and its Free Colonies—"

As you can imagine, this went on for quite some time.

When he had finally finished with the honorifics, Vermoor took in a deep breath and continued.

"I present to you, Doctor Phineas Templeton, and his band of merry Teuton travelers, as promised by Klaus the Wise Teuton several days ago."

The Empress smiled and clasped her hands together, almost in a girlsih manner. Combined with her large (though decidedly *not* fat) size, it was a funny image, and I had to bite my lip to keep from laughing.

"Wonderful! Oh how *wonderful!* What delightful little people!"

"I know, right?" Vermoor said to her before winking at us.

"Please, *do* rise." She motioned for us to get off the ground.

We each stood in turn.

"Oh—not much taller when they're standing up I see. They *are* adorable, especially this one—" she bent over and stroked the prickly stubble on Corcoran's chin.

The Commander scowled.

"Aww..." she put her hands on her hips and effected a mocking, upset tone, "Is he mad? Is he mad at mwe? Wittle cuwtie *mad?*"

Corcoran had enough. He grabbed her hand, which caused the guards to surround us and raise their tridents.

"Look lady, I ain't your pet, and I ain't your subject. So I'm gonna ask you *real* nice—don't pull that *shit* with me no more."

There was a tense moment where I thought for sure we were all about to be vaporised into thin air by a cadre of giants with plasma weapons.

Instead, the Empress started laughing. She motioned for the guards to put down their weapons.

"Or what? You'wa gownna huff and puff and *stowmp* your wittle feet... and get awl *angwy?*" The mocking tone returned. She removed her hand from his face and turned her back to him as she made her way down the line. "He's got spunk though. I like that."

I imagine Corcoran had never wanted a sidearm more in his life.

Curiously, though, Sanchez smiled for what seemed like the first time in days.

"And...*my*—" she reached Bloomington and recoiled, grasping her bosom, as if she had seen a dead possum carcass thrown off of Big Ben and ground into guts by passing lorries. "My, my, my..."

She made her way to Sanchez. "And this one—" she said, with

perhaps a bit of lust in her voice. She raised her hand to stroke her face as well, but Sanchez's patented icy stare warned her off. "What a specimen…"

She finally arrived at me—the Chief was thankfully to my right. Though I did notice a particular sparkle in his eye when looking at her. And I could have *sworn* her gaze lingered on him for an extra moment before she turned her full attention to me.

"And look at the thin one! He's awkward like a chicken who got its beak stuck in a fence!"

I was growing tired of being treated like an animal in a petting zoo for this Amazon's pleasure. Yet I decided to take a different tactic than Corcoran and Sanchez.

"Your Highness, what an honor to meet you! We have heard *so* much about you."

"Oh my! He's a charmer too." I could've sworn she blushed.

"I'm told you've made the acquaintence of my good friend, Klaus Thurbur?"

Her face lit up. "Indeed—Klaus the Wise Teuton!"

The conch instrument blew another short tune.

I bit my tongue waiting for the now-bloviating instrument to stop.

"Uh, yes, *quite.*" I adjusted my collar. "I saw that he gave you his tablet—"

She clapped twice to interrupt me. Within moments, four of Vermoor's guards brought the glass-encased tablet into the throne room, and sat it next to the Empress.

"This is called a *tablet?*" she asked.

I smiled. "Perhaps a mistranslation. You see, we have a device that automatically—"

She frowned. "Yes, yes, it translates what I say into your language. But it's still calibrating somewhat since," she took in a deep breath, "You are from Teutonia, kingdom of the north. One of the few remaining independent states, though I have *no* idea how you make it work, it's so *dreadfully* cold."

For a moment, I thought whether it was better to play along with Klaus's ruse, or to come clean with the Empress.

I decided that playing along was the better course of action.

"Yes, we Teutons *are* from quite the hearty stock—" I looked at Bloomington before changing my sights to Sanchez and Corcoran.

Sanchez picked up on it right away and shrugged. "Well, you know the old saying: if you can still feel your tits and clits, it must be summer in Teutonia."

This cracked the Empress up entirely, and I must admit, I (and the others) enjoyed a hearty laugh as well.

The Empress wiped tears from her eyes. "How delightfully… *vulgar*."

Corcoran nodded. "Yeah, she's a real hoot. Go ahead—tell the Empress some of your other old-timey Teutonic sayin's Sophie."

Sanchez's eyes went wide. "Oh, I'm *sure* the Empress doesn't want to be bored by some inbred *hick* from Teutonia." She pointed the words squarely at Ricky.

"Oh, but I do! I do!" The Empress was giddy with excitement—she clasped her hands together with anticipation like a young girl about to hold a puppy.

"Well… let's see…" Sanchez stroked her chin, desperate for an out.

"Perhaps you could tell Her Highness a bit about the custom of noodling?" I offered.

"Noodling?"

"You remember right? Our good friend, Kathleen? Kathleen *Madigan?*"

It was a gamble that Sanchez had ever seen Kathleen Madigan's standup. A real shot in the dark, to be perfectly honest—she was wonderfully famous in my own time—2032—and *always* hilarious, but I didn't know if her white-hot fame carried over to Sanchez's time as well.

However, as soon as I said it, Corcoran (of all people) got a gleam in his eye.

"You see Your Highness," he started, "Back home, in… uh… Teutonia… we have people who go out noodlin'. They wade into shallow water... Stick their hands in these big 'ol holes… and *dare* big ol' catfishes to bite on them so that they can fling 'em out of the water and suffocate 'em to death. And eat 'em."

This caused the whole crowd of Atlanteans to erupt in laughter, including the Empress.

What I wasn't ready for was the straight-up ten minutes of Kathleen Madigan's act that Corcoran proceeded to reel off, as if he had been watching it on Netflix on repeat for months.

When he had finally finished, the Empress was laughing so hard that, had it not been imprudent, I might suggest she need the use of a diaper to keep from wetting herself. To be fair, the same would apply to the guards and, quite frankly, most of us.

I was shocked. Doing the math, I wasn't sure if Corcoran even knew of "Netflix," as you and I know it, existed.

"Netflix?" I mouthed to him during one particularly raucous spate of laughter.

He furrowed his brow and leaned over to me. "I'm from outside St. Louis, remember? So is she. Plus—" he checked to make sure everyone else was still caught up in uproarious laughter, "—she's funny as *fuck.*"

No argument from me there! Though I had no idea that the hilarious Ms. Madigan was even rising to stardom as early as 2012, in hindsight it made sense for it to be true; she must have been honing her craft over decades.

As the laughter wound down, all tension that had previously been in the room had dissipated. We had gone from being the adorable petting zoo creatures to hilarious court jesters due to the simple happenstance of where Ricky had grown up, and his affinity for excellent stand-up.

I stepped forward and led a loud round of applause for the Commander. And ever the ham, Ricky took a pronounced bow.

"Now your majesty, as Klaus may have told you already, I'm also a Teutonic scientist with even *more* secrets to give to you. But before I do, may I ask you what kind of payment he received for his trouble?"

Both of her eyebrows arched skyward.

"Why don't I show you instead?"

CHAPTER EIGHTEEN

The ride in one of the monolithic stone "mass movers" was remarkably smooth. It was a perfectly-cut block (about the size of a pyramid block, come to think of it), and inside was spacious and quite luxuriously-appointed.

Stone seats had plush, aquamarine cushions on them. One ancillary benefit of the Atlanteans' somewhat large frames was that each seat seemed positively first-class to all of us normal humans, though Bloomington's shorter legs stuck stright out in front of him since the seat was so long, much like a child at the adult table for Christmas dinner.

Though the Empress travelled in her own mass mover (for "security reasons," Vermoor had said), the titanic captain of the guard was more than happy to spend the time fielding our questions along the way.

"I couldn't help but notice that everything is made of stone here?" I asked Vermoor.

He scrunched up his face. "Yes? What else would it be made of? Gold?" He had a hearty chuckle at his own presumed joke.

"Well, not *gold*, per se, but some kind of other metal perhaps? Like steel or iron?"

He shook his head. "Why would we work with those, mining, refining, all that hard work, when stone is so much easier to manipulate?"

He motioned to the window. We had slowed down to go through what appeared to be a commercial area, and a construction site was on the right side of the craft.

A team of Atlantean workers held tridents fairly similar to the one that Vermoor carried with him, with gold prongs, though the tip was made out of something angular and translucent.

"Crystal?" I wondered aloud.

Vermoor nodded. "Indeed."

Nothing could have prepared me for what I saw next though.

A large stone block sat on the ground, presumably ready to be hoisted into place. It must have weighed hundreds of tons if it weighed a single pound. A worker pointed the trident at it, and the long rod and block both shook for several seconds.

When he was done, another worker came by, picked up the stone, and threw it up to another worker further up on the building, as if it was light as a football.

Even more incredibly, the worker received it, maneuvered it into place like it was a child's building block, and zapped it again.

The stone immediately regained its weight, and fell into place.

"What in the sam *fuck?*" Corcoran was incredulous.

"What? You don't have levitation in Teutonia?" A rather fetching, large, dark-skinned female guard said. I sensed only a hint of condescention in her tone.

For some reason, this shocked my pride. "We *do*, but nothing quite *this* remarkable..."

She waited until Vermoor turned away, and winked at me. My eyes went wide in response. I was left wondering if perhaps she fancied me, or if she knew more than she let on.

And if it was the former, whether or not the (ahem) "size difference" could be a severe limiting factor in "getting to know each other better."

The Chief was a natural schmoozer, and combined with his professed adoration for the ancient times, questioned Vermoor on all things Atlantis.

"Noble captain of the guard, being from independent Teutonia, we often don't concern ourselves with the political games the big guys play. But please remind me—how did things get so bad between you guys and the Lemurians again?"

Vermoor laughed.

"Ah indeed—how presumptuous of me! I suppose it's my fault for disregarding those rather *ugly* stereotypes about the Teutonian schools..."

I looked at Corcoran and Sanchez, pride somewhat oddly bruised despite the fact that *we weren't* actually *from Teutonia!*

Instead of chiding the child-like boor, I decided to lean into his comment.

"Oh yes indeed—we could use a proper Atlantean education on

the matter certainly. If you'll deign to explain it to us as you did before—like we are simple Teutonian children."

Vermoor quickly launched into a rather thorough and comprehensive parable of all Atlantean history. Apparently Atlantis had started as a continent and gradually expanded outward onto surrounding continents. It had once been a robust democracy, but as with most political units that had to govern a large expanse of territory, gradually shifted into an empire over time.

As Atlantis gathered more territory, they came in contact with the Lemurian Republic. Made up of three enormous primary islands ("Le," "Mu," and "Ria," apparently) between Southeast Asia and Australia, the Lemurians were primarily a seafaring people.

At first, both countries traded with each other and prospered. Lemurians exchanged their seafaring technology and knowhow with Atlanteans for their levitation and stone-working technologies.

At some point, there had been "a big terrorist incident" in Atlantis. When mentioning it, the normally jovial captain of the guard's face went red, and his teeth clenched—clearly, he wasn't over it yet.

A big power plant exploded, and took thousands of Atlanteans with it. They never found the perpetrators, and even though there was a similarly large-scale incident involving one of the Lemurians' wave-power generators at the same time, each side blamed the other for picking a fight.

Tensions escalated from there. Soon there was an emigration embargo between the two countries, and then a travel pause. Several smaller terrorist incidents on both sides later, and each side was like a mad dog on the end of a chain, foaming at the mouth to get its own pound of flesh in revenge.

When he was done, I felt like I had sat through a particularly livid description of a major war by an outstanding history professor. It was testament to the captain of the guard's energy and animation, as well as perhaps his desire to show a bunch of dumb bumpkin Teutons the superiority of the Atlantean school system.

"So as you can see, there is no chance for peace with Lemuria. That is why we must continue to improve our weaponry—so that the Lemurians sense no weakness, no chance to topple us from our perch atop the globe."

"Yes!" Bloomington punctuated his yell with a violent fist pump. Apparently he had gotten into Vermoor's story quite a bit as well.

I raised a hand at the clammy mission specialist. "And Klaus was more than happy to give you *our* advanced Teutonic weaponry… in exchange for what, exactly?"

Vermoor checked outside the window. "You should be able to see it shortly…"

The mass mover slowed as we approached our destination. And when we looked outside of the window, that destination was plain as day:

Standing right where it seemingly had always been, covered in brilliant, shining white limestone, maybe a hundred yards from the mass mover tracks, was the Great Pyramid of Giza.

Except something was *off.*

Or rather, I should say that something was most certainly *on.*

The pyramid hummed with an intense energy that we could hear even inside the thick walls of the people mover. Translucent waves of multi-coloured energy pulsed through the pyramid's sides up to its top.

And atop the pyramid sat a large capstone.

Or so I thought.

Upon closer inspection, even this capstone was flat at the top. Almost as if it was the "base" for yet another, smaller capstone to sit atop it.

Was this thing ever *fully complete?* I thought.

Vermoor half-pointed his trident at the magnificent structure. "Behold! The great power plant of Africanus, located in the province of Giza!"

He allowed the scene to wash over us for several moments.

"Shitbiscuits and piss gravy," Bloomington said, wide-eyed.

"No thank you," Vermoor said, as if he had been offered it.

"So *this* is the source of power you use to move these mass movers?" I asked.

"Yes. And levitate stones, and everything else. Our technology harnesses the latent power of the Earth's *clique tan ploch* field."

"Pardon?" I asked him.

"I suppose there's no good translation," Vermoor shrugged. "It's like… negative gravity?"

I nodded. As I had suspected, they had also mastered the art of anti-gravity. And, presumably, in much the way Nikola Tesla had envisioned, though doing so without the aid of metal (aside from gold) would be quite a feat indeed. Though unless there was antimatter in the pyramid, there would be far less than enough energy to power—

Suddenly, Vermoor let out a powerful belly laugh.

"Looks like the local children quite admired your friend." He nodded at a group of teenagers leveling tridents at a nearby pile of enormous rocks.

As we got even with it, and passed it, I couldn't help my jaw from nearly hitting the floor of the car.

The kids were using their tridents to gently slough rock out of each block. Invisible bolts of energy turned parts of solid limestone blocks into sand that harmlessly fell to the lush, green garden below.

I knew from our time in Egypt that it was precisely where the Sphinx was supposed to be.

Only this was no Sphinx.

Instead, the unmistakable visage of Archimedes, Klaus's gigantic thirty-pound shi tzu, stared into the distance. Far from the placcid, implaccable head of the Sphinx we were used to seeing, Archimedes was *smiling*. His tongue hung out of his mouth, half-cocked, and slightly covered the large, pronounced snaggle tooth that made the pup so damned endearing.

I'm not a dog person normally, you see—I saw any responsibility outside of my work in the lab as usually an utter waste of time.

But Klaus loved that dog, and many times on my visits to his lab in Leipzig, we would be sharing drinks, only for Archimedes to jump up on my lap and start licking my face. *Especially* if I had forgotten to shave, and had a day or two's worth of stubble.

"Well, well, Finny—it appears Archimedes has a new friend!" Klaus would always say in his lightly-accented (yet always unusually jovial) English.

At first, I would respond by "lowering" (*not* throwing, as Klaus would often insist) the dog to the floor.

Over time, though, Archimedes secretly became one of the highlights of my trips to visit Klaus. Perhaps it was because my hermit-like existence made me long for contact of any sort with any living thing remotely capable of something halfway like "love."

Or maybe it was because he was so damned cute, and always was happy to see me.

Or, another possibility still was whenever I saw Archimedes, it meant I was seeing Klaus. He was perhaps the closest thing to a true friend (and intellectual equal) I could ever possibly know.

Regardless, who would've known that the lovable little pup was actually the model for one of the most striking, recognizable, enigmatic pieces of architecture the world had ever known?

And that the Sphinx wasn't an analog for the constellation of Leo, or a monument to a Pharoah, but just the idle workings of some artistic teenagers who wanted to show their appreciation for an (albeit remarkable) dog?

Nonetheless, we all shared a good chuckle at the realisation—even Sophia unleashed that wonderful laugh she could when she thought no one would hear it.

Moments later, we pulled into the station and were directed to a more S-shaped stone building right beside it. The sun was setting, and I must admit, that Atlantean sunset, with all of the yellows, oranges, and purples reflecting off of the shimmering stone buildings, was perhaps the most beautiful of the many sights I had seen through the course of my travels.

"I presume that you Teutons are weary from your journey? If so, we've prepared lodging here, at the Grand Giza, for you to rest your hearty little bones."

Truth be told, I couldn't remember the last time I had slept. It was always tough to tell, especially with unrestricted time jumps, when we'd often land in the middle of the day. How long *had* I been up? Eighteen hours? Twenty-four?

At any rate, fatigue was starting to take its toll, so I was happy when they escorted us to a floor of the hotel all to ourselves (minus the Atlantean guards posted around the corner at each end of the hallway).

We each had our own room, but I could tell that Sophia had been at something between a simmer and a boil since Corcoran had made a fool of her back in the throne room.

Now it was starting to bubble to the surface.

"Ricky, a word?"

Corcoran looked at me like a sixth grader getting called into the principal's office.

"Sure sergeant Suzy-Q, whatever—"

"*Do not* call me that right now!" She opened her room's door and practically pushed Corcoran through it. It shut behind them with a satisfying, almost Indiana Jones-like *calunking* of stone-on-stone.

Even after it shut, I could hear Sanchez unload on Ricky through the thick stone door. She was really giving it to him—at one point, I heard several crashes, as if furniture or lamps were being cast at one another.

It was decidedly *not* where I wanted to be at that moment.

Instead, I retreated to my own room. It was simple and stylish with trademark Atlantean stonework. All of the furniture was (of course) oversized, which did give me the distinct feeling of being smaller than normal.

It had been *ages* since I'd had a good shower, so I explored the bathroom. I peeled off my now-filthy clothing in anticipation of what kind of wondrous invention Atlantis had to make the mundane shower all the better.

Only instead of a conventional shower, there was only a large stone tub with five different faucets on it. I played with each one in turn, though for the life of me, each one seemed to be set to "ice cold."

Suddenly, I heard a knock at the door.

"Coming," I let the second-from-right faucet run, hoping that it would get some hot water flowing through it sooner or later. There was a robe next to the tub, and I put it on. It was several sizes too large, though for the short trek to the door, it allowed me to pretend that I was an all-powerful wizard.

"*You shall not pa—*" I said to no one in particular as the door swung open.

Standing in front of me was neither Bloomington, nor the Chief, whom I had expected to join me.

Rather it was the fetching young female guard who had winked at me on the mass mover.

"Doctor Templeton? Can I come in?" She batted her eyelids and seemingly couldn't bear looking at me directly in the eye. Her large (though quite in-shape) frame was betrayed by this demurre, almost delicate femininity that she projected.

"I, uh, yes, of course." I stammered.

"Thank you," she was already most of the way through the door.

"Remind me of your name again?"

"Birusha," she walked right past me into the bathroom, where my clothes were discarded on the floor as if I were but a common pig… that somehow wore clothes.

"I apologize for the mess. It's quite the long and perilous journey from Teutonia, and I'm quite weary right now—"

"Would you like to take a bath with me?" She asked, nonchalantly.

"Uh… yes. Yes I very much would!"

I peeled off the robe and stood there, stark naked in front of her. She fiddled with the knobs.

"Yes I think the hot water may be broken. Or maybe you know how to work it so—"

She turned around to me and put her finger to her lips. When she saw my state of nakedness, her eyes went wide for a moment, and looked me up-and-down. She settled perhaps two moments too long on my (ahem) for lack of a better word, "manhood," before she took a deep breath and composed herself.

Slowly, she raised her right hand, and formed it into the Vulcan time-traveller salute.

I couldn't believe it. This gorgeous Amazonian was a time-traveller?!

"You're… from the future?!"

She placed her finger in front of her lips again, then motioned downward with both hands so as to say "keep it down." She pointed at the ceiling and looked skyward.

We were being listened to.

Hence the need for a bath to cover the noise.

Whatever tumiesence had been building "down there" quickly dissapated.

Lemuiran, she mouthed.

I was shocked. My eyes went wide and I had to cover my own mouth with my left hand to keep from repeating it aloud.

She leaned into me and whispered. "I'm Lemurian intelligence. I was working with your friend, Doctor Thurbur. It seems that he made a… discovery. A trade—" she took a deep breath. "A discovery *and* a trade."

"Did he now?" I stroked my chin.

She nodded. "Doctor Thurbur found the top capstone of the power plant, made by the ancient ones."

"Oh goody," I couldn't help myself. "*More* ancient ones—?"

She shook her head. "This is a big deal. You realize that, right?"

"Seeing as though what the current capstone can do, I presume it might be."

Birusha took a deep breath. "Legend has it that the power plant once wasn't *just* used for power. It was a great weapon forged by the first Atlanteans, thousands of years ago, that allowed them to conquer other peoples with ease.

"One day, an Atlantean general sympathetic to the plight of the millions of people who had been mowed down by the power plant weapon made off with the top capstone—the *true* capstone, made from red crystal. The top capstone is what gave the weapon its power, many, *many* times greater than with the bottom capstone alone. When removed, the bottom capstone still allowed the power plant to make power, though any tactical usage as a weapon was ultimately lost.

"This enraged the Atlanteans. He must have been a 'Lemurian spy' in their eyes, and shortly thereafter, the explosion at the main power plant on Atlantis occurred. Our peoples have been at each others' throats for *thousands* of years now over this single incident."

Suddenly, Klaus's limerick rang in my ears.

One on top of the other

Almost like brother and brother

They project all the power

From high in the tower

Red crystal the key and the mother?

I got a shiver down my back. I was on the right track, though I was worried where it might lead me.

I eyed her faux-skeptically, "Why didn't Atlantis just make another one?"

She shook her head. "It was one-of-a-kind. The great architect, Illianhotep—"

"You mean Imhotep?" I interrupted.

She looked at me blankly.

"Maybe not…" I answered my own question.

She took a deep breath again, almost as if thinking how to explain this to such a dullard as myself, "As you may have seen, we use a lot of crystals. They do wondrous things with stone—levitate, carve it, give it mass again, etc.

"Dr. Thurbur told me that in your time, for whatever reason, crystals *don't* have these same properties?"

I cocked my head and thought about it for a moment. I suppose that it was possible that we simply hadn't rediscovered the same *focused* gravimetric technology the Atlanteans had. Or maybe it was something else. Something *big*. Like, say, the reduction of the Earth's magnetosphere. Though to have an ebbing of the scale that Birusha was describing would take—

"A cataclysm." I wondered aloud.

"Excuse me?" She asked.

"Nothing—no matter. It makes sense."

She centered herself. "Good. The specific type of crystals the ancients used in the pyramid's top capstone was one-of-a-kind. Red. Shimmering. Brilliant. Legend says it came from the sky."

"A meteor?" I posited.

She nodded. "And there hasn't been any found anywhere else since. Believe me, we've looked too. If Lemuria was able to secure the top capstone—"

"You could use it on your own power plants to create a weapon that was similarly devastating to Atlantis."

She lurched back, as if stunned by my remark.

"Something like that."

"So Klaus located this top capstone?"

She nodded again. "Indeed he did. The agreement he made was with the Atlantean government. Dr. Thurbur is quite the charmer—"

I nodded in agreement.

"—and he was able to bargain with the Empress. In exchange for access to where he thought the true capstone was, and an agreement not to shoot down the next metallic craft they saw, he would give them his tablet filled with his notes and formulas…*and* the true capstone itself."

"I *beg* your pardon?! Why the *devil* would Klaus make such a deal?" It seemed like he was getting absolutely *nothing* from this supposed bargain.

She shrugged. "I don't know. What I *do* know is that behind the scenes during his time here, he was trying to make contact with Lemurian intelligence. Once I caught wind of that, I approached him much like I approached you—" she paused and looked down at my naked body, "Well, not *exactly* like I approached you—"

I arched my eyebrows.

"Quite."

"But he said not to worry—the true capstone would fire, but his friend, Phineas Templeton, would be by shortly to take care of it and make sure Lemuria was safe."

I rolled my eyes. "I would think the curvature of the Earth would take care of that if they were targeting Lemuria, now wouldn't it?"

This time *she* rolled her eyes, "If you can gravimetrically alter an energy beam's flight and curve it downward at points all along the way…"

"Fantastic," I mumbled.

She bit her lip.

"What is it?" I asked.

"He also asked that you bring something along with you on your next jump. Something…subtantial."

I nodded. I had some idea what she was getting at from the limerick:

If you seek fortune and fame

The bottom one must be your game

Along for the ride

Get the stone to your guide;

Gabriel will be his name.

Though if that was the case…

"Don't you have a plan?" Birusha interrupted.

I shook my head. "Not really. Usually we kind of just… you know… fall into things…"

"Well, that shit's not gonna cut it this time," she shook her head. "The Empress herself is going to install the true capstone at the top of the pyramid at noon tomorrow. And once the crystal mirror is installed, and the beam is pointed at Mu…"

"Kaboom," I mimicked an explosion with my hands.

She nodded, "Exactly."

I thought for a moment. I still had so many questions about how the true capstone weapon operated. Though something Birusha said started a flicker of an outline of a plan.

"I have an idea," we both said at once.

I nodded at her. "Ladies first."

She looked me up and down, and perhaps lingered a second too long on my crotch. She waited one beat, two beats. Then she arched an eyebrow.

"How about that bath after all?"

CHAPTER NINETEEN

The next morning, I awoke with an extra pep in my step. I'm not ashamed to admit that I had declined Birusha's rather forward invitation from the night before. Not because I didn't want to, by the way. And she assured me that there would be no "size issues" with what I was packing down there, as well (take *that*, Ricky!).

Rather it didn't seem right, given that I had seen Cynthia again only days before. I had never felt such a strong attachment to *any* woman, let alone one I had only seen a couple of times. And while the momentary rush that bedding an honest-to-Trent Albertson-Atlantean would have brought, I couldn't bring myself to jeopardize anything that had happened between Cynthia and me to that point.

Instead, Birusha and I hashed out the broad strokes of a plan, including some parts of it that would push the time machine to its very limits.

Though I was convinced that the limericks in Klaus's journal required us to do one thing:

Bring the capstone *base* (the stone capstone with the flat top) back to Gabe Marlow… nearly 12,000 years in the future… through at least one time jump.

It was as mad as it sounded! And Klaus had given me the barest drab thread with which to weave a fucking Persian rug. But as my mind often did, I started to loop and shuttle a plan together in my mind as I went about the rest of my day.

For example, the thought that a woman would proposition *me* out-of-the-blue after seeing me naked was thoroughly invigorating! The Atlanteans were also kind enough to provide a selection of fruits and something between tea and coffee for breakfast, and a fresh set of clothes (the guard who had brought them noted that they made sure to get "child-sized" ones).

As I opened the door into the hallway, I whistled the theme song to *Star Trek: The Next Generation.* As I reached the crescendo, the door to Sophia's room opened, and she emerged in her oversized robe. Her mocha-coloured hair was mussed up, and though her neck appeared to be red and tender, the faintest hint of a smile crept across her lips… until she noticed me in her doorway.

"Oh wait I forgot—" she turned to close the door and re-enter her room, but what she was obviously trying to hide was already making its way through the door.

Trailing her, wearing only his patched up leather jacket tied around his waist, was Commander Corcoran.

"Oh—Ricky! Yes," her look turned stern for a moment. "Don't ever do that shit again or it's your ass."

Corcoran snorted and saluted her.

"Yes ma'am." I could've sworn when she turned around he pinched her arse.

"Whoa—I, uh, have to get ready," she fake-smiled at me and closed the door behind her, leaving myself, Ricky, and the leather jacket as the only ones in the hallway.

Now I will admit, to this point, dear reader, perhaps I had been a little dense. It was only then, after several moments of standing across from Ricky in the hallway that the last horse finally crossed the finish line.

I inhaled sharply. "You *did* it!"

"Did *what?*"

I shook my head. "You *fucked* her! You fucked Sophie!"

Corcoran turned his palms out and shrugged.

Something drew me to his neck. "Is that… is that a *hickey?*"

Again Corcoran shrugged. "I dunno. Pro'lly."

"You… what… don't you have anything to say for yourself?"

"What can I say Doc? You caught us. The other side of hate is—"

"Love?" I answered, perhaps over-earnestly.

"Hate *fucking,*" Ricky crassly completed his thought. "Look, we're both adults. It just kinda… happened. Do you want me to kiss your fuckin' ass and beg for forgiveness or somethin'? Cause I ain't doin' that."

Suddenly the door to Bloomington's room opened and he and the Chief emerged.

"Did you two fuck each other *too?!"* I couldn't help myself.

Bloomington rolled his eyes. "No *fartstorm,* we were just eating breakfast. I'm a *little bit* good with new languages, so I was picking the

Chief's brain about ancient Atlantean."

The Chief nodded vigorously. "Yes, young Steven here is quite the pupil. It took me *years* to develop even the most basic mouth sounds for the language of the ancients, and here he is speaking like it's his native tongue in little over a few hours."

"Yes, I suppose he *does* have *some* talents," I admitted through gritted teeth.

Bloomington looked from me, then to the Commander, and back.

"Why? Did you guys—oh, *I* see what's going on here…"

Corcoran and I rolled our eyes.

"Don't worry, I'm cool. I mean, not like *cool*, cool, you know? Not like I wanna do what you guys did or anything, but I'm not gonna make a big deal out of it. Just, you know, not that there's anything *wrong* with that… and stuff—"

I looked around the hallway to make sure that none of the guards could hear.

"Steven, I did *not* make love to the Commander!"

He shook his head. "Of course not. I mean, no offense Doc, but I always knew Ricky would be the top."

He paused for a moment to consider and arched an eyebrow.

"Or did you mean he liked it rough? Like a real good, hard fuckin—"

Corcoran was turning redder by the second, and *not* with embarrassment.

"Look, no one was sodomizin' anyone else here, okay?"

"Except for you and Captain Sanchez!" I covered my mouth as soon as the words escaped into the world.

Bloomington and the Chief reflexively did the same.

Corcoran raised his arms to his side. "Great. Yeah, real fuckin' mature, Doc. Thanks a lot."

"*You* and Sophie?" Now Bloomington was getting angry. Though he was no longer shaped like a raddish, the hue was distinctively enveloping his face.

"*Nice*," the Chief said.

Corcoran turned to Bloomington. "Yeah. What of it? Jealous little shit?"

Bloomington stuck a finger in the Commander's chest and started punctuating his words with pokes.

"Don't you *ever* even *suggest* that I'm anything other than 100% faithful to Marie!" He was quite the little ball of hate when he wanted to be; he continued pushing Corcoran back until he was up against the wall.

"And I swear to *fucking Zeus himself* if you hurt Sophie, I'm gonna kick your fuckin' *ass!'*

He reared back and took a swing, seemingly deliberately at the wall. Corcoran didn't even flinch, and Bloomington's punch landed squarely on the hard rock surface.

"*Fuuuuuuuck!"* Bloomington cried out. "That *hurt!"*

"Well don't punch the fuckin' *wall* then!" Corcoran didn't know whether to be mad, or to break out in laughter.

Bloomington reared back with the other hand, and tried to pop the Commander in the face.

A mocha-coloured hand reached out and caught it inches from Ricky's nose.

"I can take care of myself, thank you Steven."

It was Sophia. We had been so caught up in our argument that we hadn't noticed she had freshened up and made her way out of the room already.

All of us but Ricky quickly shoved our hands in our pockets, and looked up at the sky, as if minding our own business.

Ricky and Sophia both shook their heads in disgust.

"I can't *believe* you told them!" Sanchez shook her head.

"*Told* them? Shit Sophie, didn't take Doc but five whole *minutes* here to figure out what the hell was going on!"

"I wasn't *that* slow…" I protested, though I think a bit too much.

"I *told* you to wear a robe. Not your leather jacket like some fucking loincloth!"

Corcoran rolled his eyes. "Here we go! Nagging time!" He affected the people-pleasing attitude of a thoroughly whipped husband. "What are we doing today, dear? I'd sure like to hang out with the fellas. Can I? Pretty please?"

Now it was Sophia's turn to become bright red.

"Well *that* just made sure that it'll just be a *one time thing!*"

She slammed (as much as she could—the Atlantean doors were quite well-balanced) the door to her room behind her, and left us in the hallway in various states of dress.

We looked at one another sheepishly.

"Where'd y'all get those clothes?" Corcoran asked.

* * *

Unfortunately, the kerfuffle in the hallway made it difficult to plan out exactly how I was to get the "bottom capstone" (as much of an oxymoron as that sounds) to Gabe Marlow.

To do so, we'd need to somehow get access to the Great Pyramid itself. And more specifically, the control room that none of us had even known about previously, let alone seen.

How could we possibly do that? Security would surely be tight around the Great Pyramid in anticipation of the Empress firing it as a weapon and using it to wipe out all of Lemuria. And "honoured guests" though we may be, I doubted we had the kind of pull with the Empress or Vermoor to simply *ask* for access, either.

It didn't help that Sophia refused to talk to Ricky. Bloomington eyed Ricky with suspicion. The Chief tried to break down walls between aggreived parties, but to no avail.

Truth be told, perhaps *I* was most jealous of Ricky of anyone. While I was quite enchanted with Cynthia, if I was being perfectly honest with myself, Captain Sanchez had also made quite the impression on me.

Not that I ever thought that anything romantic might happen between us. But now it seemed that she had "made her choice"—that what little shot I had was now thoroughly D.O.A.

And yet… I wasn't really sad or frustrated. Just accepting. Guys like Ricky *always* seemed to have no problem making these kinds of connections with women, almost effortlessly. Even if they *hated* his guts.

Yet here I was, saving myself for a woman who would be an old lady in my own time. If not for the time machine, would Cynthia and I have even made the connection we had?

And if not, what did that say about the *luck* of it all? The random chance? A simple roll of the dice determined when we were born, and to this point, the people we could interact with.

I was beginning to understand the "trans-time" movement that Hank Fleener had told me about during my visit to Sir Isaac Newton. That in and of itself seemed like ages ago.

We didn't have any time to ponder such existential issues at the moment though; if the Empress was going to use the true capstone to obliterate Lemuria at noon, then we needed to discuss our plan as a crew, without the Atlanteans eavesdropping on us, and without tearing each other apart.

I thought of all kinds of different ways I could get the info to the group, but it would be extremely difficult without alerting the Atlanteans that something was up.

Yet the more I thought about it, the morning's revelation about the Commander and Captain Sanchez perhaps provided the ideal distraction to get *something* done, though it would have to be handled *just* so.

When we were getting ready to leave the Grand Giza, I decided it was the opportune moment to see if I could move the ball forward a bit. I tapped Vermoor on the shoulder as the Chief loitered nearby.

"Yes?"

"I was wondering if I might have a moment with my crew on my ship?"

The large captain of the guard's face furrowed.

"Why?"

"We, uh, had a bit of an issue this morning. Somewhat private but—" I took a deep breath, and affected my saddest tone before whispering. "Commander Corcoran slept with Captain Sanchez last night."

He looked at me completely blankly.

I chalked it up to a mistranslation. "They…err.. 'made love'? Copulated? Were intimate?"

Vermoor's face remained as if a stone head on Easter Island.

I rolled my eyes. "He fucked her brains out!"

"Oh!" The captain of the guard's eyes went wide. "Oh… I see…" For more than a moment I caught his gaze lingering on Captain Sanchez, who stood by herself, stone-faced as usual.

"The only problem is, the fat little one had eyes for the Captain too."

I nodded at Bloomington. Thankfully, he inadvertently played the part of scorned lover, shooting daggers at Corcoran, much like Sophia's overprotective older brother.

"What?!" Vermoor couldn't help but let out a hearty laugh.

I chided him to keep it down. "I know, I know—what ever *was* he thinking?" I let the statement hover for a moment to give it greater gravity.

"Right?" The captain of the guard chuckled. "I mean, I *guess* I can see her and the Commander together. Though maybe she had other options she didn't even know existed." He looked at her longingly.

An involuntary shiver curled down my spine.

"Be that as it may," I took a deep breath to keep from saying anything untoward to the giant, "We'd like the opportunity to—"

Suddenly, the Chief blurted out, *"Fa en tooknu!"*

"Fa en tooknu! Really?" Vermoor was simultaneously astonished and like an overeager kid on Christmas morning.

The Chief nodded. "Oh yes. *Fa en tooknu,* for sure. We just need several minutes for the airing of grievances and to prepare the combatants."

"Yes, yes—of course! My oh my—we haven't had a good old-fashioned *fa en tooknu* in *ages!* This will *greatly* please the Empress. What an amazing way to kick off the cleansing!"

The Chief and I looked at each other.

"Cleansing? You know—the renewal and rebirth of a people! When we… err… have the ceremony at the power plant later today!"

The Chief nodded. "Very good, very good. Now can you make arrangements to get us back to the ship?"

"I will get *right* on it!" Vermoor practically skipped off. *"Fa en tooknu! Fa en tooknu!"* He raised his arms out from his sides in "victory pose" and shouted with glee as he ran out of the building.

I turned to the Chief.

"Fa en tooknu?" I hoped my expression conveyed the depth of my skepticism.

He shrugged. "Something I came across in my study of the ancients. It's a way for aggrieved parties to 'settle the score,' so to speak. To prepare for it, both parties must have a private airing of greivances, theoretically one last chance to work out their problems before moving forward with *fa en tooknu.*"

"And *fa en tooknu* is *what,* exactly?"

The Chief stroked his chin. "Now that you mention it, perhaps I was a bit hasty."

"What?" I put my hands on his shoulders and gave him a good shake. "For God's sake, Your Highness, what is it?"

"Fa en tooknu… is a public fight to the death."

CHAPTER TWENTY

"Good. Let me at this assburger." Bloomington said, as we closed the ship's gangway.

"Bloomy, I ain't *wanna* kill ya, but Christ knows I will."

Bloomington reddened again. He shot a thick, sausage-like finger at Sanchez. "You have *ruined* this woman's honor!"

Sanchez rolled her eyes.

"Jesus, Steven! I do *not* need your fucking protection like some kind of fucking *princess!*"

"Now that you mention it, he *does* kinda look like a fat Italian plumber," Corcoran quipped.

"I'll plumb *you*, you giant piece of shit—"

"Enough, God *damn* it, *enough!*" I screamed. Though for an instant, I was worried that my voice got a bit overly-nasally, and overly-American as it is wont to do when I get worked up.

"Now once we're done here, you two can fucking tear the ship apart for all I care—"

Everyone looked at me skeptically.

"Okay, *please* don't tear the ship apart! But you can beat each other to a bloody, unrecognizable pulp… or say, leave one or the other back in the early aughts to rot as a fucking bum—"

Corcoran shook his head. "Of all the cheap-ass shots—"

I stuck out my hands. "Simmer down, simmer down—no hard feelings, I promise."

It was *mostly* true. I think.

"But right now, we have a mission to complete in the next," I checked the ship's clock, "Two hours or so. And, I am pleased to report, we also have instructions from Klaus."

"Instructions *from?*" It was perhaps the most insulted Sophia had been all day. "So we're supposed to chase this asshole down, and now he's giving *us* instructions?"

"My dear Sophia, perhaps there's been a misunderstanding.

Whatever you, Helene, Chronosaber—whatever you want to do with Klaus once we catch up to him, is up to you. I trust Klaus implicitly. At the moment, with all of the histrionics going on, I trust his judgment *far* more than anyone in this—" I looked around the cabin briefly to confirm that the statement was true, "—motley crew. So if you value my opinion at *all*, don't consider these 'instructions.' Think of them as 'the next step.' The next piece of the puzzle."

I tried to lock eyes with Sophia, but her gaze was too intense, too fiery. At one point, I had to check my shoulders to ensure that they weren't smoking from the heat.

She waved a hand flippantly. "Fine. Whatever. We'll do what he wants for now. And then he'll become wrapped up, owned, and pwned by *me*... and Chronosaber LLC."

She rushed through that last part, and looked disgusted as she said it. Though I wondered if it was the shame of having been caught in her little tryst with the Commander, or something else that I couldn't put my finger on as of yet...

I nodded again. "Fair enough. Completely fair. Sound good to everyone?"

Nods surrounded me. Even the Chief, for whom I may as well have popped a bucket of popcorn, such a spectator he had been since offering his comment on *fa en tooknu*. I thought I caught a nod from POLARIS as well.

"Very good. Now I think we can use this as a distraction to our advantage."

I caught the team up quickly on the double-capstone system, and how we were supposed to somehow get the bottom capstone through time to Gabe Marlow, of all people, as well as the Empress's presumed plans to use the true, red crystal capstone and a reflecting mirror to destroy Mu and bring Lemuria to its knees.

Sanchez shook her head. "Great, so *another* genocidal maniac we have to deal with?"

I raised a finger. "Correction—another genocidal maniac *who enjoys putting on a spectacle* that we have to deal with!"

Everyone looked at one another.

"What? Don't you know that Hitler was quite the fan of musical theatre and the opera? And the 1936 Olympics?"

There's nothing quite like a team full of erstwhile Nazi hunters eyeing you skeptically when discussing Adolf Hitler. Their intense gazes put the hairs on the back of my neck on-edge.

I arched an eyebrow. "My point is, we now know in a post-Trump world—"

"Donald Trump is dead?" Corcoran asked.

"He was *President*," Sanchez rolled her eyes.

"Bull-*shit* he was President." Corcoran was legitmately upset.

I nodded solemnly. "Eight full years, I'm afraid."

Corcoran and Bloomington looked at each other, then at us.

"No fucking *way*," Bloomington said.

I smirked and shrugged. I suppose they'd have to find out the *real* truth for themselves.

"Regardless, it's readily apparent now that showmanship has *always* been a part of leaders seeking to protect power. And what better way of doing so than putting on a fight to the death right before blowing your only rival to smithereens?"

Corcoran shook his head.

"Yeah, I get the idea, but what about this plan now?"

I smiled before I made my best Supervillain face. "Well, my dear Ricky… I'm afraid you'll have to die."

Everyone else gaspsed. Even Bloomington shrieked a bit.

Ricky narrowed his eyes.

"You're gonna have *him* kill *me?*" He thumbed a finger at Bloomington.

I nodded.

"That's about the damned *dumbest* plan I've ever heard'a."

Sanchez shook her head. "Actually, it's not such a bad idea. The crowd *does* like an underdog."

Corcoran rolled his eyes. "'Course *you're* gonna say that. You gotta axe to grind."

Sanchez's eyes narrowed. "This has *nothing* to do with *that*—" she pointed to the gangway.

I decided it was time to intervene.

"Sophia has quite hit the nail on the head, I'm afraid. The crowd is going to be expecting you to come out and eviscerate Bloomington. Just destroy him, gut him like a—"

I looked over at him, and found that instead of the look of dread I *thought* I'd find on his face, there was instead an almost sociopathic smile.

"—sturgeon. But we need more time than that. And that requires a far more even fight. So you two will opt for hand-to-hand combat. Ideally, they'll give you those trident weapons, or some other form of them. That way, it'll be easy enough to conceal the…err… 'gap' between you two's combat abilities."

"Hey!" This *finally* got Bloomington riled up. "I've come a *long* way since last trip, taintwipe!"

I rolled my eyes, "Oh yes, the difference is like night and day."

I hoped that someone would fetch a rag to collect the sarcasm that had dripped from the statement.

I continued, "The best *narrative* here is that there's a back-and-forth during the fight. Which will be led by—"

I turned to Sanchez.

"—you. Root for one 'suitor,' then the other. Do you think you can do that, Sophia?"

Her eyes narrowed. "It'll sure be easier to root for one of the two…"

"Get over yourself!" Corcoran blurted out.

"What makes you think it's *him?*" She nodded at Bloomington.

Bloomington pointed at Corcoran. "*He* made a *fool* of you!"

"And now *you're* making a fool of *yourself!*" she shot back.

Suddenly, a sharp whistle filled the cabin.

It was the Chief.

"What is it the Commander says? Ah yes—*GODS DAMN IT!"* He was seated in the kitchenette area and pounded the table in front of him. "We don't have time for this!"

I nodded. "Yes, thank you, Your Highness. Corcoran will die. You,"

I nodded at the Chief, "Will flatter the Empress and keep her occupied throughout."

The Chief's eyes widened. "What if…you know…" he nudged the air next to him.

"I know *what?"*

He paused for a couple seconds. "I think she *likes* me."

You would've thought he would've told an outrageously bad joke, so thorough were the groans from the rest of us.

I quieted the room and put my hands up and out. "Do whatever you want. Fuck her brains out for all I care!"

The Chief nodded. As if he very well might!

Even worse, I caught Bloomington licking his lips slightly after I had said it.

I centered myself with a deep breath. "All the while, the Lemurian spy I am in contact with will escort me to the restroom, or washroom, or loo—"

"Hurry it up!" Everyone said in unison.

I took a deep breath. "In reality, we will be making off to the Great Pyramid to sabotage the Atlantean death ray. I think if we can find a way to overload the red crystal capstone, we can cause its distruction without harming the bottom capstone.

"Then it's a matter of slipping past their various surface-to-air defenses, attaching the enormous, stone bottom capstone to the ship somehow, and making our graceful escape. All while mainlining medigel into the Commander for his immaculate resurrection."

"'If we can find a way?' 'Somehow?' Well, ain't you worked out *all* the kinks?" Corcoran rolled his eyes.

"Presumably—" I talked over him, "by using their very handy stone de-massing devices."

"The tridents?" Sanchez asked.

"Exactly," I nodded.

I will admit, the whole plan was more than a little crazy. There was little chance of success. All the odds were stacked against us.

And yet… why would Klaus lead us to certain doom? Why would he condemn me to a nameless, faceless death at the hands of an empire that few people even indulged the notion of its existence?

I had said I trusted Klaus more than anyone on the crew, and I firmly believed it. So I *had* to think that this plan, no matter how cockamamie it seemed, was going to work "somehow."

And if Ricky had to die to make it happen, so be it.

Truth be told, I was mostly over Ricky leaving me with neither time machine nor dignity in 2042 Baltimore. Yet something small and deep and dark within me hadn't yet balanced the ledger. I wanted him to feel pain—to *suffer* for what he had done. And if the cold emptiness of death was what it would take, albeit only temporarily, then so be it.

We only were able to spend a couple more minutes before the QC sounded the perimeter alert.

"Computer, turn that off for Chrissake!" I shouted. "On screen." The part of the ship by where the gangway normally lowered turned transparent.

"Wow!" the Chief couldn't help himself.

It revealed Vermoor, Birusha, and two other guards. I could've sworn that the large captain of the guard was *still* chanting "*Fa en took-nu! Fa en took-nu!*"

I looked around the cabin. "Everyone know what they're doing?"

Everyone nodded confidently. I made it a point to make eye contact with each and every member of the crew.

"Very well. Computer, lower the gangway."

Immediately that transparent part of the wall filled in, then lowered itself to allow the guards entry.

Vermoor's expression turned grave.

"Were you… were you able to work things out?"

I shook my head. "I'm afraid their differences proved to be quite intractible."

The hulking man stroked his chin.

I rolled my eyes. "They still hate each other. *Fa en tooknu* is on."

"Yes!" he clapped his hands so loudly, it may as well have been thunder. "Thankfully! It's been quite some time since we had a proper *fa en tooknu*, and with little ones no less! You know, what with political correctness and whatnot, having little people square off in a *fa en tooknu?* Forget about it! But if *you* are the ones proposing it," he smiled, "then how can anyone argue with it?"

"Yay, how will I ever stand it—" Sanchez started semi-robotically.

I shot her daggers out of the corner of my eye.

She perked up. Her eyes widened before she batted them, and affected a bimbo-like tone, "—to lose one of my passionate lovers. My… steady boyfriend," she half-recoiled when looking at Bloomington, "and my torrid love affair," she rubbed Corcoran's shoulder perhaps a little too convincingly.

"Do not worry your little brain, woman!" Vermoor beamed broadly.

Sanchez bristled. I could see her calculating how far it was to the armory, how much time she'd have before the captain and other guards would be able to bring their tridents up to fire.

Thankfully she thought the better of it.

"Oh?" She affected the airheaded bimbo persona again, presumably to keep from murdering him and butzing up the whole thing.

"Yes, soon your decision will be made *for* you. As most decisions should be in matters of the fairer sex and lust!" he punctuated the statement by raising both of his eyebrows at the Captain.

Again, I preemptively shot daggers at her. I could feel the heat radiating off her skin, boiling, wanting nothing more than to put a bullet or laser beam through the now-confirmed oaf.

"And who knows? Maybe both will fall. In which case," he sidled up next to her and removed his helmet as he took her hand and kneeled, "I'm sure you won't want for potential suitors."

He brought her hand to his lips and gave it a pronounced kiss.

Little did he know that she could likely break his nose with a flick of her wrist, and kill him in the shadow of an instant.

Fortunately, I think Sophia was too busy suppressing a full-on dry heave to act on her impulse. And by the time my attention turned to her, she had largely composed herself.

"Oh, you are too bold, captain of the guard," she pulled her hand and gritted her teeth. "Too bold indeed…"

Vermoor ignored her, "But that is later. And for now, let us begin the preparations for *fa en tooknu!"*

He snapped his fingers and Birusha and another guard carried in two sets of ornate armour. It was made out of the same shimmering material as Vermoor's own suit—base blues and greens swirled with the colours of the rainbow as it hit the LED lighting in the cabin.

The guards helped both Corcoran and Bloomington into their ceremonial garb. Unfortunately, nothing was worn underneath the armour, and only a long strip of the same material that came to their knees covered from the waist down in both front and back.

Though thankfully, being for Atlanteans, Corcoran was positively swimming in his set, which kept him almost completely modest.

Bloomington, though, wore the outfit rather shabbily. His now skinny-fat body seeped through the gaps between the shimmering plates. Even worse, when they disrobed him and found the fatteries lodged in his stomach, it prompted a round of quizzical looks from all of the Atlantean guards and the Chief.

I made my way over to Vermoor and put my hand up to my mouth.

"Old war wound," I shrugged. "He's *very* sensitive about it."

"Yes, I could tell something was off about this one. Plasma bolt to the gut?" he asked.

I shook my head. "Worse. Hand-to-hand sword fight."

Vermoor winced. Then he stiffened and brought *his* hand to *his* mouth.

"I have made a rather sizeable wager on the good-looking one. Is the toady-looking one such a skilled hand-to-hand tactician? Should I reconsider?"

I looked at Bloomington struggling with his armour. He was caught in the side straps.

"Cock-milker!" he uttered as he fell to one knee and continued his struggle.

I tried to keep from laughing, "I would say that changing your bet would be a wise move."

Vermoor nodded, without a hint of irony.

The two finished putting on the laughably oversized garb, and we were escorted as a group out to the main Atlantean square.

Here buildings were mostly stone and polished, glimmering glass that shimmered with millions of colours in the bright sunlight.

The garb of the Atlanteans milling about the plaza was similarly more exotic than the staid "blue-green" of the palace. Oranges and reds were present, though admittedly there were few yellows and purples.

"Those are Lemurian colors," Birusha said when I muttered something about the decided lack of yellows and purples aloud. "Wearing them is cause for treason here."

Her eyes burned with intensity, punctuating the statement. It hung in the air like a silent helicopter for several moments; it was all I could do to swallow and gulp it down.

"Indeed," I tried to stay as even-keeled as possible.

We arrived at a decently large colesseum hewn almost entirely out of solid stone. Glass windows made up one facade of the building, and ornate reliefs of Atlantean champions and dignitaries gave greater weight to the building's walls.

With a nudge, Birusha and another guard pushed Sanchez, the Chief, and I through a marble archway that led into the stadium.

Vermoor and one of his companions splintered off, with Corcoran and Bloomington in tow.

"Sorry it has to end this way, chaps." I nodded first at Bloomington, then at Corcoran.

Both men nodded before turning back to me.

"See you in another life, Doc," Corcoran said.

"I'll skewer this assrash like the diseased trout he is!" Bloomington said simultaneously.

Sanchez raised her eyebrows and shook her head. "Shame that *one* of them is gonna die for me…"

The Chief and I couldn't help but smile.

Birusha and the other guard escorted us up a long ramp to an ornately-carved door.

"May I present to you, the Empress's box!" She flicked the door open with hardly an effort.

"The Empress's box?" I inquired.

Birusha was stone-faced. "You have been requested as her guests of honor. Plus," she nodded at Sanchez, "*This one* still has a role to play in the *fa en tooknu*."

"Oh goody," Sanchez said sarcastically.

"Sophia, I realise you're *horribly* broken up right now about all of this hubbub with your lovers, but *do* try to keep your game face on," I levelled at her.

She narrowed her eyes at me. For a moment, I could've sworn it was the same death stare she had given Vermoor moments before. And I'm not ashamed to admit that my testicles may have retreated to the safety of my undercarriage at the thought of a pissed off Sophia Sanchez after me.

Fortunately, she batted her eyes and affected the dumb bimbo persona she had back on the ship once more.

"Oh the humanity! Oh the rank *unfairness* of it all!" She cried as she approached the Empress's throne.

The Empress seemed to delight in Sophia's "suffering" more than a little. She licked her lips and summoned her guards.

"Are we ready?" She asked.

Birusha nodded.

"Excellent! *Fa en took nu* begins…now!"

You could almost hear the curl of her sadistic smile.

CHAPTER TWENTY-ONE

I don't know if I just expected Corcoran and Bloomington to be handed tridents and told to stab each other to death, or for them to take ten paces and turn and fire.

But the proceedings instead began with quite a bit of pageantry. First there was the loud droning of the conch-like instruments, tuned at different pitches so that the result was rather like a Gregorian chant.

Once that godawful din had died down, the Empress stood up, grabbed a rather funny-looking microphone, and gave a proclamation:

"Welcome to the first *fa en tooknu* that Giza province has seen during my reign!"

The stands were filled to capacity, and erupted in cheers. For a moment, my mind wondered how in God's name they had filled the entire stadium so quickly. After all, back in 2032 Baltimore, the Ravens had been in quite a bit of good luck as of late (so the other professors said), and even *they* had trouble filling an entire NFL stadium with a gigantic marketing budget and plenty of notice to all involved.

This had become a bona-fide event in the space of little more than a half hour or forty-five minutes.

Perhaps tickets were free, but even the logistics of informing others about this "contest" for Captain Sanchez's affections remained an utter—

Almost as suddenly, I had my answer.

The best way I can describe it is that a "beam" of light hit my head. And while I could still think, move, act, and react, another "layer" of reality was broadcast over the surface of it all. Almost like a broadcast on the inside of my forehead, if that makes sense?

Regardless, I was "treated" to watching a pair of attractive Atlanteans, one male, one female, dressed up in what likely passed as formal garb. Both had the dark olive skin and almost bleach-blonde hair that I'd come to expect from Atlanteans, and both had too-white smiles that were far too overbroad. The man stared straight at the "camera."

"Good morning, and welcome to today's *fa en tooknu!* It's a *beautiful* day here in Giza, *pac tec tan nu* o'clock, and we have a *capacity* crowd at the Giza Colosseum to watch these two *savage* Teutons battle it out for the affections of this delightful, if undersized, Teuton woman."

Corcoran and Bloomington's faces flashed up on the imaginary screen that barely hovered over my mind. I looked around, and tried to shake it out, almost like I had water in my ears, but no matter what I did, the two announcers remained.

The woman announcer nodded. "That's right, Degrado, and what a tragic tale it is," her expression darkened ever so slightly, "A dedicated, very, *very* ugly mate wakes up today to find that his long-time, *far* too-good-for-him partner has stepped out on him in the middle of the night with a *much* more attractive little person, and now the grotesque, wronged husband is thirsting for *blood*."

She licked her lips in that same reptilian way the Empress had.

The crowd cheered wildly. Were they being treated to the same awful pregame coverage as I?

The male announcer nodded. "And *blood* he shall get! Whether it's the more attractive lover's, or his own remains to be seen."

The announcer was more than a bit too cheerful.

It was the woman's turn to talk. "Before we begin though, please kneel for the Atlantean war anthem."

On cue, the entire crowd dropped to a knee, smack dab in the middle of whatever concession-related filth had accumulated in the aisle already. They made their best attempt to position themselves toward the Empress, though the ones directly underneath the box squirmed a bit deciding exactly how they should align themselves.

Birusha nodded at us to do the same, and we complied.

The conch-like instruments fired up again, just as loud and annoying as always. Unfortunately, this time after about twenty seconds, a cacophony of shrieking bagpipe-sounding instruments joined them. It was every bit as maddening as the "welcome" broadcast we had received when arriving in the time period, though if the Atlanteans thought so, they certainly hid their pain well.

The high notes were so sharp and acute that I looked around the box to make sure I hadn't gone completely mad, and was somehow hallucinating the whole thing.

Sure enough, Sanchez and the Chief were writhing in pain, struggling to remain on one knee with all of their might.

I looked for something—anything—to dull the pain.

Birusha calmly caught my eye. She nodded toward the box's exit. I was more than happy to take the hint.

"I, uh, don't feel so—" the noise was nearly vomit-inducing on its own, so I only had to half-fake wretch. I ran for the box's exit, though the Empress was far too busy basking in the adulation of thousands of patriotic Atlanteans to notice.

"I'll take care of him—" Birusha said to Vermoor and the others as she followed quickly behind me.

Once we were on the concourse, she produced a luminescent canteen, and took a pull on it. She then offered it to me.

"Here—it will help with the *ballandra.*"

I heartily chugged down some of the liquid. Immediately, the volume of the instruments and the broadcast in my head decreased substantially.

"My *God,* thank you!" I wiped my mouth with my sleeve and handed her the canteen back. "What the *devil* is that *odious* commentary playing in my head?"

"It is *ballandra.* Wide-range, narrow beam broadcast directly into your brain. How else do you think we communicate over long distances?"

It finally made sense how they could have spread the word so quickly to so many people—it was like having a direct broadcast line into everyone's head. No wonder the Empress was so popular too—people couldn't avoid her if they tried. Unless…

"How much of that would I have to drink to turn off this infernal noise completely?"

She snorted. "Too much for you, little man. It might even kill an Atlantean to drink that much."

"So you just… live with that all the time?"

She nodded. "You can see why the Empress is so beloved."

I shivvered at the thought. As grimy as politics had become in 2032, they hadn't *quite* perfected that level of intrusion into our daily lives…

…yet.

She leaned in toward me.

"Come on—there is not much time."

We rushed down the concourse. Birusha nodded at the various guards as we passed them. At one point, I thought I caught her making a mocking gesture at me and gave her the stink-eye.

"It is to keep our cover!" She hissed.

"Right," I rolled my eyes.

We got to the mass mover station and selected a car. Birusha tapped several buttons and the vehicle sped off toward the Great Pyramid.

All the while, footage of the *fa en tooknu* was being beamed into my mind. If the mission weren't so important, the stakes not so high, I would have thoroughly enjoyed it.

First, they emplored Sophia to plead with each of her "lovers" as to why *he* was more important to her than the other.

"My dear Steven, we have fought Naz—" she caught herself, "Native peoples hand-in-hand, thousands at a time. Nonetheless, we survived. They threw everything they have at us, and still, we survived. They pointed the Schwerer Gustav at us, the biggest gun in the whole world—non-Atlantean world—and you took an LR-15 and showed them just how 'schwerer' it was—"

I don't know if it was just me, but it seemed like Sophia was getting *excited* talking about all of the weaponry.

She turned to Corcoran. "And you—Ricky. What can I say about you?"

She paused for a good five seconds.

The camera cut to Corcoran. "Don't be shy, Suzie Q!"

This sent Sanchez over-the-edge. "You're a goddamned, no-good, lying, manipulative, scoundrel. I *hate* how you shoot before asking even a single question. I *hate* how you just walk into everything, without any *shred* of a plan, figuring that things will just work out—"

She took in a deep breath, "And *more than anything*—" she shouted, "I *hate* how I can *still* be so fucking attracted to you. It *disgusts* me. So I hope you fucking die to take the goddamned gun away from my head."

A loud chorus of "Oooooos!" and wolf whistles rolled through the crowd. If Sophia had been acting, she had done a thoroughly convincing job of it.

For his part, Corcoran shrugged with a shit-eating grin on his face. He even stepped forward and took a bow.

Bloomington was foaming at the mouth; he had to be restrained by the guards, and even as he was, he reached for one of their tridents. The guard jabbed out with it—fortunately, it only had electricity sizzling at its end, and shocked Bloomington into submission.

"*FUCCCCCK!*" he howled. "That fucking *hurt* merman-fucker!" He scolded the guard.

We approached the Pyramid, and I braced for the vehicle to slow down.

Instead, it maintained its aceleration.

I gripped the oversized armrests on my seat, bracing for the worst.

Suddenly, the mass mover glided gently upward at a 45-degree angle.

Birusha looked at me, puzzled.

"You expect something else?"

I shook my head. "At this point, I don't know *what* the devil to expect."

We continued up the Pyramid, albeit somewhat more slowly now. I cannot impress upon you enough, dear reader, the sheer *size* of this structure. If anything, with the limestone adorning the outside of it, it seemed even larger than back (or forward, I suppose from this time period) in Chronosaber's Egyptian fuck-camp.

The female announcer interrupted the ride on the feed in my head.

"Now we have the traditional *fa en tooknu* airing of greivances! It appears the smaller ugly one has won the right to go first."

Oh dear God… I thought. Or maybe let slip aloud.

Bloomington was ready. He cleared his throat and bore his teeth somewhat.

"Obviously I *hate* that you banged Sophie," he started off with. "I hate that you just can order me to do whatever you want, and I have to do it."

Not realising the military superior-subordinate relationship that existed, the crowd laughed a bit, perhaps fancying Bloomington a proper cuckold.

"And I hate that you made me leave Doc—uh… the… uh… dog! I hate that you made me leave the dog behind where he was lost… and cold… and helpless!"

I couldn't help but bury my face in my hands. As well-meaning as Steven may have been, surely the awkwardness of it would—

"The attractive one left the *dog* behind?" the male announcer said. "Oh boy, *that* was a crucial error. I don't know how they do things in Teutonia, but we Atlanteans *love* our dogs."

A chorus of boos echoed through the stadium, directed at Ricky.

"Hey come on—" he turned his palms out, like a footballer who had been caught red-handed. "—I didn't 'leave the dog'—"

"Yes you fucking *did!*" Bloomington pointed right at his face. "You did it for that old bitch too. You were her errand boy!"

"I've had about enough'a this shit. Right until now, I was gonna say I ain't got any ill will toward old Bloomy here. But now—" his eyes narrowed at Bloomington. "You're annoying. You're nerdy. You're an asshole. You stink."

"I *stink?"*

"You couldn't get laid in a French whorehouse if your dick was made out of $100 bills!"

"What?!" Bloomington's face got positively raspberry-coloured.

"Sorry—$100 Euro bills!"

"You leave Marie out of this!" On cue, one of the guards offered a trident to Bloomington. Without warning, he grabbed it from the guard's hand and thrust it straight at Ricky.

It was all Ricky could do to spin outta the way. He grabbed the trident from the guard near him and got in a defensive stance.

"When did I ever say Marie was a *whore?*" he thrust the trident at Bloomington to punctuate the statement.

"Maybe I was mad and made a false *assumption!*" Bloomington shot back with a wild, uncontrollable swing.

The crowd was roaring with approval. Bloomington had won them over with his "dog story," and each time the little wombat would gain an advantage, the spectators went absolutely bonkers.

I will admit, Bloomington's prowess with the long spear was most impressive. I suppose I didn't exactly know how long he had been training in hand-to-hand combat; for all I knew, he had lived five years since our previous adventures, and now had a family.

I don't know what bothered me more: that I hadn't bothered to ask him, or that I felt little remorse for not having done so.

It was all Corcoran could do to "weather the storm." He parried Bloomington's attacks, waiting for a quiet moment to begin his counter-attack…

But Bloomington was relentless. His stamina had improved *tremendously* since the amount of excess visceral fat he was carrying around decreased from fifty additional pounds to fifteen. I suppose as *ghastly* as those fatteries had made him look, perhaps they were good for him after all.

I also wondered what was going through Corcoran's mind as he searched for a window to exploit in the fight. After all, he was the one condemned to death. He'd be crossing into the great unknown in mere moments.

And while I had certainly flirted with death several times during our travels, perhaps whispered something naughty in her ear at least and gotten a drink in my face for my trouble, it was nothing like the curiously crushing certainty that Corcoran was now experiencing:

"Today I *will* die."

What must that feel like? I realise that the Commander generally acts as if the thought of death doesn't trouble him. But deep down, in places he doesn't like to talk about much too often, was he afraid? Could death humble even the great Ricky Corcoran?

We reached about 80% of the way up the pyramid and the mass mover came to a stop.

"Quickly—follow me." Birusha pointed her trident at the wall of the vehicle, and the weapon shot a bolt of energy toward it. The seemingly impenetrable stone wall sifted away like sand in an hourglass and revealed a small platform jutting outside of the pyramid.

Above us was the capstone base. And above that, workers were finishing up installing what was almost certainly the true capstone.

I must admit, it was quite stunning. Made entirely out of red crystal, even before it was fully connected to the power plant itself, it was pulsing with energy—*deadly* energy, I reminded myself.

Above the true capstone was a large crystalline focusing mirror that was being pivoted into place. Only… it was somewhat less impressive than a proper glass mirror. It appeared to be cracked, or at least cleaved at wrong angles, almost as if having been cut by a thoroughly leathered jeweler.

I nodded at the flimsy-looking mirror, "That's going to allow them to fire at Lemuria? From *here?*"

Birusha nodded at the platform ahead. I chided myself for potentially giving away the entire operation, but luckily no one seemed to notice.

The platform was guarded by a cadre of Atlantean guards, dark-skinned and giant, even by Atlantean standards.

Birusha lowered her weapon to her side, and for a second I thought we might have a firefight on our hands.

Instead, the guards responded in kind. Either it was a common greeting between guards, or Birusha had more people on the inside.

Meanwhile, on the feed being beamed directly into my brain, Corcoran finally pressed an advantage. He swung the trident at Bloomington with short, deliberate strokes, though to his credit, Steven handled the barrage with aplomb.

Sensing an opening, Bloomington hesitated for maybe a tenth of a second. I could see him inhale deeply as he jabbed the trident forward deeply, into Corcoran's midsection, between slabs of armour.

There was a sharp howl—initially I thought it was Ricky, but it was actually Steven who let loose a combination of triumph and anguish.

I also thought I could hear Sanchez yelp out, almost as if she was the one being skewered, as the long weapon entered the Commander's ribs.

Corcoran was silent. He staggered to his knees. A thick torrent of blood coated the oversized Atlantean armour. He instinctively reached for the wound and brought his blood-slicked fingers up to his face.

Then, he slumped back, all slack. His eyes rolled back in his head, open. It was certainly not a peaceful death, and a very small part of me thought that in the weirdest of ways, even though I bore no true animus toward him any longer, we were now even.

Bloomington stood over the body. I had seen him ruthlessly kill Nazis as if they were houseflies mere days before, but a tear now sat perched on his cheek. He was beet-red in the afternoon sunlight, heaving deep breaths almost as if someone had knocked the wind out of him.

"Remember the medigel Steven…" I mumbled under my breath. "He *needs* the medigel…"

Before I could see what happened, the cameras turned to something else, something far darker than what had just taken place.

Loud horns blared as the image came into focus on the screen. It took the camera several moments to steady itself, but when it did, *I* nearly sobbed as well.

Dozens of ships adorned in yellow and purple appeared on the horizon. While they had sails, they were far too small to propel the ships, and the lack of steam indicated that perhaps we were dealing with an altogether different type of vessel entirely.

The ships closed rapidly on the Giza harbour. Tridents fired plasma bolts at the targets, but they were apparently being blocked by some kind of force-field.

The lead ship returned fire—a cannonade of shells, likely dozens of them, burst out toward the city, leaving contrails of thick smoke behind them.

Atlantean guards all over the city dropped what they were doing to shoot at the missiles as they sped toward the city.

"Is that what I think it is?" I asked moments before I took a deep swallow.

Birusha nodded, with a half smile that was almost proud. "The Lemurian navy has arrived."

CHAPTER TWENTY-TWO

"You didn't think *this* was a somewhat important detail of which for me to be aware?" I felt the steam rising out of my chest, up through my neck, and out my ears.

Birusha shrugged, "Was backup in case the Empress was ready to fire at Mu."

I looked at the ships. The largest one turned a rather massive gun barrel directly at the Pyramid.

I pointed at the ship, "*That* doesn't worry you either?"

She waved me off, eyes glazed over. Guards rushed past us first out to the platform, then into the stone people-mover down the side of the Pyramid.

Well at least that *part of this whole brouhaha just got a bit easier...* I thought.

It took several seconds before Birusha snapped out of it.

"The Empress is saying to use the—"

Before she could finish, the large focusing mirror above us pivoted several degrees. Birusha pulled me along the platform to the inside of the Pyramid. Notably, the floor was made out of yet *another* different stone than the sandstone, quartz, and granite surrounding us.

Indeed, this room wasn't one that had been on the Chronosaber tour conducted by Cynthia and Amaranth. Instead it was further up the Pyramid, and had several stone pillars and columns that were being manipulated by a couple of Atlantean workers in jumpsuits. The way they moved the large stones reminded me more of the omni-yoke than levers—sometimes they removed rods from the floor, twisted them, and re-insterted them. Other times, they changed the orientation and direction of these rods. It was like watching a gigantic 3-D puzzle being put together, though one where the pieces should have been *far* more difficult to move than these seemed to be.

There was a loud "charging" sound—as if the entire building was focusing energy through the walls. While the floor beneath us wasn't charging, the walls radiated a blue-green energy that appeared to be travelling upward at an increasingly fast rate.

Suddenly, a rumble and sharp, deep *WHIIIIIINE* filled the

chamber.

I watched through one of the "windows," though it was really just a wide slit in the wall, careful not to touch whatever force had just passed through the sides of the pyramid.

A bolt of energy like an oversized laser beam shot out from above, and instantaneously vaporized the Lemurian ship that had targeted the pyramid. The sea churned where the vessel had just been, and pulled the rest of the flotilla closer together.

"My *God*..." I inhaled as I said the words and spit out a low, deep breath with a hint of a whistle.

"Bastards!" Birusha spat the words. I imagined that for her, seeing a battleship full of her countrymen utterly destroyed in the blink of an eye was rather like what it must have been like to be at Dunkirk for an Englishman.

Birusha's rage swirled inside of her--a minor eddy quickly becoming a hurricane of anger.

I reached out to put a hand on her shoulder, but it was too late. She raised her trident and shot bolts of concentrated plasma at the two guards that remained in the room.

The first guard dropped like a sack of oversized potatoes, instantly dead. Only the second one had any warning his life was about to end; he tried to hoist his trident up to the ready, but the bolt hit him before he could bring it down to fire.

Birusha rushed over and appropriated the guards' tridents. She flung one over her shoulder, and kept the other trident and her own trained on the two technicians operating the machine.

"Step away from the controls," her tone was somewhat more than "deathly serious."

The technicians looked at her momentarily, then their expressions went blank. Their eyes glazed over, and it was only then that I realised that they must be getting communications on targets from higher ups, or even the Empress herself.

A low rumble rocked the Pyramid. Maybe one of the missiles from the fleet had gotten through? Though if so, it hadn't done much damage—the stone rods and pillars continued to move and pulse as directed by the techs.

Birusha wrinkled her nose. She lodged a plasma bolt in one of the techs' chest.

"Are you *mad?!*" I grabbed my hair and feigned pulling it out for several seconds. "We *need* them to operate this death ray!"

She levelled the trident at the remaining tech.

"We don't need *shit,*" she said, "But I'm feeling generous right now. Last chance—step away or I waste you."

The tech ran off toward the ledge, got in the newly-arrived mass mover (which had somehow automatically replaced the one we had arrived in that had been used by the exiting guards), and receded down the side of the Pyramid to relative safety.

"Fantastic. Now we have no means of escape." I raised my hands out to my sides.

"Who said anything about escape?" Birusha snorted. "I want *revenge.*"

She started manipulating the stone pillars and rods as the techs had moments before.

"If I'm right—" she reached for the left most horizontal pillar and pulled it to the right, "—this one should move the mirror side-to-side... And this one—" she moved to the vertical-most pillar on the right and manipulated it up-and-down "—should control attitude…"

"And what controls the firing mechanism?"

She didn't answer immediately. Instead she looked through a crystaline tube that hung down from the ceiling. Presumbly, it was some sort of targeting mechanism, like a periscope.

"What are you looking for?" I tried a different tactic.

"Where is the Empress?" she manipulated the pillars, searching for her intended target. "In the palace? No wait—she'd still be at the—"

She feverishly maneuvered the pillars, presumably to target the stadium, where not only the Empress, but also my crew—my *friends* were. And Ricky's body not yet even cold.

"Wait—wait you can't! My friends!"

She stepped away from the controls momentarily and grabbed me by the collar.

"My person—my… my *mate* was on the *Tanogi.*"

She pointed out to the swirling empty spot where the Lemurian ship had been vaporised.

Did he also know about you casually propositioning Teutons for sexual baths? I had to literally bite my tongue to keep from throwing out the smart arse remark.

"I am so sorry for your loss," I took a deep, uneven breath. "But we *must* stick to the plan. Overload the true capstone. Destroy it. Destroy the mirror. End this war once and for all."

"I feel like those are two different things!" She stepped away from the controls and turned so her back faced me. "I have the power to cut the head off the snake right now! These Atlanteans' blind devotion to their Empress is both their strength and weakness. They fight for her, they *die* for her, but without her—" she turned toward me and raised a finger, "—without her they are rudderless. Who will lead them? Her child? That boor Vermoor? I can lay waste to her, the city, this whole province *right now!* And *that* may just end this war once and for all!"

I stroked my chin, if only for a moment. I needed just a little more time—

"Can you give me one minute?"

"*One* minute—" she said. She fiddled with the controls dialing in her target once more. "Starting *now!*"

I rushed out to the platform. There was little time to waste. I looked around and saw missles and plasma bolts flying all over the place. More than a few buildings had taken significant damage, and several were starting to collapse.

"POLARIS—Care Bear! Care Bear! But do *not* track *me!* Go to the colesseum and load up the rest of the crew, including Commander Corcoran. Then come find me and come out with the original Care Bear plan as soon as they're loaded up. Understood?"

I don't even know why I asked—it was a one-way channel so it wasn't like the maniacal robot could even respond if it wanted to.

Within seconds though, I saw the ship rise from its landing pad and quickly make its way over to the stadium. It landed right near Corcoran's body, best as I could tell.

"Time's up." Birusha said without a hint of emotion.

"No—wait!"

It was too late. She heaved the largest horizontal bar forward. Within moments, the low charging noise and rumble started again. The blue-green energy pulsed up the walls. I thought of threatening her with the trident, but I was sure it was too late, and that antagonizing her would only draw her ire.

I looked on helplessly out the small window as the focused beam of energy *WHINED* and carved out a swath of the city in a wide, irregular arc. It was close to the stadium, but not exactly dead-on, and the building (and more importantly the time machine) remained unscathed.

"Damn!" She pushed the large bar away and turned from the controls.

I heaved a sigh of relief.

"One more shot—" She stood at the crystal periscope gadget and fiddled with the controls.

I put a hand on her shoulder. It took all of the strength in my forearm, but I turned her away from the controls so we were face-to-face. I levelled my gaze at her.

"Look, Birusha, I understand how upset you are. I know what it's like to lose a loved one. My father died in much the same way; here one minute, then gone the next.

"But we *must* follow the plan. Maximize the power and destroy the mirror and the true capstone. You trusted Klaus, right? And he trusted me. So what I'm telling you is now that you've done a fair bit of damage to the city, it's only a matter of time before the whole fucking palace guard is on its way up here. And if they get here and that death ray is still operational—"

Her pupils dilated ever-so-slightly. I hoped I was getting through to her.

"—then they'll *still* have the death ray. And my guess is their first target will start with an 'M' and end with a 'U.'"

Her eyes shot up toward her forehead in contemplation. It was easy to discount the intellectual abilities of these large people because they were so damned *big*. I had to remind myself that any culture that figured out how to levitate stone and create a death ray of this scale was not a stupid one by any stretch.

She finally let out a loud scream.

"Gods curse it! You're right..." she pulled a row of rods up out of the left side of the ground. Each made several clicking noises, and the clicks got quicker and higher-pitched as they got closer to being fully extended out of the floor.

There were half a dozen of these stone rods that she had to extend to their maximums. All the while, I stole glances at the door to the chamber, hoping against hope that we'd be able to finish before—

"That should do it!" Birusha exclaimed. She reached for the large horizontal beam—

And slumped over it. A large, empty plasma wound occupied the space her heart had moments before.

I looked in the doorway to find Vermoor levelling a still-sizzling trident at Birusha.

"Lemurian filth!" He rushed over to me, flanked by several guards. They surrounded me, tridents out, surely waiting to get their own retribution.

Vermoor scowled at me for a moment. Then his face dropped, and became one of deep concern.

"Doctor Templeton—are you okay?" His ever-present earnestness would be his downfall.

I rubbed my head for effect, "I—uh—just had a nasty bump on the head. Nothing major."

He spat on Birusha's corpse. It was all I could do to keep a straight face.

"I knew we had a Lemurian mole in the guard for quite some time. But Birusha? I would never—" he paused in momentary contemplation before he turned to me, "—and to kidnap our honored guest on a day of *fa en tooknu,* well that's… that's just *wrong."*

I nodded. I stole a glance at the stone pillars. The death ray was ready. I needed a way to push the large horizontal pillar, and escape with the capstone base. *That* was going to be quite difficult with Ver*moron* and his band of merry men using it to take out Lemurian battleships.

That was it!

"I do believe she mentioned something about one of the ships having some sort of 'doomsday weapon' on it before you so—" I took a breath and smiled, "—heroically rescued me."

"Where? Which one?!" the Captain of the Guard thundered.

I feigned confusion, "I—I don't rightly know. She didn't say," I shrugged, "Better destroy them all then."

Vermoor nodded. He turned toward the controls. He spied the ships through the crystal apparatus, and maneuvered the targeting mechanism into place.

That's it... just push the bar now big boy... I thought. If the oaf would just push the "trigger" bar to engage the laser, it would overload the mirror and shatter it. And the death ray would be no more.

He reached for the trigger bar.

"Gods forgive me," he said.

He started pushing the trigger bar forward.

"Wait!" the darkest-skinned guard on his right tapped him on the shoulder. He nodded at the vertical pillars extended on both sides.

"Oh my!" Vermoor half-jumped out of his sandals. "Clever girl—she turned this to maximum power! If I had fired it, it would have—"

There was no more time. I couldn't let them power the death ray down, or it would be permanently in Atlantean hands.

Without thinking further, I lunged myself into the hulking guard's midsection, in a full-on rugby tackle.

It must have taken him by total surprize. He lurched backward, staggering several giant steps in but a moment. His ample backside connected with the horizontal pillar, and pushed it forward into firing mode, turning the Pyramid on once more.

The rumble and charging noise began again. Only this time, the sounds were more pronounced, deeper, like the building itself was reaching down deep into its bowels for what was to come.

The energy surged through the walls more quickly. Ripples of blue-green power poured up through them like an upside-down waterfall, cascading to the Pyramid's apex.

Then...silence.

But only for a moment. This time, the deep *WHIIIIIIIIINNNNNNE* was nearly eardrum-shattering. We all reeled in the control room as the building went into a full-on earthquake.

I heard glass shatter above us, and looked outside. The crystal mirror was floating in millions of shards outside of the chamber.

Then, a loud *CRASH* and *POP!* The energy whooshed back down the sides of the Pyramid, and the room went dark.

"What have you *done?!*" Any remaining geniality Vermoor had toward me vanished. He raised his trident and thrust it around wildly, hoping to hit me in the extremely low light.

I dodged to the left, then rolled right. I sprung to my knees, but noticed the large guard winding up his trident, levelled squarely at my chest. He half-smiled, and I returned the gesture.

Dead to rights.

Suddenly, the room illuminated for three short bursts.

Vermoor stood, poised, ready-to-strike…

And turned so I could see the cauterized wound that had cleaved its way clean through his chest.

The other guards quickly dropped as well. More illuminating bolts followed.

I looked at the landing and saw a vaguely human form filling it, growing larger as it approached. It carried a large mishmash of tubes by its side as it advanced on my position.

When it was a mere ten feet away, the form's eyes illuminated.

"Did I do good MASSSSTTTER?" POLARIS's mechanical voice asked, seeking approval.

"You did great, POLARIS."

For once, I meant it, too.

CHAPTER TWENTY-THREE

POLARIS and I raced back out to the platform. I fully expected to see another cadre of Atlantean guards storming up the side of the Pyramid in the mass mover, but what I saw outside was far more fearsome.

The sun appeared to be *bleeding*.

Actually, that's not 100% accurate.

The sky *surrounding* the sun appeared to be bleeding.

A pale brown halo enveloped the sun, and grew noticably larger with each passing minute. It wasn't necessarily that the sun *itself* seemed dimmer; rather it was that the area surrounding the sun was beginning to obscure the rays that normally were visible on an otherwise bright and sunny day.

"I don't like the look of that," I nodded at POLARIS and pointed at the sun with the Atlantean trident I still carried.

"Nnnnnoooo Ssssshittttt..." it replied.

The gangway was still lowered, so we hurried onboard the time machine. Bloomington, Sanchez, and the Chief were all gathered in the dining area, heads hung low, expressions dull and lifeless, even though POLARIS and I had made it back on-board safely.

"Who died?" I asked.

Sanchez nodded at the table in front of them.

Ricky Corcoran's lifeless body lay completely limp, a bag of meat. At least someone had the decency to close his eyes; I still recoiled when thinking of that grotesque expression—

"What? He's *dead* dead?"

The Chief nodded, "Yes, your miracle herbs have had no effect."

"We gave the medgel to him about fifteen minutes ago and—" Sanchez bit her lip for a moment before she shook her head. I could've sworn her eyes went glassy for an instant before she composed herself once more.

"I *killed* him!" Bloomington banged on the table next to the corpse, waking all of us except the Commander (and POLARIS).

Sanchez raised her eyebrows at him and wiped a quick hand across her face.

"Uh, yeah—you did."

Bloomington was trembling, "I didn't mean to… you know… *kill him*, kill him. I just was so pig-fucking *mad* at him… and they gave us those tridents…"

I didn't quite know what to say. And despite knowing that in such situations I should generally keep my mouth shut, I decided against my thirty-six years of experience in that regard.

"It's okay, Steven—he knew the risks."

"He *knew* the *ris*—" he ran a pudgy hand through his thinning black hair, "I died back when we were with those assgoblin Mayans, and you wanna know what happened?"

We all looked at him expectantly.

"Jack fucking-*shit*, that's what. It was just one minute, a fucking axe through the back, the next, I'm staggering back to my feet and they acted like they saw a ghost. Just no afterlife, nothing—it didn't exist. *I* didn't exist."

It was an odd statement from Steven both for the vulnerability he was presenting, and because I had never thought about *his* experiences with death. Admittedly, like most people, I was terrified of death as some far-off "end point" where I would surely someday cease to exist. But I hadn't approached it as a scientist yet. I hadn't tried to gather any data about it.

Though to be fair, even my own pursuit of time-travel was clouded by my emotional reaction to my father's death all those twenty-odd years before. Thinking I could somehow "cheat" death, if not on my own behalf, then certainly for my father's benefit, taken from me (what I considered to be) before his time.

And now, presented with a single data point, Steve Bloomington's personal experience with death no less, I couldn't help but feel a chill wriggle down my spine. It was as if someone had lowered the cabin temperature by a solid 12 degrees, or (worse still) as if Death himself had somehow replaced Corcoran as a member of the crew.

We were all jolted out of the somber moment by the now-familiar sound of an alarm klaxon.

(Though I suppose I was rather thrilled for any kind of distraction.)

That would change as soon as I made my way to the command chair.

WARNING: Coronal Mass Ejection Incoming! flashed on the QC's display.

"Coronal mass *ejection?!*" I said aloud.

The QC's blocky animated avatar appeared on-screen.

Did I stutter?

"No I suppose not," I rolled my eyes.

Was it possible? A massive solar flare *caused* by *my* actions in the pyramid? I suppose it *had* been high noon when the Pyramid made its final "grand finale" of a discharge that shattered the mirror and went straight into the air. But how many millions of miles did it have to travel? It seemed to me like a rifle shot taking out a mosquito from halfway around the world.

Unless... I furrowed my brow. Could the blast radius have been angled opposite the shape of the Pyramid itself? That would mean it would start as an isoceles triangle and continue out for millions and millions of miles potentially, which would give the Pyramid's final, dying blast a chance to hit the sun, and begin the cascading coronal mass ejection.

The implications were *staggering*. I would normally say that Klaus goaded us into doing this (in hindsight) terroristic act.

But I knew better—this *had* to happen somehow. If I hadn't pushed Vermoor to start the enormous energy surge that destroyed the mirror and the top capstone, some other causal event surely would have. There had to be *some* catalyst for this mass coronal ejection.

And, even worse, since "whatever happened, happened," we were *always* the ones who started it!

I had an intense hankering for scotch, though I could only steady myself against the command chair.

"You *can't* be serious—" Sanchez elbowed her way past Bloomington to the front of the ship.

"What does that mean?" The Chief asked.

"It means that there's an enormous solar flare headed right for us," I turned to the Chief, "and I think we may have caused it."

He looked back at me blankly.

I sighed. “It means the sun is angry, and we may have provoked it.”

The Chief stroked his now-stubbled face, “The sun is angry… the sun is angry…”

Bloomington grunted, exasperated, “It means this fucking ship is cooked if we’re on this side of the planet too long!”

I nodded, “I’m afraid Steven is correct, though—” I paused momentarily for reflection, “—I think we might have up to twenty-four hours before things get really hairy. But yes, it potentially could fry all of the electronics on-board should we be on the wrong side of the planet when it hits.”

The Chief remained somber, “Ancient legends say that the time of troubles began when the sun got angry, and the sky grew dark and grumpy. Soon enough, the thunder gods grew tired of the ancients’ wicked ways, and started lobbing a non-stop lightning barrage at the earth’s surface.”

He looked at me with wide, earnest eyes.

“Is this the beginning of the time of troubles? Did *we* cause it?”

I patted the short, stocky man on the shoulder, “Well—” I looked at the other two reminaing companions, “—We can’t be *completely* sure—”

Bloomington pounded the table again.

“Fuckmuffins! So now I’ve got *all of Atlantis* and this piss-soaked time of troubles on my conscience too?!”

I’ll admit a chuckle may have leaked out when Bloomington had the temerity to utter “fuckmuffins” with complete seriousness.

I put my arms out to steady my completely unstable colleague.

“There, there, easy now Steven. Whatever happened happened and whatnot—”

“Yeah, only because this Klaus assresident *told* you it had to happen—”

“Now see here about Klaus!”

I raised an arm to point accusingly at Bloomington, but our argument was interrupted as the ship took a deep lurch.

“What the hell was that?” Sanchez asked.

"Computer, 360 degree view please!" I bellowed.

The walls dissolved away to reveal a full platoon of Atlantean royal guards standing on the platform. They had their tridents pointed at the ship, and were unleashing powerful bolts of plasma at the side of it.

I couldn't see the damage they were causing to the outside of the ship, but if it was enough to cause the inertial dampeners to fail, then it must be some rather serious firepower indeed.

"Computer, take us up to the top of the Pyramid—now!" I yelled as I strapped myself into the command chair.

"Top of the Pyramid? Get us the *fuck* outta here!" Sanchez implored.

"I can't—we need the capstone base!"

Sanchez rolled her eyes and scrambled into the gunnery seat to my right.

"Well, we aren't gonna make it very far with those Atlanteans using us as target practice either!"

She levelled the laser cannons at the platform and opened fire. Some of the bolts found their targets—they turned the enormous soldiers into little more than glorified hamburger meat. The other bolts tore through the platform as if it was a cannonade on a sandcastle.

The soldiers were dispatched within seconds, though Sophia kept firing on the platform. Her hatred boiled up in her eyes, and what started as a low, glutteral yell turned into a mighty roar as she continued pulling the triggers.

"That's enough, Sophia!" I yelled. I put a hand on her shoulder and steeled my tone. "That's *quite* enough!"

She finally relented and let the triggers go. The brilliant white limestone facade had been eaten away around the platform, revealing the familiar blocks of duller heavy limestone beneath it.

"Are you okay?" I asked.

She looked at me; her trademark placcidity returned remarkably quickly, almost the same as I'd expect from a hardened sociopath.

And that was *before* the small smile crept over her face.

"What do you mean? I'm *fine!*" She affected a soft chuckle.

"Yikes. I've seen you do some fucked up shit Sophie," Bloomington scampered over as he talked, "But *that* was cold."

She shrugged, "Kinda a stressful day guys..."

"Computer, engage cloaking device," I said, just to be safe.

We were now directly above the Pyramid, though for the life of me, I had no earthly idea of how we'd transport such an enormous object. True, technically the ship operated with an anti-gravity drive, so the mass wouldn't be a problem if I could enlarge the gravimetric field somehow to encompass a greater area.

But still, positioning the multi-tonne stone into place would be near-impossible. Unless...

"Can we use that trident thing of yours to make it so it floats?" Sanchez asked.

I nodded, "I was thinking exactly the same thing, Captain Sanchez."

"But how do we attach it?"

I shrugged, "I haven't the faintest idea. But I know who might—" I turned to POLARIS. "POLARIS, if I told you we needed to attach that rather large capstone base atop the Pyramid down there to the ship, can you come up with a workable solution?"

"Proccccccesssssssingg..." the robot said. *"Proccccccesssssssingg... Proccccccesssssssingg..."*

"Jesus Christ," Sanchez said.

"Shitbucket is worse than my netbook back home," Bloomington said. He turned to the robot and cupped his hands over his mouth, "Hey dumbfart! *Hurry... the fuck... up!* We don't have all day here!"

"Yesssssssss Massssterrrr..." POLARIS said. *"Solution complete. Chance of succcccceessssssss 79.1%"*

The robot picked up the trident.

"Lower gangway pleassssssse..."

The ship did nothing.

I rolled my eyes, "Computer, please lower the gangway."

WARNING: Lowering the gangway here may affect ship attitude displayed on the screen.

"Just lower the fucking gangway goddamnit fucking pretty please with sprinkles on top!"

The ship *finally* relented, and did as it was told.

POLARIS wasted little time. It thrust out the trident, and shot waves of gravimetric energy at the capstone base for several seconds. When the capstone was light enough, POLARIS jumped out of the ship and hoisted the immense stone over its head with ease.

The robot bounded up like Dick Fosbury on top of the ship, which was somewhat jarring since the cloaking device was engaged, so POLARIS for the life of it looked like it was bounding through thin air. The robot held the capstone base with one hand, and with the other, it raised the trident up to the capstone's bottom. Some debris fell out of the bottom of the capstone, presumably hollowing out the bottom somewhat.

POLARIS's maniacal grin was omnipresent as it jammed the trident into the bottom of the capstone base, then welded the trident to the top of the ship with its hand.

Finally, the robot slid down the side of the craft, hung on the doorframe of the gangway, and swung itself into the ship.

"Allll done," POLARIS announced.

Perhaps three minutes had elapsed since the ship lowered the gangway.

"Well done, POLARIS," I said, "Though for some reason I thought you were going to attach the stone to the base of the ship."

"Gannnngway would not opennnn," POLARIS said.

"Quite right," I nodded. "So the ship will fly with this, errr… setup?"

"Chance of succccceesssssssss 79.1%"

"What? Fuckin' *lame*—" Bloomington said. "You can't do any better than that?"

"It wasssss the optimal ssssssolution given the perammmmetersssss."

I nodded. "Good enough for me."

It must have looked positively insane from afar; the capstone base flying through the air as if possessed by demons, so I asked Sanchez and Bloomington to work on configuring the cloaking device so that it could cloak the capstone base as well.

Meanwhile, since we had taken off from the top of the Pyramid, the Chief had seemed somber, and detached. He certainly wasn't his normal jovial self. While I had an inkling as to what was the matter, I decided to confront him to make sure we were on the same page moving forward.

"What's wrong, Your Highness?"

He shook his head. We were still in 360-degree mode so he pointed toward the city.

"The battle rages on—"

Yikes. I had forgotten that there was an all-out, honest-to-God, "end of civiliazation" *war* happening as we were absconding with a priceless and quite irreplaceable part of history and Atlantean culture.

"—and yet, I feel like I must do more."

"Now, now, Your Highness, you can't blame yourself for what happened—"

He shook his head, "I don't. I don't know who to blame for this… but I do know what I have to do about it. Forgive me Dr. Templeton, you've been more than hospitable up to this point… but can we make one more stop before leaving? I promise we will be done in plenty of time for your crew to get to safety."

I thought about it for only a moment. At this point, I thought of the Chief as a full member of the crew. He had been invaluable in securing a safe landing in this time period, and establishing contact using Atlantean—it was probably the least I could do to indulge him in a short side trip.

I nodded, "No problem at all. Name your favor, Your Highness."

"I want to go back in the city to get the Empress."

"Are you *fucking mad?!"*

I covered my mouth with my hand reflexively after I said it.

"I… er… mean with all due respect, Your Highness."

He stuck out a palm, "No offense taken. I realize it'll be dangerous down there. But—"

"Stop thinking about getting laid, man!" Bloomington popped off.

"It's not *about* getting laid!" the Chief was indignant for a moment before his eyes widened. "Well… not *completely* about getting laid anyway."

Sanchez and I looked at each other for a knowing moment.

The Chief shook his head out of it and pointed at the city once more, "Look, a lot of innocent people are gonna die from a lot of different things, okay? But I know how to save them. The ark—the safe space. The… uh… what did you call it again? In the ground? Many miles from here, but safe—"

"Gobeckli Tepe?"

The Chief snapped his fingers, "Right! Gobbelty-gook! If the legends are correct, the time of troubles will make the surface no place for humans. But—" he raised a finger, "—underground will be safe for quite a while, as long as we can get organized, get supplies, get people, skilled workers—"

"And to get those," Sanchez interrupted, "You need the Empress."

The Chief winked, "Exactamundo."

I took a deep breath and looked the Chief in the eye. He was just as honest and earnest as usual. His eyes pleaded with me for a chance to "make things right," at least in some small way in his mind.

"Very well. Computer, POLARIS, scan the area for the Empress."

"Thank you, Dr. Templeton!" The Chief jumped up to give me a big bear hug.

"Don't thank me yet, Your Highness. As you yourself mentioned, this plan of yours is quite fraught with danger."

"Yes, but would you have it any other way?"

Even though I smiled in reply, truth be told in fact I *would* rather have things quite a bit safer. With Corcoran slowly rotting on our kitchenette table, and the ripsaw pace of our time in Atlantis already, I was exhausted. I could use some good solid sleep, a shower, and a shave.

Unfortunately, those activities would have to wait until we were safely in a time period where a good-sized chunk of the sun *wasn't* speeding toward the planet.

"Found herrrrr—" POLARIS pointed to a stretch of road between the colosseum and one of the government buildings in the area, that looked like a miniaturised (and somewhat less grand) version of the palace.

"Computer, interface with POLARIS, lock on the location he's indicating, and take us in."

Within seconds, we were zooming off through the skies toward the Empress and what remained of her personal guard. Honestly, aside from a couple odd wobbles here-and-there as the inertial dampeners got their bearings, you would've never known we had a stone weighing hundreds of tonnes atop us.

Whilst in transit, Sophia, Bloomington and I raided the armory. I'll admit it: it honestly felt good again to have my dual-holsters strapped to my sides—reassuring even. Especially since this time, one of my custom laser pistols occupied one of them. POLARIS picked up the LR-15 and readied it.

Bloomington put a finger on the robot's forehead.

"Now shitbucket, the Chief wants to *protect the Empress,* okay?"

"Yesssssss Masssssster..."

"That means only shoot the purple-and-yellow ones, okay?"

"Yesssssss Masssssster..."

"Okay, good." He punctuated the statement by releasing the safety on his laser pistol. Steven seemed to be pulling out of his funk somewhat—he was likely glad to have something to think about other than the dead body laying on the nearby table. Especially when that dead body was the one who would have made a "crack" or "remark" about how *terrible* Bloomington was with weapons (evidence from Leipzig notwithstanding).

I worried about Sanchez though. She was obviously only a couple degrees from a full-on boil at this point. I hoped she didn't blame the Empress too much for Corcoran's death; if so, and she let her emotions get the better of her, this could be quite the hairy little encounter indeed.

We landed perhaps thirty metres from the Empress and her guards. They were pinned down behind the remains of a gorgeous fountain in the middle of a four-way intersection, engaged in a firefight with several soldiers in yellow-and-purple armour; apparently at least some Lemurians had made landfall.

We wasted no time; I lowered the gangway and we were immediately in the thick of things. POLARIS was first off, and laid down a volley of covering fire.

Before we could follow him though, one of the Lemurians picked up an enormous block off the ground. He threw it casually at the robot, and while it was in the air, he levelled a trident at it, and shot pulsing gravimetric waves at it.

The block instantly gained mass. POLARIS turned the LR-15 on the block, and it split into several large chunks. One of them hit him squarely in the laser rifle, utterly destroying it.

The others bombarded the robot, taking out its (newly-remade, mind you) knee joint. It was all the robot could do to drag itself back up the gangway as we poured out of the ship.

"POLARIS is down!" I yelled.

"Noted!" Sanchez said. She took cover behind a nearby stone planter. Bloomington and I followed suit.

Several plasma bolts flew overhead. While I still winced at these near-misses, I noticed that Sanchez and Bloomington both were cool as cucumbers. Sanchez coldly lowered her rifle and started picking off Lemurians one-by-one.

Her precision with the large gun allowed Bloomington, the Chief and me to move from behind the planter to a pile of debris, maybe ten metres from the Empress.

It was close enough that the Empress was within hearing range, and the Chief called out.

"Your Loveliness?"

"Nothon? Is that you?"

No-thon? I mouthed at Bloomington, and he shrugged. I thought the Chief's name was Octoc. Though I suppose that could have been his family name, while "Nothon" was his horrificly *awful* given name.

"Yes darling, it's me! Your Nothon, come to save you!"

"Oh my! What a pleasant surprise!" the Empress seemed genuinely thrilled to see the short, stocky Chief, whom she still likely thought to be the most charming Teuton she had ever met.

Sanchez had depleted the squad of Lemurians down to just three. Bloomington winged one, and when another went to help him, they lined up in such a way that Sanchez took out both with a single headshot.

The last one seemed to be a bit more slippery. He was the one who had taken out POLARIS, and he kept using his same trick, again and again—hoisting up rocks with his trident, then giving them mass to try to take out the Empress's position.

I noticed that many of the rocks he was using came from the ruined second floor of the building next to him. One particularly large boulder seemed to be teetering on its edge.

I took out my laser pistol and inhaled sharply. I held my breath as I squeezed the trigger, and unleashed a torrent of laser bolts at the rock perched above him.

Dare I say that what happened next seemed to be right out of a Wile E. Coyote cartoon; the rock started teetering, then shaking, and then rolled right over, hitting the Lemurian right as he was raising his trident to stop it.

"Brilliant!" The Empress clapped her hands together. "Simply brilliant! Our Teutonian friends have saved the day once more—hoora—"

She looked at the ship, which was still cloaked, so it appeared that the capstone base was floating in mid-air.

"What have you done with my capstone base? And the true capstone?!"

The Chief rushed over to her side and took her hand, "My dear, do not worry yourself with such matters now. We have far more pressing things at hand."

She put her hands on her hips, "What could be more pressing than a death ray to eradicate this Lemurian *scum*—" she spat in the general direction of the poor fellow I had just crushed, "—which *requires* the capstone base?"

The Chief explained the mass coronal ejection as best he could, which is to say by shortcutting with a lot of "the sun is angry"-type nonsense.

The Empress absolutely ate it up.

"My goodness… so in twenty-four hours *everything* here—my buildings, my people—will be *gone?"*

"I'm afraid so, my darling. And it gets worse if you believe the ancient legend—err, prophecies."

She furrowed her brow, "What prophecies, exactly?"

I rubbed my chin, "The prophecy that soon the continent of Atlantis will be swallowed up by the ocean."

Dread crept over the Empress's face, "Lies… these must be horrible lies—"

Sophia was just now joining us; she shouldered her rifle and approached the group.

"You there! Funny woman! This is a joke, isn't it?"

Sophia shook her head, her mouth level and stoic, "No joke, Your Excellency. Our, uh, Teutonian scientists—" She looked around at us, and I think caught Bloomington picking his nose, since she scrunched up her nose and made a face at him, "—have forseen it."

Sanchez lowered her weapon and started to clean it.

"I can't… I won't…"

"Death to Atlantis and its wretched tyrant!"

The cry came from one of the Empress's own guards. He raised his trident at the Empress from perhaps thirty metres behind. The weapon shot out a gravimetric beam at a nearby boulder, and pulled it toward the Empress. With just one flick of the wrist, he could kill the whole lot of us, including the other guards.

The Empress turned to look her accoster in the eye, as her stern, authoritarian expression faded in the face of true, immediate power.

One shot rang out. Then another.

Instantly two red dots appeared on the rogue guard's forehead. Blood gushed from them within moments, as the body crumpled lifelessly to the ground, and the boulder fell harmlessly away from us.

I looked around at the group. The Chief didn't have a weapon, Bloomington and I were still reaching for ours, and Sophia hadn't been able to wrangle her large rifle into place.

As I looked past her, though, a well-muscled form staggered at the base of the ship's gangway. The person fell to a knee and steadied itself on the pistol it had just fired from some thirty metres away.

It was Commander Corcoran.

And he looked like hell.

"Scotch!" he croaked. "I need *scotch* for sam fuck's sake!"

CHAPTER TWENTY-FOUR

"Ricky!" I couldn't believe how jubilant I sounded to see him.

"Holy shit!" Bloomington said.

"You're okay!" Sanchez and Bloomington rushed to his superior's side; each one took a different arm and hoisted him up to his feet.

"Scotch!"

"Sounds like Doc after about 9 a.m. on a Wednesday," Bloomington said.

For once, I had no retort—it was actually one of the better jokes the little toady had ever made.

"I am *so* sorry!" Bloomington gave him a hug as he helped carry the Commander up the ramp.

"Don't... worry... about it..." Corcoran heaved each word with a its own breath.

"Let me fix you a drink, buddy—" they carried the Commander on the ship.

After the Commander's heroics, it wasn't much work to get the Empress to listen to the Chief. He told her about the location of Gobeckli Tepe.

"I'm not aware of any underground caves there..." she stroked her chin in contemplation.

The Chief thought for a moment. "You know..." he snapped his fingers again. "The ark was built to weather the time of troubles! Since the time of troubles hasn't happened yet—"

"Then the ark still has to be built," I completed his thought.

"Yes! And—" he grabbed for one of the remaining guards' tridents. The guard held strong; he refused to let the little man have it until the Empress nodded at him, at which point he finally relented.

"This thing can carve through all kinds of stone, correct?"

The Empress chuckled, "Nothon, don't make me make a 'dumb Teuton' joke in front of your friends."

He shook his head, "With a couple of these, we should be able to carve it out in no time. A week, tops. What I need you to do," he turned to the Empress, "—is get on that fancy broadcast thing of yours, and start rounding up people and supplies. Evacuate the area. Trusted people only—" he looked at the corpse of the dead guard on the ground to make his point.

The Empress nodded. Though she clearly wasn't used to taking orders from anyone, she actually seemed to be listening to the Chief, taking in what he said. Dare I say there was a genuine affection developing between the two.

The Empress turned to leave with the remainder of her guards. She took several steps before she thought the better of it and turned around.

"Doctor Templeton, thank you. For everything. Especially for bringing Nothon here to save my people."

My eyes must have gone as wide as dinner plates for a moment before I composed myself; it was probably best not to mention what had happened at the top of the Pyramid an hour or so earlier.

I shook my head, "Think nothing of it!"

I reached out a hand toward the Chief, "You're quite sure about this?"

The Chief nodded and took my hand in his own, "Whole-heartedly."

He pulled me in and embraced me in another big bear hug. This time, though, it was equal parts gratitude and the sadness that comes with knowing that this is almost certainly goodbye.

"Hey, you've got a time machine, right? Don't be a stranger."

Normally I would've lied to the Chief with an "I won't," but I respected him too much to verbalise such a blatant falsehood. Instead, I simply nodded my head and smiled.

"Goodbye, Your Highness. Safe travels."

I turned to head back to the ship. I only made it a few feet before the Chief called to me again.

"Doctor Templeton?"

"Yes?" I turned around.

The Chief threw his trident through the air in a high, deep arc.

Now, know that there was no malice behind the Chief's throw—he was simply trying to give me a going away present. But the simple matter was, it *was* a trident. It *was* sharp on the end.

So forgive me, dear reader, if I say that I shrieked a bit and took several harried steps back from the incoming weapon.

The Chief laughed as the trident hit the stone pavement with a clang, and came to rest next to me.

He nodded at it, "You might need that, and—" he pointed at the remaining guards, "—I've got plenty more. Good luck, Doctor Templeton."

"Good luck, Your Highness."

I picked up the trident and practically ran back on-board the ship. It wasn't that I was worried that *another* guard might prove themselves a traitor, or that Lemurians would start raining rubble on us any second, but I had had *quite* enough of Atlantis for several lifetimes.

Fortunately, when I arrived back on the ship and secured the gangway, a very welcome sight awaited:

Ricky Corcoran sat in his gunnery seat, taking deep gulps on a glass of Macallan 18-Year. As soon as he drained it, he held the empty glass out, and Bloomington dutifully refilled it. I didn't know if it was the effects of the medigel needing more toxins to "repair," or if he just wanted to get a bit pickled.

"My *God* Ricky, it's good to see you alive!"

I ran over and embraced the man whom I had wanted nothing more than to kill a few short days before.

"Owww! Fuck!" He sucked in a deep breath, "Watch the side god*damn* it!"

I practically jumped away from him.

"Sorry—" I rubbed the back of my head reflexively and took a deep breath, "—we just thought—"

"You were dead as *fuck!*" Bloomington kind of half-sobbed out the words. He went over and embraced Corcoran on his bad side.

Even though Corcoran gritted his teeth, he patted Bloomington on the back.

"There, there, Bloomy. Everything's gonna be okay…"

"I'm *so sorry!"* Now Bloomington was in full-on wails. Sanchez and I looked at each other, not in horror, but rather surprized to find each other smiling. We were just glad to have the big oaf back.

"And now *I* owe *you* one, I think," I breathed in deeply, "That rogue guard there surely would have crushed us all if he had even one more second on this earth."

Corcoran shook his head, "Don't mention it."

I shook my head right back at him, "No, truly—I want to make good on my promise."

Corcoran tilted his head to the side, with an "Is he serious?" expression on his face. He inhaled sharply.

"Okay. You wanna do something for me? Maybe if you write another little book, you could name it after me."

I nodded, "Done."

Truth be told, to that point, I hadn't even really considered doing a follow-up to my first book; the sales of the first one had proven quite dismal, and this ghostwriter was *extremely* difficult to work with.

"Oh and one more thing Doc—"

I nodded, "Anything. Name it."

Corcoran grinned, "I get to pick the music this time."

He thumbed through my tablet for several moments before he settled on "Hooked on a Feeling" by Blue Suede.

"Big *Guardians of the Galaxy* fan, are we?"

"Guardians of the *whatnow?*" Corcoran furrowed his brow and turned to Bloomington, "Is that one'a those nerdy movies you're always watching?"

Bloomington shook his head, "No. Never heard of it."

It was so hard for me to remember sometimes that Corcoran and Bloomington had come from 2012, before many of the Marvel Cinematic Universe movies had been released.

Though in a weird way, I envied them.

"You *haven't seen Guardians of the Galaxy?"* Sanchez and I said practically in unison.

Both Bloomington and Corcoran shrugged.

"I'll tell you what—" I nodded at my tablet in Corcoran's hands, "It's right there on that tablet. Why don't you two go watch *Guardians of the Galaxy* and some of the other… uh… 'new' Marvel movies, cough, cough, **Infinity War**, cough, cough—"

Sanchez nodded, eyes wide.

Corcoran offered his glass to me, "Need a nip, Doc? You know… for the cough?"

I gave him my best, most practised look of annoyance.

"And rest up, and I'll set us to get out of here post-haste."

Bloomington and Corcoran retired to the crew quarters, leaving Sophia, POLARIS and I to make the ship ready for our next time jump.

Both Sophia and I were utterly wiped out—we both had seemingly been through the ringer the past few days. So thankfully POLARIS was available to boss around (though perhaps somewhat more politely than Bloomington might), and after fixing itself once more, I was able to enlist its aid in making sure everything was "up-to-snuff" for the jump.

First thing was first though; we needed to get into space ASAP and get to a safe place, somewhere on the other side of the planet (or even solar system). I told POLARIS the parameters of our predicament, and it was able to calculate a spot outside of the blast radius of the solar flare. A few button presses later, and we were soaring through the sky, and back into space.

"Hooked on a Feeling" led to the rest of the *Guardians* soundtrack, and I found myself pleasantly upbeat and thankful for our situation. After all, it could be *quite* a bit worse than things had turned out. If "destruction of two advanced civilisations that few others would ever know existed" was the worst thing to happen, but we escaped with all of our crew… was it really all *that* bad?

I silenced the answer in my head a hundred times before I could fully form it.

When all systems were go, I flipped to the applicable page in Klaus's journal. The next time jump seemed oddly out of place, both for the time period and location:

23-12-1749, Paris, France: Count Your Blessings R.I.P.

Of course, being a student of classic literature, my mind immediately jumped to Dumas's *The Count of Monte Cristo.* But the time period wasn't right—that book took place in the early 19th century. Not to mention that it seemed rather unlikely that Gabe Marlow might catch a ride in a time machine simply to meet us there and receive the capstone base.

It *was* one of Klaus's favorite works though, to be sure; he especially enjoyed the turn-of-the-21st-century film starring Jim Caviezel and Guy Pearce.

"It's so much more upbeat, don't you think, Finny?" He said to me one night as we were working on drinks several years before.

One of Klaus's trademarks was his boundless enthusiasm. If you told him he had a day's worth of shovelling shit in front of him, he'd smile and get a gleam in those frosty blue eyes which, with his short-cropped grey hair and stubble, made him look like a wily young grandfather. He would simply nod and say that "at least it's not two days of shovelling shit!"

"I don't know, Klaus—there's something to be said for carefully-crafted revenge carried out to its natural ends."

At the time, Klaus waved a hand in front of his face, "So much hate Finny! And for what? Who has wronged you so badly in your career? You have a wonderful job, a fantastic lab, a generous benefactor—what's the matter?"

I took a draught of my scotch, "'What's the matter' is that I haven't received the faintest lick of recognition for any of it."

He raised an eyebrow, "You mean your work with… 'lasers and optics'?"

I nodded.

He frowned, "You know, I think we may be able to help each other out here one day. I can't say too much about it just yet… but I think there may be some parts to each of our work that are, how do you say? Complimentary?"

This caused *my* eyes to go wide, worried that perhaps I had said too much to Klaus already.

"Really? What do you mean?"

"Well, for one thing, I can see why you might need a cloaking device for whatever planes or vehicles you're working on. But… there might be another application where such a device would be far…

more… valuable…"

I didn't want to say anything, lest I give away the fact that I was working on a bloody time machine!

"Yes?" I asked, as innocently as I could.

"Indeed…" he said, and let the pause afterward hang in the air like an overloaded lead ballooon for several seconds. "I know you're working on something having to do with espoinage."

"Oh," I tried to mix in a heavy amount of worry to offset the ample relief in my reply.

"Blowing up nukes from behind enemy lines, or something like that, eh?"

I nodded and shrugged, "You got me!"

We had a good chuckle and segued into our favorite spy books and movies. Yet something stuck with me for the years since. It was the look that Klaus gave me after I had said, "You got me!"

It was a look of "Yes, I do… and not in the way you might think…"

The other side of this clue he had written was that Klaus enjoyed a good fiction as much as anyone. He would make up elaborate stories for his own entertainment, and for a scientist he was quite charismatic, and able to convince most people of these fanciful stories' veracity.

So I *hoped* that perhaps we would finally catch up with him, and this was all just some elaborate masquerade he had set up for his own amusement.

Though I still *prepared* myself for another intense, firefight-laden jump against God-*knows*-what kind of abomination. Perhaps it would be mermaids this time… or an army of elves riding pegasi.

Regardless, I was ready to jump if the QC was.

I keyed the coordinates into the QC. Unfortunately, instead of the "99.9%" probability of success icon I was accustomed to, there was instead a graphic for "WARNING: Time Jump Parameters Changed. Execute additional payload checklist before jumping."

"Lousy buggar," I practically spat the words at the QC. "POLARIS? I have another checklist for you…"

It took the robot an astonishing two hours to work its way through the "Additional Payload Checklist." I suppose it made sense—though the capstone base didn't have any mass of its own *per se* at the moment, the geometry of the ship might require a different-sized wormhole, which in turn could affect the energy output required, along with how the gravity drive operated within the earth's gravity well.

If even *one* of the parameters was slightly out-of-whack, it could spell disaster for the entire mission and crew.

All the while, I made sure that we were in a stationary orbit on the far side of the planet per POLARIS's caluclations—the absolute *last* thing I wanted was for the massive solar flare that was brewing to sneak up on us and fry our electrical systems. And while it was likely big enough that the planet might not even provide full refuge, it might give us a little more time with which to work.

That made the work quite dark, and more thankless than ever. Sophia was a great help as well, don't get me wrong—but we both were kind of "punch drunk" with fatigue, and made several errors we normally wouldn't.

Thankfully, POLARIS caught them. I honestly didn't know where we'd be without the grotesque robot. What a find by Bloomington—I'd have to ask him who added it to the loadout for this mission and get them a scotch on me.

We were finally ready to go.

I asked the computer how far away the solar flare was, just for kicks.

"Solar flare approaching in 3 hours, 57 minutes, 26 seconds," it flashed on a screen.

My God! Had we been working for 18 hours on this already? No wonder Sophia and I were beat—we were beyond what any human should be asked to do.

I pulled up the coordinates for our next jump. The QC's output for the probability of success was somewhat less than reassuring:

82.6%

"Computer, *why* are we so far off on our chances of success?"

The computer listed off a long list of variables it couldn't fully account for.

"How long will it take to get the chance of success above 90%"

The computer crunched the numbers for several seconds.

5 days, 14 hours, 23 minutes, and 6 seconds.

I pounded the console, then hit the QC panel with my fist.

"Damn you!"

Ouch! the QC output on its screen.

"I mean, " I took a deep breath, "I'm sorry. This is the best we can do before the solar flare hits?"

The QC was fast in its reply, "Yes."

I nodded, "Very well. Bring up the coordinates screen again."

The QC showed the picture of the planet, as well as the coordinates and time we were jumping to.

The big green "Engage" button flashed on the screen.

I didn't hesitate to hit it.

The ship flew to a safe distance away from the planet and spun up the tunneling lasers. Within seconds, we were in the familiar confines of the wormhole.

The ship began to shake almost immediately as we entered the time vortex. It started as mere turbulence, and reflexively my fingernails dug into the soft armrest of the command chair.

Then the shaking became more violent, and less predictable. Sanchez strapped into her chair, and POLARIS literally dug its feet into the bulkhead of the ship. I was reminded of my initial trip back to dinosaur times, when the then newly-comissioned time machine was pushed to its limit by a jump of some 65,000,000-plus years.

Now though, it apparently strained under the size of the capstone base above it. Perhaps the Atlantean graviton waves were starting to lose their potency. Or maybe the wormhole had its own gravity well, which now pulled at the capstone base through the ship, daring to crunch it like an aluminum can under a well-heeled boot.

I was quite sure that when I had designed the time machine, "piggybacking hundred-tonne pieces of limestone-plus-God-knows-what on top" was *not* in the machine's specifications.

Nonetheless, the old girl soldiered on. A bolt from the side of the ship flew loose. Then another. I was convinced that it was only a matter of seconds until we were all floating in space, satellites long before people below would know what that would even mean.

Finally, just when I thought the time machine couldn't take anymore… the shaking stopped, and the ship emerged from the wormhole.

"Damage report!" I bellowed. I wasn't quite sure what I expected the QC or POLARIS to come up with, but it sounded like something Jean-Luc Picard might say, and I wanted to maintain the appearance of control given the bowel-emptying levels of uncertainty we had just experienced.

"Structural integrity 86.7%" the QC flashed up on the screen.

"Any chance of hull breach? Or other major problems?" I asked, my voice tremulous.

"Negative," the screen flashed.

I allowed my neck to relax and looked up at the ceiling of the ship. I puffed out a long, loud breath—it was like releasing a pressure valve for about 15% of the tension throbbing through my head and neck.

"POLARIS, can you start fixing the ship?"

"Yessssss Masssssterrr."

"Wonderfuuu—," I said. I think I passed out before I could even finish the word.

CHAPTER TWENTY-FIVE

I awoke to the wonderful smell of eggs and bacon wafting in from the kitchenette.

I quickly rubbed the sleep out of my eyes, unstrapped myself, and walked over to the source of the delightful smell.

There, clad in aprons (where the *devil* did they find those?) were Sanchez and Bloomington.

"Hey Doc!" Sophia was about as cheery as I had seen her.

"Turdmonkey! Broke *another* yolk!" Bloomington chided himself.

I made an overly theatrical sniff at the air, "My, smells wonderful! My compliments to the chef. Is this… what you two do when you're not hunting Nazis? Or whatever it is you do normally?"

They looked at each other, grinned, and chuckled too cheerily, like a couple of morning talk show anchors.

"By the way Doc, you weren't kidding about that *Guardians of the Galaxy* movie—it was the *tits!*"

I don't know if Steven noticed how Sophia's expression changed on a dime to her usual, "mildly annoyed" self.

I still couldn't help myself, "Indeed! I only wish I could go back and watch them again for the first time…"

He ignored the comment, "And *Infinity War?* Totally *did not* see that coming! And how they ended it in *Endgame*—I mean—"

"Spoiler alert, Steven," I looked at Sophia.

"What? I saw those movies bunches of times back in the day," Sanchez shook her head.

That was all the green light that Steven and I needed. We spent the next twenty minutes gushing about the various Marvel films Bloomington had apparently binge-watched through the turbulence and night.

How long was *I asleep?* I wondered.

At a lull in the conversation, I decided it was time to change the subject.

"Where's Ricky?"

Sanchez shrugged, "I saw him a few hours ago. He grabbed a couple of bottles of scotch out of the pantry, and grumbled back to his bunk."

I frowned and my eyes went wide, "Yes, well… that medigel-induced toxicity *can* really do a number on people." I poured myself a nip from one of the opened bottles on the table and guzzled it down greedily—I needed it after the previous evening's theatrics.

"Uh-*huh,*" Sanchez rolled her eyes.

A pregnant pause hung in the air for several moments.

"I say, POLARIS—damage report?"

"Ssssyssssstemsssss at 97.8% and risssssing…"

"And the capstone base? Will it crush us when we re-enter?"

"Neggggativvvve."

"Good show! Excellent work old boy!" I don't know why exactly I was playing up my Britishness at that particular moment, but it just felt *right* in the then-and-there.

I heard the *WHOOSH* of the crew quarters open, and Commander Corcoran came struggling out of his bunk.

"God *damn* it…" he felt his forehead, "…I feel like one'a Bloomy's *shits.*"

"That bad, huh?" Steven asked, completely serious.

"Maybe third bottle of scotch will be the charm," Sophia deadpanned.

Corcoran narrowed his eyes at her, "You know what? Why don't *you* try dyin' and comin' back to life real slow-like, with medigel, and cravin' booze that your body is usin' to make you feel even *more* like shit."

"Rain check?" Sophia didn't skip a beat.

"That's what I thought."

"How *are* you feeling, Ricky? Getting *any* better?" I decided to offer an olive branch.

He shrugged, "Ribs still hurt like a motherfucker. One'a them feels like it's made outta cartilage. Maybe some other organs moved around to places they shouldn't be… but other than that—" he affected an overbroad smile, "—I'm just peachy."

I nodded, "Glad to hear it." I hoped my tone conveyed how deadly serious I was. I felt like Ricky had repaid me in spades and then some.

By this point, the ship had put us into a geosynchronous orbit with our destination coordinates. Honestly, I could've used another couple of days of rest and relaxation after our ordeal in Atlantis, but I was absolutely *convinced* that Klaus awaited us below. And while I had a million questions for him, more than anything else, I was curious.

Curious about *why* he'd done everything he had. Curious about his goals. Curious about what he wanted to accomplish. After all, there wasn't much he could do to change the past. So why steal a Chronosaber time machine in the first place?

The questions tickled my mind as I showered and changed into era-appropriate clothing: the QC had pulled a sort of three-piece suit, made out of a luxurious blue silk-like material. Gold piping adorned the sleeves and edges, and an oversized blue coat completed the ensemble. It felt surprisingly comfortable, though the long white socks were a bit much for my liking.

Corcoran and Bloomington had similar ensembles. Sophia had a rather elaborate dress made of red silk with gold patterning on it. It was fashioned as a rather hoop-skirt-like apparatus, though thankfully modern technology (or at least "future technology") had made it much easier to put it on.

Still, she was unable to zip up the back by herself.

"Can someone help me get into this?" She asked.

"I'd rather help you get out of it," Corcoran said with a chuckle.

She glared at him, though in a sort of "mock-perturbed" way with a sly smile underneath.

He zipped her up.

"Now for the important part," she said, raiding the armory with the zeal of a polar bear searching for a seal pup.

"Yeah I was wondering when you'd get back into the guns Sophie," Bloomington said. "When you were talking about hunting Nazi's back there, it was like I had asked Marie—"

Sanchez held up a hand, "Stop. Just stop—whatever disgusting thing you're about to say? You probably shouldn't say it, okay?"

Bloomington thought for a second, then opened his mouth anyway.

"Nope," Sanchez said without looking at him.

He looked down one more time. He raised a finger and prepared to speak again.

"Not a chance," Sanchez had found a scoped rifle and was sighting it.

Bloomington waddled away.

"Thank you," I whispered to her.

"Don't mention it," she said.

As we appraoched the planet, I was actually thankful to see all of the usual continents back where they "belonged;" Atlantis was long gone.

Yet at the same time, I couldn't help but think what a tragedy it all was. Maybe the Chief helped preserve the human race. Or maybe he saved thousands of people.

But when you're talking about a civilisation-destroying event, one that likely affected millions and millions of people, it was tough to feel anything but a sinking pit in one's stomach. That was especially true when I bore at least some (and maybe all) of the responsibility for doing so.

Fortunately, I hoped I would soon have the opportunity to see exactly what Klaus was up to, and to ask him if it was all worth it.

We approached Paris for the second time ever in the time machine. I asked POLARIS and the QC to try to track Klaus from above, much like we had the Empress in Atlantis, but there were far too many people scattered about for that to be effective. Not only that, but Klaus could have very well been indoors, and we would have been none the wiser.

Suddenly, Sophia's eyes went bright.

"Computer, can you track any gravimetric distortions or particle traces from the past several days?"

My eyes went wide for a moment—I suppose to a scientist seeing someone say something like that was akin to what Sophia felt when describing all of the various weapons and ways she and Steven had mowed down Nazis in the past.

"An old trick from my Chronosaber days," she said.

"I thought you were still in their employ?" I arched an eyebrow.

She scrunched up her face and shook her head, "Of course. It's just... easy to forget sometimes when you have a crew like this!"

Her feigned excitement far from sold me.

The QC made quick work of the scan, and it led us to a large field directly below the curved "arch" of the Seine.

"Very well—follow that trail to a close landing spot," I thought for a moment, "And by all means, *do* engage the cloaking device!"

I hoped that the modifications had been successful in cloaking the capstone base as well.

We continued to soar over mid-18th century Paris. The differences between World War II-era Nazi-occupied France and the current city were stark and immediately apparent. Though buildings were shorter and streets paved with stones or not at all, there was more *life* in the city—more *vibrance*—even at the lofty heights from which we viewed it.

Maybe it was the flickering lamps that dotted the streets instead of the electric lights I was used to.

Or maybe it was being under the yoke of a different tyrant than Adolf Hitler; in this case, the King of France (Louis the XV, if I wasn't mistaken).

More than anything, what stood out was the lack of the Eiffel Tower. In fact, as we approached the city, it became increasingly clear that we were set to land exactly where *La Tour Eiffel* was to be built at the end of the green space!

Knowing Klaus, he had done it on purpose just to get a rise out of me.

"POLARIS, you stay on-board and make the remaining repairs," I ordered.

"Yesssssss Masssssterrrr," it croaked.

"The rest of you, with me. Sophia, is there any way—"

She nodded, "I've already modified my tablet to pick up on the gravimetric particles that Dr. Thurbur's body would have absorbed in transit. We should be able to track him the same way we tracked the ship."

"Very good. Splendid, in fact!" I could've hugged her, though I thought the better of it—one never knew how Sophia Sanchez would respond to physical contact.

I ordered the ship to lower the gangway, and we walked out into the large knoll, perhaps the most heavily-armed dandies *Gay Parie* had ever seen.

It was a somewhat different scene than you might expect: the vast tract of land was filled with rotting little vegetable plots that appeared poorly tended-to, even factoring in that we were in the winter months. Large houses clustered around the wide-open park. Most of them were quite grand in their own way, though some had been left to dilapidate. The subtle flicker of candlelight danced in many of the windows, giving off a rather calm, peaceful, and dare I say "romantic" vibe.

Oh how I wished Cynthia could join me here! The places we'd go—the adventures we'd have!

And yet… I couldn't for the life of me see how it would ever be possible. Still, if my travels through time had taught me anything, it was to expect the completely unexpected again and again.

Sanchez held her tablet out in front of her and led the way. We approached one of the "sides" of the park, and in particular, one very tony house. It was wonderfully French stone-work, with a turret and grey tiled roof atop it. I wondered how long it took craftsmen of the era to fashion it—especially since a couple of Atlantean teenagers could probably whip it up in a couple of days.

A man with a long French face and protruding nose stood outside of the doorway. His powdered wig and impeccable posture gave off the distinct impression that even though he was not nobility himself, he had been surrounded and influenced by it his entire life.

He had a rather large, leather-bound book opened up to the middle that he stared at as if it was a crystal ball, and he, a fortune teller.

"Name?" He asked curtly, without looking up.

"The Doctor Phineas Templeton party," I replied.

The man snorted. "New money…" I thought I heard him mumble under his breath.

"The *fuck* you say?" Corcoran asked.

"Templeton… Templeton…" he ignored the Commander too as he continued to thumb through pages, which I thought might be at his own peril.

Suddenly, his expression brightened.

"Ah yes! Phineas and party! Sir, you are on the Count's personal invite list. And I have been instructed to treat you like no less than the Count Himself. Please, please—do come in!"

He finally looked up from his book and saw the hulking, rough-around-the-edges monster he had just ignored, and his eyes went wide with fear.

Corcoran snorted his approval at the tiny Past-ie's reaction. He decided to have a little fun, and made an aggressive fake "bite" through the air at him.

"Right this way… right this way!" the worry crept into the man's voice as he led us inside.

It was all the rest of us could do to keep straight faces.

We walked down a rather gaudily-wallpapered hall to a large room. It was painted dark—purple perhaps? Though tough to tell in the muted candlelight—and contained high ceilings and one large, round table in the middle. Various chairs and couches dotted the sides, and a cloud of smoke wafted up toward the soot-stained ceiling.

Inside, a small crowd gathered—maybe a half-dozen people. Shockingly, among them were two women. I say "shockingly" because it appeared by all accounts that these women were being included in the discussion, and being treated as equals by the men in the salon. It was thoroughly refreshing, and dare I say the most "modern" I'd felt in all of history.

Not to bury the lede, but sitting at the table, on a large, gold-leafed, honest-to-God *throne,* was Klaus Thurbur.

His eyes met mine and instantly caught a flicker of candlelight.

"Now, what were we discussing? Oh yes—the ether that propogates the heavens and holds the spheres above," he said to the rapt crowd. It was dark in the room, but I could've sworn he winked at me.

"But Your Grace, with all due respect, how can you be *so* certain that this fluid, this *ether*, so exists?"

"Because Francois, my good man, I have met Jesus Christ *himself!* And he of all people should know what keeps the stars in the sky, and the spheres in place."

Half of the guests tried to mute their chuckles, while the other half scoffed.

"*You* met *Jesus Christ?*" one particularly short and stocky mustachioed Frenchman asked.

"Indeed I did," Klaus was grinning like an idiot.

"So tell me then, Your Grace," the man punctuated the statement with more than a little sarcasm, "What is 'Jesus' like?"

"Oh, he's very kind, very kind," Klaus was really hamming it up now, "Gentle… and fun-loving. Into… uh… 'exotic plants.'"

The guests all raised eyebrows.

"For their… medicinal properties. It's one of the ways he healed the sick after all—" Klaus feigned looking at us standing in the doorway once more, "—My guests have finally arrived… late as usual," his German accent sharpened the words, though his good nature ensured they remained largely benign.

He turned to his guests, "Ladies and Gentlemen, we shall continue this another time perhaps. Although," he looked at each of us in turn, and was visibly taken aback when he got to Bloomington's hollowed-out, formerly pudgy face, "I may be taking a rather long trip in short order. So if this is truly goodbye, then I say to you a hearty and meaningful, 'good bye.'"

The guests all bid their farewells and adieus, though the mustachioed man tried to re-engage Klaus in the debate, he politely and deftly declined to do so. Once they were all gone, Klaus nodded at the long-faced man who had let us in, and he closed the door behind him.

He sprung out of his throne and practically sprinted across the room at me.

"My dear Finny, it's been too long!" He extended a hand and held the other out for an embrace. I smiled and gladly accepted, though I got a nasty static electricity shock when we shook hands, perhaps from the extremely plush carpet underfoot.

"We keep missing each other," I said with a chuckle. He held the embrace for a couple of seconds, and then disengaged so we were face-to-face.

"How are you, old chap?"

"Fine, fine," he beamed. "Entertaining myself by trolling 18th

century French nobles in my little salon."

"Yes, it's *quite* the operation you have here," I nodded at the door and the long-faced man who had just closed it.

"I *thought* you'd like that, especially with Commander Corcoran in tow! What an honor!"

He made his way over to the Commander and vigorously shook his hand. Corcoran smiled a sly grin and gave Klaus a firm (if under-powered by the Commander's standards) handshake in return.

"Nice to meet you too, Gerry!" Corcoran said.

Klaus chuckled, "American military—charming as ever… And you must be…" he cocked his head as he made his way over to Sanchez, "The lovely Captain Sanchez of Chronosaber?" He took her hand and gave it a long, lingering kiss. "Very charmed."

"I wish I could say the same, Doctor Thurbur. You have something that belongs to us."

Klaus blew out a loud raspberry.

"Belongs? To *you*? We can talk more about that in a minute—I assure you that the only thing that rightfully 'belongs' to that *hag* Helene is a sharp wit, love of money, and a sadistic streak that would make Hannibal Lecter cringe."

Klaus looked over at Bloomington and the German's eyes went wide again once more, presumably with disgust. He brushed back his (much longer than I remembered) hair, and let out a huff.

"Now, I know you're all wondering what the hell I'm doing here, and—"

Bloomington scrunched up his face and stuck out a clammy hand.

"Steve Bloomington. Nice to meet you Klaus!"

Klaus eyed Bloomington's hand for a moment before putting his hands firmly at his sides.

"Great!" he forced a curt smile at him before turning back to us. "I know you're all wondering what the hell I'm doing here, and all will be explained in due time. I apologize for all of the theatrics and hoops I made you jump through with that scavenger hunt, but given your shared experience together, it was the only way I could be sure that Helene would be on-board sending *you all*—and *you all* specifically—back to find me."

We looked at each other skeptically.

"And *that* is why I've come back as the Count of St. Germain!"

Of course! I should have known as soon as I heard the name of the time machine he stole.

"Don't tell me that's the reason you stole *this particular* time machine?" I asked.

He grinned and shrugged.

Sanchez, Corcoran, and Bloomington looked at me as if I was speaking Atlantean.

I rolled my eyes, "The Count of St. Germain was a charming, mysterious nobleman who paraded around Europe making *outlandish* claims about living for thousands of years, meeting historical figures, the future, etc. I fear that Klaus here simply couldn't resist the opportunity to come back and have a little fun at the expense of some unsuspecting Past-ies."

He nodded, "Quite right, Finny! But only partially so. You see, part of my voyage of course was to toy with some of these simple folk I might meet along the way. And I always had this as a sort of 'endpoint' for the journey, where we could all meet up and get down to *the real* business at hand—"

"Which is?" Corcoran interjected.

"*That* is what I am about to tell you, my good Commander. Please, everyone have a seat at the table..."

CHAPTER TWENTY-SIX

"Let us start with Chronosaber," Klaus said. "As unpleasant as Helene may be, it's undeniable that they have quite the lucrative racket going on. Shuttling wealthy time-travelers this way and that—it's turned them into a multi-hundred-thousand Bitcoin company."

Sophia and I nodded. Bloomington and Corcoran looked at each other, puzzled.

Klaus arched an eyebrow and continued, "But what if that's *not* the way things are supposed to be? What if Helene found a way to exploit a loophole in the universe, one that never should have been opened," he looked square at me, and I flinched backwards, "And one that we can repair *right... now?"*

"How in the sam *fuck* is that possible?" Corcoran asked.

"Yeah, great story Dr. Thurbur, but there's only one problem," Sophia said, "You can't change the past!"

I nodded, "And Klaus, by now you of *all* people should know that firsthand. Even if you hadn't travelled through time before, now you have. You've *seen* how utterly impossible it is. How bloody *fixed* everything is. No going back to change history, no saving ones you've loved..." I let my voice trail off, choking back a stuttering sob.

Klaus put his arm around me and beamed, "There there, Finny. Not to worry. And yes, I admit, that is 'the way things are,' given the current time travel technology we have."

This brought me out of my funk and perked up an ear, "Whatever do you *mean?"*

Klaus was on a roll now—his curiosity was infectious and his enthusiasm radiated throughout the dimly lit room.

"Finny, your time travel technology uses tunneling lasers to stir up spacetime, and then break it apart to make a wormhole, right?"

"Well..." I looked around at the audience and thought the better of having a long argument about the finer points, "...there is *slightly* more to it than that, but yes, those are the broad strokes."

"Did you ever ask yourself how that time rip is repaired? How it resolves itself?"

I felt a bit stupid, "Well... no. I can't rightly say I did."

Klaus nodded, "Okay! Good! It is my hypothesis that the *reason* that you can't change things through time travel is that somehow, spacetime, the universe, whatever you want to call it, its number one job is to repair these rips in space time that have been so casually left by you, me, and every other fat slob time traveler who decides to take a trip into the past or future."

I looked at Sanchez; she was deep in thought. Corcoran leaned in skeptically, while Bloomington for once appeared to be conteplating something other than grabbing a snack from his nostril.

"When whatever this mechanism is makes these repairs, it seeks to repair the entire timeline, and keep things 'the way they were.' Therefore, you cannot change the past when you go back in time through this mechanism."

We all pondered the statement for several moments.

"Yeah, that's all well-and-good," Sanchez said, "But Dr. Thurbur, forgive me, I've traveled *extensively* through time. Shit, I ran a dinosaur safari base for asshole tourists," she looked over at me, and I nodded, not recognizing that she may be indicating that I was the very kind of arsehole tourist of which she was complaining, "And the fundamental paradox still remains—*if* you can change the past, *then* you could start a series of events that cascaded and resulted in you never *existing* in the first place."

"Yes, yes! Thank you Captain Sanchez—right on cue!" he stuck a finger in the air. He turned to Bloomington as if he was explaining things to a small child. "The idea is, if young Finny here went back to meet Jesus, he steps on a rock, somehow stepping on that rock makes it so that Finny's mom and dad never meet and never had him, so how can he then come back in time to kick the rock if he never existed in the first place, correct?"

"Exactly," Sanchez nodded.

"I'm getting there… and I have a theory. But to be perfectly honest, I won't be perfectly sure until we can *test* the theory."

"So what's your theory?" Corcoran asked.

"What? About the true nature of time? Or an alternative means of time travel?"

I opened my mouth to speak, but as he so often does Klaus filled the void with words.

"I suppose they are one and the same," he said, eyes upward in thought. Klaus looked around and took a deep breath.

"As you may know, I am a specialist in the field of optics."

We looked around the room and nodded at one another.

"And Finny, I helped you design the cloaking device for the time machine, correct?"

I nodded. I did mention that earlier, dear reader, did I not?

"Indeed. It was *brilliant* work. Simply brilliant."

"Thank you," he took a minor bow. "*But*, it is not the whole picture! The cloaking device works by bending light *around* the time machine. Light bends enough, past the index of refraction, voila! No more time machine can be seen! Still gotcha?"

We all nodded again.

"But what if space-time was no different than light? What if it could be bent far enough so that you bend and bend and bend, and then," he clapped his hands and then extended them out wide, "It snaps back. No repairs to space-time needed. "

It took me only a moment to realize the full gravity of what Klaus had just described.

"A *time cloak?*" I was incredulous.

Klaus nodded, "By my calculations, with enough power, you can," he made a wrenching hand motion, "bend and wring space-time without ripping it. *And*, more importantly, I *think* you can do it in a way that you *can* change the past."

The room went dead silent. Somewhere in the house, a dog barked three times in rapid succession.

"Ah—Archimedes!" he clapped three times in rapid succession. The door opened, and the tank-like, oversized shih tzu ran through the door. He went over to Klaus and gave him a couple quick licks, and then ran straight over to me, jumped on the vacant chair next to me, and pawed at me for pets.

"Hey boy! Been a while!" I said as I ruffled his soft fur. Truth be told, there was something metatative about it—petting the dog gave me time for my brain to rapidly process all of this new information.

"Great! So why the *fuck* did we have to go through Egypt, those fuckin' aliens, and honest-to-*God* Atlantis? Why not just make the fuckin' thing, travel back, do what you wanna do, and bam! You're done?"

He wagged a finger at Corcoran, "Ah, but my dear Commander, that's the problem—there is no way to create enough energy to bend space and time to that extent, even some 70 years into the future! Or at least, I thought there wasn't…"

We all leaned in now, on the edge of our seats. Even Archimedes was listening to his master.

"One day, in my office, I received a very peculiar package from an anonymous source. There was no return address, no note, no nothing, just four things in there.

"The first was labeled 'True Schematic of the Great Pyramid of Giza.' It contained all of the rooms with which you are now familiar, including the capstone platform, and several others that are hidden that you may not have found. It was extensively and professionally labeled, and looked like the real deal.

"The second was an old-fashioned photograph of a stone that had 'Discovered 2089 - 10-5-9203' and some coordinates on it—those turned out to lead me to the village of your friend, Chief Octoc. On the upper half, it had Atlantean script, and on the lower half, it had an ancient language that resembled Aramaic. Using this, with a little work, and perhaps a trip or two to visit Trent Albertson in Ancient Judea, I could translate Atlantean into German or English via Ancient Aramaic."

My eyes bulged into saucers. *Maybe Trent Albertson isn't quite the dumb patsy that he seems?*

"Of course, Albertson was as big of a doofus as you've seen, so that plan was mucked up. But I had a backup plan—a little more on that in a minute."

I nodded, sufficiently satisfied that Trent Albertson *was*, in fact, entirely the dumb patsy that he seems.

"The third was a treasure map—honest to goodness—leading to an underground chamber in the Giza province back in Atlantean times. It had a short description of what would be found: 'Pyramid's True Capstone - Damaged,' and some calculations about the energy output it could achieve if activated. Plus a date, which, as you can guess, is very close to the one I gave you for Atlantis.

"And finally, the fourth was a flash drive, and on it was a short news video about a Marlow Aerospace mission capturing a rare asteroid with ruby crystal inside, and bringing a rather large sample back to their facility outside of Cairo, Egypt, for further study."

"Marlow…" Corcoran struggled with the name, trying to place it.

"The disheveled, mustachioed fellow who met us at my laboratory in 2032 after we dispatched those odious Nazis in Leipzig," I said. "So you think Marlow is behind this whole thing? Hence the rather cryptic wholesome limericks in your secret journal imploring me to bring the capstone base back with me to his time period."

Klaus nodded, "Precisely, my dear Fin. Precisely! Putting it all together, I came up with my plan: One, investigate the Great Pyramid to ensure that the structure was as the schematic said it was. I did this with that lovely Egyptologist Miss Hess and that old mule Ms. Amaranth."

I couldn't help but chuckle at the comparison, and neither could the others; Sanchez practically let out a loud guffaw.

"And it was as it should be. Two: since Albertson was of little help deciphering the Atlantean script, I made the supposition that the date and coordinates on the Atlantean stone picture might lead me to someone who could help decipher it. And, again, I was proven correct. It took more than a little back-and-forth, but your friend the Chief was an excellent teacher of the Atlantean language. And, for his trouble, he got exactly what he bargained for: the ability to soar through the skies like a bird, albeit with your crew instead of mine.

"Three: once I was able to speak and translate Atlantean, I needed to actually go get the capstone. But again a problem: it was allegedly damaged! So I needed to find a way to either repair it, or make a new one. So I traded access to the hidden chamber for the actual top red crystal capstone itself, damaged as it may be, and did a detailed scan of that damaged true capstone, how it was put together, et cetera and so forth, so that I could fabricate it at a later date. And wrote up those rather distasteful *clean* limericks in that journal to lead you to *exactly* what needed to be done, Finny."

I nodded, somewhat more gravely than intended.

"You just assumed Atlantis *wouldn't* use the true capstone to destroy Lemuria?" Sanchez asked.

Klaus smirked, "I assumed nothing, my dear. Some of this I had to play by ear, some of it I divined by speaking to that guard, Birusha for example. She sought you out, correct? How is she doing?"

"She's… uh… rather dead, I'm afraid," I said.

"Yes, yes, I know, but—" he blanched for a moment, "Oh. You mean the time of troubles…"

I put a finger to my lips in thought, "Well… not exactly…" I decided to change the subject just a bit, "Though that does raise an interesting point: how the *devil* could you—or we—all of us—condemn an entire civilization—*two* whole *advanced* civilizations—to *extinction?!"*

"We condemned nothing!" Klaus shot back, his temper rising as I had rarely seen it before. "If we're successful now, with this next phase of the plan, then perhaps we change the timeline and they need not suffer at all!"

I thought for a moment—it actually made a bit of sense.

He smiled to calm himself down, "So seeing as how the true capstone was damaged, and would likely malfunction or be destroyed when sufficiently charged with energy, I decided a fourth step was needed: use the scan I had made in Atlantis with the red crystal that Marlow Aerospace brought back to craft another true capstone. A true capstone that would be structurally sound... and powerful enough to harness the *real* power of the Great Pyramid to power up my greatest invention: the time cloak!"

"So you think this guy, Marlow, is in on it somehow?" Corcoran asked.

Klaus allowed himself a thin smile, "My dear Commander, that is *exactly* what I think. I think he's trying to do some kind of 'end around' on Helene. He certainly does not seem to care for her, that's for *sure."*

"But how the *devil* would he know what you were working on, Klaus?" I said. "I mean, no offense, but it wasn't exactly like you were broadcasting the fact that you were working on a time cloak to all comers..."

Klaus stroked his chin, *"That* is the multi-trillion dollar question, isn't it, Fin? All I can say for now is I have no idea *how* Marlow learned of my work, nor *how* he acquired these materials, nor *how* he was able to smuggle them to me. But the simple fact of the matter is... he apparently did! And now, it is up to *us* to unpack his true motivations."

"So you *don't* know for sure that Marlow *is* in on it then?" I asked.

Klaus stroked his bearded chin and gave me a mischievous grin, "No. No I suppose I don't."

"And I take it you don't know what side he's on either?" Corcoran asked.

To this, Klaus nodded vigorously.

"Actually of *that*, I'm quite certain. Marlow is certainly no fan of

Helene. And by ponying up the financial support for this trip, he'd assemble the only team capable of taking down her entire time-travel empire. So at best, he's a kind-hearted billionaire doing 'the right thing' for humanity by getting rid of one of history's greatest monsters. At worst, it's an 'enemy of my enemy is my friend' situation. Either way, I am quite sure he is on our side. And let's say I'm about 80% sure that he's the one who sent the package to me."

My mind raced. Klaus's explanation *seemed* rational, logical, and well-thought-out. But that was the problem with someone as naturally charming and charismatic as Klaus—he *always* presented his ideas in such a persuasive manner, even when he knew he was dead wrong, or just outright fucking with people.

Sophia drummed her fingers on the table to break the silence.

"So what's your ultimate goal then?"

"Pardon?" Klaus was caught partially off-guard.

"Why do you want to use the time cloak? What's your goal?"

Klaus smiled, "Of course my dear! Of course—*why* do we need this time cloak? What shall we do with it? Well, I'm glad you asked…"

He sucked in a deep breath.

"I want to go back in time and stop this time travel madness from happening in the first place."

"And you think that will 'make things right?' All this crazy shit we've been through—it'll be okay then?" Corcoran asked.

"Well," Klaus gauged our reactions thus far, "Not exactly. We would need to go to several points in time, and at each one, there's a catch."

"Of *course* there is," I rolled my eyes ever-so-briefly.

"You see, changing the timeline could only occur in a very limited period of time. Like when a rubber band is snapped, and it goes backward, and then forward beyond the point at which it originated, and then settles. We would do the same thing, to bend space time, and it would bend, then snap, then settle. It's this brief period between the snap, and the settle that we'd be beyond the 'index of refraction' of the universe, and able to change the timeline."

"Okay. Beautiful," Corcoran nodded. "So we work quick then."

"I suppose I should say *two* catches," Klaus stroked his chin. "Because once the universe catches up, and the timeline is changed, that will set that 'butterfly effect' in motion. It'll kick the proverbial rock when visiting Jesus. So if we're back in time, and we change the timeline to where one of us isn't born? Not only won't that person exist… but everyone else will have *no recollection* of that person *ever* existing.

"If, say, Bloomington over here—" he extended an open palm at Steven, "—went away, then probably no one would notice anyway. But Commander Corcoran? Or me? Or Finny? Those are *major* changes to the timeline. And if Finny wouldn't exist, then dare I say the mission would end right then-and-there, since the time machine would no longer exist, and we'd all be blinked out of existence as we know it."

He paused for several seconds to let what he was saying roll over us.

"So we'll just—*poof*? Gone?" Corcoran asked.

"Maybe. It's a strong possibility," Klaus said.

"Like the *rapture?*" Bloomington asked too seriously.

Klaus rolled his eyes, "Yes, exactly like the rapture."

"Cool!" Bloomington's eyes went wide.

I shook off his ridiculousness, "So *why* should we risk everything to do this, again? I don't mean to speak for everyone, but I rather prefer existing to… not."

"Because this universe is *wrong*. Because Helene shouldn't control it—" he looked at Sanchez, "—no offense."

She shook her head, "None taken."

"Because we might be doing irreparable harm to the fabric of spacetime itself. If thousands of time travelers each make a little rip in the fabric of spacetime, time-and-time again, what becomes of spacetime after all those rips? Have we stopped to ask ourselves? I surely have *not*."

His expression darkened, "And we must know that our reality—*this* reality—likely *is not* the real reality!"

Corcoran knocked twice on the table, "Seems pretty fuckin' real to me."

Klaus laughed, "Delightful Herr Commander. Simply delightful," he clapped his hands together and continued, "It is *a* reality, but not *the* reality. We are in a very precarious position here; time doesn't change on a micro-level. And yet on a macro, big-picture level, perhaps it does.

It's the *only* outcome that makes logical sense: *this* kind of time travel should not be possible. But we—or *you*, I should say," he nodded at me, "found a loophole. And it's precisely *because* the universe doesn't allow any single event to change that our entire timeline has been irreparably damaged."

That one even hurt *my* head. Though I thought I knew what Klaus was getting at.

"So you're saying that theoretically, time travel *should only* be possible via your 'time cloak,' bending spacetime solution. Which does allow for *some* changing of the timeline. But, it should *not* be possible via my 'tearing' method, which forces us into a static, unchanging timeline that *never* was supposed to happen in the first place?"

"Correct!" Klaus was getting excited. "Good for you, Finny!"

"My head fucking hurts," Corcoran shook said head and banged it on the table.

"I just want to put things back the way they were without time travel. Or at least this barbaric form of time travel. No more Chronosaber. No more *Helene*," Klaus spat the word out. "And maybe, just maybe, we can right some very real *wrongs* along the way."

We looked at one another. I can't imagine that *any* of us were thrilled with the current state of our lives, and how the current time travel scheme had affected them... with two notable exceptions.

I nodded at Sanchez and Corcoran, "What do you two think? You probably have the most to lose out of all of us."

"Finny, I ask you not to take any one person's thoughts or feelings into account over those—"

I cut him off, "Klaus, if you're going to ask us to make this big of a shift—a *life-changing* shift for all of us, in the truest sense of the word, where the very question of *existence* is at stake? I think that requires some input from everyone."

I went around the table, and all present nodded. Even Archimedes gave a bob of his head.

"Very well then—Commander?"

"Well... I mean I love layin' on the beach and fuckin' hot chicks as much as anyone," he scratched his chin. "But I did plenty of hangin' out on the beach and bangin' hot chicks *before* all this time-travel shit. Ladies love the SEALs," he raised an eyebrow at Sanchez, and she shook her head in disgust, "So I'm all for it if you think it'll put things the way they're supposed'ta be."

Sanchez composed herself and looked at each of us in turn, "I'm not gonna sugar-coat it: you all think I'm one of Helene's loyal footsoldiers, right?"

Corcoran, Bloomington, and Klaus all practically *screamed* "Yes!" at the same time.

"The thought *had* crossed my mind, Sophia," I confirmed with a wan smile.

She shook her head, "Right. Well, there are only so many demanding asshole millionaires you can deal with before Chronosaber loses its shine a little bit. I was a glorified concierge, having to smile for *hours* at a time—"

Corcoran and I looked at each other and chuckled, as if to say *If she thought* that's *smiling…*

The anger continued to boil into her pores, and reddened her normally flawless caramel-coloured skin, "—and making their most *ridiculous* requests happen: 'I want to hunt dinosaurs using only a machete!' Fine! Don't cry to me when the goddamned thing rips your fucking head off and uses you like a chew toy! And then there's the paperwork that came from that, the depositions, the lawyers—oh *God!* The fucking *lawyers!* Poking and prodding for any kind of hole in your story, even if you were up until just 2 hours before deposition because one of the 'guests' decided to proposition every female employee on base, and you had to decide whether to make a big stink to corporate for the 5,642nd time, which wouldn't do *jack shit* and might get you shipped off to Chronobase Upsilon, or to sweep it under the rug like a 'good little girl' for Helene and her rich-ass, spoiled fucking cronies!"

She stood up, picked up the chair she was sitting in, and flung it against the wall like she was Bobby Knight. To my complete and utter surprize, it shattered into several splintery pieces.

Sanchez heaved out a couple of deep breaths, a full-on, raving lunatic. She steadied herself, and took in one more large deep breath through her nose.

When she let it out, the same stony expression as usual was back on her face.

"So you could say this trip we've taken? Despite some of the...unpleasant happenings on it—" she looked at Corcoran and scrunched her nose.

For his part, the Commander smiled like a feral cat that had eaten a whole nest of canaries.

"--has been the fucking *highlight* of the last *five years* for me! So yes, the universe has turned out 'slightly-less-than-optimally' for me. And *hell* yes, I'm all for changing it to the way things should be."

We all exchanged worried looks for several moments.

Klaus broke the silence, "Very good—very good! And you, Finn? I assume I know the answer already, but—"

I nodded sharply, "Of course I'm with you Klaus—this universe is like a hellhole wrapped in a shit-covered blanket in Fresno."

I didn't expect the remark to garner the laughs it did.

"Perfect! How exciting! Everyone is on board then?"

"What about me?" Bloomington's frumped-up face reminded me more than a bit of a pug, minus any of the innate cuteness one might have.

"*Everyone* is on-board? Wonderful!" Klaus clasped his hands together.

"I mean, I dunno—" Bloomington was far too concilliatory to Klaus, who seemed to have it out for the toady scientist for some reason.

I nodded at Steven, "Klaus, I hate to say it, but we *must* consider Steven. After all, he met his wife *solely* because of time travel! Changing things around—they might never meet. He might never raise a family or find true love."

Klaus turned toward Bloomington and at least acted startled when he saw him.

"Oh! Of course Mr. Bloomington, forgive me—I didn't hear you. Explosions in the lab and whatnot have made me oddly and persistently deaf."

I know for a fact that unless Klaus had been secretly shooting guns and blasting dynamite in his lab, this was a bald-faced lie.

Bloomington, though, was deep in thought. I don't know that he had considered to date what a profound effect time travel had on his life. One could even make the argument that aside from Corcoran and Helene, Bloomington was the most successful time traveller of all-time—at least that I was aware of.

And now, Klaus was asking him to give everything he held dear away. To forfeit the odd happiness he had discovered between traveling through time, killing Nazis, and his family life. And for what? On a hunch? On the *chance* that things would be better for everyone else?

This was perhaps the *true* reason that Klaus was trying to avoid talking to Bloomington throughout the conversation—he wanted to avoid this very difficult, very *real* conversation with him.

Bloomington cleared his throat.

"I mean, you know, obviously time travel has been fucking *awesome* for me. Marie and me—we're on the same page, like asshole and asshat in the dictionary—"

I couldn't believe that it was Sanchez struggling to keep it together after that—she bit her lip to keep from guffawing.

"—I mean I *kinda* get you Doc Thurbur. I see what you're saying. I'm not stupid, you know—"

Klaus beamed, "Of *course* not, Steven. Who was saying anything of the sort?"

Bloomington snorted. I wasn't sure if it was out of derision or just his normal disgusting bodily process at work.

"I know that Marie and I are connected. We're *meant* to be together. So I'm just gonna ask you once—" he turned to Klaus, "—if we do this, you *promise* you'll be able to get me back to Paris to meet Marie again?"

"Well—" Klaus stroked his now-bearded chin, "—I can't use the word *promise* since there are too many variables at play. After all, we make one false move, or even one *right* move, and we could blink ourselves out of existence. *But—if* you and I make it through this next phase of our journey intact with the time cloak available, and our memories of this conversation haven't been scrubbed by the time changes…then absolutely, you have my solemn promise that we will do just that."

Bloomington nodded.

"Good enough for me."

I couldn't *believe* it! Maybe Bloomington was a better man than I. But you can better believe that had I found a way to somehow spend the rest of my days with Cynthia, I would've less-than-politely told Klaus to fuck right off, with both middle-fingers fully extended.

Or maybe it was something else. He was, after all, a romantic at heart. Maybe he honestly thought that love—*true* love—transcended space and time. And no matter what happened—if we all somehow forgot each other entirely, then somehow, someway, his beloved Marie and he would end up together, "as they should be."

There wasn't too much time to think at the moment though; Klaus clapped his hands together several times with glee.

"Wonderful! Wonderful wonderful! Excellent—now there's only one more aspect of my plan we have to cover. Something absolutely terrifying that you'll *never* expect was hiding amongst you this entire time...

CHAPTER TWENTY-SEVEN

We scrambled up the gangway, eager to see what the *devil* Klaus was so eager to show us. He seemed to think that he had really "pulled one over on us," but I could tell exactly what his master "surprize" had been as soon as he boarded the ship and his face went long.

"Masssssster Thurrrrburrrr!" POLARIS ran over to Klaus like it was a lost puppy being reunited with its owner.

"Oh—you guys found the robot already?" He asked, ignoring POLARIS even as it enveloped the professor in a long bear hug.

"Yeah—we found the fuckin' robot already," Corcoran nodded at him.

"Damn! I was fantasizing about the 'big reveal' ever since I saw you for the first time. Of course I needed a way to craft whatever I needed for my little plan, and as you may have seen, POLARIS is quite the gifted craftsrobot. I had one of my students in deep cover with Chronosaber smuggle it on your ship before you left. It is, as we say in German, a big old letdown."

I didn't know if Klaus realised that we all had holotrans on, and thus whatever German he spoke would be instantly translated into English.

Bloomington blew a loud raspberry.

"I saw it in the cargo hold like three weeks ago. Your student didn't do a very good job of hiding it."

Klaus ignored Bloomington, then turned to the robot and offered a wan smile.

"Good to see you too, POLARIS. Did they treat you well?"

"Allllll exccccccept the uggggly onnnnne."

"Fuck you, you circus freak-show bearded lady's ass-licker!" Bloomington kicked at the robot, but found its rhenium-reinforced knee joint to be quite sturdy; Steven hopped around in pain, clutching his toe for more than a few seconds.

"Yes, I can see how that might have grown tiresome," Klaus said.

"Verrrrry Tirrrresssssome," POLARIS echoed.

We settled in. I offered Klaus a tour, but he demurred.

"If you've seen one time machine, you've seen them al—*holy shit!*"

I was pretty sure the holotran translated that as well.

Klaus rushed over to the gunnery seat, "This little pony has a little bit of kick to her, huh?"

Corcoran looked on with a glint in his eye, "Damn skippy she does. Kicked the asses of three Annunaki fighters no sweat."

Klaus's eyes went wide, "No!"

Corcoran nodded, "Yep. Blew up all three. 'Course, the gunner may've had somethin' to do with that—" he dusted off his shoulders only half-mockingly I think, "—but yeah, this thing can kick some ass."

Klaus ran a hand over the seat, almost like Sanchez cleaning her rifle. Slowly, methodically, almost sensually, as if he were to move too swiftly, he might "scare the cat" and send it running.

"*Very* nice," he said.

Sanchez, Corcoran, and I looked at one another with arched eyebrows.

"Ah, I almost forgot!" Klaus rushed outside with the speed of a man half his age. "Did you get it?"

"The capstone base, you mean?" I asked.

"Yes, yes—where is it? Did Birusha not tell you to—" even though the ship was cloaked, he looked at the ground and saw a much deeper indentation than one normally would from a standard time machine. "—oh you clever devil you! You cloaked the capstone base too?!"

I nodded, "Yes! Well—not exactly me. It was Captain Sanchez and Bloomington—they're the ones who figured it out."

I looked over at Sanchez and Bloomington, and I could have sworn both blushed.

"Nicely done!" Klaus was downright giddy. "Excellent work even by my standards. Tell me, how did you compensate for the index of refraction—"

At this point, the four of us launched into a highly detailed discussion of cloaking the capstone base, and the various challenges that doing so had provided; I will happily spare you the details, dear reader.

"Nevertheless, better work than Chronosaber, to be sure!" Klaus finished with a flourish.

We all had a good chuckle at that. I looked over at Ricky and noticed that he had fallen dead asleep in his chair.

I decided to have a little fun. I took off one of the shoes that had been provided, and tossed it at him, knocking him decidedly *out* of his reverie.

"Aw *fuck!*" he unholstered his pistol and cocked it instinctively all in one motion. "Son of a *bitch*—that… that was just *rude*."

"So is falling asleep on your friends," I retorted. I turned to Klaus, "So, if we give you the specs, will you be able to implement this on the *Saint Germain?*'

Klaus ran a hand through his long, thinning-on-top grey hair.

"Yes… about that…"

A bead of sweat ran down his brow.

"I'm afraid the *Saint Germain* is quite full already with all of the time cloak apparatus inside of it. Based on what Captain Sanchez and Mr. Bloomington have told me here, the modifications required at least *some* additions to the gravimetric matrix, correct?"

"That's right," Bloomington nodded.

"What a shame," he said. "The gravametric matrix is used extensively by the time cloak equipment. After all, we are generating a *massive* gravimetric field to quite literally bend spacetime. So, unfortunately, all of the output slots are already taken.

"Additionally," he rubbed his hands together, "how is the capstone base attached to your ship?"

We all turned to POLARIS.

"Modifieddd Atlantean Gravamettttric Devicccccce jammed into the sssssshhhhhipppp…" the robot said.

Klaus nodded, "As I feared. Any sort of modification to the outside of the *Saint Germain* could cause irreparable harm to the time cloak. I'm afraid the exterior is… uh… 'modified' quite a bit already—though perhaps I should show you instead."

Moments later, we were at the other end of the enormous park.

Klaus looked around, and, seeing no passersby, he disengaged the cloaking device on the *Saint Germain*.

Now know, dear reader, that I am not a design snob by any means. I find form *far* less important than function.

That said, there was a simple elegance to most time machines out there: spotless, brushed metal, nice clean round curves for the most part.

Klaus had taken that original design… and essentially painted a moustache on the Mona Lisa.

Large casings covered the frame now like a mechanical spider, or one of those claw machines that allowed children to spend tons of money on trying to get a $1 stuffed animal. Large industrial-grade wires ran under the casings, and atop the ship there was a giant, ugly, mechanical bolt, that flashed with various coloured lights and holographic panels.

"Gross!" Bloomington (of all people!) said.

"Isn't she a beaut?" Klaus ignored him. "But as you can see, there is simply no way to attach the capstone base to the top of the ship."

I nodded gravely, "Indeed."

It was all I could do to swallow my disgust.

"Here is the problem though Finny: unfortunately we cannot run two simultaneous wormholes to the same exact time period."

I nodded, somewhat *less* gravely.

"The ripple effect."

"Pre-*cisely*," Klaus said.

"So why not, you know, go like 15 minutes before us or somethin'" Corcoran asked.

Klaus shook his head, "Unfortunately my dear Commander, it's not quite that easy. Whomever goes first yes, would likely make it no problem. But that wormhole would 'ripple' out, like the proverbial stone that's thrown into a pond, and make it so that the second ship misses its window by up to a decade or more."

Sanchez nodded, "It's actually something Helene uses as justification for the regulated monopoly Chronosaber operates under."

"Under which Chronosaber operates," I corrected her.

I suppose I deserved the chorus of "Ughs" and "Harumphs" that followed.

"So here is what I propose," Klaus once again assumed a more "whimsical" persona, "Someone will make the jump in your time machine. I, and anyone who wishes to join me, will follow closely behind in the *Saint Germain*. We will keep a comm channel open between the ships for the duration of the jump. One wormhole this time for both ships. When we emerge, we rendezvous in Cairo and plot our entry into the Marlow Aerospace facility to abscond with the red crystal. Sound good to all?"

We exchanged nervous glances. Klaus seemed to have an answer ready for *every* question we threw at him. Though, to be fair, he *had* been stuck in 18th-century Paris for Trent-knows *how* long, with his only form of entertainment trolling Past-ies, so perhaps he had done all of his planning quite in advance.

I was the first one to nod.

"Sounds like a plan Klaus. But I must say I'd rather prefer to stick with my ship. Tough for me to abandon it at this stage in the game and whatnot."

"Yep—me too," Corcoran said.

"For sure," Bloomington replied.

"Uh huh," Sanchez added.

Klaus smiled, "Very good then! Just me alone at the wheel, on the open vaccuum, as usual!"

I got the distinct impression that he was rather trying to cheer himself up somewhat, and perhaps failing at it.

We readied the ships and prepared for takeoff. I set the time coordinates in the center console:

20-4-2102, Cairo, Egypt

I was more than a little anxious about the whole "end of the world" business Helene had discussed all the way back in 2032 Baltimore.

More than anything though, I sure hoped that Klaus was correct about Gabe Marlow. Klaus's argument as to why he would help us *seemed* sound. And I suppose up to this point my complete and utter trust in Klaus had been rewarded with… what, exactly? Alien invasion? Genocide?

Though to be fair, should his theory of time travel be possible, and we could go back and change the past, and restore it to its natural state, theoretically *all* of the madness we had experienced would revert "back to normal."

But if that was the case, was *that* enough for Marlow to cast his lot on our side? Or was there something more driving him? Something beyond a common hatred of Helene to which he could hitch his proverbial horse?

It seemed like with every time jump, we encountered more questions, and never any *real* answers.

With how poorly the last jump had gone, I decided to go against Han Solo's advice from *The Empire Strikes Back*, and asked the computer for the odds of a successful jump.

"79.3%"

"But that's lower than last time!" I protested.

"Operational variables have shifted," the computer displayed on the screen.

"Con-fuck-it," I said, to no one in particular. "Will making any further adjustments increase the odds at all?"

"Negative," the computer flashed on the screen.

"Very well then," I shook my head. I headed for the pantry and opened a fresh bottle of Macallan Eighteen-Year from the crate. I poured myself out a healthy amount, then did the same for the rest of the crew. I even found myself pouring one for POLARIS, then realised what I was doing, and stopped. It *was* already in the glass though, so I picked it up, tilted it, and slugged it down in one fell swoop.

"Attention all crew!" I yelled. "You are needed in the kitchenette on a matter of the utmost ship's security immediately!"

I emerged from the pantry to find the others already seated around the kitchenette table.

"Excellent!" I passed out the drinks to everyone.

"Thanks Doc," Corcoran said. He guzzled his down greedily, perhaps still recovering from the effects of the medigel.

"Nothing of it," I poured him a refill, and he again downed it.

I looked at him skeptically. I poured him a smaller pour.

He downed it again.

This time, I poured him a sip, and held back his shoulder.

"Hang on a goddamned second, okay Ricky?"

He glared at me. No matter.

"Here's to the best damned time travel crew I've ever had the pleasure of serving with. And one of the craziest fucking plans I've ever been a part of."

"Here's to the time heist," Corcoran said. Perhaps he *had* watched *Endgame* after all…

"Here here!" Everyone clinked glasses and we enjoyed a brief drink, retelling stories from the voyage so far.

"Remember when Trent Albertson introduced us to Charlton Heston?!" Everyone was downright giddy with laughter.

Several minutes later, "And so there's POLARIS, armed to the teeth, and this little Past-ie cripples it!" Sanchez said. More laughs.

Even later, "And in the palace in Atlantis, when Sophie told that joke, and then I egged 'em on, and damn near did Kathleen Madigan's whole fuckin' routine?" Corcoran launched into the bit about noodling again, exactly as he had done before. And we all just about pissed ourselves with laughter.

Truth be told, it was the best I had felt in *months*. And I don't think it was just because we were all hilarious semi-comedians who entertained one another readily.

No, there was something else more there. Something that I only realised at that very moment.

I picked up a spoon and clinked it on my glass several times.

"I just wanted to say that… well…"

"Spit it out!" Sanchez wolf-whistled at me.

"I don't know if you all have noticed, but I'm not very good expressing my emotions."

"*Quite,*" Corcoran said in his overly-affected British accent. More laughs.

"I just wanted to say, when I first started building my time machine, all the way back when I thought Jacob was the one bankrolling me and *not* Helene," (I still couldn't help but spit the word), "More than anything else, I wanted to get my family back. My father... my mother... I just wanted that feeling of 'back together.' As if I'd go back in time, clap my hands, and 'Whoa! Family's back again!"

Everyone else chuckled, even if it was perhaps a bit forced.

"Call me naive, but I firmly believed that my family was there to be found in the past. However, now I know I was wrong. *That* family—the one I originally went in search of, is gone for good. Even if somehow this cockamamie plan of Klaus's re-knits it, I'll have no idea that's the case.

"So before we embark on the weirdest stage of this journey yet, I just wanted to let you all know that along the way, I *did* find a family. I found you, Ricky," I turned to the Commander, and we exchanged a nod.

"And you, Sophia," I nodded at her, and she kept her lips tight, eyes glassy, as she imperecptibly blinked a nod right back at me.

"And you, Steven," I nodded at him, but the little wombat bolted out of his chair, and gave me a big bear hug around the back.

"And yes, even you, POLARIS."

The robot paused for a moment.

"I lovvvvve yooooouuu Doctor Templetttton..." the robot barked.

"Aw, no you don't," I was fighting back the tears now, "That's just some assinine program Klaus probably wrote for you telling you to say that. But I *still* appreciate the gesture."

"No probbbblemmm," It said.

"The point is, *you* all are my family now. And going into this next jump, perhaps the *last* jump as we know it, *that* is what I am *now* most afraid of—losing my family!"

By now, everyone was blubbering, except for Ricky. He tried his damndest to keep a stoic face, but I even caught a single tear running down his cheek.

POLARIS even croaked out several sob-like noises, which oddly pulled me out of the conversation a bit.

"What about me?"

It was from the ship's speakers. And it was Klaus.

It jolted me out of the universal love-fest, and I couldn't help but smile.

"Of course! You too Klaus!"

"Right back atchya, Finny!" I could hear his smile through the comms. "But I'm afraid I've made all necessary preparations and I'm ready for takeoff. So perhaps we can finish this later?"

I dried my eyes and headed for the command chair. The big bright green "Engage!" button was still flashing on the screen.

In hindsight, I suppose it was a tad "irresponsible" to do what I did next. Though then again, who among the crew would have been impatient or dastardly enough to do so, and ruin the rather wonderful moment we had all just shared.

"On my mark. 3…2…1…engage!"

I pointed forward as I said it and hit the button, (obviously) mimicking my hero, Jean-Luc Picard.

The ship took off and sailed through the Parisian sky. It was nearly daybreak now, and the first pink hints of a sunrise crept over the horizon.

It was quite lovely in a truly *timeless* way—not with the panache of the time vortex, or the shimmering beauty of the skyscrapers back in Atlantis, but rather as a sight that I all-too-often took for granted. Especially given the somewhat "less-than-100%" odds that we'd reach our destination.

We ascended to a safe height. Bloomington and Sanchez took their seats, and POLARIS braced itself. Corcoran was already strapped into the seat next to me.

"So whatchya think?" He asked as we approached the safe distance for time travel.

"What do you *mean*, what do I think?"

"You know… all this end'a the world talk? It doesn't seem a *little* odd that we cause this big time of troubles the Chief was talkin' about back in Atlantis, and now we're headed to a time period where everyone thinks it's the end of the world again?"

I shook my head, "Not *everyone* Ricky. Just Chronosaber. And that's only because none of their ships have returned from beyond that year horizon. Correct me if I'm wrong, Sophia?" I asked over my shoulder.

She nodded, "That's right. It's one of Chronosaber's most closely-guarded secrets—strict 'need to know' basis."

Corcoran arched an eyebrow, "So then why did we need to know?"

"Pardon?" I responded.

"Suzie Q, you told Doc about this back durin' dino times last trip, right?"

She rubbed her chin, "Yeah, I guess I did."

"So who told you to tell him? If it's just 'need to know?'"

Now Sophia was looking at the ceiling, deep in thought.

"I don't know. Instructions came from corporate. It could be Helene, or Burnham, or anyone up there really."

"Burnham?!" Bloomington, Corcoran, and I shouted simultaneously.

"Burnham?" Klaus asked, genuinely curious.

"The Sage of St. Louis?" Bloomington asked rhetorically.

"He was a fabulously wealthy time traveller we met back in St. Louis last trip, 1985," I said. "Used his knowledge of the future to get rich picking stocks. And apparently, one of Helene's top cronies."

Corcoran shook his head, "Last time I saw that old *fuck*, I beat the shit out of him with a hand dryer and left him for dead in a men's restroom."

We all arched an eyebrow at the Commander.

Sophia shook her head, "No, he's... very much alive," she rubbed the back of her neck, then decided to move right past what the Commander had said, "But Ricky's right, Finny—*someone* in Chronosaber wanted you to know that. So we should be *very* careful moving forward."

I nodded. I don't know that I appreciated the full gravity of the situation right at that moment. Though as you shall see shortly, it was perhaps a bit "hairier" of a situation we were getting ourselves into than I ever could've imagined.

The button for the time jump appeared on the console in front of me.

"Okay Klaus, I'm go for time travel."

"As am I, Fin."

"3…2…1…Engage!" I made the finger motion again. The rest of the crew was likely getting sick of it by then, but I could say a hearty and well-earned, "Bugger off!" to them, emotional speech be damned.

The tunneling laser came to life and carved out a fairly standard-sized wormhole in front of the ship.

"Everybody hang on to something," Sophia said. The authority she projected was simultaneously reassuring and terrifying that she felt the need to project it.

We entered the event horizon first, and Klaus followed directly behind.

As soon as we entered the wormhole, all hell broke loose.

The ship dipped sharply "downward," or at least as much as there *were* directions in a bloody time vortex!

"It's just like the last jump!" Bloomington yelled out.

"Computer, compensate for gravimetric anomoly!" I shouted.

"Attempting to compensate," the screen flashed.

The ship listed to the right, desperately trying to regain attitude. The inertial dampeners made absolutely no difference with the hundred-plus tonne capstone base atop the ship. The ship groaned from the strain—almost as if she was crying out in agony.

"Computer, can you please right the fucking ship?!"

"Attempting to compensate," the screen flashed.

"Fucking worthless," I pounded the screen. The ship didn't like that at all—it took a sharp yaw the other direction, and the ship's localised gravity became intermittent. I felt the straps of the command chair alternately tightening up and holding me down, and loosening up, and allowing me to float.

It was positively stomach-churning, though I wasn't about to lose my cookies when there was a decent chance we wouldn't even survive the jump.

"Finny? Come in Finny? You must set your—"

There was a violent shudder throughout the ship. Now the groans were turning to shrieks—whatever metallic parts made up the ship's skin were being absolutely pushed to their limits.

"Yes? Klaus?" I shouted at the top of my lungs. "Come in, Klaus? Set my *what?"*

I waited several seconds for a reply, but found only static on the other end.

"Damn it!" Corcoran gritted through his teeth.

"Computer, how much time to the mouth of the vortex at current speed?" Bloomington asked.

"4 minutes 11 seconds," the computer flashed on the screen.

"I don't think we *got* 4 minutes 11 seconds," Corcoran said.

"We *definitely* don't," Sanchez said.

I racked my brain—there had to be *something* we could do! After all, I had *built* the goddamned ship. But for the enormous rock that sat atop it now, we'd be safely cruising to whatever awaited us in the 22nd century.

"But it isn't the *rock* now really, is it?" I asked aloud.

"Huh?" Corcoran shouted back at me.

"It's not the rock—it's the gravity in here—in the wormhole. We need to clear it as soon as possible if we want to make it all in one piece."

"Sounds great Doc! How the *fuck* you wanna do that?"

I knew *exactly* what we had to do.

"POLARIS, prepare to vent antimatter from the reactor directly behind us."

"Doooooing thatttt could be hazzzzzzardousssss—"

"I don't give a tinker's shit! Get down in the maintenance hatch and do it."

"Yesssssss Massssterrrr…"

The robot hustled down into the maintenance hatch, and the hatch shut tight behind it.

"Hang on," Bloomington said. "If you vent antimatter inside a time travel vortex, then that's gonna—"

A loud explosion rang the ship like a horrible gong. The ship immediately went into a shaking tailspin, and the gravimetric field was shut off. Glasses shattered and silverware flew about the cabin--I found it ironic that the whisky-filled glasses from which I normally derived the most stress *relief* were now causing me an insane amount of panic.

Nevertheless, our speed *was* clearly increasing. The timer sped up... *1:34... 0:58... 0:27...* The QC was having trouble accurately gauging time; after all, how long *was* a second when you were travelling hundreds of years in a relative instant?

I gritted my teeth. It felt like I could reach out and *touch* the end of the wormhole now. Only a few more short seconds...

There was another *BOOM* from outside the ship. The klaxons seemed louder. It was as if the ship was going to burst apart at the seams...

And then, all of a sudden, the shaking stopped.

We had exited the wormhole, and now were weightless.

"Report!" I shouted at the QC.

"Attitude and ship control failing. Initiating crash procedures."

That was most certainly *not* what I wanted to display on the screen. Unfortunately it was a bit tough to read as the uncontrolled spin of the craft rotated us in all 360-possible degrees.

"Computer, align breaking thrusters beneath us! Divert all power to breaking thrusters!"

"Breaking thruster power at 45%." Now it felt like the QC was mocking me.

"POLARIS, are you still with us?" Sanchez asked.

"Yessssss Missssstressss," he said.

Corcoran and I exchanged an arched eyebrow—under different circumtances it would have at least garnered a chuckle.

"Do you have manual thruster control down there?"

"Yesssssss Missssstressssss. Thrussssterrrrsssss only 32% ffffunnncttttional."

"Calculate how to get us out of this spin with current thruster power and execute!" She was so calm and collected, and dare I say in command.

"Yessssss Missssstressss."

At first it was hardly noticeable—the occasional "kick" from outside the spacecraft as the odd thruster fired here or there.

Then the kicks came more often. And after a while, the front of the ship was pointed directly at the earth.

It was rising rapidly.

"Hey rust nuts, position us so the fucking *breaking thrusters* can fire!" Bloomington said.

"Yessssss—"

"Finny? Finny come in?"

It was Klaus, interrupting.

"Yes! I hear you Klaus, go ahead!"

"I am initiating a deep dive to try to—"

But before he could finish, it was too late. I felt one last big "kick" beneath us.

And the time machine crashed into pieces.

* * *

I don't know how long I was out. It may have been seconds, may have been minutes. My head was a jumble of scrambled thoughts combined with a dull, low ache.

I looked around the cabin. Everyone was still strapped in their seats. Corcoran and Sanchez were just coming to as well. Bloomington was out, but most definitely breathing from the honking snores emanating from his half-plugged nostrils.

"PO-POLARIS?!" I shouted.

"Yessssss Massssterrrr," Its reply was faint, but it was still with us too.

I instinctively exhaled. At least everyone was (nominally) okay.

Almost everybody, that was.

"Klaus? Come in, Klaus?"

No reply. Not even static.

"Computer? Computer open a channel to Klaus!"

Yet the display didn't change. It was just the QC's blocky avatar with the eye pixels replaced by "X"s and an "Out of Order" displayed somewhat cheekily across the bottom of the screen.

I sighed. Hopefully I (or POLARIS) would be able to fix it.

I took a deep breath and unbuckled myself from my chair. My entire torso ached, like someone had hit me repeatedly with a cricket bat right in the solar plexis. Each breath took a *staggering* amount of effort; presumably because of the mililitres of blood that seeped into my lungs.. I heaved my way toward the gangway, which could no longer be lowered, in large part due to the gaping hole where it used to be.

I stumbled out into the daylight. It appeared to be morning, though I tried to steady myself and figure out which way the sun was moving.

The capstone base was (miraculously) intact, and no longer cloaked. It sat on the ground, askew, seemingly still without mass.

Yet immediately beyond it was something that was so unexpected, so *bizarre,* that dare I say it unsettled me more than anything else I had seen before.

Perhaps a hundred metres off to the side of the capstone base was a large crowd of people, adorned in somewhat futuristic clothing—lots of spandex and neoprene-based fabrics, as I recall (unfortunately, "athleisure" most certainly did *not* die out in the future, but rather had gained traction like a terminal cancer on society's falsely-well-crafted bottom.)

Next to the crowd was a stage and a podium. And above it was a holographic banner, that read:

"April 20, 2102: Happy Phineas Templeton Day!"

As I staggered out, my mind struggled to put two-and-two together.

WHO day? What now?'

"Oh my God! It's him! It's really *him!*" someone in the crowd shouted.

Shrieks followed. I think one or two people fainted. The chorus of cheers was deafening.

I finally had my well-deserved recognition, after all.

CHAPTER TWENTY-EIGHT

I suppose that old bat Helene *had* said that should I embark on this mission, I would achieve all of the fame and notoriety I felt I deserved…

But this was altogether too much! The throngs of adoring masses?! The boisterous cheers?! The (ahem) women who were riding on peoples' shoulders, exposing their *bosoms* to me?!

(Okay… maybe I lied. Maybe this was *exactly* what I had in mind!)

I'll admit, amidst the foggy confusion in my head, part of me thought I had died and this was, perhaps, the afterlife.

My second thought was that I expected the future to be more mature, perhaps more sedate. But then somehow I remembered that often our own view of the future is coloured by our own experiences. As *I* went into the future, year-by-year, *I* matured. *I* got more sedate.

Why on earth should the rest of humanity be the same?

On the stage, Helene and Victor Burnham beckoned me over. Burnham had affected his kindly grandfather persona, and Helene was unlike I had ever seen her: smiling, almost certainly *falsely* cheerful, playing whatever sick part in this plan of hers to perfection as always.

"Ladies and Gentlemen, I present to you, Doctor Phineas Templeton! The *true* creator of time travel!"

More raucous cheers filled the Egyptian air. The weather was as pleasant as Egypt had been in Atlantean times, likely in large part to whatever terraforming efforts had been in place to remediate the Middle East after World War III.

I slowly made my way through the crowd toward the podium. I knew I had all manner of other responsibilities at the moment—like my wrecked ship, banged-up crew, and even determining if Klaus was, in fact, still alive.

But I was being presented a classic "Deal with the Devil," both in terms of spirit and the actual individual with whom I was dealing.

Helene had promised me the only thing I ever wanted: recognition. And now that she had come through on that point, it was like what I imagine black tar heroin must be like. There I was, clasping hands with total strangers, posing for pictures, flirting with attractive (*very* attractive) young women, throwing themselves at the black-suited, yellow-eyed Chronosaber guards making a path for me through the crowd.

And for what? Just to say they had *touched* me? (Though in hindsight, I suppose the list of women who had laid a finger on me to that point was a rather short one, so perhaps they wanted to become members of a *very* exclusive club indeed.)

Eventually, we reached the stage, and Burnham gave me a hand up onto it. I was shocked at how strong the little old man was, as he was able to pull me around as if I were a rag doll.

He outstreched both arms at Helene, and she did the same to me. It was sickening really—she had a big smile on her face like she was fucking *Oprah*, the motherly old leader of Chronosaber finally welcoming home their lost hero they had missed for so long.

I affected a broad smile and gave Helene a half-hug, half-pat-on-the-back with one arm. She rather awkwardly tried to pull me around for a full bear hug, but I maintained a steady wave at the crowd so that she couldn't complete her embrace.

"I always keep my promises, darling," Helene hissed into me ear as she tried to pull me in, "*Always.*"

I inadvertently checked near me for venomous cobras so serpentine was her voice.

"Indeed. Thank you Helene—I *do* mean that," I tried to be as genuine as possible. I knew there was *something* Helene was up to here. Her enmity for me ran so deep, she wouldn't *dare* do *anything* to help me unless there was something in it for her. I just needed to probe a bit as to what, exactly, it was, so that I had some kind of leverage for when she eventually tried to spring her trap.

That moment most certainly was *not* now, in front of this enormous crowd of people, though. I was basking in the adulation like I was on holiday in Bermuda (one of my absolute favorite vacation spots in the world, mind you), and once at the podium, I raised and lowered my arms several times just to wring out every little last bit of applause I could.

Helene yanked the microphone over to her.

"Doctor Templeton has been on a top secret assignment for Chronosaber all these many years, helping track down one of the most dastardly criminals space and time have ever seen."

Muted gasps and whispers went through the crowd.

"A mission that was *wildly* successful, mind you!" She was controlling the crowd with her tone and expressions like Jim Henson with his hand up Kermit the Frog's arse.

The wild, raucous cheers resumed, to the point where she had to beckon them to quiet down so she could continue.

"And with the help of his partner, Commander Corcoran, and several other Chronosaber assets, Dr. Templeton has finally cracked the mystery and the case, and I have just been informed, the time criminal he has been tracking has now been brought to justice!"

I must've turned ghost white. I hope my look didn't betray my confusion. Had she captured Klaus somehow? After all, she seemed to know I would be landing in that exact spot. Did she know where Klaus's ship was? If so, where had she taken him?

"For now, though, I will let Dr. Templeton make a few brief remarks. Ladies, Gentlemen, and all other genders present, I present to you, Dr. Phineas *Templeton!"*

She pushed the mike over to me and raised her arm above my head.

"Now's your chance, darling. Your moment in the bright lights. Don't fuck it up."

I nodded.

"Just don't get mad when I upstage you, you old nag," I said through gritted teeth as I waved to the crowd.

"Fop," she shot back, and waved herself.

"Succubus," I did the same.

We went back-and-forth for several more insults; if the crowd sensed something was up, they didn't show it. The thunderous applause continued for quite some time.

Finally, with what I like to think is a showman's sense of timing, I stepped up to the podium, cleared my throat, and began to address the crowd.

"Ladies and Gentlemen, thank you. And thank you, Helene, for that *wonderful* welcome!" I stood to the side of the podium and gave a golf clap in Helene's direction. The old shrew stood up and courtsied *slightly* too deeply, and showed off a little too much in her thin dress.

It was all I could do to swallow my own vomit and prepare myself to speak on, even with that sour, acidic taste in the back of my throat.

"It is true that *I* created time travel. And I trust that you all enjoy my creation?"

Another wild round of applause. I could *certainly* get used to this!

"You are all *quite* welcome then! I must say, I have been 'on assignment'" my eyes darted to Helene—I hoped the poison in my words wasn't *too* noticeable, "For quite some time now. And while I certainly *did* invent time travel… I had no idea *how* it would impact this world. How it would impact *lives*. How it could help people make sense of their place and time in the universe."

I paused and looked out toward the wreckage of my ship, which was slowly becoming engulfed by passersby. I tried to make out Bloomington, but I could only make out one larger person who appeared to be Ricky.

"And honestly, while I would like to take *all* of the credit for this fantastic achievement in human history, others deserve quite a bit of it as well. Commander Corcoran—Ricky, can you give everyone a wave?"

I looked out toward the ship, and Corcoran did just that. The crowd erupted once more.

"You know, when I first met Ricky, I thought he was quite the scoundrel." A smattering of laughs. "But now that I know him better, I'm *quite* certain he's an incorrigible degenerate."

That line got a somewhat bigger laugh.

"And Captain Sophia Sanchez of Chronosaber. Sophia is maybe the baddest ass person I know, and yet she does it all with such an effortless grace that it can be easy to underestimate her. As I and several Lemurians can tell you, do *not* make that mistake or you will pay dearly!"

Confused murmurs from the crowd. *So they don't know about Lemuria yet? Good…* I thought.

"Of course, Mission Specialist Steve Bloomington of… well I don't rightly know of what, now do I?" A few laughs. "He has again and again proven himself an invaluable member of the team, and dare I say an excellent… err… friend."

I was as shocked as anyone when the word escaped my mouth. I was even more shocked by the assorted "Awww"s of the attractive women in the audience.

"And then of course, there's—" I was going to mention POLARIS, but then I remembered that Klaus had smuggled the robot on the ship, "—all of you!"

(I pivoted somewhat deftly, I think.)

The crowd cheered very wildly—even crowds couldn't escape the rampant narcissism that seemed to be a part of the human condition whenever we went.

"I *do* appreciate everyone making it out here today. You know, if we're being completely 'on the level' here, I would say that your recognition and adulation has been the foremost on my mind since I started this project. And now that it's here—"

Should I tell them the truth? Or a fib designed to play to their vanity?

"—It's every bit as wonderful as I anticipated."

I went with the fib.

Truth be told, already I was getting sick of the incessant cheering, the waiting on them to finish, and the utter *predictability* of their reactions to every little line I said.

"Now, if you'll excuse me—and you too, Helene—" I looked over at her, and she raised an eyebrow in reply, "I have important scientific business to attend to. Onward and upward!" I ended my speech with a flourish and looked to scramble off the stage.

Unfortunately, I felt a heavy hand around my midsection. I looked down to find Burnham grabbing at my belt.

"Just a moment, my good doctor!" his tone was grandfatherly, but his eyes betrayed his enmity toward me. "Helene has one more thing for you."

She approached the podium once more. "Thank you, Doctor Templeton. We have one more thing for you—it's your payment for services rendered to Chronosaber."

She snapped her fingers, and two of the oversized Chronosaber soldiers in black uniforms with the glowing yellow eyes somewhat comically carted over an oversized check. It was made out to me, and for the amount of 1,000 Bitcoin.

"I present to you, 1,000 Bitcoin. Of course, it is being wired safely to your wallet, but I thought it would be worth it for the crowd to see just how much we appreciated you at Chronosaber!"

As the crowd cheered, she stepped away from the mike and

whispered to me.

"And now every crackpot in the audience with a half-baked idea will pitch it to *you* for once in your life."

"My how *magnanimous* you're getting in your old age," I shot back, and started walking away from the podium.

"Leaving so soon? Have somewhere else to be?" The wry smile on her face indicated she thought herself a step or two ahead of me.

"Oh, you know…places to go, people to see," I replied. Truth be told, I desperately wanted to contact Klaus somehow, were he still, in fact, not captured by Helene's goon squad.

She nodded, "Oh indeed. It's just… well… no, a hero of your stature doesn't want to be bothered by such trivialities…"

"What?" My curiosity had been sufficiently piqued.

"It's just… well with these *adoring* crowds," She mocked innocent moreso than O.J. Simpson, "it would be a real *shame* if you would get held up moving across town, wherever you're going."

And suddenly, something clicked into place.

"Yes, well, for now I was planning on spending some of my newfound fortune, you know? Enjoying myself a bit."

Helene nodded, "As well you should. Take your time—Dr. Thurbur isn't going anywhere. Enjoy yourself! And when the time is right… we'll bring you in for a proper debriefing."

All I could do was nod my (false) assent. She quickly pulled me in close with one hand, her mouth next to my ear, each breath damp and warm on my neck. I didn't no whether she was going to kiss me or prod at me with her forked tongue.

"Thank you," she hissed.

"Nothing of it," I backed off instinctually. She lingered perhaps two seconds too long before finally letting me go.

I scrambled off the stage and rushed toward the ship. Unfortunately, every Tom, Dick, and Harry was mobbing me now, asking for autographs, begging for pictures, and, to a lesser extent, money.

I was shoved one way, then the other. I dug into the soft, rich earth with my heels, trying to find *some* kind of "center" as I reeled from side-to-side.

Of course. That was why Helene had done this—the crowd that had gathered would make it difficult to go *anywhere* around Cairo, especially now that the ship was busted into pieces.

It gave her time to… well, *what*, exactly? Find Klaus? Get Marlow?

That raised the other question that was gnawing at my mind: How much *did* Helene know, exactly? Had she orchestrated *everything*? Including getting us to Marlow Aerospace later on? Perhaps even sending Klaus the packet of information to begin with? And if so, why?

My head was beginning to hurt—I needed space to think. But unfortunately space was the one thing that was at an absolute premium at that very moment.

I was getting fed up. I reached for my Baretta—not wanting to *hurt* anyone, mind you, but perhaps just to scare some folks—

I felt a strong hand on my shoulder. Then another one on the other shoulder.

"Okay folks, show's over. Important Chronosaber business—"

It was Sophia. She pushed through the crowd and pulled me after her.

I looked at the other side, and found Corcoran on my left, sopping up at least some of the attention that had been meant for me.

"Commander! A hologram, please?"

"I want to marry you!"

"Have my babies!"

"Not right now," Ricky somehow maintained that devilish grin throughout the trek back to the ship, even while he was practically accosted by everyone in his path.

"We need some privacy," I said, "We need somewhere we can talk *without* the hoi palloi and *without* Chronosaber listening in. The ship is—" I nodded at the still-smouldering hulk of twisted metal, "—I was going to say 'compromised,' but I suppose 'totally fucked' would be more accurate."

"What about the crew quarters?" Sophia asked.

"They ain't exactly 100% sound proof, especially in its current swiss cheese config," Ricky said. Unfortunately, the crowd continued to swell and surround us.

"Is there enough power to engage the cloak?" I asked.

"Robot's probably the one to ask about that, if we can find it," Ricky said.

We finally approached the ship, though the crazies and their flying camera drones still followed us. The term "weirdo" seems a bit "underpowered" for all of them; each one had a thoroughly colourful hairdo with bright yellows and reds that would have likely set Atlanteans on tilt.

Not only that, but it was clear the ship was in *no* condition to host a "secret meeting." The crew quarters were carved open like a gutted tin of beans thrown in-between two bums having a knife fight. Not to mention that POLARIS was nowhere to be found.

"Ship ain't gonna be so private after all," Corcoran said.

We continued past the wreckage more to escape the mounting rabble than anything else, and made our way onto a wide boulevard that was alight with all manner of bright neon signs, and garish advertisements—all of which were oddly tailored precisely to me:

Dr. Phineas Templeton: Enjoy an Ice-Cold Pepsi

Kol Kalash, Dr. Templeton? 34% Off Today Only

Visit the Underworld for a Delightful Macallan Twenty-One

Have a Drinking Problem? Connect With One of Our Specialists Today…

That last one notwithstanding, I wondered how the devil these messages could be so on-the-nose targeted to me.

Then I remembered the smart contact lenses that Sophia had given me back at Chronobase Igloo, and I shot her daggers.

She gritted her teeth and shrugged sheepishly.

"Helene?" I asked.

She nodded, "Helene."

"Wonderful. So am I to assume that she can track my every movement now via these… these damned *things* in my eyes?"

Corcoran nodded behind us at the fast-moving crowd, "I think she can track us a lot easier than all that."

I dug at my eyes to remove the damndable hololenses from them; it took a bit of prodding, but eventually I was able to get the mini-homing beacons out of each one, and stepped on each surreptitiously on the groud.

Unfortunately, this left me somewhat more blind than a bat; the world instantly went blurry, though thankfully without the smart specs, the gaudy adverts also faded away.

"Emergency! Optician! Emergency!" I tried to raise my voice above the rabble continuing to mount behind us.

Sophia shook her head.

"Do you know your prescription?"

"-5.75 with a cylinder of astigmatism in the right, and -6.25 in the left."

Sophia tapped a button on her wrist and a holodisplay overlayed her arm. She tapped several "buttons" on the display, and looked into the sky.

Within minutes, a drone carrying a small Warby Parker box silently darted above us and matched our speed. It dropped the package gently into Sophia's waiting arms, and flashed a green laser over her face.

"Thank you," she nodded at the machine. It tilted its "head" at her slightly, and flew away.

She opened the package and produced a set of smart spectacles that was quite stylish; it was perhaps a little bit flashy for my tastes, being a brushed platinum hue with rounded rectangular lenses, though I must admit it looked quite stylish and in-line with the current fashion of the times. She tossed the glasses at me, and thankfully, for once in my life, I caught them, albeit with several bobbles.

"Thank—" I put them on my head and immediately the world went sharp and crisp once more… though the obnoxious adverts returned to my field of view as well.

"—you."

Sophia waved her hand at me.

"Don't mention it. You owe me $5,741 when you have a sec."

I swung my hand up to cover my mouth.

"What? You're a billionaire now—remember?"

"Of course, of course—thank you, Sophia."

Mind you, this entire time we were zig-zagging through the streets of Cairo, being chased by an adoring mob of people hoping to get "just a quick holopic" with myself or the Commander.

"Maybe I can find a safehouse—" Sophia scanned the streets. She pointed down an alley, and led us to what seemed like a fairly inconspicuous cafe.

We were able to catch our breath only for a moment before we opened the door, and were greeted with raucous cheers, balloons, and a "Happy Dr. Phineas Templeton Day!" banner.

As the previous mob converged on our position, and the new mob at the cafe greeted us with open arms, it was clear that out of all of the precarious positions in which we had found ourselves this voyage, *this* was going to be the most difficult from which to escape *by far.*

I took a deep breath, put a broad smile on my face, and approached the first imbecile for a holopic.

While the people may have been taller and more beautiful than they had ever been in the past, and their hair colours were as varied as the bins of ice cream at a Baskin Robbins, they also seemed to be quite a bit *dumber* than people had been previously, as well.

"Was it hard to invent time travel?" one of them asked me.

I blew an ironic raspberry, "No, no—not at all! Did most of the *hard* work in an afternoon, honestly. After that, it was all downhill from there."

"Are you friends with Jesus?" Another one asked.

"I... uh... well... I mean 'friend' is a rather *strong* word—"

One particularly dim bulb came up to me and asked me to autograph his "First Edition" copy of *Jesus Was a Time Traveler*—"the one with all of the typos."

"My good man behind me can help you with that," I nodded at Bloomington.

He looked as if he had just smelled a fart.

"Fuck off, losertaint," he said to the heartbroken fan.

We carried on like that for what must have been hours. It seemed like we'd never get through the entire crowd, now quite literally coming at us from all angles. I thought about firing my pistol into the air to disperse the crowd, but the place was packed so tightly it was all I could do to protect my sidearm from being lifted by a nefarious tourist.

To his credit, Ricky was able to affect his smiling, folksy Midwestern persona the entire time. And if I may say so myself, I thought I was able to grit my teeth and muddle through it rather well also.

By the time the final ghoulish-looking, pasty-faced basement-dweller had secured a picture with the two of us, and we were able to make a path to the exit of the it was getting dark. Since we had the ceremony at probably about nine or ten am, with her little scheme she had concocted, Helene had somehow managed to keep us occupied for a full *eight-plus hours.*

Not only that, but the entire time we hadn't heard so much as a peep from Klaus. I had no idea if he had even survived the crash, or if he had, whether or not that shrew had sunk her pointy little teeth into him.

"Thank *God,*" I shook myself off, like a dog getting out of a bath.

"What? Didn't ya say ya wanted to be famous?" Ricky's smile was broadening.

"Yes, but… more in an Einstein sort of way, and less of a common Trent Albertson-manner."

Corcoran shrugged, "Fame ain't always what it's cracked up to be, Doc. I coulda told you that."

"Yes, well I've now received an appropriate dosage for one lifetime, thank you very much." I shook my head to get my bearings.

The old-fashioned bell attached to the door rang once more. I rolled my eyes at what I was sure was *another* fame-worshipping rube hoping for a lock of my hair, or a vial of my blood.

"Well, what have we—"

"Masssssterrrr!"

The robot's grotesque visage was unmistakable. I didn't know if I welcomed it for the rather Data-like habit it had developed of bailing us out of impossible scenarios, or because its presence meant that there was at least a possibility that Klaus was not in Chronosaber's clutches quite yet.

"POLARIS you beautiful bastard! So good to see you!" I ran up and gave the robot a hug.

"Goooood to sssssssee you ttttoooooooo, Masssssssterrrr!"

"Is Klaus—Dr. Thurbur—is he still—"

Suddenly, the robot's eyes glowed red. It stared straight forward, like a terminator now focused single-mindedly on its target.

"Murrrrrrderrrr mode engaged. Murrrrrderrrrr mode engaged…"

"Oh my *God!* The robot's going to kill us all!" The adoring fan who had asked me to autograph his copy of *JWATT* screeched.

With that, the room cleared of most of the rabble, including the lone clerk behind the cash register.

All of us grabbed our sidearms, and levelled them at our erstwhile companion. Was this some kind of "hack?" A Chronosaber ploy to use our own trusty "do everything" robot to finally cut us down?

POLARIS's grin deepened. It reached out both hands. Ricky and Sophia unlatched the safeties on their weapons. Sweat dampened my brow, and my own finger started to squeeze the trigger.

The robot turned from us, and in one motion fashioned a makeshift "lock" for the door by welding a table to the door frame.

Then it turned back to us, its eyes back to "normal," and did something I'd *never* seen it do before:

It laughed.

"Finnny? It'sssssss meeee Klausssssss, come innnnn," POLARIS said.

"Ha ha, very funny," I was more than a bit perturbed at the robot's dark sense of humour.

"Thissssss isssss noooo joooooke," the robot replied. *"I outttttfittted itttt wittthhh a speccccciially encccrrrryptted comm linkkk for thisssss verrrry reassson."*

I stroked my growing beard, "I'll be damned… if it's *really* you, what's Archimedes's favorite dog food?"

"Achimeeeedeeessss doessssn't eat dog food. He eatssssss sssssteak… and cheeeessssse."

I caught Corcoran, Bloomington, and Sanchez exchanging pained, "get a load of this guy" looks.

I only smiled, "Klaus my good man! Where shall we meet you?"

CHAPTER TWENTY-NINE

I quickly gathered everyone in the storeroom of the cafe. It was the most "private" room available given the circumstances, and given that we were hashing out a plan with a very wanted fugitive at the time, it made sense to take all reasonable precautions, encrypted channel or not.

The conversation was made quite a bit more arduous by POLARIS's rather metallic, half-lisping way of speaking. So to spare you from reading pages and pages of "s"s and "r"s and "t"s, I shall summarize the conversation henceforth:

Klaus landed his ship (undamaged) several kilometres away from us, and (unsurprisingly) was soon thereafter met by a cadre of Chronosaber troops.

Sensing that he could buy more time for us by allowing Helene to think that he had been apprehended, he had allowed them to put cuffs on him, take him into "custody," and communicate with Helene to that effect.

"Whatttt they didnnnnnn'ttttt know wassssss thatttttt POLARRRRRISSSSS heeeeerrrre wassssss waittttinnnnggg forrrrr themmmm innnn my carrrrrgooo bay."

(You can see why I wished to limit your exposure to such "conversation"—you are *quite* welcome!).

From there, he relocated to a quieter suburb of Cairo, cloaked the ship, and sent POLARIS out to look for us while he pondered the next steps of his plan.

"Well, thanks for gettin' here so quick," Ricky narrowed his eyes.

"Herrrrrr Commmannnnnnderrrrrr, I asssssurrrrre you I made gooooooood uuuuuuuussssssse of thatttttt timmmme. Heeeeeerrrre's whaaaat weee'rrree goingggg to doooooo:"

Klaus noted that in the diagram of the Great Pyramid as a power plant that he had, there were vast subterrainean caverns and pools underneath the structure. Somehow, using the "physio-electricity" (which is to say, electricity obtained through movement, much like the hydroelectric station at Niagara Falls) of these pools, along with the natural electrical power stored within the earth postulated by Nikola Tesla and others, with the capstones at the top, the Pyramid is able to generate and discharge truly staggering amounts of power and electrical energy held within the earth itself.

These pools were obviously operational back in Atlantean times (*"though not necesssssssssarrrrrily with waterrrrrrr,"* Klaus/POLARIS cryptically warned us), as their death ray still worked brilliantly. But we would have to check and ensure that the pools were still "up to spec," as Klaus put it, before trying to turn on the Pyramid as a power source. Klaus volunteered to do that from a safe distance away from the Pyramid itself (since he could still fly there), provided he could use POLARIS's advanced sensory technology to do so—much how we had used the robot to find rhenium back in the Chief's village.

While they were doing that, the rest of us would be tasked with pilfering the red crystal meteorite from the Marlow Aerospace facility. We would need to find a way to break in, disable any security they might have, locate the meteorite, steal it, and somehow transport it to the Pyramid.

Once there, POLARIS would fashion a new true capstone based on the specs that Klaus had scanned from his time back in Atlantis.

Then, we would actually have to position the capstone base in place. This would have normally been no tougher than flying my time machine up to the top of the pyramid, and allowing POLARIS to gently lower it into place… were my time machine still functioning! Instead, the massless capstone base still sat atop the ship, like an enormous massless paperweight made out of papier mache.

After that, we'd have to position the true capstone in place, and operate the Pyramid's controls, for which I was (unfortunately) uniquely qualified, having observed the techs and Birusha in Atlantean times.

Finally, Klaus would fly to the top of the Pyramid, soak up the requisite power we needed to operate the time cloak, grab me from the control room, and jet off to change the past.

And *where* were we headed on our first jaunt back to "make things right?"

"Chronobase Alpha?!" Sanchez was, unsurprisingly, the most shocked.

"Innnndeeeed my dearrrrr," "It'ssssss the furrrrrthesssst baaaack Chronossssssaberrrr hassssss sssssuccccesssssfully gone."

"And I'm guessin' we ain't goin' to shoot up a bunch'a dinosaurs, neither?" Corcoran asked.

"That'ssssss rrrrrright, Herrrrr Commmannnderrrr. We will

desssssstrrrroy it."

Bloomington and I gasped. Surprisingly, Sanchez just nodded.

"Figured as much."

"We mussssst desssssstroy all *targetttssss in orrrrderrrr to rrrrrepairrrr the timeline. I will exxxxxplain it morrre when we have accomplisssssshhhed the missssssion."*

I nodded. I wondered where all else we would need to travel to and "incapacitate" things (for lack of a better word).

With the broad strokes of the plan laid out, and night quickly descending on Cairo, we all agreed to try to meet up at the Pyramid by 11:00 pm. That would give us enough time to power up Klaus's ship, and hopefully make our first time cloak jump before Helene and her minions could get wise to what we were doing.

We bid POLARIS farewell, and watched as its grotesque form bounded out into the streets of Cairo, ostensibly toward the coordinates where Klaus was waiting for it.

The rest of us slowly nudged our way out of the cafe and into the streets of Cairo. We moved as discreetly as we could through the alleyway, hoping against hope that the robot had sufficiently scared the ever-living shit out of people enough that we might be able to move about the town largely unhindered.

That lasted for all of about five seconds.

"Oh my *God!* It's *them!"* a rather attractive woman in her forties yelled out.

Immediately, several passers-by swarmed our position.

"Doctor Templeton! A word please!" One member of the press yelled out.

"Take me back in time with you! Please!" An older man latched onto my leg, causing me to recoil as if he was a scorpion!

It was all a little *too* convenient: whenever we went out in public now, we were treated like the Beatles or Rolling Stones or Clive Hendrickson. It was almost as if Helene had turned *my* greatest wish to *her* ostensible advantage. Though to what point and purpose remained a mystery.

"Ain't got time for this shit—" Corcoran unceremoniously raised his pistol in the air and fired three shots in rapid succession.

The small crowd startled and dispersed. Within moments, drones with flashing red and blue lights surrounded us. They looked rather like large flying hockey pucks with robotic arms attached at the bottom, though there appeared to be a mini-minigun at the end of the arm as well.

"Gun crime reported! Gun crime reported!" the deep, metallic voices of the drones said in unison.

"Great—way to *go*, Ricky," Sanchez said.

"Processing," the drones said. They scanned Corcoran with a bunch of green beams. I would've been more scared if Corcoran wasn't hopping around, giggling like an idiot.

"God *damn* it stop! That tickles!" He was a proper lunatic with laughter as the beams scoured every inch of him.

"Identity confirmed: Corcoran, Richard. United States Navy. Special clearance granted. Result: not guilty. You are free to go."

The beams unfortunately ended, and Corcoran fell to one knee, itching his skin wildly.

"Wow—for a second there, I thought you might piss yourself," Sanchez said.

"You'd like that, huh?" Corcoran shot back.

"Marie certainly—" Bloomington tried to interject.

"Stop!" Sanchez and I waved him off in unison.

The toady wombat frowned.

"I *never* get to say funny shit like you guys do!" he protested.

"That's because it's not 'funny'—it's just shit," Sanchez said.

He looked at me and I raised my eyebrows to confirm it.

Bloomington shook his head, "Whatever, Ass-squirrels! Fuck all of you."

"Same to you," I affected my most British accent possible.

"Just…keep that thing holstered and be careful with it, will ya?" Sanchez nodded at Corcoran's hip.

"Shit—we hookup once and she's already my naggin' girlfriend," Corcoran grinned.

I thought Sanchez might shoot him right then-and-there.

We finally made it to a main road, and noticed a man outfitted in what can only be described as a business silver jumpsuit simply wave a hand, and all of a sudden a mini flying saucer descended from the sky, opened its door, and allowed him inside.

"Guess that's the 22nd century version of a taxi?" Corcoran asked.

"Let's see if it is," Sanchez waved her hands above her head. Sure enough, within seconds, one of the mini-saucers dipped down from the sky and opened its door for us.

"Where to?" the voice that prompted us was British, pleasant, and male. Though obviously there was no driver; it was simply the "voice" as it had been programmed into the vehicle, and as our holotrans translated it.

"Marlow Aerospace hangar. Main research facility, Cairo," I said.

"The fare is 3 Satoshis. Continue?"

Sophia and I rolled our eyes at one another and grinned. That was perhaps a few pennies in my time, and little more in hers.

"Of course," I nodded. The saucer asked for my casual Bitcoin wallet hex address (you'll find out about this soon enough, I'm sure), and within moments we were off flying above the city.

"What the *hell* is a 'Satoshi'?" Corcoran asked.

"Bitcoin, ferretshit for brains," Bloomington said. "I mined a little in my spare time before I became a fucking time-traveling special forces Nazi-killer."

I arched an eyebrow, "Do you know your address off-hand, Steven?"

"No. Why would I?"

My eyes went wide, "Because you're from 2012, correct? By now, whatever pittance you invested into it would likely be worth quite a fortune…"

Now it was Bloomington's turn for his eyes to bug out. I suppose he had collected his phone from the ship's wreckage, and he was desperately combing through notes and apps to see if he could find it. Unfortunately, his phone was operating on something known as "4G," and thus wasn't compatible with the cellular networks of the day.

"Dog shit-filled condom tiny cock substitute elephant camel

asshole double-fuck nutless screwjob—"

The longest string of Bloomington curse words I've ever heard ensued.

Within a minute, we landed softly in front of Marlow Aerospace's front gate and exited the cab.

I couldn't imagine a more intimidating scene to passers-by:

A thick, concrete wall surrounded the area with barbed wire attached to the top. A couple of old-school, World War II-era pillboxes guarded the front, along with several robots that made POLARIS look like an ineffective wimp. They were at least eight feet tall, for the life of me looked like enormous, reinforced T-800s from the Terminator movies, and (needless to say), they were heavily armed.

But one thing and one thing alone let me know this might be somewhat more difficult than anticipated:

Among the terrifying terminators, fences, and guns, were a platoon of Chronosaber soliders, all decked out in their night black uniforms with the glowing yellow eyes we had first encountered by Klaus's laboratory in Leipzig.

"Not an *entirely* surprising twist," I said to no one in particular.

"Well Suzy Q, looks like you're up," Corcoran nodded at Sanchez.

She squinted at him, as if to say, *"Really?"*, and strode confidently up to the gate.

"Sergeant, I'm Captain Sophia Sanchez, escorting these guests of Chronosaber into the Marlow Aerospace facility for a debriefing."

She nodded at us, though I must say we were quite a distance away and as I mentioned it was getting dark, so it might have been somewhat difficult for the guard to see to whom she was referring.

The guard stared back blankly.

"You can look up my service number, SS-78952-Bravo-Igloo-Hotel."

This time, the guard snorted.

"Sorry ma'am, we are under strict orders to lock down the area. No exceptions."

"No exceptions, huh?" Corcoran hurried up to join his one-time lover at the gate. "Not even for an American hero?"

The guard didn't so much as flinch. He looked Ricky up-and-down for a moment before shaking his head.

"Sorry Commander—I can't even let *you* through on this one…"

Bloomington made a move out of the shadows, but I clasped him on the shoulder and shook my head at him.

I had an idea.

I jogged up to the gate and put my arm around both Sanchez and Corcoran.

"Ah, sorry there old chap. These two and I had a little bet. You see, I bet them that you had this area on lockdown, even for such," I cleared my throat perhaps a bit too much, "*luminaries* as they are. But for me, *Doctor* Phineas Templeton, father of time travel, whom Helene practically just gave the key to the city—"

The soldier saluted and came to rapt attention.

"Doctor Templeton, *sir!* I didn't know they were with *you, sir!* Please proceed with my most sincere apologies."

I raised my eyebrows at my incredulous crewmates, and punctuated it with a hearty salute right back at the sergeant.

"No worries at all—just see to it that we're treated more… *amenably*… once inside?"

"Of course, sir. I will alert the patrols. You are to have Orbital Level clearance. Enjoy your stay."

The sergeant motioned to several of the large terminator-type robots, and they opened the heavy blast gate.

I practically skipped inside! Oh what a change for the better—to have all of the fame (and benefits associated with said fame) as I desired!

It was as if *finally* the universe was catching up… *finally* making things right… and *finally* allowing me to take my rightful place in it.

And I'm about to throw this all away because… WHY, exactly?

The thought *had* crossed my mind, more than once. Why go through with Klaus's plan when I was treated like a veritable rock star in 2102?

But then I thought back to earlier when the mass of people surrounded me… the constant requests and threats… not having any space to breathe…

Not only that, but I absolutely *knew* that Helene was up to *something*. She *had* to be… and I had a sneaking suspicion that we were all playing right into her trap.

Though again, what did she have to gain by making things more difficult for us, then allowing us to waltz on in to this maximum-security facility? Something didn't add up…

We entered the facility, which appeared to be made out of sparkling glass and a lucite-like material that was every bit as awe-inspiring as something out of Atlantis. What was markedly different, though, were the stark, clean lines that made up pretty much every plane in the facility. It was in stark contrast to the almost Gaudi (*not* "gaudy")-style of some of the Atlantean buildings we had seen and visited; this was much more "modern," much as if Jonny Ive himself had designed it.

The guard from outside walked us right through security, which was a delightfully *Total Recall*-like x-ray wall behind which the guards had us proceed. Though alarms sounded for the variety of firearms that we carried, they were promptly turned off by the enormous terminator-like robots that manned the machine.

Past security was a long, *very* wide hallway with a T-intersection in the middle. Chronosaber guards manned all four corners of the intersection, and it was soon apparent why:

Helene was waiting there, in a bright red women's business suit.

"There are my heroes!" I swear she almost gave me diabetes so saccharinely sweet was her cadence.

"You mean her*o*," Sanchez said.

Her insubordination frightened *me* a little bit.

Helene laughed it off, "Just having a bit of fun, my *dear*," the old crone was close enough now that she did something I would have *never* thought to do—at least if I wanted to keep my testicles firmly ensconsed in my scrotum.

She reached out to Sanchez's cheek and pulled on it, like an overbearing aunt.

And Sanchez just took it! I suppose the alternative was to get in a big fight with the guards, the terminator robots, Helene, et cetera and so forth, but *still*… I had *never* seen poor Sophia Sanchez so humiliated in her life!

If there was any doubt where Captain Snachez's loyalties now lay, I think that cheek pinch eliminated even the most fleeting thoughts of loyalty she still had to Chronosaber.

Helene then turned to Corcoran and reached out a hand toward his cheek, but the Commander grabbed her by the wrist.

"Not a fuckin' *chance*, lady."

Somewhat oddly, he brought his second hand to cover *his* crotch.

She flinched her head toward him, but he maintained his resolve, almost as if he was chewing nails.

Finally, she looked at Bloomington, who smiled at her. She shuddered with revulsion before she turned back to me.

"How did you know where to find me, dear?" She asked me. She seemed genuinely curious and suspicious.

"Ah, well, you know…" I rolled my eyes, "That Klaus is a slippery one. I had heard he had gotten away, and you know," I clucked my tongue a couple of times, "Now that you mention it, he *had* mentioned 'Marlow Aerospace' a couple of times, and I just wanted to make sure we could find *him* if—"

Her eyes went wide, mocking innocence, "Oh? I thought that was the purpose of your little transmission from that bodge of a cafe—to give us his location?"

I stopped dead in my tracks, causing the Chronosaber guards to bump into me from behind.

"I… uh… yes, of course," I picked up my gait. "The transmission—"

"Posh now!" she flexed out a wrist in front of her, "Whatever device you were using was *very* traceable--2050s technology, correct?"

"I'm not sure," Sanchez said through gritted teeth.

"And while the transmission itself was quite encrypted, we were able to pinpoint the source of it to within 100 metres, give-or-take. My soldiers are closing in on Dr. Thurbur's position now. Which means, you've held up *your* end of the bargain, and *I* mine. How did you like your *adoring* public?"

She was *really* starting to get on my nerves. Of course there would be Chronosaber agents in the crowd in the cafe, and one of them likely was listening in on us the entire time. If Chronosaber was on their way to get Klaus with a mere *handful* of the soldiers patrolling this facility, I feared that even POLARIS wouldn't be able to avert a rather unhappy ending for my German friend. It moved the timeline up quite a bit.

"Well I—"

Before I could finish whatever pithy one-liner I had cooked up, alarm klaxons went off. Smoke filled the hallway, and it was followed just as quickly by the sprinklers going off.

"What the devil?" Helene asked. "Secure the heroes!" she barked at the soldiers.

Before they could get in formation though, I heard the *pew pew* sound of a laser pistol fill the air. The rear guards dropped quickly, and the terminators soon followed. The front guards hustled Helene off ahead of us.

We instinctively looked for cover. Laser bolts still chased Helene and her guards down the hallway. Every so often, a new terminator robot came rushing up from behind us, trying to establish a perimeter, though whenever it did, it quickly was turned into swiss cheese by whatever was shooting down the hallway.

I ducked and covered my forehead with my arm. Wouldn't *this* be just a *capital* way to go out?

The shooting got closer. Sweat ran off my brow like a waterfall. Corcoran and Sanchez stood back-to-back, guns up, ready to repay whomever assualted us in kind.

Suddenly, I felt a hand on my shoulder. It wasn't a Corcoran or Sanchez-level grip. It was more like Bloomington, soft, and "suggestive" instead of "commanding."

The figure's other hand banged on the wall, and a hologram dissolved to reveal a secret door in the otherwise stark, white wall. The shadowy figure opened it, and thrust me inside. Corcoran, Sanchez, and Blooomington soon followed.

After we were all safely in the room, four POLARIS-model robots took up positions directly inside and outside the door. Occasionally, the exterior robots would volley off a few laser pistol shots, presumably at Chronosaber terminators.

Finally, as the smoke from the hallway cleared, a shorter, stout man rushed into the room. He was dressed in his trademark tweed jacked, and his now-obvious mussed toupee and unkempt mustache gave him away immediately.

"Gabe *Marlow?*" I asked.

"I told you whenever you're in a pickle, I have your back, Dr. Templeton…" he replied.

CHAPTER THIRTY

I was shocked that the funny disheveled man from the conference room in 2032 Baltimore now stood before us.

"Thanks for the assist there," Corcoran nodded at Marlow.

"Don't mention it. Nor shall I solicit a 'thank you' for getting POLARIS aboard your ship. Or for getting Dr. Thurbur that packet of information before he stole the *St. Germain* and took off to right the *horrific* wrongs that time travel and *that woman* have wrought on history."

We all looked at one another, stunned at his social awkwardness more than anything else.

"I really *do* hate her, you know?"

"Join the club," we all said in unison.

"How'd she come to overrun your facility then?" Sanchez asked.

"As much as it pains me to say it, I suppose her massive privately-funded army is better than mine. Although," he nodded at the POLARIS robots guarding the door, "These old things still have some tricks left in them."

"We…err… know," Sanchez said.

"Did she say Klaus's position has been compromised?" The billionaire's mustache twtiched as he spoke.

"Quite," I nodded.

"Well then we don't have much time. Follow me to the meteorite. Once we're there—" he motioned for the POLARIS robots to escort us into the still smoking, smouldering hallway with various alarms blaring, threatening to pop our eardrums.

"—all *hell's* gonna break loose."

I unholstered my sidearms. Walking beside Corcoran and Sanchez, I sensed if not perhaps a "relief" that they'd finally get to shoot at moving targets again, then at least a welcome familiarity. *This* was their habitat. *This* was their purpose. Anything else they excelled at was purely incidental.

We followed Marlow through a maze of T-intersections. As we

passed by open doorways, I was *shocked* at some of the things I saw in passing: revolutionary new propulsion systems far more advanced than the simple gravity drive in the time machine I had designed. Lightweight body armour the thickness of a t-shirt that was being blasted with laser fire, and that proved more than equal to stopping it cold.

And then there were the robots! One room I ducked in momentarily had what could best be described as a giant mechanical ape. Technicians in white jumpsuits with thick, green goggles took turns slicing off the ape's arms. The beast did *not* care for this, and swatted at the techs, who (quite nimbly, I thought) scrambled for their lives. Within seconds of losing an appendage, a new arm would appear in place, seemingly crafted out of thin air.

I felt a hand on my shoulder.

"Pretty cool, huh?" It was Marlow.

"I *know*, right?" I felt like a runway model in a cocaine factory.

"Nanotech and advanced materials development. We've found that one of these mechanical apes could potentially wipe out dozens of conventional annihilator-class robots, like the ones Chronosaber uses."

"Sooo… *why* aren't we letting it loose? You know—to do its thing?" Sanchez asked.

Yesssss, I thought. I hadn't the stones to ask myself, even though I hoped against hope that someone might.

Marlow shrugged, "I guess you've got a point, Captain." He whistled at the techs, "Let her *loose!* Targeting Chronosaber-uniformed soldiers and robots only."

The techs nodded. I could practically see their smiles and the gleams in their eyes through the dark, greenish goggles they wore. One of them tapped several commands on a holotablet, and the mechanical ape's eyes changed from green to red. It pounded its chest and reared back on its legs, howling a devilish cry that sent shivers down my spine. Lord only knows *what* the scream did to any Chronosaber troops in the area.

"We might wanna—" Marlow jumped out of the doorway, only to land where the mechanical ape decided to bust through the wall. Corcoran dove and pushed the eccentric billionaire out of the way, and then rolled to safety himself.

As if sent by God Himself, four Chronosaber terminators (or "anihilators," I suppose, as Marlow had called them) appeared from a nearby T-intersection. They riddled the mechanical ape with laser fire; its torso was so filled with holes we could see clean through it, from one end of the hallway to the other.

The ape was unfazed. It beat its chest, then lunged at the first anihilator. It grabbed the massive robot by the head and twisted it off. It then used the appendage to dig into the robot's midsection; each bash dimming the anihilator's eyes until they went dead black.

It wasted no time grabbing two other anihilators, and smashed them together repeatedly like rag dolls being forced to kiss by an overbearing young lady.

The ape ended its symphony of violence on a riveting and beautiful crescendo by corraling the final anihilator, raising it up in the air like an offering to the sky gods, and then bringing it down over its knee, smashing it in twain like a baseball bat.

"Oh my God… *yes!*" Bloomington was the first to speak. "That was *so* fucking cool!" he turned to Sanchez, "We could kill *so* many Nazis with that thing!"

"I know, right?!" Sanchez licked her lips.

Marlow turned to the techs, "Set ANNIE to respond to my voice commands, and *only* my voice commands."

The tech nodded and tapped out a few lines of code on his tablet.

"ANNIE?" Corcoran asked.

"Ape-like Nanotech something or another," Marlow responded, like a proud (if disinterested) parent.

ANNIE's eyes changed colour once more—this time, they burned a bright, intense orange. It turned its attention to Marlow.

"ANNIE, clear a path to where the red meteorite is being stored."

I half expected the ape to reply with POLARIS's voice, but it just nodded, let out a simian roar, and bounded down the hallway, using its hands to pull its feet forward.

Marlow and the POLARIS robots followed it, with the crew and me shortly behind.

"Didn't think to use the killer ape robot…" Corcoran shook his head and pointed a thumb at Marlow.

"Yes I suppose he seems a bit," I raised my hand horizontally next to my head, and shook it up into the sky, "spacey. But he *is* on our side."

Corcoran nodded as we ran, "Any friend of the giant killer ape robot is a friend'a mine."

We continued along the maze of T-Intersections. Thankfully, after one Chronosaber soldier was dumb enough to challenge ANNIE in our path, and was literally ripped limb-from-limb for his trouble, the rest of the human Chronosaber soldiers decided to scatter when they saw the ferocious mechanical ape bounding toward them.

We finally arrived at a rather non-descript corridor with the usual gleaming white lucite walls. Marlow put his hand on a spot on the wall, and a hologram gave way to another doorway.

"LA-9824 - Astromining," the sign next to it read.

"Quickly, quickly," Marlow said as he opened the double doors. "Not much time."

Somehow ANNIE was able to scrunch itself through the doorway. A couple anihilators were waiting on the other side and opened fire.

ANNIE bounded over to one, and bit its head off with great fanfare. It then used that anihilator's limp body to beat the other erstwhile warrior robot into a silent submission.

White-suited techs scrambled around the room. They were being ordered about presumably by scientists, who wore shimmering silver jumpsuits covered by traditional white labcoats.

"Protect the meteorite! Protect the meteorite from that… that *thing!*" One of the scientists screamed.

"Everybody calm down!" It was another scientist…but… could it be?

"Dr. Tyson? Is it *you?*" I covered my mouth as soon as the words came out. How uncharacteristic of me, but pardon me if fucking *Neil DeGrasse Tyson* didn't warrant a little bit of hero worship, as slack-jawed and rube-ish of me as it may seem.

The doctor simply nodded and smiled, "I get that a lot, actually."

"So you're *not* Neil DeGrasse Tyson then?"

The scientist shrugged.

Apparently that was all I was going to get out of him.

"Doctor Templeton, please—" Marlow made his way over to the

meteorite, which was surrounded by force fields at the center of the room. It was every bit as ruby red as described by the Atlanteans, and then some. It shone under a bright white spotlight, each angle cleaved into its face shimmering like the side of an Atlantean building at sunset. It was truly breathtaking…

…which made it all the more odd that I simply couldn't turn my attention away from the erstwhile Dr. DeGrasse Tyson.

"It's just—the resemblance is *uncanny*—"

"I don't think so," It was Bloomington.

I made a sour face at him.

"Lower the forcefield," Marlow raised a hand at the meteorite, as if commanding it to drop. Several *more* alarm sirens went off, and added to the cacophony.

"That's going to cause a new round of alarms," Marlow said.

We all narrowed our eyes at him, still apparently oblivious to the alarms that had started moments before. He remained non-plussed.

The billionaire turned to ANNIE. "Quickly—take that meteorite to the loading dock. And *protect it!*"

The ape nodded and bounded back through the door, followed closely behind by the POLARIS robots.

We ran after it once more.

"Don't you guys have a segway or something we can use?" Bloomington asked.

Marlow looked at him with eyes bulging overwide. His mustache trembled ever-so-slightly.

"A what?"

"It's this rolly…thing… we used to have—"

"I do not. What I do have—" he nodded ahead, "—is a fucking killer ape robot. Good enough?"

"I guess," Bloomington sounded defeated.

ANNIE bounded ahead; it cradled the meteorite like an American football in the crook of its elbow. Occasionally, it stiff-armed the odd annihilator or two, but it did not slow down.

Of course, that meant that we had to keep up. I must say, even *I* was feeling rather winded at this point, and hoped that wherever this "loading dock" was, it was somewhere nearby. Though to be fair, Bloomington and "Dr. Tyson" both lagged behind me.

After a half-dozen more corridors and turns, we finally stopped along another hallway. Marlow dissolved the hologram, and "LO-0003 Loading Dock" appeared next to the new doorway.

"Everyone inside—quickly! Very quickly now!" Marlow commanded.

We emerged in a large room that for the life of me appeared to be a hangar bay. A large tanker vehicle of some sort powered on as soon as Marlow entered the room. It had another cargo container hitched to the back of it. Two *very* snazzy-looking motorcycle-ish contraptions surrounded the tanker; I say "motorcycle-ish" because they had no discernable wheels!

"ANNIE, take a position in the cargo container, and for the love of *Albertson*, protect the crystal!"

The ape nodded, and bounded into the cargo container.

"What's in the tanker?" Corcoran nodded.

"Now's not the time, Commander," Marlow shook his head. "Besides, you'd never believe me if I told you."

"Try us," Sanchez said.

Marlow sighed.

"It's quartz."

"Pardon?"

"Liquid quartz crystals. It acts as a—a reagent with the water underneath the pyramid. We pump that into the tunnels and caverns in and underneath the Great Pyramid, and it should boost the power levels to what you need to power Dr. Thurbur's time cloak."

Of course! Quartz crystals! I thought it odd that the Atlanteans had built the Great Pyramid with a large granite "sarcophagus" in the King's Chamber.

"Granite contains quartz," I mused to myself, rubbing my bearded chin. "Quartz focuses the energy from the earth into *usable* energy in the Pyramid!"

Marlow paused and turned to me, "*Very* good, Doctor."

I nodded, sufficiently basking in approval.

He nodded in return, though this time at the bike-like vehicles.

"Captain Sanchez and Commander Corcoran will drive the hoverbikes. Specialist Bloomington and Doctor Templeton will ride shotgun, respectively."

"What about you?" Corcoran asked.

"My collegaue," he nodded at "Dr. DeGrasse Tyson," "and I will fly the tanker to the Pyramid. Hopefully we still have time…"

He let the words fade and entered the cab of the tanker. I quickly climbed on the back of Corcoran's hoverbike. It was well-built, to be sure, though being my first hoverbike, I didn't know exactly of what it was capable.

Neither, apparently, did Corcoran.

"Hang on to your ass," he said. He pressed at several buttons on the clear HUD screen of the hoverbike, but nothing happened.

I nodded at the lever extending from the steering column, with a big red button that had an "ON" sign next to it.

He snorted and pressed it. The bike came to life, whirring up what sounded for the life of me like a magnetically-enhanced gravity drive.

"Be careful—if that's what I think it is, it's going to have a *bit* of kic—"

He turned the handlebar and the hoverbike jumped to life. We bolted through the hangar bay forcefield and into the streets of Cairo. It was all I could do to hold on to Ricky for dear life.

"Yeeeeee-fuckin'-haaaaa!" Ricky called out to no one in particular. The HUD flashed with coordinates and a preferred route to get to Klaus's position near the Pyramid.

Surprisingly, right behind us were Sanchez and Bloomington on the other hoverbike, and the tanker truck followed closely behnid them.

0:51 to destination… the HUD read. *0:50… 0:49… 0:48…*

Suddenly, three flashing red dots appeared on the screen.

WARNING: Chronosaber vehicles ahead. Altering route.

Three large metallic spheres blocked the route ahead. They looked like giant ball bearings, though they just *sat* there, lifeless for the moment.

"Are we to be *afraid* of these—"

The giant ball-bearings seemed to "bounce" briefly off the pavement, and came alive. Without any sort of noise at all, they eerily started following us, first matching our speed, and then seeking to overtake it.

I felt more than a bit like Indiana Jones with the boulder bearing down on him in *Raiders of the Lost Ark!*

"Can't we go *faster?*" I implored the Commander.

"Gee, why the *fuck* didn't I think of that?" Corcoran shot back. "These big brass balls got all *kinds'a* get-up and go!"

"Well in about five seconds, we're going to be crushed!" I couldn't help but think that my estimate may have been over-generous.

"Hang on—I've got an idea—"

Corcoran wrenched the bike to the side. I nearly lost my grip on the bike's footholds, not to mention the eggs that Bloomington and Sanchez had cooked up earlier that morning.

Nonetheless, the ball bearing took a moment to correct. If nothing else, it bought us some time.

That is, until I turned my attention forward. Corcoran had (inadvertently?) turned so that we were hurtling toward a rather imposing metal wall at a frightening speed!

"Ricky? Ricky! Godamnit Ric—"

"God*damn* it Doc trust me a bit won'tchya?"

"To what? Purchase sufficient life insurance for me in the next three seconds before we're flatter than—"

I could see the scowl on the Commander's face through the back of his head. He balled up his fist, and his forearm trembled. For a moment, I thought I might finally fall victim to the full force and impact of Ricky's famous temper.

Suddenly, he jammed his fist down on a big purple button with some upward-looking symbols on it.

The bike whirred. Perhaps all of a foot away from the wall, we stopped moving forward on a dime, and launched into the air for what seemed like a full minute.

"Rickkkkkyyyyyyyyyy!" I screamed, perhaps three octaves higher than usual. Forgive me, dear reader—I fear my arsehole may have puckered up all the way into the back of my throat.

Almost as suddenly, we stopped our ascent and traversed the, in hindsight, humourously short top of the wall, which was all of a meter wide.

Finally, the pit of my stomach dropped like a stone. We free-fell down the other side of the wall for several heart-stopping seconds. I tugged on every handhold I could find, searching for… what? A parachute? Some sort of eject mechanism? Truth of the matter is, when your life is flashing in front of your eyes, a very powerful and base survival instinct kicks in.

It was powerful enough to dispel any notion of "God" or "the afterlife" from my mind. After all, if paradise awaited on the other side, why would the prospect of shuffling off this mortal coil be quite so awful?

On the other hand, were we to consider "the universe" more broadly as a "God" of some sort, then I had no doubt in my mind at that very moment that God was, in fact, all too real.

Finally, we reached near the ground again. Our descent halted with a sudden *JOLT* so powerful that I was immediately re-assured that my arsehole was back in its ordinary position, and *quite* bruised to boot.

Then, as if we had just gone over a mere speed bump, the bike raced ahead back at full speed, the giant ball bearing a distant memory… for now.

CHAPTER THIRTY-ONE

"You okay Doc?" Corcoran yelled back.

I opened my mouth to respond, but unfortunately all that came out were more of the eggs Bloomington had cooked that morning. They covered the Commander's back in a sticky, yellow-and-orange pastiche.

"God *damn* it!" he shook his head. "Ain't got time for this shit, Ricky," he yelled at himself.

"Sorry!" I croaked out. The back of my throat still felt acidic with sick.

"Hey computer, how much time to target?" Corcoran asked.

9…8…7… flashed on the screen.

I looked up, and sure enough, the pyramid was right there in front of us. I had forgotten that before the War, Cairo had extended almost fully to the Giza plateau. Since its subsequent bombardment and rebuilding, the city now extended to mere meters away from the ancient structure.

After having seen it in all of its glory in Atlantean times, it now seemed somehow old and decrepit; a shadow of its former self. Like when seeing a reclusive actor many years after his last big role, now just playing out the string, and waiting for "the next step" that awaits us all.

Hopefully, that next step puts things back as they're supposed to be… I thought.

We arrived at the pyramid at the same time as Sanchez's bike. Ricky "slid" the hoverbike sideways to stop its momentum, presumably to look cool.

Sanchez did the same, though she cut it much closer to the side of the pyramid, and thus, looked much *cooler*.

The Captain nodded at me. "Rough trip?"

"Bad *driver*," I corrected her.

"You ain't a pancake, are ya?" Corcoran shot back.

The tanker truck peeled around a corner, and barreled toward us.

It was followed closely behind by several of the large ball bearings. Glowing projectiles flew from the back of the truck at the metallic spheres, though it was only as the truck got closer that I realized that ANNIE was quite literally *throwing rockets* at the spheres.

The truck stopped several meters from us. Without much fanfare, it extended a long arm from its chassis toward the ground, and shot a laser straight downward. Within seconds, the beam stopped, and what appeared to be a robotic hose extended into the cavity and began pumping liquid quartz into the ground.

Marlow jumped down from the cab.

"Quickly—find Klaus! He *must* be somewhere around here."

"What about the unwanted company?" Corcoran nodded at the ball bearings barreling toward us.

Marlow shook his head, "Let ANNIE worry about that! You find Klaus—*now!"* He pointed at the near corner of the Pyramid. Instinctively, the four of us ran toward it.

Perhaps curious to witness more of the robot ape's carnage, I looked over my shoulder to see how it would deal with these curious, seemingly sentient ball bearings.

ANNIE ran toward the ball bearings. It stood tall and beat its chest at the spheres.

The nearest one didn't slow down—if anything it increased speed as it approached the mechanical ape.

ANNIE didn't flinch. The nanotech-reinforced beast raised its arms in front of it and grasped onto the giant sphere. It dug its heels into the ground as it moved backward. ANNIE found its footing and picked up the giant orb, as effortlessly as if it were a beach ball. It threw the giant orb perhaps half a kilometer and let out a satisfying roar.

"Yes!" I couldn't help but let out a cheer and pump my fist at the feat.

Only… the ball bearing came roaring back. It stopped perhaps twenty meters away from the robotic beast. Several other of the ball bearings joined it, side-by-side, as if preparing a firing squad to take on the beast. In all, there were probably nine of the ball bearings joined together in a straight line directly across from ANNIE.

ANNIE cocked its head to one side, confused, if only for a moment. It doubled down on its roar and beat its chest even more wildly than previously.

Suddenly, one of the ball bearings on the end seemed to melt. It turned into a sideways cone-shaped structure, before a tongue of liquid metal shot out from the side. Yellow eyes formed on it, and fangs extended out from the "mouth" that was being carved into the metal.

The ball bearings had joined up to create a giant, metallic snake!

I shivvered as I pondered just how *ghastly* this fight was shaping up to be.

ANNIE roared forward. It launched at the snake, teeth beared—

"Hey, Doc! Keep the fuck up, will ya?!" Corcoran snapped.

"But… but!" I stammered. "The robot fight—"

"Yeah! This is gonna be cool…as…*fuck!"* Bloomington said.

Corcoran smacked me once, hard, in the face.

"We gotta get to Klaus, God *damn* it!"

I waited for the similar slap for Bloomington as well… but it wasn't forthcoming.

I shook my head, ruefully. Perhaps some other time there'd be a chance to see such a spectacle. Though I wondered if such an opportunity would occur in my lifetime.

My dejection quickly turned into relief as we came upon Klaus's hodgepodge of a time machine. The capstone base was uncloaked, and attached to the top of the ship.

"So, children! Have fun?" he asked, in his cheerily-accented English.

"I could ask the same of you," I formed my mouth into a tight smile. I put a hand on Klaus's shoulder. "Helene didn't find you, did she?"

He shook his head, "No, thank *Got!"* His German accent settled on the word more pronounced. "She would've filleted my scrot—"

"We get the idea, Professor," Corcoran shot back at him. He collected himself with a deep breath, even while still moving at a brisk walk. "So what's the plan now?"

Klaus nodded at the tanker truck. I couldn't help but steal a glance at ANNIE, which had raised one of the giant metal balls over its head, and was throwing it at the rest of the gigantic metal snake like a football throw-in.

The giant metal ball hit one of the other orbs at a startling speed, and the mechanical ape let out a reverberating roar.

But as soon as it hit, the ball stopped and fell to the ground. The snake reared up and hissed.

Another hand cracked me across the face, with even more force.

This time, it was Sophia.

"Ow! What the *devil—*"

"Hey," she snapped her fingers several times in my face, "Eyes on the prize Finny."

I nodded.

Klaus activated the holodisplay attached to his smart watch.

"POLARIS, come in."

"Yesssssss Massssssterrrrr."

"Secure the red crystal from Mr. Marlow near the tanker truck and bring it to the *Saint-Germain* for fabrication into the true capstone, per the specifications in program Thurbur Alpha."

"Yesssssss Massssssterrrrr."

Klaus clicked off his holodisplay.

"And now we wait…"

Unfortunately, the fight between Annie and the gigantic Chronosaber ball-bearing snake had moved firmly into suburban Cairo, and thus was no longer visible. From time-to-time, I heard incredible noises that made it sound like something *incredibly amazing* was happening; the whirring of a saw blade… several high-pitched hisses and mechanical roars… the odd plasma-based explosion here or there…

Bloomington and I looked at each other like the only children forced to sit out Christmas that year.

Finally, POLARIS bounded over to the ship, repaired leg and all. It carted the red crystal above its head, and Klaus hurried up the gangway and quickly emerged with a box of other materials.

"Thankkkk you Masssssssster." POLARIS said. Within a minute or two, it went to work cleaving and carving the crystal to spec. We all

stood nearby, mouths agape at the quick work the robot was making of the project.

A laser bolt flew overhead. I instinctively ducked as Corcoran and Sanchez unholstered their weapons.

A cadre of anihilator robots was advancing on our position, perhaps 500 metres away. While Marlow's POLARIS robots were stalling their advance somewhat, the Chronosaber robots pressed onward toward the ancient building. Soon enough, the hulking, maniacal robots would be in range to target and hit us.

Fortunately, POLARIS itself was nearly finished fabricating the true capstone out of the red crystal meteorite.

"Proccccccesssss Compleeeeete." POLARIS said.

"Excellent! Well done POLARIS and thank you!" Klaus said.

"You're welllllllcome Masssssterrrrr." The robot looked at the rest of us as if to punctuate the fact that we hadn't so much as offered it a "thank you" for all of the help it had given us.

"I swear to *God*, if this *shit* doesn't work…" Bloomington of course saw it as another opportunity to threaten the robot and "put it in its place."

POLARIS stared back, as expressionless as its maniacal face could be.

Klaus nodded at the tanker truck once more. "By my calculations, the liquid quatz crystals should be 90% in place by now, underneath and inside of the pyramid. So, Finny—" he turned his attention toward me, "—we'll cut a way into the control room at the top of the pyramid. Commander Corcoran, Captain Sanchez, and some of our friendly robots will lay down covering fire on the advancing Chronosaber troops and beasties. POLARIS will attach both the capstone base and the true capstone to the top of the pyramid, and you, Finny, will get out into the control room and, as you say in America, 'get this show on the road' by pushing that sideways bar forward, or whatever it was you said they did to turn it on. Good?"

I nodded, "Absolutely."

We climbed aboard Klaus's ship. Until that moment, I didn't realise just how damned *alien* it seemed to me. To use a Star Trek analogy, if the clean lines and brushed aluminium of my original design were meant to evoke a perfect, Enterprise-D-era Federation vessel, then the monstrous renovations Klaus had made to his machine to add the time cloak made it look downright *Cardassian* by comparison. Ugly brown metal claws surrounded and cradled the ship with all of the love and tender care of a tarantula. Gaudy flashing lights and harsh angles completed the rather *Terek-Nor*-style of the craft.

Once we were aboard, I found myself in the somewhat awkward position of trying to climb in the Captain's chair at the same time as Klaus. We bumped heads and exchanged curses.

"Old habits die hard, my friend," I said, and extended a hand outward to the chair.

"Thank you, Finny." Klaus nodded his approval.

Klaus immediately took control of what appeared to be an enhanced omni-yoke.

"Computer, execute program Thurbur Beta."

"*Executing program Thurbur Beta.*" The computer said in reply, with the honest-to-God same voice as the computer in *Next Generation*.

"*Super* cool!" Bloomington blurted out. "The old ship just had a fucking dumb-ass *screen*—"

"Don't speak ill of the dead!" I shot a look at Bloomington, perhaps a bit overly forcefully. He frowned and looked downward at his shoelaces.

There was little time to feel sorry for the old QC that had bit the dust earlier that same day. The ship floated up to the level of the control room within seconds. Several more seconds and it had carved out the near-exact size and shape of the pyramid's doorway. And moments later, the ship had maneuvered into position next to the pyramid, and extended the gangway down to the carved-out blocks of stone.

Klaus nodded at me.

"That's wonderful and all, Klaus, but those blocks weigh several tonnes, and—"

"Ah—almost forgot!" he reached down and produced the trident we had brought with us from Atlantis. He held it out to me, and I gladly grabbed it. "Thought this might come in handy, so I had POLARIS pull it from the other ship's wreckage."

"Always a step ahead, eh old chap?" I asked. I extended the trident toward the block, and then pushed the button I had seen the teenagers using to carve the sculpture of Archimedes back in Atlantis.

The blocks started to slowly sift away into sand, revealing the familiar control room in which I had nearly croaked back in Atlantean times.

Suddenly, the craft lurched with a jolt, though I moreso "saw" it out of the extended gangway than felt it.

"We've got incoming fire from Chronosaber aircraft!" Sanchez nodded at the front of the ship. Three menacing-looking time machines floated to triangulate our position. Unlike my original version of the time machine that we had grown to love, these were outfitted with several "non-tunneling" lasers, as well as what appeared to be some kind of missile or torpedo tubes.

Corcoran unbuckled himself from the gunnery seat and practically threw Sanchez into it.

"Don't fuckin' let us die, darlin'," he grinned at her and planted a (rather long and lingering, I thought, given the circumstances) kiss on her lips.

Before their lips had disengaged, Sanchez's hands were flying over the console, deploying whatever weaponry with which Klaus had outfitted his ship. Even as she fired the first laser blast at an enemy ship, she allowed herself to bite down on her lip for the shortest of moments.

Corcoran stormed toward me. He didn't have to say anything—I extended the trident toward him, and in a single motion he levelled it at the carved out blocks, and hit them with a graviton beam.

He ran down the ramp, and lifted the blocks out of place, almost as if they were movie props, and flung them out, seemingly indiscriminently toward the ground below.

I couldn't have imagined what happened next if I had tried; Corcoran turned toward the now-weightless stone blocks flying through the air. He picked up the trident with one hand and held it out in front of him. With his other hand, he made a "V" between his thumb and forefinger, and held it out at arms length.

He waited… and waited… two seconds… three. Finally, when I was about to say something fully smart-arsed about getting on with it, he unleashed another graviton beam at the falling rock.

It immediately regained its heft, and plowed into a group of Chronosaber anihilator bots that were trying to flank some POLARIS-class bots on the ground.

"Woo-*hoo!*" I couldn't help but let out a child-like scream of joy.

Ricky turned to me and flashed a grin ever-so-briefly before he nodded at the hole in the pyramid.

"Go on Doc—take us home."

I nodded and took a running start as I leapt the short distance onto the platform. Ricky covered me from the ship, LR-15 in hand. He shot off several laser bolts into the air, presumably trying to help Commander Sanchez defend the ship.

I found myself in the familiar control room from Atlantean times.

"Lights!" I ordered to whatever Atlantean-era computer might still be listening.

Nothing happened.

Maybe it was that the holotran wasn't translating into proper Atlantean yet since it had no frame of reference.

But it was far more likely that I had a far larger problem to deal with. One that wasn't readily fixable given that we were some 12,000 years from the last time this grand machine had operated:

The Great Pyramid was dead.

CHAPTER THIRTY-TWO

"Klaus? Come in, Klaus?"

"Yes, Finny—have you started the machinery yet?"

A loud crash came over the open channel. I hoped it wasn't Klaus's time machine being smashed to bits.

"I have *not*—we have a slight problem. It appears the mechanism in here is quite dead."

There was a delay for one second… two. I started playing out awful fantasies in my head, wondering what the *devil* I was going to do if Klaus's time machine had been shot out of the air and was disabled (or worse).

"Roger that, Finny. POLARIS is crunching the—"

Someone muttered something on the line in a low, muted (yet nasaly) tone that I couldn't make out.

"What was that?" I asked.

"Well I'll be damned Bloomy. It's just crazy enough to—" Corcoran said over the line.

Suddenly, the time machine darted away from the hole in the side of the pyramid. It performed perhaps two dozen quick maneuvers in the span of ten seconds, dodging laser fire with each precise movement. The evasive maneuvers were acrobatic enough (and I was high enough on the platform) that my fear of heights momentarily took over, and made me feel quite ill.

I shook my head out of it.

"Hang on—it's going to be close—"

The ship moved in as close as it could to the hole in the pyramid. Suddenly, a small, wombat-like form darted out of the craft. It landed with surprising grace, tumbling into a somersault before Steve Bloomington hit the ground running.

Right behind him, several mechanical hands grasped the side of the entrance to the chamber. Within moments, three Chronosaber anihilator bots had hoisted themselves into the room. They unholstered their weapons and levelled them on Bloomington and myself.

Instinctively, I reached for my Baretta. The ship came about and spun its turrets to face the opening.

"For *fuck's* sake—" I said, to no one in particular. "They *can't* be planning to—"

The turrets whirred to life. Bloomington leapt at me and used his momentum to fling both of us toward one of the side walls. Laser fire illuminated the ancient corridor, and immediately two of the anihilators were "semi-vaporised" as best I can describe it; their torsos were completely disappeared by the laser fire, while assorted limbs and head parts only remained behind.

Somehow, the third robot avoided the same fate. Its gun was trained directly on us now; the barrel spun up angrily and its eyes appeared to narrow, almost as if the damndable machine was hellbent on avenging the "deaths" of its comrades.

"Not today, boltcock!" Bloomington let out a weird, glutteral shriek as he unloaded his laser pistol on the angry-looking robot.

The bolts pelted the anihilator and threw off its aim with each hit. As the droid was forced to recalibrate, I couldn't help but think that the only thing keeping me from being turned into pure ash was Steve Bloomington's itchy trigger finger on the laser pistol that I had designed.

Every time as the robot was about to fire, a new volley from Bloomington's laser pistol hit it, and though it wasn't damaged, the robot couldn't ever seem to come to a firing solution and pull the trigger.

"I say, Sophia, now would be a good time for another one of those—"

The laser pistol beeped. I recognised the tone within a split second—it meant that the power source was becoming overheated.

"Fartnuggets!" Bloomington screamed. "Fucking dumbass piece of *shit*—" He hit the handle of the laser pistol against the ground several times. It was a testament to my (ahem) amazing construction that it didn't break on the spot.

That was the opening the robot needed; it levelled its weapon at the two of us once more. I fired my Baretta indiscriminently, hoping against hope to hit something critical.

Then, as the anihilator's gun spun up, signaling our imminent demise, I shut my eyes tight. For a brief, fleeting moment, I was back as a happy-go-lucky child sitting on my father's shoulders, walking joyfully up-and-down the banks of the Thames.

Father jostled me up-and-down rapidly.

"Oh no—damned cobblestones!" He teased as he picked up his gait.

"Dad! No—stop!" I said in-between gleeful laughs.

As we passed the familiar alleyway in which I had spent the better part of several months, dressed as a bum, I saw my older, pitiable form come into view. It was me alright, but I looked awful. It wasn't just the malnutrition, or the excessive whisky consumption either; rather it was the sick, twisted *glee* on the bum's face. How my older self was *relishing* getting a verbal beat-down by my father week-in and week-out.

My father turned beneath me to address the bum. And I was certain what his next words were going to be.

I was wrong.

"Someone's coming to save you—" he said to the bum, in his firm, even tone. "—Someone's coming to save us all."

I was jolted out of my reverie by the sound of a laser gun. Only it wasn't the whirring of the minigun bolted to the anihilator, but rather the familiar sharp whine of an LR-15.

The anihilator stumbled back several feet as it turned to face its new assailant. But the LR-15 was firing on automatic, and slowly, but methodically carving its way through the metal skeleton of the wretched robot.

Finally, several laser bolts connected with the anihilator's head, and sent it flying far away from the rest of the robot's body.

I dared to heave a sigh and looked down the corridor.

There, with the laser rifle flung casually over his leather-jacket-clad shoulder, wearing sunglasses was none other than—

"Ricky!" Bloomington shouted.

"You two called for help?" he grinned and extended a hand down to me.

I accepted and rose to my feet before dusting myself off.

"I suppose I owe you another one now," I said. I looked at him semi-sideways, "Though were the sunglasses *entirely* necessary

Ricky?"

He shrugged, "Yeah. If you wanna look cool. As. *Fuck.*"

"Badass!" Bloomington blurted out.

I couldn't help but nod my approval.

Corcoran turned to Bloomington, "Now what was this about a 'jump start,' or whatever Bloomy?"

Bloomington nodded, "Yeah, I mean this shit hasn't been used for thousands of years, right? So whatever power source it used probably needs—"

"—Another power source to get it going." I interrupted.

He nodded, "Yep."

I frowned, "But Steven, as sharp as your observation may be, we have no way of knowing what kind of connector Atlanteans used for power. It's not like we can use a USB cable or AC plug or even a pair of jumper cables and start this pyramid like a dead automobile."

He snorted. "Duh! But you said this thing absorbs power from the Earth, right?"

"I suppose that's how it works. I'm not sure—other than what Klaus showed all of us, I got a ten cent tour from a Lemurian spy and that blonde himbo Captain of the Guard."

Corcoran instinctively turned to survey the hole in the pyramid's facade. Though there weren't any anihilators trying to force their way in *yet*, I understood the hidden subtext of his glance:

We had to hurry.

"Well, let's just assume that's the case." Bloomington pulled out a packet of medigel from his pocket and casually flung it at me.

"Medigel? Steven, I don't know what you know about the properties of medigel, but I'm *quite* certain that the chemical reaction inside doesn't contain enough energy—"

Bloomington clasped a clammy hand on my shoulder, "Doc, Doc—I love you man. Seriously, I do. But that said, can you *please* shut the *fuck* up for a second? Just like one second, literally, I'm about to solve all our shit, okay?"

I was taken aback by Bloomington's abrupt show of confidence, *true* confidence, as opposed to his usual bravado.

I bit my lower lip and forced a thin smile and nod.

Bloomington rolled his eyes—at me!—and continued.

"I'm not gonna try to use the medigel to blow some shit up, *r-tard!*" He raised his shirt up.

I recoiled involuntarily.

He started to pull at the PEBBLE (or as you likely remember them, the "fatteries") from his midsection.

"Jesus *Christ* Bloomy—are you okay?" Corcoran grabbed his arm.

Bloomington slapped his hand away.

"*Yes...*" He let out through gritted teeth. The fatteries inched out from the piles of white, hairy skin that surrounded them.

"Steven—are you quite sure?" I asked him.

"Just open the medigel and pour it on me once I get... this...*fucker*..."

He gave the fatteries one last yank, and they came flying out of his stomach. Blood started to fly everywhere as his guts and internal organs were exposed for all the world to see.

I quickly tore open the medigel with my teeth and poured the teal goo on the gaping wound.

"...OUT!" He flung the contraption across the room. It landed near the stone control console for the pyramid and beeped a couple of times.

Then, the device pulsed several times and exploded.

The flash forced our eyes away and the force of the blast pushed us up against the side walls. My ears pounded for three or four seconds as a loud whine filled the room. All three of us cursed for different reasons until we were able to turn back to the source of the blast.

For a moment, there was nothing. It appeared that Bloomington's plan had been a dud.

Then a finger of electricity crawled across the control console. Then another. Soon the bolts turned to the coloured patterns of energy that had filled the room back in Atlantean times.

"My *God* Steven—I think you did it!" I said.

Bloomington, though, was sprawled out on the ground, moaning in pain.

"Owwww! The *fuck!* It hurts!"

The blood was at least beginning to pool and mix with the medigel on his stomach. Corcoran attended to his fallen comrade, who by all accounts was near the threshold level of pain he could endure.

"Hey. Hey come on now buddy. Steve? Everything's gonna be okay now, ya hear?" Corcoran put a hand on his shoulder, while steadying the LR-15 at the gaping hole in the pyramid in his other hand.

"I—I don't know if it will." Bloomington croaked out.

Corcoran turned to me, "Bloomy did his part, Doc. Now do your thing with the—" he nodded at the stone levers and rods on the control panel, "—whatever the sam *fuck* that thing is."

I hurried over to the control panel and racked my brain to remember how Birusha had set it up for maximum power.

Actually, that brought up a good point.

"Klaus? Come in, Klaus."

"Ja Finny."

"How much power do you need from the pyramid to charge up the ship."

He paused in thought.

"All of it you can spare. Full power. That's the only way to ensure we get enough. Then when we're topped off, we'll let the crystal destroy itself and the pyramid go dormant. It's the only way we can ensure that Helene won't follow us."

I nodded, "Roger that. See you in a few."

"Roger that. Positioning the ship now."

I extended the vertical rods as fully as they would go to get to the "full power" position that Birusha had shown me back in Atlantean times. A noticeable hum filled the room and the lights that danced along the wall intensified.

"Hey Doc, hurry the *fuck* on up now, will ya? Sophie says we got Chronosaber anihilators fixin' to climb up the sides of the pyramid, lots of 'em. And I ain't think they're makin' a social visit, catch my drift?"

I nodded.

He scooped up Bloomington and carried him toward the hole in the side of the pyramid.

"Klaus, come in? Are you in position?"

"Not quite… not quite… okay! POLARIS finished installing the capstones atop the pyramid, and is back inside. We are in position. All set Finny—let her *rrrrrip!*"

I took a deep breath and heaved my body into the giant horizontal stone bar that served as the pyramid's on/off switch.

It moved, but barely a twitch.

At this rate, it was going to take forever to get the pyramid going again. And we had *slightly* "less-than-forever" in which to do it.

I knew what I had to do. I hated it. Hated putting him through it, but—

"Hey Ricky? Steve? I need your help."

Corcoran visibly snarled as he looked over his shoulder.

"Kinda busy saving Steve's life here, Doc."

"I need your help to move this bar," I pointed at the large horizontal stone that had to be pushed forward. "It hasn't been moved in *centuries*—millenia even! And I need your help—both of you—to do it."

Bloomington let out a loud groan.

"I don't think Bloomy's gonna be much good to ya, Doc," Corcoran said.

"We *need* to do this, or the mission fails. Simple as that." I punctuated it with a forced shrug.

"God *fuck* it all," Corcoran said. I could practically feel his eyes rolling at me, even though his face was turned away from me at present. "Come on Bloomy. Let's help Doc finish this."

He helped Bloomington hobble over to me as quickly as he could. It seemed like Bloomington was gaining more mobility and function by the minute, but his skin was especially pasty. Sweat beaded on the tips of the thick, coarse body hair that coated every exposed inch of his flesh. He half-whimpered with each step closer to the beam.

Finally, both reached my position. Corcoran and I helped steady

Steven in a way that he could exert maximum force on the stuck sideways stone pillar. I took the opposite end, and Corcoran hopped in-between us.

"Okay, on the count of three," Corcoran said. "One... two...*three!*"

We pushed against the stone bar with all of our might. It moved more than it had with my solo effort... but just barely.

"Oh my God! Oh my *God!* That fucking *hurt! Shit! Fuck! Wart-fuck!"*

Corcoran patted him on the back, "It's okay buddy... it's okay... deep breath now."

I resteadied myself and braced for another push.

"One...two...*three!*"

The stone bar picked up slightly more momentum. It was about halfway there now. I could feel the mechanism on my side loosening and unlocking.

"Titty-*fuck!*" Bloomington said. "Titty-titty-titty-*fuck!"*

"Feeling better, are we?" I couldn't help myself.

Corcoran glared at me.

"One... two...*three*!"

This time, the bar gave way. All three of us fell forward, flat on our faces. Bloomington started to unleash a string of curse words, but they were muffled by the sounds of the pyramid gearing up to unleash the enormous untapped power within it.

The walls crackled with colour and electricity. The massive structure vibrated, then shook as it charged up for one final spectacular discharge of power.

"We need to go!" I yelled above the din.

"Let's get the fuck *out* of here!" Corcoran yelled, apparently not hearing me.

Corcoran and I took up either side of Bloomington and practically carried him toward the open hole in the side of the pyramid. It was all we could do to keep from breaking out in an all-out sprint as we reached the old platform, and felt the cool nighttime desert air on our faces.

Three bright flashes went up inside the pyramid, and the capstone released a torrent of energy toward the sky. It was rather beautiful; not nearly as focused as a laser beam, but kind of with a weird, lava-lamp-like array of reds and purples that arced skyward into the clear starry night.

The blast hit the time machine and enveloped it, cradling it in nourishing energy. The ship pulsed and spun, soaking up as much as it could like a homeless kitten lapping up milk left at a stranger's door.

"70 percent power… 80 percent… 90 percent… 100 percent!" Klaus said triumphantly.

The three of us couldn't help but quickly partake in what Corcoran would later call a "man hug." We raised a fist in the air and cheered for what seemed like a good ten seconds.

"110 percent… 120… 130…" the jubilation turned to trepidation in Klaus's voice in mere moments. "Have to get out of here—stand-by!"

Suddenly, the ship did a backflip out of its position atop the pyramid, tumbling end-over-end toward us. It was sure to take us out if we waited, so we grabbed Bloomington and dove back inside the pyramid.

We waited for the collision with the giant structure.

But it never happened.

I wrenched open an eye and mustered up the courage to walk to the hole and look outside.

There was the time machine, back under Klaus's control, slowly inching toward the hole to pick us up.

The gangway deployed.

"Quickly! Get on board—the anihilators are closing on your posit—"

As if to punctuate the statement, a volley of laser fire carved up the facade of the pyramid directly over my head.

I scrambled back inside and put my arm around Bloomington. Corcoran took the other side and we pulled him into the opening. With his free arm, Ricky shot cover fire in the general direction of the robots.

They answered back. The bolts came more quickly this time, almost as if they were right… on… top of us…

"Make a run for it!" Corcoran said. He heaved Bloomington ahead, then ran in front of the wounded scientist to protect him as he stumbled up the gangway.

"Come on, Doc!" he yelled at me. I dodged one laser bolt, then another as I ran full speed toward the craft.

Just a few…more…steps…

Something compelled me to stop, and a half-dozen laser bolts carved up the space immediately in front of me.

The ship's turrets turned on the source of the laser bolts and returned fire of their own. I had neither the time nor the presence to see whether or not they hit their mark, but at least they bought me enough time.

I scrambled on board, and fell to the floor, in a heap.

CHAPTER THIRTY-THREE

"Computer, please close the gangway right now!"

I thought Klaus picked a rather ridiculous time to continue his practised politeness toward all things machine.

I stumbled to my feet, and made my way to the control deck.

"You did it!" Klaus said. He extended a hand upward and I grasped it awkwardly, as you might imagine two men who had spent more time with books than people might.

"No—*we* did it!" I corrected him. "All of us. From the good Captain's covering fire," I nodded at Sanchez, "To POLARIS doing the heavy lifting," I acknowledged the robot, "To Corcoran and Bloomington's abject heroics back there," I nodded at the two men who I now considered my long-term compatriots, and dare I say, my closest friends (other than Klaus, of course).

"Yeah, we can all have a nice little circle-jerk once we're the hell *out* of here," I was only half-surprised that it was Sanchez.

"Quite right, Captain Sanchez!" Klaus punctuated the statement with a clap of his hands. "Now as I mentioned before, the ideal place to start is probably your old stoimping grounds, Chronobase Alpha. Way back in dinosaur times since that time cloak jump will require the most energy, and—"

Bloomington pushed the glasses up on his face. With all of the pain he must have been going through, it was telling that he sat up wordlessly off the ground, and pointed at the scene unfolding in front of us out the command deck viewscreen.

The pyramid still belted red and purple energy into the night sky. Only at some point away—far, *far* away, that energy crackled and jumped in wide, long, irregular arcs.

As it did so, the night sky began to "crack," like a glass dome being chiseled away by a sharp pickaxe. The cracks grew longer and more intertwined as the sky rippled and undulated.

Then, to my amazement, the sky shattered. Millions of pieces danced for a split second, rather like the holographic Chronosaber logo that shattered in that promotional video I had first seen back at Chronosaber Alpha, all those months ago.

And when the holographic pieces had fallen, all that was left was…

…an identical night sky?

It's hard to describe though; the stars twinkled more, and seemed a bit more vibrant against the utter midnight darkness of the sky set next to it.

"What in the sam *fuck?*" Corcoran whispered.

Then the *really* weird stuff started happening.

One gigantic cigar-shaped craft seemed to flash into existence out of nowhere in the sky above us.

Then another odd ship appeared, this one a massive top-hat that dwarfed Klaus's time machine.

Ships started popping up around us, one per second. Their sizes, shapes, and colours were as varied as all of the combined minds of all of the science fiction writers throughout history.

Finally, one massive saucer-shaped craft materialised directly above us. It was purple, and had a cyllindrical band of lights around the sides, and one massive light in the middle on the top and bottom.

It hovered over our position for just an instant before the large light underneath it shot out and hit our ship. The noise with which it hit started as a mere buzz, then built up to a cacophony of hums, clicks, and dare I say voices.

"What's going on?" I looked around at Klaus, then at Corcoran, then at Sanchez, utterly clueless.

"What the *devil* is going on?"

Then I heard a sharp crack.

And everything faded to black.

TO BE CONCLUDED...

THANKS FOR READING!

Sorry this has been so long in the making! I promise that the final volume of the trilogy will be out much sooner—hopefully by the end of 2021. I've already made good progress on the start, and I think you'll really enjoy it as the conclusion of this part of the WATT universe's saga.

A couple things before you go though.

If you'd like **a special bonus chapter—the fight between ANNIE and Chronosaber's big ball-bearing snake in all its glory**—subscribe to my newsletter at:

https://www.djgelner.com/anniefight

And I'll shoot it right on over to you.

Also, if you enjoyed this book, please consider leaving a review and telling others about it. Word of mouth really is the best kind of marketing, and I'm always looking to connect with you and your networks of like-minded WATT-heads.

Thanks again, and *Templeton Was a Time Traveler* (might need to work on that acronym) will be out within a year-ish!

ACKNOWLEDGEMENTS

This book was even more difficult to finish up than the eight year gap between books might indicate. I was all on-track to release it by the end of March, 2020… and then the COVID-19 pandemic hit.

Not only that, but my trusty buddy, Sully, lost his battle with a debilitating degenerative disease just as this book was getting ready for final publication. To those that know me, he was the inspiration for Klaus's dog, Archimedes, and I miss the heck out of him.

Also, my father-in-law, Jim, passed away unexpectedly as *CWATT* was getting finished. Jim was always one of my biggest fans and champions—he bought paperback copies of all of my books to hand out at our wedding, among other things. He did get an advance proof copy of *CWATT* before it was finished, so I sincerely hope that he had the chance to read it before crossing over, and it was to his liking.

So that's all my way of saying "Sorry it took so long—even at the end here." I'll do my best to get the next book out much more quickly.

On to the acknowledgements!

Right up front, I want to thank my beautiful, funny, smart, wonderful wife, Kate. Without her gentle prodding, beta reading, and support, there's a good chance this manuscript would've sat in a drawer for another five years or so before I got around to finishing it. Love you babe!

My wonderful daughter Kara, you are the light of my life. I love you more than words can ever express. I hope that someday (not *too* soon) you're able to enjoy this series without earmuffs.

To any other kids Kate and I might have someday… sorry kiddos, missed the boat on this one! Maybe the next book we'll get you.

To the rest of my family, thanks for your guys' support and encouragement. My brother, Grant, especially—he may have meant it as an off-hand comment, but at Thanksgiving 2018, he mentioned that, "Well, *JWATT* should definitely be a best-seller, if more people knew about it!" That was really kind of the kick in the pants I needed to finish the stretch run here.

To Chris Boucher, who's wonderful and delightful performance of *JWATT* also gave me a little extra push to keep going with this one. His spot-on renditions of the characters helped me get back inside their heads whenever I felt lost.

To Geoff Colman, perhaps my greatest reader and Facebook buddy out there. Thanks for all of your guidance and help putting this thing together, even with all of the stops and starts.

And finally, to you, the reader who decided to check out this book. Thanks for continuing along with me on this special journey—if you and your friends keep buying these, I'll keep writing them.

ALSO BY D.J. GELNER

Jesus Was a Time Traveler

In case you missed it... you can find it here:

https://www.amazon.com/Jesus-Time-Traveler-WATT-Book-ebook/dp/B00AHHVC94/

ROGUE

Men and women huddled hundreds deep, hoping to will their way into the secretive facility. Struggle or interfere on the long desert trek and they're shot. Getting in is tough; thousands will be turned away. Once inside, hard labor and years of servitude await.

Far fewer still will accomplish their ultimate goal, a whisper of a shadow of a dream in the face of soul-crushing hopelessness.

So why do those who make it inside consider themselves the lucky ones?

Available in Paperback and Kindle Formats on Amazon and Kindle Unlimited HERE:

https://www.amazon.com/Rogue-D-J-Gelner-ebook/dp/B00D0F8D9W/

HACK: THE COMPLETE GAME

Hack" O'Callahan is angry. Even though he's managed four World Series-winning teams over a career spanning more than forty years, he's finally encountered a foe he can't beat: Liver cancer.

Armed with a supply of his favorite cheap whiskey ("Old Reliable") and with his sharp tongue zipping off callous remarks from his foul mouth, Hack decides to spit in the face of his impending demise by worming his way into managing the AA Hoplite Magpies, a team divided and at odds with each other and the rest of the Northern League. As Hack instills a little "old school" discipline in this rag-tag bunch, he comes to find that his players are keeping secrets of their own, shocking secrets that threaten to tear his clubhouse and the world of sports apart at the seams.

A comedy similar to *Major League* or *Bull Durham,* but with several dark twists, the *Hack* trilogy will keep you laughing and guessing until its shocking conclusion.

D.J. Gelner is a "web property developer" (don't ask) from St. Louis, MO. He currently lives there with his wife and daughter.

www.ingramcontent.com/pod-product-compliance
Lightning Source LLC
Chambersburg PA
CBHW051330250626
47155CB00007B/2540

* 9 7 8 1 9 3 9 4 1 7 0 7 7 *